BIBLE
TIME TRAVELERS

BOOK ONE: A GIANT PROBLEM

KARLY MULLEN

The Bible Time Travelers
Book One: A Giant Problem

Text Copyright: Karly Mullen 2023
Illustration Copyright: 2023
Publishing Rights: Kaio Piublications, Inc.
2023

All Rights Reserved. Printed in the United States of America

ISBN: 978-1-952955-40-2
Kaio Publications

www.KaioPublications.org
Graphic Design: Colton Wells
Illustration: Jeremy Pate

Dedicated to Evelyn Ruth. May you always stay curious and love God.

CHAPTER 1

Riley Carson sat on her front stoop, anxious for her parents' blue van to pull around the corner and into the driveway. Today was the day that her father was coming home from his first trip with Biblical Expeditions, a company with a mission to find items from the time of the Bible. She had heard her dad saying to her mom that this was a trip of a lifetime. He had apparently been trying to get on with Biblical Expeditions for months, and now his time had finally come. He had only been gone for four weeks, but to Riley, it felt like forever.

    Riley's mom had left to go pick him up from the airport about an hour before his flight arrived. Riley's older sister, Reese, stayed home to babysit, "because ten is still too young to be by yourself." Riley wanted to play soccer with her, but she was inside talking on the phone

with her gross boyfriend, Stone. Teenagers are weird, thought Riley as she heard Reese giggle from her open bedroom window. I'm never getting a boyfriend!

"Could you keep it down a little?" Riley yelled up at her sister.

"Leave me alone, Riley!" Reese shouted back as she popped her head out the window and stuck her tongue out at her sister.

Sisters are the worst, Riley concluded in her mind.

She was very eager for her parents to get home. Her foot started tapping the ground, and she began to mess with her hair. Riley looked over at the sound of footsteps and saw her best friend and next-door neighbor, Gabe Donovan, walking up to her. "Is your dad home yet?" he asked.

"No," she said. "He should definitely be home by now."

"Well I know what will distract you," Gabe said, stealing the soccer ball from her side. "Betcha I can score a goal on you before you can me." He pointed to trees on either side of the yard as goalposts.

"But I can't win." Riley sighed. "You're stronger and faster than me. I'd lose in an instant."

"That's the point," Gabe said, laughing, "I'm challenging you because I know I'll win." Riley made a hmph noise and crossed her arms. It wasn't fair. Riley couldn't help that she wasn't as good as him, but he still liked to pick on her. As Gabe laughed, the Carson family van parked in the driveway.

"He's here!" Riley launched from the steps and ran to the car. As soon as her dad stepped out of the car, she jumped into his arms.

"Hey, sweet girl," he said, his scruffy beard tickling her shoulder.

Riley pulled away and looked at her father. "You're so tan!"

"I know! The sun is ten times hotter in Israel than it is here!" Her dad lifted a hand up toward Reese's window, where she was waving. "And I have so much to tell you," he continued. "But let's talk about it over dinner. We stopped and picked up pizza on the way home."

Mrs. Carson was carrying the pizza in the door when she passed by Gabe. "Gabe," she said, "you are welcome to stay for dinner, too! I know you are excited to hear Mr. Carson's stories."

"Sure, Mrs. Carson!" Gabe's brown eyes lit up with excitement. He ran into the house, leaving the soccer ball behind in the yard. Mr. Carson and Riley pulled his suitcases out of the trunk.

"Was that boy picking on you, Riley?" asked her dad.

"Kind of," she said, "but it's okay. He just likes to tease me because he's better at soccer."

"You know," said Mr. Carson, "a little faith can go a long way in being a better player, no matter the game."

Riley shrugged. "If you say so, Dad. But I don't think it'll work in this case."

Mr. Carson laughed. "One day you'll see," he said. "I promise."

CHAPTER 2

"So," said Riley's dad as the Carsons and Gabe settled in to eat, "we went to this place called the Valley of Elah. It's near Bethlehem over in Israel. And let me tell you, it's hotter than our worst Ohio summer!"

"Reese," interjected Mrs. Carson, "no phones at the table, please. Stone can wait." Reese rolled her eyes, then put her phone down and turned her attention to her dad.

"The Valley of Elah," Mr. Carson continued, "is the place where David fought Goliath. And we think we know its present-day location."

"Like we learned in Bible class?" Riley asked, eyes wide with wonder. Even Reese looked impressed.

"Exactly like you learned in Bible class," replied

Mr. Carson.

"So, was it actually, you know, the real deal?" asked Gabe, his mouth full of pizza.

"Well," said Mr. Carson, "we dug for about three weeks and found nothing. Just more and more dirt. But then," he said, reaching behind him into his backpack, "we found this." He pulled out a black box, and inside was an object wrapped in a thin brown cloth. When
he opened the cloth, there lay an old, leather slingshot with thin straps.

"Whoa." Riley and Gabe said this in unison.

"What if a tourist just had that there?" asked Reese. "Or it was, like, from another time or something? Not Bible times."

"Well, that's why I have it here." Mr. Carson carefully put the slingshot back in its wrapping and box. "See, Biblical Expeditions asked me to take it to an artifact specialist in Cleveland tomorrow to see if we can date it more accurately. But I and several others on our team think it might be, as you kids say, legit."

"Whoa," Riley and Gabe said together again.

"I hope it is real," said Riley, "that way the world has something that awesome."

"Me too," said Gabe, "but because that would make it the coolest weapon of all time!"

Mrs. Carson laughed, picking up everybody's empty plates. "Now, you two go wash your greasy hands and play a little bit before it gets dark. You need to get all that energy out."

Reese, instead of going to play, too, ran back up to her room to continue the phone call with her boyfriend.

Riley and Gabe made their way back outside and sat down on the front step. "Do you think," asked Gabe, "that that slingshot killed a giant? It seems a bit impossible to me."

"Well, I don't know. But if it's the real one, then the Bible says it did. And the Bible tells the truth."

Gabe shook his head, messing up his hair in the process. "Nah, nothing that little can defeat a big old giant."

"Hey," Riley whispered, scooting closer

to Gabe, "if we wait a little bit, we can probably sneak into my dad's office and get a closer look. That's where he always keeps important things."

Gabe nodded quickly, smiling in excitement. "I am so in. Let's do it."

They kicked the soccer ball around for a while, Gabe scoring on Riley every time and Riley caring about the game less and less. After Gabe had scored his tenth goal, they sneaked inside.

The late summer sun was starting to set. Riley's parents were on the couch watching some sort of comedy show, and Reese was still talking to Stone, and the two friends knew that this was their chance. Riley and Gabe tiptoed carefully down the hallway all the way to Mr. Carson's office. Riley slowly turned the knob, and she and Gabe entered the room.

The walls were lined with what seemed like hundreds of books about history and time. There were empty display cases all around, waiting for Riley's dad to fill them up with other lost treasures. In the middle of the room was her dad's big brown desk, complete with

a lamp and laptop. Next to his laptop, though, was what they were really looking for: the black box.

Riley opened the box carefully and peeled back the smooth brown cloth to reveal the slingshot. It looked more worn down and beat- up when they were closer to it, but it still made them feel excited to be that close.

"I don't know if we should touch it," whispered Riley, "Dad acted like it was too precious to touch. Like the china Mom has in the high cabinets."

"Oh, don't be such a sissy," Gabe hissed back, and before Riley could stop him, he took hold of the slingshot. That's when the world began to flash.

Riley put her hand on top of Gabe's, which was holding the slingshot tightly. "What's happening?" Riley covered her eyes from the brightness while what sounded like a roar rang in their ears.

"I don't know," Gabe shouted. "Just hold on!"

The air around them began to rush, making their hair fly all around them. The lights

got brighter, the roar got louder, the wind got faster, and then, just as quickly as it started, it stopped.

CHAPTER 3

For a moment, Riley just stood there, her hand over her eyes. Her skin was starting to feel warm, and it felt like her shoes had flown off in the rush. She heard Gabe gasp next to her, and that's when she uncovered her eyes. They definitely were not in her father's office anymore.

All around them were small hills and grassy fields. The sun was shining like it was morning and there were short but wide trees scattered around them. Birds were singing above them and below them was a dirt path.

"Gabe," said Riley, "our clothes."

Gabe looked down like Riley was and, to both of their surprise, they weren't in their tee-shirts and sneakers anymore, but in rough tunics that went down just past their knees and thin sandals. Gabe tugged at the blue fabric

with his free hand. "Aw great, a skirt?!"

Riley giggled at how Gabe was reacting and then her eyes widened in horror. "Gabe," she said shakily, "where's the slingshot?"

Gabe froze in the place, and looked at his hands...the slingshot was gone! However, in its place, wrapped in Gabe's clenched fist was a small, crumpled note.

"Open it," encouraged Riley, "and make it fast."

Gabe opened the note and read it out loud. "The one who delivers must deliver the slingshot to you."

"Weird," said Gabe. He scrunched up his face in confusion. How is this all happening? He thought. Is this all a dream? He turned to Riley. "Pinch me," he said. She reached out a small hand and pinched his arm tightly. "OUCH! Not so hard!" He shook his head. "Well, we can rule out this being a dream."

Riley's face quickly turned worried. "What do we do? Where even are we?"

"Definitely not Ohio," laughed Gabe uncomfortably.

Riley looked around for any indication of

where they were, and that's when she spotted a wooden signpost a few yards away. "This way!" She ran towards the signpost, Gabe eventually passing her and making it there first. In one direction pointed an arrow that said

"Bethlehem" and on another pointing the opposite way said the word "Gath."

"Bethlehem…" said Gabe, "isn't that where your dad just was?"

"Yeah," said Riley, "but that's impossible, right? How can we be all the way over there?"

"Well, we already know it's not a dream," whispered Gabe. Reality sunk in. This was real life. "And, Riley," he said, "since it's not a dream, then we have to ask another important question. We know where we are…but do we know when we are? Because these weird dresses are not for sale back home."

Before Riley could answer, a low growl came from somewhere near her. She looked at Gabe and laughed. "You had, like, 4 slices of pizza," she said, "there's no way you're still hungry." She stopped laughing when she saw the look of fear on her friend's face.

"Riley," Gabe said, his voice cracking,

"that wasn't my stomach."

The two friends turned around slowly, goosebumps creeping over their arms. There, lying in the grass, crouched down, was a big, ferocious, lion. Its tail was rigid and its shoulders rolled as it stalked the two kids.

"Gabe," said Riley, both of them slowly walking back as the lion crept forward, "what do we do?"

Gabe didn't answer. His mouth was open, but no words were coming out. The lion bared its teeth and crouched down low, ready pounce.

CHAPTER 4

"Don't run! Start shouting!" A mysterious voice echoed across the clearing. Without taking their eyes off of the lion, Gabe and Riley decided to listen and started yelling at the top of their lungs. The lion seemed to be startled, and began to retreat a little bit, but it still stayed in it's hunting position. The kids kept shouting as loud as they could, and then, suddenly, the lion was tackled to the ground.

    The kids darted over near a tree and watched as a young man wrestled with the lion. How he had knocked it totally off balance, they didn't know. But they watched as the lion pawed at the man and the man fought back. There were roars and shouts from the tangle on the ground, but pretty soon Riley and Gabe could tell that the lion was obviously losing the battle. The young man untangled himself from

the lion and started yelling at it to go.

He then pulled out a slingshot, no, the slingshot, and started firing rocks right at the lion's head. That was enough for the beast, and he ran off into the valley, never to be seen again.

Gabe and Riley both felt stuck to the ground, amazed at what they had just witnessed and still recovering from the fear. That stranger had SAVED them. A total stranger! And one who had the slingshot!

The young man tucked the slingshot in his belt, shook out his hair, and jogged over towards the kids. "Are you guys alright?"

The two were surprised to see that the man was actually a teenage boy, not much taller than Gabe. He had curly auburn hair and his skin was tanned from the sun. He was thin, but muscular, and wore a tunic just like theirs, but his garments were brown.

"I...I think so," Gabe managed to respond.

"What are you guys doing out here in the open anyways?" Asked the boy. "Kids like you shouldn't be on your own in the valleys."

Riley gulped. "We're just lost," she said,

"we were, um, we were..."

"Separated," Gabe interjected, "We were separated from our family on the way home. And they live that way." Gabe pointed out in the opposite direction that the stranger came from.

The stranger nodded and panted, out of breath. "Well, let me help you," he said, "I'll help get you home."

"First," said Riley, "we should probably get you some water. You look EXHAUSTED."

The stranger laughed. "You're probably right. Follow me," he said, "Martha is just over by those trees."

The three walked over to a cluster of trees where a donkey and carriage stood hiding in between them. The stranger pulled a jug from his cart and began to drink in big gulps.

"Thank you," said Riley, "for saving us back there. We owe you our lives!" Gabe and Riley sat down on the grass across from the cart.

"Oh," said the stranger, "it's nothing I haven't done before. I take care of my father's sheep and have to deal with wild animals all the

time. I'm just glad this one didn't get a good scratch on me!" He took another big gulp of water. "I'm David, by the way."

"David? Like the David?" Gabe nudged Riley in the ribs hard.

"She means that in a good way."

David laughed. "Well, I am the only David in Bethlehem, so I guess I am the David. Now, what are your names?"

"I'm Gabe, and this is Riley."

"Well, Gabe and Riley, why don't we get you home, alright? There's just one thing I have to do first. See, my brothers are fighting the Philistines right now, and I have to drop off some supplies. Is it okay if we make a stop there?" The two kids nodded in agreement. David stood up. "Well, let's go, then. We should reach the Israelite camp in the afternoon." He helped Gabe and Riley to their feet, and the trio began the journey to the camp.

"So," Riley asked as they walked, "who in your family is fighting again?"

"My three oldest brothers," said the boy, "they're the strongest so they get to go fight. My father, Jesse, sent me to bring some bread

and grain. Martha is just here to help me carry it all." He patted the donkey on the neck.

"How long have they been gone?" Riley continued.

"It feels like forever," David sighed, "I've just been at home taking care of the sheep. Don't get me wrong, I love those little lambs and would do anything to protect them, but still, sometimes you just need a change of scenery to make the days go faster. At least we get our Sabbath day and our rest as a change of pace."

"I like Sundays because that's when we go to chu--" Gabe shot Riley a dirty look, "--I mean temple. We go to the temple."

"I like going there, too," said David, "it's so comforting to know God resides among His people isn't it?" The two children nodded in agreement. "It's also nice to spend time in His word. Always remember that God's word guides you if you stay in it, understand?" Riley and Gabe nodded before continuing the rest of their journey.

At one point they came to a stop so David could feed Martha the donkey and let

her drink some water from the creek. Gabe pulled Riley to the side. "We have to stay close," he whispered. "We have to get that slingshot!"

"I know, said Riley? But it has to be delivered remember? We can't just grab it!"

"Well, it can't hurt to try. Maybe time is the deliverer. Just, try to grab it when you can."

Riley agreed with Gabe's plan, both of them making a pinky promise to try their best. They rejoined David, who was finishing hitching the wagon to Martha, and set off once again. They walked for hours up and over hills and around sharp corners, the path winding all around them, until finally they reached the top of the largest hill yet.

CHAPTER 5

"That, my new friends, is the Valley of Elah." Riley and Gabe looked down at the deep valley. Near them, just over to the left, were hundreds if not thousands of large brown tents. To the right, what seemed like a mile away, stood red tents. "Those are the Philistines over there," said David, pointing to the red tents. "They are vile and cruel and do not serve the God of our fathers. Their god is just an idol, a statue of a being named 'Dagon'. It makes me sad, that they are missing out on the blessings of the Lord."

David pointed to the brown tents. "Those down there are the Israelite tents. Remember that there are a lot of people, so make sure that you stay close to me."

The trio walked down the base of the hill to the edge of the camp, where David talked to a guard and quickly set up a small

tent. While he was finishing laying out bedrolls for the three of them inside, there came a great shout from the camp around them. David rushed out of the tent. "Come! Hurry and stay close! They are going into battle."

David quickly grabbed Riley's hand, who in turn grabbed Gabe's, and they began to wind through the sea of tents, campfires, and people bustling around. From all sides of them, soldiers in heavy and shiny armor began forming a single file line that wove around the camp.

Gabe looked over his shoulder across the valley and saw the Philistines doing the same thing and filing out onto the field in straight rows. He gulped, taking in the size of the Philistine's massive army. Riley struggled to keep a grip on David's hand as they ran throughout the camp. She didn't even have time to notice all the formations that the soldiers were taking. She just didn't want to get lost.

Not only that, but Riley could tell David was looking for someone, or anyone he knew. He kept examining the faces of the soldiers passing by him. After a few minutes of running,

they finally came to a rapid halt next to a particularly muscular group of soldiers. Gabe and Riley literally fit inside one of the men's shadows because he was so huge.

"Eliab! Abinadab! Shammah!" exclaimed David. "Brothers, what's happening?" Gabe, Riley, and David fell into step with the three brothers, who acknowledged David's voice with a smile, but kept their eyes straight ahead.

"It's time to fight, but today is not the first day we have gone into the valley like this," said one of the brothers, "it's been forty days and not a single fight has occurred." "Yes," said the brother behind him, "Abinadab is right. We go out and stand, but that is all we have accomplished, other than being afraid."

"But why Shammah?" Asked David, "Why are all of you afra--"

"WHY HAVE YOU COME OUT TO DRAW UP FOR BATTLE?" They had made it to the open section of the valley. As the lines of Israelite soldiers came to a halt, the three friends turned around and saw, in the middle of the valley, someone that could only be described as a giant.

The giant was as tall as a full-grown elephant. His bronze helmet shone in the sunlight-just like his armor. His spear was taller than he was, with a huge, pointed, sharp stone at the top. He had a sword on his hip and an evil grin on his face. The only other person in the middle of the field carried a gigantic and sturdy shield. David moved Riley and Gabe protectively behind his back.

"His name is Goliath," whispered Abinadab, "Goliath of Gath."

"AM I NOT A PHILISTINE? AND ARE YOU NOT SERVANTS OF SAUL? CHOOSE A MAN FOR YOURSELVES," Goliath roared, "AND LET HIM COME DOWN TO KILL ME, THEN WE WILL BE YOUR SERVANTS. BUT IF I PREVAIL, THEN YOU SHALL BE OUR SERVANTS AND SERVE US!" All of the Philistines cheered while the Israelite army shifted around, all of them very afraid to face the giant. "I DEFY THE RANKS OF ISRAEL THIS DAY! GIVE ME A MAN THAT WE MAY FIGHT TOGETHER!" The Philistines cheered again from across the valley, this time banging their shields, the noise thundering between the

surrounding hills.

Then, slowly but all at once, the Israelites turned away and retreated, each of them admitting that they did not want to face the giant. Some of the soldiers began running, the terror clear on their faces. Riley quickly followed David's brothers, not wanting to be the last ones left on the field. When they reached the edge of the camp, they turned around to see David slowly walking back, not in a rush at all.

Shammah stooped down next to Gabe and pointed at Goliath. "Do you see that man who has come up?" Gabe nodded. "Surely he has come up to defy Israel. And the king will make the man who kills him rich. He will give him great riches, his daughter to marry, and he will give freedom to his family."

"What shall be done for the man who kills this Philistine and takes away Israel's reproach?" David had finally joined the line of the camp where his brothers, Riley, and Gabe stood. "Who is this Philistine? Who is he to defy the armies of the living God?" David's face was angry, upset that all the men in the army

were letting Goliath defy them and God.

Abinadab stood up and repeated to David what he had told Gabe, and his angry face was replaced with a thoughtful one.

"David, why have you come down?" This time, it was the brother Eliab that spoke. He was big, bearded, and very obviously annoyed. Riley thought that he looked like a manly version of Reese whenever she found Riley eavesdropping. "Who did you leave the sheep with? I know the evil in your heart, David, and you've come down to see the battle!"

David shot a frustrated look at Eliab. "What have I done now? Was it not just a word?" He turned to Riley and Gabe. "Come now, let's leave Eliab and my other brothers with some peace, and we'll turn in for the night."

Gabe and Riley turned and followed David, Riley giving a halfhearted wave over her shoulder.

"Oh," said David, "my siblings can make me so upset! But sometimes, it's better to walk away than to argue."

"I understand," laughed Riley, "my sister

drives me CRAZY. All she cares about is her silly boyfriend."

David looked at Riley kindly and placed a hand on her shoulder. "Oh, Riley," he said, "sometimes people think that their world is the only world, just like Eliab thinks this camp and this battle are his world. But do you know who's world it is, really?"

"God's?" She responded, doubting her answer.

David nodded. "Yes, God's. He'll help you through all your disputes. Even the ones with my brothers or the ones with your sister. He's there."

Riley smiled to herself and the trio finally made their way to the tent.

The three climbed inside and each found a bedroll. "Now, come morning, I know God will win," said David. "Be sure to pray for Israel tonight, friends. And good night."

CHAPTER 6

"David?! David, son of Jesse?!" Riley was jolted awake at the sound of David's name being yelled all around the camp. She looked around to see David and Gabe had empty bedrolls and hurried outside. There stood the two boys, waiting for the shouting to get closer. The slingshot was still in David's belt. Riley could almost reach it, her fingers touched the leather, but then--

"I am David!" He stepped forward as a carriage holding a man in very fancy clothes came around the corner.

"Very well," said the man, "I'm here to take you to King Saul of Israel. He requests your presence at once." Riley and Gabe gasped. The king?!

"I will go," said David, "but I must bring these two with me. They are under my watch."

"Very well," nodded the man, "climb aboard. I'll take you to his tent." The three friends climbed into the carriage.

"Saul heard about what you said yesterday to your brothers and your friends," said the man, "he thinks your bravery is something to be admired."

"The Lord is my salvation, so why should I be afraid?" David replied.
The man nodded, taking in David's wise words. "I understand you and the King have already met?"

"Yes sir," replied David, "I've played the harp for him for a while."

"That's so cool," Gabe said.

"Actually," said David, not understanding what Gabe meant, "the palace is actually pretty warm in the summertime. I'm sure his tent is just as nice."

Within a few minutes, the carriage had made it to Saul's tent. It was right in the middle of the camp, and it was definitely the largest. They followed King Saul's messenger inside to where a large throne sat. And there sat King Saul.

King Saul was dark and tall--so tall his head nearly touched the ceiling. His eyes were brown and deep, and they looked worried. His brown hair fell to his shoulders and his beard cradled his chin. His bronze armor and thick black sandals looked sparkling new, and the crown on his head looked big enough for Riley to fit around her waist.

"Hello again, David," said King Saul as David bowed. Gabe and Riley bowed, too, following David's lead. "And hello, friends of David." Saul looked at them with his big eyes. "You are very blessed to be in the hands of such a good young man." He turned his attention back to David. "Now, my boy. I'm sure my messenger has told you that I have heard your brave words. Do you not fear Goliath, Giant of Gath? None of my soldiers, not even the best ones, will fight him."

"Let no man's heart fail because of Goliath," said David. "Your servant will go and fight this Philistine."

Saul let out a booming laugh. "HA! You are not able to go against this Philistine to fight with him! For you are but a youth, and he has

been a man of war from his youth."

David straightened up a bit, more resolute than ever. "Your servant used to keep sheep for his father. And when there came a lion, or a bear, and took a lamb from the flock, I went after him and struck him and delivered it out of his mouth. And if he arose against me, I caught him by his beard and struck him and killed him. Your servant has struck down both lions and bears, and this Philistine shall be like one of them, for he has defied the armies of the living God. The Lord who delivered me from the paw of the lion and from the paw of the bear will deliver me from the hand of this Philistine."

"It's true, Your Majesty," said Gabe abruptly, "he saved us on the road to this camp from the biggest lion I've ever seen." Riley nodded quickly in agreement.

Saul inclined his head to Gabe in acknowledgment and Gabe seemed to sweep with pride that the king gave him attention. The King paused and thought for a moment. "Alright, go. And the Lord be with you! But first, we must get you in armor to fight."

At once three servants came rushing in, forcing Gabe and Riley over to the side of the tent. One servant put a bronze helmet over David's head, which fell in front of his eyes so he couldn't see. Another brought him armor made out of chains, which caused David to trip when it was put on his shoulders. The last servant brought a sword that David strapped to his side. The armor seemed to swallow David whole and make him look tinier than he already was. He tried to take a step, but lost his balance, swaying in the armor. Riley let out a little giggle before clapping a hand over her mouth.

"Girl," said King Saul, "Why do you laugh?"

Riley felt her cheeks flush red. "I'm sorry, Your Majesty," she said quietly, "it's just, he can't fight with armor that doesn't fit him."

"She's right," said David, struggling while taking off the armor and sword. "I cannot go with these, for I have not tested them. Assemble your soldiers, and I will prepare myself. Thank you for your kindness." David bowed, which caused Gabe and Riley to do so

as well, before the three left the tent of the king.

"David!" Gabe called as the two sped up to catch up with him. "What can we do? How can we help?" They approached a small creek running through the middle of camp.

"Please," said Daivd, "help me look for the smoothest stones you can find. That would be a great help."

The three of them spent several minutes combing through the rocks that were in the creek. They came up with about twenty stones, and from out of those David chose five that would fit in the little pouch on his side. Then, the friends turned around towards the valley and the shouting armies that were, once again, lining up there.

CHAPTER 7

"Do you remember where Abinadab was standing?" David asked. The children nodded. "Go stand with him. I will go fight the giant." Even though the children knew how this story ended, they both began to feel very afraid. Riley felt tears beginning to well up in her eyes.

"Oh Riley," said David, wiping the tears that started to fall, "be brave and have faith. And you as well, Gabe." Gabe nodded, standing strong and puffing out his chest a little to show his courage. David then kissed both of them on the forehead before running off into the fray. Gabe and Riley rushed to find Abinadab.

"You two," said Abinadab as they approached, "where's Dav-"

"AM I A DOG THAT YOU COME TO ME WITH STICKS?" Abinadab, Riley, and Gabe looked out and saw a laughing Goliath

approaching David with his shield-bearer at his side.

"Oh no," whispered Abinadab.

Gabe and Riley exchanged a worried look. "Have faith," he mouthed to her. She nodded, but, still being afraid, took her friend's hand for comfort.

The Philistine let out a growl that felt like it shook the surrounding ground. Riley and Gabe could almost hear his big yellow teeth grinding in rage at the Israelites. In front of him stood David, who looked like an ant next to a big oak tree when compared to Goliath.

"COME TO ME," Goliath said, "AND I WILL GIVE YOUR FLESH TO THE BIRDS OF THE AIR AND TO THE BEASTS OF THE FIELD."

Then David said to the Philistine, "You come to me with a sword and with a spear and with a javelin, but I come to you in the name of the Lord of hosts, the God of the armies of Israel, whom you have defied. This day the Lord will deliver you into my hand," the Israelites cheered, "and I will strike you down and cut off your head, that all the earth may

know that there is a God in Israel, and that all this assembly may know that the Lord saves not with sword and spear. For the battle is the Lord's, and he will give you into our hand."

Without warning, the Philistine roared like thunder and began to move like lightning. He moved in great strides towards David and began to draw his arm back to launch his spear. Just as quickly, David stepped forward and loaded his slingshot with a single smooth stone. Abinadab quickly covered Riley's eyes by tucking her into his side, but Gabe watched as David released that one smooth stone...it went higher and higher until....

THUNK. It hit Goliath right in the middle of his forehead. Goliath came to a fast stop, his eyes wide with shock. Slowly, he dropped his spear and wobbled a bit before falling to the ground face first, dust flying all around him.

CHAPTER 8

Everyone stood in silence, mouths open. You could feel the shock in the air as all of the stunned soldiers, both Philistine and Israelite, stared at the fallen giant, defeated by the young shepherd boy...

"For the Lord God of Israel!" This cry rose from a soldier in the middle of the army, and soon the other soldiers joined in the cheer.

Abinadab quickly set Gabe and Riley on a nearby boulder, just above the heads of the troops, before joining the Israelites in a massive charge toward the Philistines. The Philistines, now that their champion had fallen, ran away as fast as they could from the hundreds of soldiers running their way. The victory belonged to God and Israel.

When the valley cleared, David left the side of Goliath and jogged over to where the

two were sitting. They jumped off the boulder and Riley launched into David's arms. "You did it! You really did it, David!!" Riley shouted.

David laughed and hugged Riley tightly, spinning her around in a circle. "No," he said, setting her down, "that victory belonged to God. Another thing to always remember." He reached out and shook Gabe's hand. "With faith, God works wonders, doesn't he?" Gabe nodded, a huge smile beaming across his face.

David's eyes drifted over their shoulders. "But, my dear friends, I'm afraid our time together is drawing to a close." The kids turned around and saw King Saul standing near the camp's edge, waving David over to him. "I have a friend, Menah, who lives one mile down the road in the direction we were going. He's a very good and just man. Follow the path to his house, and he'll help you rejoin your family."

The two kids nodded, and Riley began to tear up, not ready to say goodbye. David took notice and knelt down in front of her, reaching for his belt.

"Before we part, Riley, I want you to have these." David took the small pouch containing

the four unused stones and placed it in her open hand. "Take these and remember that the Lord can do a lot with a little.

"And you, Gabe, take my slingshot." Gabe looked in wonder at the rugged, worn down leather. "Because with faith, Gabe, you have your greatest weapon against any foe."

David kissed both of them on the cheek. "Good luck on the rest of your journey. Remember, it's one mile to Menah's house, and he will help. And take care, both of you. God guide you." With that David turned and walked away, stopping by Saul and looking back to give one final wave goodbye before following him into the camp.

That's when Riley and Gabe began to feel the wind pick up around them. "Riley! We did it! David delivered Israel, and he delivered the slingshot to us!"

"We did it!" Riley shouted back, light starting to shine around them and the roar getting louder. "Now we can go home!" They grabbed on to each other's hands one more time and closed their eyes tightly. When they opened them again, they were home.

CHAPTER 9

Gabe carefully set the slingshot back in the box just how they had found it and replaced the lid. They were both very relieved to be back in their normal clothes.

"I'll meet you back outside," said Riley. They both snuck out of the office, careful to shut the door behind them. The sun was still just starting to set in the sky--it was like no time had passed at all.

Outside, Riley met Gabe with a large pink jewelry box. "My mom gave me this for Christmas," said Riley, setting it down between them in the grass, "but Reese is definitely the one who likes jewelry! It hasn't had a use for me until now." She knelt down and opened the box. At the same time, she reached into her pocket and pulled out David's pouch of rocks. Riley put the pouch inside and closed

the box, locking it with a key that she had on a necklace. "There," she said, "now we know they are somewhere safe." Riley put the box back in her room, making sure it was in a safe hiding spot before coming back outside, key necklace secure around her neck.

"Let's both promise that this stays between us," said Gabe, holding out his pinky. Gabe interlocked his pinky with Riley's.

"Yeah, my dad would go crazy if he knew we snuck into his office! And then he'd think that we had gone insane if we told him what happened!"

"I wish that we could've stayed in touch with David somehow," said Riley, "he was such a nice guy."

Gabe laughed. "You know we can just read what he has to say, right? It's like he left behind letters for us in the Bible."

"You're right!" Riley beamed, "He did write in the Bible! That's so cool--it'll be like he never left!"

"If this happens to us again, which if your dad brings home more artifacts to be examined, it's definitely a possibility, we may

even see him again. Who knows?" They both sat in silence for a moment, lost in thought.

"How do you think all of that happened?" Gabe asked.

"I don't know," said Riley, "but I agree. I do think it can happen again. We'll just have to wait for my dad's next expedition. I think I heard him tell my mom that his dream location is a place called Babylon, but we'll see!"

"Well, hopefully, he finds something," said Gabe. He paused. "Do you think the artifact expert would believe us if we told him it was for real?" Gabe wondered out loud.

Riley just laughed and shook her head no. "Come on," she said, kicking the soccer ball towards him, "We still have time for another round of soccer. And I think I'm ready to take down my Goliath."

Discussion Questions and Activities

Use these questions with your children for comprehension, thought, and conversation! These questions are perfect for a small group setting as well.

1. If you could go back to any Bible story, which would you choose and why?

2. David was very brave in facing Goliath. What would you do if you came face to face with the giant? What weapons would you choose? How would you react?

3. Has there ever been a time where you felt small compared to a challenge? How did you face it?

4. What advice would you give Riley and Gabe for their next adventure?

5. David reminded the children that "they can do a lot with a little." What do you think that means?

6. What are some ways you can show your faith daily, even if it is in a small way?

Acknowledgments

This book wouldn't have been possible without the help of a good family and great friends. To Kitty, Sue, Tammy, Brandon, Carolyn, and Terran: without your helpful edits and wise words this dream of mine would not be a reality. Riley and Gabe's story is my child, and it really took a village to raise it up.

To my parents, who always encouraged my dreams and lifted me up when I could've given up: your support is everything to me and I'd be lost without it.

Grandparents are often overlooked, but I'd like to mention mine. They've always instilled a love for God in my heart, and for leading me to Him I am eternally grateful.

Katie, Matthew, and Sarah, also known as the best cheerleaders ever, you guys are awesome.

Some of David and Goliath's dialogue comes from the Bible, and being able to incorporate it into this work is a blessing.

And finally, this whole book is a love story to the best book ever written. God is at the heart of this book, and I pray that everyone who reads this will come to follow Him and His Word.

Karly Mullen was born and raised in Ohio by a God-fearing family. She attended Freed-Hardeman University and graduated with her B.A. in English in 2017. Karly loves God, her family, working with kids, and her dog, Laci. She still resides in Ohio today with her wonderful husband while pursuing her passion for writing.

Printed in the USA
CPSIA information can be obtained
at www.ICGtesting.com
JSHW041932180224
57340JS00012B/83

GHOST EYE

DARK WATER
BOOK 2

XANTHE WALTER

Xanthe Walter

For Penny
My beloved pink, sparkly girl

AUTHOR'S NOTES

Content Advisory
This book contains **mature themes and explicit sexual content, including scenes of sexual violence.** It is intended for readers 18+ only. For detailed content information, please visit the content advisory web page for this book before reading. Chapters containing sexual violence or explicit reference to it: Three, Five, Seven, and Nine.
https://www.xanthe-walter.com/content-advisory/dark-water-book-2/

Language Note
This book uses British English spelling and grammar conventions throughout.

Quality Assurance
While this book has undergone extensive proofreading to ensure the highest quality reading experience, should you encounter any errors, please report them to my PA at XW@xanthe-walter.com for prompt correction.

Join Walter's World

AUTHOR'S NOTES

Subscribe to my newsletter for exclusive content, including a FREE spicy gay pirate novella, priority updates on new releases, giveaways, and more. Sign up here: https://geni.us/ww-bm

Chapter One

JUNE 2088

Alex

Nothing shall serve him longer, not strength nor comeliness, nor his fine armour,
which indeed shall soon be lying low in the deep waters covered over with mud
– The Iliad

Alex lay on the polished oak floor, gazing hazily at the ceiling. He'd fallen so far, so fast, that he couldn't catch his breath, which was coming in staccato gasps. His vision slowly clearing, he saw Tyler pacing around the room, heard him crowing about his victory. Over to one side was Solange – so beautiful, so deceitful – sitting as still as a statue, gazing at him sadly.

Tyler strode over and gazed down at him. "Are you listening to me?"

Alex forced himself to look up at the man who now controlled every aspect of his life. Tyler thrummed with a lean, wolfish energy, savouring his power over his victim.

"Yes," Alex rasped. His voice sounded strange, as if he were hearing it from a great distance.

"These are your bodyguards," Tyler said, beckoning. A tall,

muscular man with a scarred face and a big fat man with a shaved head stepped forward. "One of them will be with you at all times. They'll accompany you everywhere during the day and guard your bedroom door at night."

"Bodyguards?" Alex snorted. "You mean they're to stop me escaping."

Tyler laughed. "Oh, you can't escape, Alexander – and you wouldn't get very far if you tried. You're chipped, and you have one of the most famous faces in the land. You'd be captured within five minutes and returned to me – and I promise you that the consequences wouldn't be pleasant."

"How could it be worse than this?"

"Try escaping and you'll find out," Tyler gloated. "Besides, how long do you think you'd last out there without my protection? The entire country hates you. You're safer under my roof than anywhere else. I'm a registered houder – the IS Agency inspectors can visit at any time, when I'll have to account for your safety, prove that I'm feeding you, and treating you... if not exactly well, then at least adequately. You should be grateful."

"Forgive me for not seeing it that way."

"Oh, I'm never going to forgive you," Tyler said emphatically. "Now, get up. It's time to start your new life."

Alex heaved himself slowly to his feet, shaking with the effort. His body felt heavy, as if it didn't belong to him – as if he'd been shattered into a million pieces and glued back together in a poor facsimile of himself. His tongue felt leaden, his head ached, and his limbs moved in a slow, dreamlike way.

Tyler was bouncy by contrast, still running on the adrenaline of his victory. He strode to the lift with Alex following slowly, painfully, behind, his new "bodyguards" falling into step beside him, one on each side. A couple of floors down, the doors opened onto another suite, decorated more plainly.

"No smartwalls here?" Alex raised an eyebrow, glancing at the plain magnolia walls.

"Oh, these are smartwalls, too." Tyler touched the wall, and it created a spangled pattern around his hand before reverting to its orig-

inal colour. "All the walls are." Alex looked around, startled – the walls upstairs had been alive with colour and vibrancy, but this looked like a regular wall. "I can change the colours whenever I feel like it. Tomorrow it might be blue." Tyler shrugged.

"Must have cost a fortune," Alex said facetiously. "And wasted on us lowly servants, surely?"

"It's not for *you*. It's for my guests." Tyler grinned. "This is where you'll live from now on." He bounded around the space, making the dull throb in Alex's head even worse by his sheer exuberance. "Here's the kitchen – your diet will be controlled by my chef and your meals cooked for you." Tyler gestured at gleaming white cupboards, a break-fast bar with stools, and a small dining table with four chairs. "You'll have to ask permission from the chef if you want anything outside mealtimes."

"Really?" Alex drawled. "Isn't that taking your power trip a bit too far?"

"Wake up, Alexander! Having power over you is precisely the point. That's why you're here." Tyler grinned.

"I know why I'm here. I'm a toy." He shrugged. "Your revenge toy, to play with whenever you're bored."

"Not only when I'm bored." Tyler winked. He strode into another room, and Alex, flanked by his bodyguards, had no choice but to follow. "As you can see, you have a nice big living area. There are plenty of books and a generous movie and music library – although no internet access, obviously." He pulled a mocking sad face. "You aren't allowed to contact anyone from your old life – though that won't be a problem as you don't have any friends, and your family don't want to know you anymore."

That hit like a punch to the gut.

Tyler seemed satisfied that he'd landed a blow and moved on.

"This suite isn't only for you – it's also where you'll entertain my specially selected guests. There's a dining area here..." They entered a large room, furnished with a massive mahogany table and ten plush upholstered chairs in a shade of deep purple. The walls radiated a deep red glow. "It's only for when you're entertaining – the rest of the time you'll eat in the kitchen. And down this hallway is a gym where you'll

work out to stay in shape for my guests." He led Alex into a spacious, light-filled space, full of gleaming equipment.

"I don't do gyms," Alex said flatly.

"You don't have a choice," Tyler snapped. "You'll 'do' whatever I tell you. Your trainer will devise a workout plan for you."

"Good luck with that," Alex muttered under his breath as Tyler continued on down the hallway.

"And here is your bedroom." Tyler ushered him into a large, airy room with several floor-to-ceiling windows. "They don't open, obviously," he said, gesturing.

"Obviously," Alex said, looking around. There was a huge bed, made up with cream satin sheets, a plumped-up duvet, and a plum-coloured coverlet. Opposite the bed was a bank of wardrobes with mirrored doors.

"View this as being the most exclusive of hotels," Tyler advised him. "Your room will be cleaned, towels replaced, and your clothes taken away for laundering daily. Most servants would be damn lucky to live in such luxury. You should be grateful."

"I'll work on it," Alex sniped.

Tyler opened one of the wardrobes to reveal several sets of exquisitely tailored clothes: formal suits, shirts, and ties, also jeans, tee-shirts, jackets, coats, and gym apparel. Shoes, boots, and trainers were lined up on a rack along the bottom. "All in your size – I had them made specially." Tyler smiled.

"There's something for every occasion. For example." He withdrew a pair of white linen trousers and a red silk V-necked sweater. "If I'm entertaining on my yacht, these would be appropriate. Or if I want you in a business meeting, just sitting there, looking beautiful, helping to sweeten a deal, then this." He pulled out a stunning charcoal-grey suit and an iced-violet cotton shirt.

"Who wouldn't want to sleep with the infamous Alexander Lytton?" He reached out and tousled Alex's hair. "Who wouldn't want this beautiful bad boy at their mercy, lying naked on this bed, begging to be fucked?"

"I think you overestimate my sex appeal," Alex said.

Tyler laughed. "We both know that's not true. How many times

have you used your looks and fame – or should that be notoriety? – to seduce some idiot into kneeling at your feet to suck your dick? I've seen the photos; I've watched the interviews with your discarded conquests. You despised them. You used them for sex, and drugs, and sometimes both. Now it's time to see how you like being used in return. Come over here – you'll enjoy this."

He opened another cupboard door, and Alex saw an array of sex toys, dressing-up clothes, and bondage equipment.

"You're here to supply any fantasy my guests want. Let's be clear on one thing." Tyler looked him straight in the eye. "These people are my clients and business associates, and you are their reward for giving me contracts, closing deals, or coming down on price. So, you will give them whatever they want. If they choose to tie you up and whip your sorry arse until you bleed, that's fine by me. If they demand you to do the same to them, then you do it. Hell, if they want to dress you up like Hudson Brink in that god-awful movie about alien space eggs and fuck you up the arse while serenading you in Martian, then you'll be only too happy to oblige. Understand?"

Alex looked at the contents of the cupboard and then back at Tyler. "Yes. I understand," he said, filling the words with as much derision as he could.

"Good. By the way, the smartwalls... they record everything that takes place in this suite." Tyler waved his hand at the pale green walls. "That's why I keep the decoration low-key, so my guests don't realise they're smartwalls, as you didn't – and therefore they don't know they're being recorded."

"Blackmail?" Alex raised an eyebrow.

"I'm not a charity," Tyler snapped. "If people want a night with you, then I want some collateral to hold them to their deal."

"Just good business practice, then," Alex commented dryly.

Tyler smirked. "I didn't get to own this place by being nice."

"Recordings can be deep-faked," Alex pointed out.

"Not these recordings. My smartwalls contain state-of-the-art truth-marking tech that can tell if something has been AI generated. It's so good they're even using it to verify evidence in court these days."

Alex gazed at him glumly. Of course he'd thought of everything.

"You'll be shaved, styled, and dressed by your own personal stylist every day. He'll decide what you wear."

Alex felt a pang of loss. He'd always felt his choice of clothing defined him to others, but now George Tyler would do the defining instead – and he had a feeling he wouldn't like the person Tyler wanted him to be.

"There's no razor in the bathroom," Tyler said suddenly. "And the smartwall footage is monitored 24/7, just in case you're thinking of suicide."

"Don't flatter yourself that being your IS, kept in luxury, forced to wear expensive clothes, and made to fuck people for my supper is bad enough to drive me that far," Alex retorted witheringly.

"It shouldn't. It's not so different to how you lived before." Tyler patted his cheek. "Only now, you don't have the freedom to fuck up your own life, or the lives of the people around you. That's an improvement."

Alex bowed his head; Tyler had scored another hit.

"Now, when I said you'll let my guests do anything they want, I meant it. The IS Detention Centre updated your STD vaccinations, and you'll be tested regularly, so there's no reason for our guests to be inconvenienced by having to wear condoms."

"God forbid," Alex muttered.

"Of course, if they want to be on the safe side, or if they get a kick out of wearing rubber on their pricks, they're more than welcome to do so." Rubbing his hands together, he took a step back. "Oh, this is going to be fun!"

"I don't see how," Alex replied sullenly. "You've got me. That was the fun bit. Now I'm just another IS for you to order around."

"Oh no, you don't understand." Tyler took his face in his hands and gazed at him intently. "You have no idea how often I've dreamed about what I'd do when I got you here. I've had five long years of fantasising about it. You killed the love of my life – making you my servant is good, but it's not nearly enough to make you pay." He wore an expression of terrifying zeal. "Losing Isobel nearly broke me, so that's what I'm going to do to you. I'm going to break you, and you

know what?" He leaned in close and breathed in Alex's ear. "I'm going to enjoy it."

Alex felt a shiver run down his spine.

Drawing back, Tyler was all geniality again. "Now, I have a business to run. I'll give you some time to settle in and then introduce you to your first assignment." Leaving the room, he took the guards with him.

Alex stood there, chilled to the bone. What did Tyler mean by "breaking" him? Surely he was broken enough? He certainly felt it. He'd lost everything. He rubbed his arms, trying to comfort himself. He was going to survive. In fact, he'd make survival his mission. Whatever Tyler threw at him, he'd find a way to endure.

Glancing into the en-suite bathroom, he found a tub big enough for an orgy. The taps were gold-plated, there was a bidet next to the toilet, and several fluffy white towels hung from a gold-plated rail. This was his gilded cage, and he was the beautiful bird trapped inside, ready to sing on demand.

Slumping onto the bed, he gazed blankly out of the window. He had a glorious view over the lost zone. Far beneath, he could see the ghostly outline of the decrepit London Eye, lying forlornly in the water. There was a sudden sound at the door, and Solange poked her head around it.

"Hello, Alex," she said quietly.

He looked at her for a long moment, realising he had nothing to say to her.

"Alex, please, I need to talk to you." She tiptoed nervously over, and he realised she was afraid – not of the guard outside the door, who must have let her in, but of him and his reaction. "I know you must hate me right now." She sat down gingerly on the bed beside him and put her hand over his, but he pulled away. Biting her lip, she tried again. "I want you to know that he had cameras and bugs in my apartments and on my clothes. He listened in to all our conversations. His men followed me wherever I went. They were always with us – in bars, restaurants, and clubs – everywhere. I had no way of letting you know you were being played."

"Did you even want to?" he asked bitterly.

She chewed on her lip again, then shook her head. "Not at first, but

I didn't know what I'd got myself into. I grew up in the Quarterlands, Alex. I was desperate to get out and make a life for myself. Tyler's men were trawling around the Quarter where I lived – they approached me and asked me to meet him. He was charming and persuasive – you know how he can be – so I signed myself into his service for seven years."

"Didn't you ask what you'd have to do as his IS?"

"Oh, I knew. I'm aware of how I look." Solange shrugged. "He had me polished up and trained for the role he wanted me to play. I was coached to be exactly what you wanted. I asked him what would happen after he was done with you, and he said I'd be useful in his business dealings. He wanted someone who could talk to his clients – who'd be interesting and entertaining, as well as look good."

"Not just talk to them; you couldn't have been that naïve." Alex snorted.

"No. I knew he wanted me to sleep with them. He was honest about that." His face must have registered his shock, because she shook her head impatiently. "Alex, women like me have always been courtesans. It's often the only career path for bright, pretty girls who have no other way of getting on in the world."

"What about your art? Your paintings?" he protested.

She burst out laughing. "Don't be an idiot, Alex. I can't draw for toffee! I thought you'd seen through me when you noticed I didn't have any of my work in my Oxford flat."

"But you were awarded an art degree from one of the most prestigious universities in the world." He frowned. "I was there on graduation day – I saw you collecting it."

"Tyler bought it for me – he made a huge donation to the university. He was torn at first about whether to put me in for an art or business studies course – he wasn't sure of the best way to reach you. Then he decided that although you were doing a business degree, your first love was clearly art and design – his people reported that you went to art lectures. He thought if I was an artist, it would make me more attractive to you."

"Fuck." Alex ran his hands through his hair in disbelief. "He went to a lot of trouble to get you into my life."

"If he wants something, he goes for it; he doesn't do anything by halves. You have to understand that if you're going to survive here."

"Was any of it true?" he asked her quietly. "Any of what you told me about yourself? What about your parents being killed in that duck accident?"

"My mum ran off with some bloke when I was fourteen, and I never even knew my dad." Solange dipped her head. "The duck accident thing was specially designed to appeal to you because of what happened to your mum."

"Christ. You're a real piece of work."

"I'm not ashamed of becoming Tyler's IS," she said hotly, her chin jerking up. "But I *am* ashamed of what I did to you," she added in a smaller voice.

"Forgive me if your apology doesn't sound very convincing."

"It's not an apology, it's an explanation."

He turned to look at her properly for the first time. Her face was pinched, and her lower lip red where she'd chewed on it. She looked genuinely upset.

"Explain it to me, then. I'm listening."

She nodded and took a deep breath. "Okay, so at first, he told me to get close to you and find out what makes you tick. Like everyone else, I thought I already knew all about you. That you were a spoilt rich kid who screwed up his family. So it didn't bother me when he told me to feed you croc and make you fall in love with me." She gave a tight little smile. "You fall in love with me? That's ironic, isn't it? You always told me it'd never happen, and you were right. I wanted to hate you, because I envied you. I grew up with nothing, but you had it all, and were pissing it away on drink and drugs."

"Yeah, that's what everyone thinks. Maybe it's even true." He hunched his shoulders miserably.

"No, see, I started off feeling that way, but I changed my mind when I got to know you. I saw then that this fucked-up world had chewed you up and spat you out the same way it had me. Just because you had money didn't mean your life had been better than mine – it was just different. You were sent away to boarding school when you were just a kid, and your family was so obsessed with your shiny older

brother that the only way you could make them see you was by acting out. I wanted to hate you, Alex, God knows I did, but I couldn't."

"I can't trust a word that comes out of your mouth."

"I know, and I deserve that, but it's true all the same." She reached out again to take his hand, and this time he let her. "Despite what everyone thinks, you're the least arrogant man I've ever met. You're messed up, but you aren't wicked. You're just... lost."

"If I wasn't before, I am now. You've seen to that."

"I wish I could change the past, but I can't. I did try to help you. I started to feel sorry for you and even to..." She flushed and looked away. "I fell in love with you, of course, just like Neil and so many others. I knew how much you hated it when people fell for you, and I hoped that if I acted clingy it'd drive you away. I wanted you to escape from Tyler's clutches. He was very angry about that."

"What did he do to you?"

"Well, he has a temper, and he's very focused on getting what he wants, so I'm sure you can guess."

"If he hit you, it's illegal, and you could go to—"

"Oh, Alex, don't be so naïve." She shook her head impatiently. "They aren't all like your father, building pretty villages and playing lord of the manor, handing out largesse and getting off on the gratitude of their serfs."

He stared at her. "You know, I never saw my father that way."

"That's because you have no idea how the rest of us live. Tyler doesn't care what's legal. Do you think he ended up living in a place like this, with his massive fortune, by following the bloody rules? His father and mother were both indies, for God's sake. He dragged himself up to where he is now. While your father obeys the law, people like George Tyler play the system. Of course he hits me – and he'll do the same to you, and worse, if you don't do what he says."

"I honestly don't care." He shrugged.

"I know, and that's why I'm here." She took his face between her hands and looked into his eyes. "I'm frightened for you. I care about you. I'd do anything to help you."

"I'll pass on that, thanks, considering who the offer comes from." He jerked his head away.

"I thought you'd say that, but the offer stands anyway."

"You do know he's watching all this?" He gestured at the wall.

"Yes, but I'm used to that. He's been watching us alone together for years now." She got up and walked to the door. "Please, Alex, for your own sake – do what he says and don't antagonise him. Please."

"One thing," he said as she opened the door.

She glanced back.

"Did you know what he was planning to do to me? Did you know this was the endgame? Being his whore to be pimped out to sweeten his deals?"

She shook her head vehemently. "No. He didn't share his plans with me. At first, my orders were to get close to you and pump you for information that he could use against you. Later, I thought that maybe he was intending to steal your designs and cause a rift between you and your father. I had no idea he envisaged doing this. If I had..."

"What?" Alex demanded. "What would you have done, Solange? What *could* you have done?"

"I don't know, but I did try to warn you, Alex. I told you to stop trying to win the affection of father figures. I wanted you to walk away from Tyler and be your own person, but you couldn't do that. You wanted his approval too much – and look where it's got you." Giving him one last, sad smile, she turned and left.

He ventured out later that day to explore his surroundings. He was smart – if there was any weakness in Tyler's security, he was sure he'd find it. Then what? Escape? First things first...

His door wasn't locked, but the tall thin guard with the scarred face fell into step behind him the moment he exited his bedroom. He walked to the lift, but found it could only be opened by the retina scan of one of the guards. Access to the stairwell was similarly restricted, and there were no other exits. The guard followed him the whole time, without comment on his expedition, and he soon realised that nobody was stopping him because there was no point; there was no way out. Returning to his room, he threw himself back on the bed.

Outside, the sun was setting, bathing the lost zone in an eerie

orange glow. Placing his finger over the chip in his wrist, he wondered if he'd ever get used to how it felt, pulsing under his skin. Finally, exhausted by the day's events, he fell asleep.

He was woken at 8 a.m. by a small plump man wearing a pair of white trousers that were far too tight and a flamboyant top in shades of orange and green so bright they hurt.

"Morning, darling! I'm Lorenzo, your personal stylist," he said in an extravagant Italian accent. My, you're just as beautiful in person as you were onscreen! Alexander, my love, it's going to be a pleasure working with you."

Lorenzo bundled him into the shower, fussing and cooing. When he emerged, the stylist was waiting outside, ready to shave him with a cut-throat razor. "Come on, my love, and let me give you a proper shave," he said, seating Alex at the dressing table. "I want your skin to be as smooth as a baby's bottom."

Alex made a face into the mirror.

Lorenzo laughed at him. "Don't mind me, I like to talk. I'll shave you once on ordinary days, and twice if you're receiving guests in the evening – unless those particular guests would prefer you looking rakish, sweetheart." He lathered Alex's chin and began his task.

Alex wondered what it would be like to move his head a fraction and feel the sharp blade of the razor slip into his jugular.

"I'm an expert on Mr Tyler's guests," Lorenzo told him as he worked. "I research them all, so I can create precisely the right look to appeal to them, because, as I always say—"

"What's your real name?" Alex demanded.

"What, dear?"

"All your camp bullshit is wasted on me, *sweetheart*. I've been in more gay bars and slept with more queens than you've had manicures." He glanced contemptuously at the man's impeccably polished finger-nails. "What's your real name? It's sure as hell not Lorenzo."

"My real name's Brian, and I'm from Braintree. Does that make you feel better, love?" Lorenzo replied in a harder tone.

"No. Does it make you feel better to pretend you're some hotshot Italian stylist?"

"Listen, handsome, I'm an IS just like you." Lorenzo gestured at his

identity tag. "But unlike you, I didn't steal a truckload of money from my own father to end up this way. I have a proper contract that entitles me to, amongst other things, walk out of that door without a guard trailing me everywhere I go. Yeah, I could have held on to my freedom and be working in an army shop, but I wanted more. I may not be dressing Hollywood stars, but by swallowing my pride and taking Mr Tyler's ID tag, I get to work with the next best thing – and in this country, right now, that's you. There isn't a stylist in Britain that doesn't want to be dressing you, but that honour goes to me. So you'll have to learn to suck it up, big boy."

Alex stared at him in the mirror and then broke into a wide grin.

Lorenzo stared back haughtily for a second, and then joined in.

"We're going to get along just fine, Alexander, my love, trust me," he told him with a wink. He finished shaving Alex and then pulled some clothes from the wardrobe. "I want to try out some different looks on you, darling, so we know what to go for, depending on who we're entertaining. You must have a repertoire – just like Solange. Luckily, you're incredibly versatile. See, you can be an innocent young lad..." He flattened Alex's hair down and pressed a tie up to his neck, making him look like a fresh-faced schoolboy. "Or a debauched sex god." He ruffled his hair into a just-got-fucked tousle and held a scarlet shirt under his chin. "You're wonderful – so many looks, such great bone structure. You'll be a joy to work with, just like our beautiful Solange."

Alex had no interest in different "looks", especially as none of them corresponded with his own style. But his bohemian clothes, loose hair, and stubbled jaw were gone; when Lorenzo was finished with him, he was a clean-shaven, beautifully dressed mannequin, his hair artfully styled into waves with handfuls of product.

"Now, don't you look beautiful," the stylist exclaimed.

"I don't look like me," Alex said, trying to find some trace of himself in his reflection.

"Psh! What was so good about being you, hmm?" Lorenzo asked, patting his shoulder kindly. "We all want to be someone else, really, don't we, sweetie?"

Clearly, this was all part of Tyler's plan to erase Alexander Lytton

and construct the perfect IS in his place. But Alex refused to be erased. As he gazed at himself in the mirror, he decided that he would seek out some trace of himself every day, even if it was just a sardonic smile or ironically raised eyebrow. He saw it now – beneath the hair product and unfamiliar clothing, there was a glimmer of his real self in the contemptuous curl of his lip. He exhaled. He was still here. The day he couldn't see any sign of himself would be the day George Tyler had won.

After the styling session, he was escorted to the kitchen. The chef, who appeared to have no name other than "Chef", placed a plate of eggs and toast and then a bowl of fruit and yoghurt in front of him. It smelled and tasted delicious, but he wasn't hungry; he barely managed a couple of mouthfuls.

After breakfast, Chef spent a couple of hours going through the foods he liked and disliked, and any food allergies and intolerances, making copious notes. Chef was a small dark energetic man with a heavy French accent; like everyone else Alex encountered, he was wearing an ID tag. Alex wondered if he was a refugee – plenty of people had fled the warlords in Central Europe to sign a rich person's IS contract in Britain. It guaranteed they'd be fed and clothed, if nothing else.

When Chef was finished, Alex was escorted to the gym and introduced to his personal trainer. Mason was a short man with unfeasibly huge muscles, and a moustache that sat on his upper lip like a fat brown slug.

Alex had always found anything to do with fitness utterly tedious, after hours spent listening to his mother and Charles discussing training regimes over the breakfast table. Mason didn't look as if he was going to make the subject any more interesting.

First, he was made to run on a treadmill attached to a heart monitor. Then he was taken through various strength, speed, and agility trials that were both boring and exhausting.

"You're in appalling shape for a man your age. It'll take months to get you to where you should be," Mason complained, and set to work

devising a personal fitness programme that sounded like nothing short of torture.

He was the kind of man Alex had always hated – humourless and relentlessly heterosexual. The former made him dull, and the latter rendered him immune to Alex's attempts to charm his way out of his exercises.

"You'll report here every day, and you won't be allowed to leave until you've performed every single exercise I set for you," Mason barked.

"What if I'm ill, or, you know, can't be arsed?" Alex said petulantly.

"I don't care if you're fucking well dying – you'll do every single exercise I've given you," Mason retorted as he uploaded the programme to the smartwall, which displayed every exercise, complete with guide videos showing him how to perform them. "Understood?"

Alex shrugged.

Mason took two threatening steps towards him. "Understood?" he barked again, his moustache so close that Alex could almost feel the bristles.

He stepped back and gave Mason a withering look. "Oh, yeah. I understand," he said, as insolently as he could manage.

"You're a sorry excuse for a man," Mason yelled. "If I have to drag you from your deathbed to make you work out, then I will. Don't fucking try and pull any shit with me, or you'll regret it. I'm not one of the pussy boys you're used to – you'll soon learn who you're dealing with."

"Aw, bless. You think you're special, darling," Alex drawled in his best camp voice. "Listen, Muscleman, I've been expelled from three of the top boys' boarding schools in this country. I've eaten their shitty food, run their lousy cross-country courses, and been bawled at by their sadistic phys ed teachers. I've met plenty of men like you. You're not special, you're not unique – you're not even close." Leaning forward, he planted a kiss on Mason's cheek, then ducked out of reach.

However, much like his old PE teachers, Mason soon took his revenge by making him do press-ups for the rest of the session.

. . .

When he returned to his room, he was startled to see that the walls were now a vibrant orange. Tyler, true to his word, was showing him just how much control he had over Alex's environment. His bedroom walls changed colour every day thereafter – sometimes several times a day. The walls might be blue when he left to enter his en-suite bathroom, only to be yellow when he returned half an hour later. If Tyler meant it to be disconcerting, it backfired. Alex was glad of the variety, because otherwise everything was the same. The same monotonous routine every day: breakfast, gym, lunch, downtime, and then dressing for dinner. This last was enforced, even though it was just him and Solange sitting down to eat.

He went along with each and every indignity, aware that they were minor compared to what awaited him. It was one thing to allow Lorenzo to shave and style him, but was he really going to sweet-talk one of Tyler's "guests", take them to bed, and fuck them? Could he do that? And what would happen to him if he refused?

He didn't consciously stop eating, but a great lethargy came over him in the following days. He'd lost several pounds in prison as his stomach seemed to have stopped telling him when he was hungry – or if it did, he wasn't listening. He would walk to the kitchen three times a day and sit down. Food would be put in front of him, but he'd push it around the plate, barely able to manage more than a few bites.

Solange tried to make conversation, but when he could be bothered to reply, he only wanted to hurt her.

"Is this place just for us whores?" he asked one morning. "I mean, I've been here a fortnight, and the only other indies I've seen are Lorenzo, Mason, Chef, and the goons, and none of them seem to live here." He gestured in the direction of his two guards. One was standing by the door, while the other sat at the breakfast bar, sipping a cup of coffee. They did have names, but he couldn't be bothered to remember them, so he'd taken to calling them Scarface and Fatso instead. Neither of them had so far risen to the provocation. They did shift rotations with two other guards, to whom he'd given equally facetious nicknames.

"It's the suite Tyler keeps for entertaining his clients," Solange told him, pouring a glass of orange juice. "It's our job to make them comfortable; we're the only people who actually live here."

"Where do the rest of Tyler's indies live?" he asked.

"There's a dormitory level on the floor below. Most of them sleep there, in shifts. Conditions up here are much nicer."

"Aren't we the lucky ones," he said bitterly.

"As a matter of fact, we are. Downstairs, nobody even has their own bed, let alone their own room. The major-domo, Mr Drummond, runs Tyler's IS programme like clockwork. They're assigned a bed at night depending on who is working where. The beds are packed in, dozens to a room. They're just a place to sleep when the indies aren't working."

Alex noticed Scarface peeking over the top of his coffee mug, gazing at Solange intently as she spoke.

"You don't want to get on the wrong side of the major-domo, sonny," the man said, getting up to pour the dregs of his coffee into the sink. "He might look like a banker, but he hits like a boxer. No IS gets on his bad side, not even the security detail – and we don't scare easy."

"Thanks for the unwanted advice, Scarface," Alex snapped.

"You should listen if you want to get by in here." Scarface glanced at Solange. "You tell him, Miss Solange," he added in a gentler tone. "For his own sake."

"He's right," Solange said.

"Seriously?" Alex rolled his eyes. "Come on! George Tyler's IS programme gets monitored by the IS Agency, just like my father's and everyone else's. It might not be nice, but it can't be as bad as you're making out."

Solange gave him a worried look. "Tyler doesn't run his IS programme like your father runs his, Alex. Most people don't. If you hadn't walked through life with your eyes closed, then you'd know that. You screw up here, and the consequences won't be pretty."

"Forgive me for not taking the advice of the person who lied to me for years on end," he snapped.

"You should listen to her," Scarface advised. "She knows what it's like here. You need to get your head around the fact that you're not

free anymore, sonny. You're just an IS with a job to do now – and Tyler will make you do it."

"Be his whore you mean, like her?" Alex jerked his head at Solange, noticing the little wince that passed across the guard's face at his choice of words. "When does the whoring actually start?" he asked, throwing the word out again to enjoy Scarface's reaction. "So far, all I've done is work out and sit around in this place."

"Tyler's guests are important people, and he needs them onside for a reason," Solange said. "I doubt he'll let you get close to one until he's sure you'll... perform."

"I'll be interested to see how he's going to make me," Alex drawled, with more bravado than he felt. "I mean, it's a bit different for you. My anatomy might not actually work to order."

"You'd better hope it does," Scarface said. "Would you like more coffee, Miss Solange? Mason will be here soon."

"No thanks. I'm good." She shot him a grateful smile, and Alex noticed how his cheeks reddened.

After breakfast, they went to the gym for their daily session with Mason. The trainer viewed fitness as a quantifiable resource to be measured, weighed, and achieved with the help of copious charts and spreadsheets that he updated daily and displayed on the smartwall. Baiting the dour despot had become one of Alex's favourite pastimes. Mason had a habit of barking orders that Alex liked to pretend he hadn't understood, causing Mason to repeat them ever more frenziedly. He hated completing Mason's charts showing how many weights he'd lifted and how far he'd run each day, so he took to making them up, filling them with false data whenever Mason was busy supervising Solange, and enjoying a small thrill of triumph from the rebellion.

Today, though, it appeared that rebellion hadn't gone unnoticed, because Mason wasn't alone: Tyler was with him, and they were both studying Alex's charts on the smartwall. Beside him was a tall, muscular, bald man dressed immaculately in the Tyler livery of black shirt and tie – Alex noticed a thick leather strap hanging from his belt.

Solange stiffened and gave a little jerk of her head in warning, so Alex assumed the bald guy must be the major-domo she'd referred to at

breakfast. He wasn't afraid. He'd endure any beatings Tyler and his sidekick wanted to hand out; he had nothing left to lose.

"So, we have a problem," Tyler said as Alex and Solange entered the room.

"Do *we*?" Alex emphasised sarcastically.

"Yup. Mason says you're fucking with his charts, and you don't do your exercises properly, and Chef says you don't eat a bloody thing he puts in front of you, so you're skin and bone, which..." Tyler took a step back and surveyed Alex for a second. "While lending you a certain waifish charm, can't go on. You need to eat."

"I'm not hungry." Alex shrugged.

Tyler glared at him. "I expected a certain amount of bullshit to begin with, but I didn't spend a hundred and sixty million quid to watch you starve to death. You'll do what I want, when I want."

"Make me," he challenged.

The entire room suddenly went very quiet.

"This is my major-domo, Mr Drummond." Tyler gestured to the man beside him. "You might have noticed his strap. Do you know why he uses this particular one?" He held out his hand, and Drummond passed him the length of leather.

"I don't know, and I don't care," Alex said defiantly, waiting for the first blow. At this point, he thought he'd actively welcome the pain.

"Because it hurts like hell but doesn't leave many marks," Tyler said.

"And you don't want me marked when you hand me over to be fucked by one of your stupid guests?"

"You?" Tyler laughed. "Oh, I'm not going to beat *you*, Alex. You're too thin and wasted, and I spent too much money to risk harming a hair on your pretty little head. No, I'm going to beat *her*."

He turned as he said that and lashed out at Solange. The strap cracked down hard on her shoulder, and she screamed.

Alex reeled back, taken by surprise. Collecting himself, he said as nonchalantly as he could, "Why should I care about her? She spied on me for five years. She betrayed me. I don't care if you hurt her."

"Good – so you won't mind watching."

Drummond picked Solange up and held her against the mirrored

wall, while Tyler whipped the strap over her shoulders repeatedly. She was only wearing a thin workout vest, and she screamed again and again as each stroke hit home.

It was so raw and brutal that Alex didn't know what to do. He didn't love Solange – he wasn't even sure he liked her – but he didn't know how to stand by and watch a woman take a savage beating in front of him. He tried to harden himself, to find the core of darkness in his soul that everyone was so sure he possessed... but it simply wasn't there. Watching two big people hold down and whip someone much smaller brought back vivid memories of his schooldays. His only weapon against the bullies who'd tormented him then had been his sharp tongue. But although it might have brought him some satisfaction, it usually only made the beatings worse. If he was lucky, his brother intervened, but there was nobody to protect Solange – except him.

He saw Scarface take a step forward, and then pause, a surprised look on his face as if he hadn't even realised he was moving. He caught Alex's eye with an expression of mute appeal.

"Stop!" Alex cried out shakily.

Tyler paused, his arm still outstretched. "Are you going to eat whatever is put in front of you?" he demanded.

"Yes."

"Are you going to do every single exercise Mason gives you?"

"Yes." He bowed his head.

"Good." Tyler handed the strap back to his major-domo and walked over. "And are you going to fuck any person I tell you to fuck?"

"Yes," he mumbled.

"Again, so I can hear it," Tyler ordered. "Are you going to be the good little whore we all know you are?"

Alex looked at Solange, still pinned to the mirrored wall by Drummond, her body shaking with quiet sobs.

"Yes," he said in a louder voice, his throat dry.

"No – say it properly," Tyler ordered mercilessly, waving his arm around the room. "I want them all to hear you say what a whore you are."

GHOST EYE

21

"Yes, I'll be a good little whore," he shouted, his heart beating crazily in his chest. "And I'll fuck anyone you want me to fuck."

"Good boy." Tyler grabbed his head and kissed it.

Alex froze.

Tyler laughed and released him. "Oh, don't worry – I'm not going to fuck you. Not yet, anyway." He winked, and Alex felt a flash of revulsion. Tyler patted his cheek, still laughing. "Aw, and to think you used to find me so sexy. One day, you'll beg me for the pleasure and mean it – and on that day, my victory will be complete." With that, he turned on his heel and left.

Drummond dropped Solange and followed him, and she sank to the floor. Alex ran towards her, but someone else got there first. Carefully picking her up, Scarface carried her to her room. Alex trailed along behind them and then stood back, helplessly watching as Scarface placed her on the bed and examined her shoulders. They were red and looked sore, but the strap had done its work with as few traces as Tyler had promised. Despite that, Alex knew she'd be in pain for days.

"I'm sorry," he said, lying down on the bed beside her.

"Don't feel sorry for me," she said, shivering in shock. "I deserved it for what I did to you. I deserved it and more. You should have let him keep on beating me."

"I couldn't." He stroked her hair away from her forehead. "It turns out I'm not such a bad boy after all."

"I don't think you ever were, really," she said softly.

"I'll go and get you some painkillers," Scarface said, leaving the room.

"You do know he's hopelessly in love with you, right?" Alex said.

Solange gave a feeble smile. "Yeah, I know. Poor guy. He was first assigned here about three months ago, and he's been my unwanted puppy dog ever since."

"Hey, don't write him off – you two have a lot in common."

"Like what?"

Alex gave a little grin. "Well, you both have a tendency to fall for the wrong people."

She managed a shaky little laugh. "So, are you really going to do it?

When the time comes, are you going to willingly sleep with Tyler's guests?"

He gave a dismissive shrug. "Oh, I've always sold myself; Tyler was right about that. But now, I'll be doing it to keep you safe, instead of to score some drugs or to keep Neil happy. I just have to keep remembering that."

"I hope you can, Alex." She reached out and curled her fingers around his hand. "For your sake more than for mine, I really hope you can."

Chapter Two

OCTOBER 2095

Josiah

The sun was already creeping around the edge of the curtains when Josiah woke. He glanced at his bedside clock in surprise: 8.33 a.m. He hadn't slept so late or so deeply in ages. He felt relaxed and peaceful... until he caught sight of his lacerated hands and memories of the previous night came flooding back in. He groaned as he remembered allowing Alexander into his bed; what on earth had possessed him? Two days! He'd had the IS for two days and already the man was sleeping beside him. What the hell?

He rolled over in trepidation, but there was no sign of his IS. A delicious scent wafted up the stairs from the kitchen, and he realised, with relief, that he wouldn't have to face Alexander just yet.

He reached for his holopad and saw that Reed had posted an update. He read it as he cleaned his teeth... then stopped and put his toothbrush down in surprise. The court records on Alexander's servitude had been released, revealing his first houder to have been George Tyler.

Josiah took a moment to consider that – Tyler was a household name, a famous businessman, and fabulously wealthy. The surprising element was that Alexander had been working for Tyler when he stole that money. Why on earth had Tyler forked out

£160 million for a man who had deceived him so appallingly? Reading on, he saw that Tyler's family had a long history with the Lyttons. Josiah wiped a towel across his face absently – this was starting to feel personal. He finished the update and put his holopad away, wondering what it meant for the case and his understanding of Alexander Lytton. This would clearly take some time to digest.

He took a shower and shaved, enjoying the fact his head didn't feel tight and fuzzy anymore and his eyes weren't stinging from lack of sleep. He felt like himself again, which made the intense emotions of the previous night seem distant and alien, as if they belonged to a different person. He winced at the memory of that wild, passionate kiss; he would have to apologise to Alexander and make it clear it wouldn't happen again.

Dressing in a charcoal-grey suit with a lilac shirt, grey waistcoat, and purple silk tie, he glanced at himself in the mirror. He looked better than he had in days: the shadows under his eyes had disappeared, and his eyes were clear and bright. There was some colour to his skin, too, and the bruises on his jaw weren't nearly as stark. The knuckles of his aching hands were in far worse shape, but he could hide them behind gloves again.

He almost had a spring in his step as he jogged down the stairs. He paused at the bottom; his shoes, which had been covered in mud and gravel from his trip to The Orchard the previous day, were neatly positioned at the foot of the stairs – clean, gleaming, and freshly polished. "Alexander!" He picked them up and strode into the kitchen, brandishing them.

His indie was standing in front of the hob, washed, shaved, and dressed in a pair of jeans and a tight blue tee-shirt that showed off his toned arms and chest. "Did you do this?" He waved the shoes.

"They were dirty, so I cleaned them," Alexander replied with a shrug.

"What time did you get up?" He sat down at the kitchen table to pull on the shoes.

"Six. I did my yoga, polished those, tidied up down here, took a shower, and then came back down to prepare breakfast."

"You didn't have to do all that," Josiah chided. "I've looked after myself perfectly well for years. I don't need help."

"I know, but you work hard, and isn't it nice to have someone to do the boring stuff?"

"It's too nice. That's the damn point. I can see how people get so used to this kind of thing they come to expect it, and before long..."

"They have a whole team of indies taking care of their every need? Yeah, I can see it, too." Alexander grinned at him. "But honestly, it's nice to be useful."

He cleared his throat, feeling awkward. "So... about last night."

"Hmm?" Alexander arranged two plates on trays and began serving breakfast.

"I want to apologise."

"Why?" Alexander glanced at him curiously.

"Because I lost control."

"And that's such a bad thing for you, right?" Alexander raised an amused eyebrow.

"Yes," he said firmly. "I'm not going to make excuses. I was upset and confused, but I shouldn't have behaved like that."

"I didn't mind." Alexander shrugged.

"Well, I do – and I want to be clear that it won't happen again."

"Okay." Alexander shrugged again. "Are you ready for breakfast?"

He felt wrong-footed by Alexander's complete lack of reaction to what had been such a huge deal for him. "Um... yes."

"Good. Here." Alexander handed him a tray. "I thought we'd eat in the dining room as it's such a nice day." He jerked his head at the sun shining through the kitchen window. "Unusual for this time of year – we should make the most of it."

Josiah followed his indie into the dining room, which he never used because it'd always seemed pointless when there was only him, eating alone. Besides, it was where he'd shared many long, convivial meals with Peter through what felt like the perpetual summer of their marriage, with the patio doors open when it was warm, and Hattie flopped out on the cool paving stones leading to the lawn.

The table was already set for breakfast – there were even fresh flowers in the vase on the big oak table. Alexander opened the patio

doors, while Josiah sat down silently because he couldn't think of a good reason not to. His indie was right – it was a lovely day. The trees in the garden were a glorious mix of oranges and yellows, and the lawn was green and fresh from the recent rain.

"When did you last even come into this room?" Alexander asked. "To sit, I mean. You obviously clean it regularly, but then keeping everything neat, tidy, and firmly in its place seems to be your thing."

"I don't remember." Josiah took a mouthful of food. This morning it was a tasty paella – Alexander clearly had a repertoire.

"Don't close up again," Alexander said softly, pouring him some orange juice. "Last night…"

"Was a bad night for us both," Josiah said firmly, thinking how easy it had been to talk to his IS in the dark as he sat on the swing, and then to share a bed with him. Too easy. "Today is different."

"Yes, indeed – but you *are* very different with your armour on." He gestured to Josiah's suit. "All these years of seeing you onscreen, looking so strong and self-assured – I had no idea you were still so locked up in your grief."

"If you think it's a weakness you can use against me, think again."

"I would never do that," Alexander said sharply. "I was surprised, because I made the very mistake I'd warned you against making – of believing in appearances. I was glad to see that side of you last night, to be honest. It makes you more…"

"Pathetic?" Josiah suggested.

"Human," Alexander said softly.

"Hmm."

"Are you ashamed of your grief?" Alexander studied him for a moment. "No, that's not it. You're only ashamed I saw it. That's the real reason you didn't want me in your space, I think."

"Yes," Josiah agreed honestly.

"Well, I won't tell anyone."

"I'd never ask you to keep secrets for me."

"Nonetheless." Alexander shrugged.

Josiah busied himself eating his breakfast, feeling profoundly uncomfortable.

"I love the vase," Alexander said, pointing at the glazed green

ceramic vase, filled with flowers, at the centre of the table. "The inscription is beautiful." He brushed it with his fingertips and read out loud. "'To my dear friends, Peter and Josiah, on your wedding day. With all my love, Liz.' Who is she? She sounds nice."

"She is."

"Did she make the vase herself?"

"Yup."

"Are you still in touch with her? How do you know her?"

"She's an old friend."

"So, you *do* actually have friends; I was starting to wonder."

Josiah glared at him, but he couldn't hold it for long in the face of Alexander's cheeky wink.

"What's she like?"

Josiah smiled. "Very sweet, very kind, and very pretty."

"Did you ever have a thing with her?" The indie's eyes were gleaming, but Josiah found he didn't mind the mild teasing.

"I've been gay since the day I was born, so no, I did not have a 'thing' with her. I've never had a thing with any woman. How about you?"

Alexander nodded. "I've only been with men for the past few years, but before then I slept with women, too. Of course, I'm an IS, so I sleep with whoever I'm ordered to sleep with."

"That's not entirely true. You offered to sleep with me, and that certainly wasn't my order," Josiah pointed out.

"I find you attractive." Alexander flashed him a smile. "Besides, I'm an IS – it's my job to keep my houders happy."

"And I told you that you don't need to keep me happy in that way."

"I know, but it's been a long time since I was given any choice in the matter."

"You know how wrong I think that is," Josiah told him quietly.

"Do I?" Alexander raised an eyebrow. "Your husband was brutally murdered by an IS, and you seem to have dedicated your career to tracking them down for crimes they may or may not have committed. You're so good at it you've even earned the title 'indiehunter'. Now, I get the feeling you don't like that name, but maybe I'm wrong. You do give out some very mixed messages."

"I've never once sent anyone for trial without believing they were a hundred per cent guilty," Josiah told him firmly. "IS or not. I've caught plenty of murderers who weren't indies, but the media doesn't care about them."

"Justice means a lot to you, then?" Alexander leaned forward, his grey eyes blisteringly intense. "Whoever the victim is?"

"I don't give a damn who the victim is – I track down killers. That's my job."

"And do you give a damn who the perpetrators are?"

"No," Josiah replied flatly. "I don't care if the perp is the prime minister, some Quarterlands drug lord, or an IS – my job is to catch killers, whoever they are, and I do it very well."

"And if the killer is justified in taking a life?"

Josiah put his fork down. "Are you confessing?"

"No. It's just a question. You seem like a man who wants everything to be black and white – I wondered how you felt about shades of grey."

"Well, I don't make the rules, but every society needs laws against murder, and every murder has to be accounted for, regardless of circumstance. If the killer has a good reason for committing the crime, then that's up to the courts to decide, not me. Solving the case and sending it to trial is my job – nothing more or less."

Alexander nodded slowly. "Thank you. Now, let's change the subject. Your friend Liz – did she also make those funny little objects up there?" He waved a hand at the sideboard, which displayed half a dozen little jugs, cups, and bowls of varying degrees of wobbliness.

Josiah glanced up at them with a smile. He dusted the little knick-knacks carefully every month, but it had been a long time since he'd actually taken any pleasure in them. "Yeah."

"They aren't so good, but this one – the one she made for the wedding – is flawless." Alexander ran his fingers gently over the vase on the table again.

"She'd had time to practise by then."

"She has a good eye for design – once her skill caught up with her creativity," Alexander pronounced, studying the vase on the table critically.

"You're an expert?"

"In design? Not exactly an expert, but I've studied it and had some ambitions in that area once. Your friend is artistic. I had a friend like her once, too – very sweet, very kind, very pretty."

He glanced up, wondering if he was going to learn something important. "What happened to her?"

"That's a story for another time," Alexander dismissed softly.

Josiah gazed at him searchingly. "You don't trust me."

"I don't know yet – I'm still trying to decide – but you don't trust me, either."

"I don't know yet – I'm still trying to decide."

Alexander gave an amused grunt.

Finishing his breakfast, Josiah stirred his tea thoughtfully. Alexander had quickly learned of his sweet tooth, and he knew there would be a teaspoon of sugar in it, just the way he liked it.

"So, are you still going to take my life apart, piece by piece, like you said yesterday?" Alexander queried.

"Yes," Josiah said flatly. "Any suggestions as to where I should start?"

Alexander's mask sprang back into place in an instant, his eyes emptying of all emotion. "Well, you've already done my family, so the next logical place to investigate would be my first houder," he said. His tone was offhand, but Josiah noticed the tight lines of tension in his body.

"George Tyler?"

Alexander's mask barely stayed in place. "It seems like you've already made some progress in taking my life apart," he commented neutrally.

"Yup. What can you tell me about him?"

"Nothing." Alexander shrugged. "You'll have to form your own opinion."

"Okay, but I'm not here to run around doing your bidding. I'm here to solve a murder and bring a killer to justice."

"I want that, too." Leaning across the table, his mask slipped – his eyes were blisteringly intense. "You have no idea how much."

"Then help me with my investigation."

"I am!"

At that moment, Josiah's holopad buzzed, Esther's face flashing up in the room. "We're not finished," he told his indie as he picked up the call.

"No, we've barely begun," Alexander replied, standing up to clear the table.

Josiah didn't have time to wonder what he meant as Esther started speaking hurriedly.

"Joe – sorry, but the media have found out that you've taken Lytton as your temporary IS, and they're all over it. You can expect some fireworks."

"Any idea how they found out?" Moving into the living room at the front of the house, he flicked the curtain open an inch and was immediately blinded by camera flashes.

"No idea, but they're on their way over."

"They're already here."

"Do you need me to send Reed to escort you in?"

"No. I'm not coming into the office today. I have another line of inquiry."

"A lead?" she asked hopefully.

"Not exactly, but it could turn into one. I'll speak to you later."

He returned to the kitchen, where Alexander was stacking their breakfast crockery into the dishwasher. "Grab a sweater. You're coming with me today," he ordered.

"I am? How exciting. Any reason why?"

"Yeah, there's a horde of reporters outside the door trying to get pictures of you. There's no way I'm leaving you here alone with that mob outside."

"Where are we going?" Alexander grabbed his sweater from the back of one of the kitchen chairs.

"I'm taking you up on your suggestion; we're going to pay George Tyler a visit."

He took a certain grim satisfaction from the way the blood drained from the indie's face. Alexander took a deep breath and then squared his shoulders in a determined way.

"Okay," he said.

. . .

Josiah was thankful he'd parked his duck in the garage the previous night, instead of leaving it on the driveway as he sometimes did. It meant he could get Alexander into it without being seen.

"There's a blanket on the back seat," he threw over his shoulder, striding towards the duck. "You can put it over your head so they don't get a picture. I'll tell you when the coast is clear..." He stopped in the process of opening the duck door when he realised Alexander wasn't behind him. Turning, he found his IS standing in front of Peter's red car, a stunned look on his face. "Don't tell me you're one of those people who loves these useless lumps of old metal?" he sighed.

Alexander blinked, his eyes bright and wet. "She's beautiful," he said. "Anyone with an eye for design can see that." He reached out a finger almost reverently towards the vehicle. "May I?"

"Go ahead."

He left the IS to it, mystified by how anyone could be so deeply affected by the sight of an old car. He put through a call to Reed to ascertain Tyler's current whereabouts, watching out of the corner of his eye as Alexander gently caressed the car. He stiffened when Alexander walked around to the driver's side and peered in through the window. "Nosy?" he growled, striding over.

Alexander jumped. "A little," he admitted, shamefaced. "This is where it happened, isn't it?"

"Yes. There's no blood, if that's what you're thinking. I had the seats replaced, and I cleaned every single inch of the interior with the specialist equipment Mel gave me." He opened the driver's door to illustrate that point, and they stood there in silence until he suddenly became aware that Alexander wasn't looking inside the car anymore – but at him. "What?" he demanded.

"Nothing," Alexander said, but there was a quizzical expression in his eyes, as though he was expecting something. He shook his head. "Just... I'm surprised you kept her, after what happened. Doesn't she bring back memories of that night?"

"No." Josiah slammed the car door shut.

"Thank you for showing her to me," Alexander said softly. "She really is very beautiful."

Josiah grunted. Peter's car was sacrosanct – he never showed her to anyone, and he was keen to move Alexander away.

Escorting Alexander over to his AV, he settled him in the footwell of the passenger seat with a blanket over his head. Then he clicked open the garage door and backed the duck out onto the driveway and then onto the street at top speed. The media scattered as the duck thundered into the road. Dozens of cameras flashed, but they didn't get what they'd come for. They were in too much disarray to organise a pursuit, and he soon left them far behind. When he was sure they weren't being followed, he pulled the blanket off the indie and threw it onto the back seat.

"You do know what they'll write about you now that you've taken me as your IS, don't you?" Alexander said, sliding up into his seat.

Josiah tensed. "Yeah, I know, but I don't care what they think."

"You're their hero – they've built you up, and now they'll tear you down. That's what they do."

Josiah gripped the steering wheel tightly and increased his speed.

"I think you care a bit," Alexander murmured.

"The press have been telling lies about me for years. Why should I care about another one?"

"Then why haven't you ever sued them?"

"What's the point? I do my job, and I don't bloody well answer to them."

"They could make your life difficult. So far, the lies they've told about you haven't made your job any harder – the opposite, probably – but this one might."

"I'll deal with that if it happens."

"I believe you will." Alexander settled back. "But now you're in a bad mood, and we were doing so well over breakfast."

"Do you want to play twenty questions again?" Josiah growled.

"No, I want you to tell me about your wedding day."

That took the wind out of Josiah's sails. "Why the hell do you want to know about that?"

"The vase – I'm intrigued. I'm wondering how the aloof Josiah Raine ever got so far as making vows to spend the rest of his life with someone."

"It wasn't like that." Josiah slammed his foot on the accelerator.

"Then what was it like?"

He had no intention of sharing something so private with Alexander, but he retreated back into the easy comfort of the memories as he drove.

———

It had taken them a week to return to the convoy after leaving Geneva. Big Jen had been left in temporary charge of restocking the trucks and getting things on the road again. She looked rather pleased with herself as she sauntered over to greet them. The rest of the unit followed, delighted that their popular commanding officer had returned.

"Remember," Josiah warned Peter, "we're telling them about us. I'm not skulking around your tent at night."

Peter rolled his eyes. "I know, I know. I'll tell them when I go through our orders later."

"We'll tell them," Josiah said firmly. "Both of us. Together."

They jumped out of the jeep, Hattie keening in excitement behind them. Big Jen greeted Peter with a salute, and he returned it.

Much to Josiah's surprise, she let out a loud whoop and turned to face the rest of the unit. "Finally! Pay up," she yelled, pointing at the ring on Peter's finger. "What took you so long, Sarge?" she asked cheekily, spinning back around to face him. "We opened a book on you making an honest man of the captain months ago."

Josiah stood there, his mouth open, dumbfounded.

Peter let out a howl of laughter that went on for so long he almost choked. "We're not actually married," he spluttered eventually.

"We're engaged," Josiah corrected stonily, uncomfortable with the fact that their relationship had been the subject of gossip.

"Your secret is safe with us, sir," Big Jen said, tapping the side of her nose.

"No," Josiah said sharply. "We won't ask you to keep our secret or to lie for us. If you want to report us, we understand."

"As if," Big Jen laughed. "We look after our own."

And that was that.

. . .

The convoy resumed its slow journey across the war-torn countryside, but this time it was different: conditions were far more dangerous since the scavs were more numerous. It took them much longer to make progress as they were forced into pitched battles every few days, and the need to remain ever vigilant took its toll.

They were, therefore, exhausted a couple of months later when they stopped at the base camp to resupply – and surprised to find a lumpy package waiting for them.

"What is it?" Josiah asked, feeling the weight of it.

"No idea, but it's addressed to us both." Peter ripped open the box to discover a small, misshapen pot inside, carefully wrapped and accompanied by a handwritten note:

Don't laugh! It's a first attempt. Uncle Simon is teaching me the family business. Hope you're both well. Lots of love, Liz.

"Yes, but what actually *is* it?" Josiah held it up and studied it.

"A jug? Maybe?" Peter grinned. "Good for Liz."

"How did she know where we'd be?"

"I keep in touch." Peter shrugged.

"Isn't that risky?"

"It's all risky." Peter shrugged again, a gleam in his eye.

"Hang on. I know that look." Josiah took him by the arm and dragged him out of earshot. "Is there anything you should tell me, Peter Hunt?"

"I was going to – just as soon as I was sure." Peter handed him his nanopad. "It's a message from Elsie. She can get a new shipment out of England by the end of next week if we can get the convoy to Normandy in time."

"It'll be tight," Josiah said slowly. "But we can do it if we drive a hard pace. I reckon we can clip a day off the time if we take that new route I told you about yesterday."

Peter raised an eyebrow. "No lectures?"

"No. This is who you are; I knew that going in. I'm not going to try and change you – my job is to keep you safe while you fulfil that saviour complex of yours."

"My hero." Peter pressed a grateful kiss to his cheek. "You know, Joe, this is going to be a lot more fun with you on board."

"You and I have completely different ideas of fun." Josiah rolled his eyes, although he couldn't deny he felt a thrill all the same.

When they arrived at the supply camp in Normandy, another misshapen package was waiting for them.

"What do you think? A cup?" Peter held it up.

"Hmm... I think so. It's better than her last attempt; it doesn't topple over when you set it down." Josiah demonstrated, placing the ceramic object on a chair. "Anything from Elsie?" he asked in a softer voice.

"Yes. Our guests will be waiting for us in a warehouse an hour away from here. We'll take one of the trucks out this evening and pick them up."

After it had grown dark, they slipped out of camp.

"Why do they need our help once they've arrived?" Josiah queried as they drove. "They're out of the UK; surely that's the hard bit?"

"It is, but all the port towns over here are teeming with bounty hunters. It's big business tracking down escaped indentured servants. We can't just dump them here and wash our hands of them. If they get picked up, they might betray us. So, we take them on to safer areas, and hand them over to people we can trust to look after them until they find their feet."

"Who organises the other side of it?" Josiah asked. "The getting out of the UK bit? Is that Elsie?"

"Elsie's a little too old for that. She's our liaison – she takes calls from escaped indies and arranges collection. We have a network of volunteers in the UK that Elsie runs. They pick up the indies and care

for them until we can arrange shipment out. We have a number of routes for that. I'm just a small part of a much bigger operation, Joe."

"Yeah, but it's your operation, isn't it? You set it up. You know where all the bodies are buried – metaphorically speaking."

Peter grimaced. "We all do our bit. I work the convoys most of the year, so I have people I rely on back home."

"It's a miracle you haven't been caught."

"Planning and logistics." Peter grinned. "The army taught me well."

The warehouse held around twenty indies, and the volunteer who'd spirited them out of Britain. Peter exchanged a few words with her, introduced her to Josiah, and then they loaded the escapees into the back of the truck, where supplies of food, water, and medication were waiting. They were a poor, huddled mass of humanity, visibly scared, some in poor shape physically, while others were clearly struggling with the stress of their escape. All of them were pathetically grateful.

"I can see why you do this," Josiah said quietly as they drove back to camp with their human cargo.

"Yeah, I knew you would." Peter squeezed his hand.

Josiah was on tenterhooks for the duration of their mission, worrying constantly about the indies being discovered in the back of the truck.

"Relax. I've done this before," Peter laughed.

"It's nerve-wracking."

"You get used to it."

Josiah brought supplies to the indies every other evening, taking it in turns with Peter. He waited until the camp was quiet before slipping into the truck. Some talked to him, while others were just silent, pinched faces in the dark. Nonetheless, each of them had a story, and Josiah was almost sorry to say goodbye when they reached LKG.

He breathed a sigh of relief when the indies had been safely dispatched to their contact in the sprawling barge city. He hadn't slept properly since picking them up, unlike Peter, who snored the nights away peacefully.

GHOST EYE   37

That night, Josiah fell into a deep, relieved slumber the minute his head hit the pillow, only to be woken in the early hours by the sound of gunfire. Peter was already jumping out of bed, reaching for his gun; Josiah wasn't far behind.

The camp was awash with what at first he took to be scavs – except that these attackers were well organised and had guns.

"Militia," Peter snapped grimly as the unit fell into a line of defence around the trucks. "Run by the warlords."

"So close to the Barkhausen camp?" Josiah hissed, hunkering down beside him.

"The warlords are winning at the moment; we might not have the camp for much longer. I've called for backup, but we'll have to hold them off until it comes. Think we can do that?"

"I was at Rosengarten, remember?" Josiah shot him a grin and turned to instruct the unit.

The fighting was fast and intense, but there was no sign of the promised backup. Finally, Peter had no choice but to order a retreat. The convoy was lost, all the trucks and medical supplies surrendered to the militia. Josiah was just glad they'd got all the indies out in time.

Their opponents fired at them furiously as they fell back, and it was chaos. The unit scattered, running in the dark with gunfire flashing all around. Keeping his head down, Josiah sprinted as fast as he could towards a patch of woodland in the distance, Peter always in sight beside him. He saw Little Jen go down in a hail of bullets, then heard a sharp crack and saw Peter stumble, his leg suddenly covered in blood. Picking Peter up, he slung his arm over his shoulder and dragged him towards the cover of nearby trees.

"I can't walk. You should leave me," Peter protested, panting heavily as Josiah propped him up against a trunk and fastened a makeshift tourniquet above his wound. "There's no chance we'll both get out of this alive."

"Then we'll both die, because I'm not leaving you." Looking back through the trees to see if they were being followed, he caught sight of a group of militia in the distance and took hold of Peter again.

"Leave me!" Peter growled. That's an order."

"You're not the only one who can disobey orders, you know," he retorted. Heaving Peter onto his back, he set off again.

He wasn't sure how far he ran, or for how long, dodging bullets along the way. One of them must have hit home, because his shoulder suddenly started to hurt, but he paid it no attention. He was still running when another bullet hit his leg, and he went flying down the side of a hill, coming to rest at the bottom with a thud. Confused, he looked through a curtain of blood to see Peter crawling towards him.

"Joe... Joe!" Peter's face appeared above him, framed by the light of the moon... no, that wasn't the moon... that was...

"Helicopters," he croaked, pointing up into the air.

"Oh, thank God for that," Peter gasped, looking up. "Joe!" He turned back. "Stay with me, Joe."

"I'm fine," he lied, his tongue feeling thick and lazy in his mouth. He must have lost consciousness for a moment, because when he came to, he could hear himself groaning, and Peter was leaning over him.

"Just rest easy. I've radioed our position. They'll find us soon. Look – I can see them coming." The bright lights in the distance grew closer and closer, the wind from the helicopter blades making the trees rustle violently.

"About fucking time," Josiah said, and then he passed out.

When he woke, the first thing he saw was Peter, sitting beside him.

His leg was heavily bandaged, he had several days' worth of stubble on his chin, and his face was etched with weary lines. Hattie was sitting patiently at his side.

"How long...?" Josiah rasped.

"Have you been napping? Three days." Peter held a glass of water to his parched lips.

"Where...?"

"Army hospital in Salisbury. We're back in England. They airlifted us here when they realised how badly we were both wounded."

"Convoy?"

"Gone." Peter shook his head. "First one I ever lost."

"Sorry." Josiah knew he had to be devastated by that. He moved his

arm, gingerly, and rested his hand over Peter's. "What about the rest of the unit. Little Jen?"

"She's dead. Most of them are."

The news wasn't unexpected, but it hurt all the same.

"We've lost control of the whole region; that's why backup took so long. They've dismantled the peacekeeping missions with immediate effect. We're being transferred back into the regular army," Peter said despondently.

"What?" Josiah tried to sit up, but a wave of nausea forced him back down.

"Yeah, you shouldn't do that. You have a broken fibula, several cracked ribs, a bullet in your shoulder, another in your ankle, and concussion," Peter said.

"Nothing serious, then." Josiah managed a ghostly grin.

"The bullets are flesh wounds, luckily. The rest are nastier, but you'll live."

"Feel half-dead," Josiah said hoarsely.

"That's twice you've saved my life," Peter said, almost accusingly.

Josiah gave a wry grin. "And there's you always telling me how easily you managed to stay alive before we met. I'm not seeing it, to be honest."

"I was an idiot."

"Yeah, but you're my idiot, and keeping you alive is my job."

"Then you're the idiot. Your life is important, too." Peter squeezed his hand.

"Can't live without you. No point," Josiah muttered. "Better to keep you alive."

"Oh, you'd be fine. You'd find some other worthless fool to save, I'm sure. I just hope they deserve you."

"Don't." Josiah reached out, wincing, and put his finger over Peter's lips. "Don't even joke about it."

Peter nodded while gently stroking his hair. "I'm sorry. It's okay," he said quietly. "I wouldn't want to live without you, either. I won't joke about it again."

"You look like crap." Josiah studied his fiancé's drawn face. "Couldn't they find you a bed?"

"I wouldn't leave in case you woke up. We've been here the whole time." Peter rested his hand on Hattie's head.

"How did you get her out?" Josiah asked, smiling as Hattie licked his fingers.

"Big Jen turned up with her. No idea how. She's fine – thank God. A bit smelly but none the worse for wear – Hattie, I mean, not Big Jen, although actually, she didn't smell too savoury either. Oh – I've got something that'll make you smile!" He reached into his pocket and pulled out a small ceramic jug covered in light cream swirls. "From Liz."

"She's improved. It does actually look like a jug." Josiah grinned. Then a thought occurred to him. "What about me? Am I being transferred back into the regular army, too?"

"Yeah. I told them all about us. This." Peter pointed to his ring. "They weren't exactly delighted, but they don't have enough good officers to throw any away. As long as we don't work together again, it's fine. So, maybe now's the time for you to join the MPs like you wanted?"

"I'd like that," Josiah said, nodding slowly. "What about your business with Elsie?" he asked quietly.

"I don't know." Peter gave a washed-out smile. "It's all on hold for now."

"I'm sorry. I know how long you spent building it all up."

"Yeah." Peter gazed down at the ground for a moment, then looked up again and grinned. "Fuck it," he said. "Let's get married."

They didn't want a fuss, so they didn't tell anyone. Six weeks later, Josiah hobbled into the registry office on crutches to find Peter waiting inside looking... completely unlike Peter. He'd ironed his uniform, polished his shoes, put gel in his usually messy hair, and pinned his medals to his chest for the occasion. Hattie was beside him, proudly wearing a white bandana around her collar.

When they got back, they found they hadn't done such a good job of keeping it a secret as they'd thought; Big Jen and the other survivors

from the unit were waiting for them with a crate of booze and a pile of wedding gifts, including…

"It's beautiful." Josiah held up the smooth emerald-green vase and read the inscription on the side. Then he glanced at the note that accompanied it.

So happy that my two favourite men are getting hitched. I wish I could be there, but I'm sending this instead. I think it's my best to date – it doesn't even wobble. Congratulations! Liz

They partied until dawn. After everyone had gone, they sat outside on the grass to watch the sun come up.

"I'm not giving up on the Kathleen Line," Peter told him. "I'm just taking a break until I work out what to do next."

"I never thought for a second that you'd ever give it up." Josiah shrugged. "I don't want you to change. I kinda love you the way you are, even though you're a complete idiot most of the time."

Peter grinned. "That's good, because I'll still ignore the rules, and do stupid stuff, and probably get us both into trouble."

"Don't you know that I'm a Quarterlands kid?" Josiah snorted. "I can handle trouble. Now, shut up and kiss me."

––––––

Even after all these years, the memory was still vivid, making his heart ache with loss. Josiah took the next corner too fast, and the AV screeched in protest. Alexander reached out and gently touched his hand. Josiah steadied himself. He had to stop thinking about the past and focus on the here and now. He was going to meet George Tyler; he needed his wits about him.

Chapter Three

JULY 2088

Alex

Alex gazed at himself in the mirror. His thick brown hair had been blow-dried into a bouffant style, he was clean-shaven, and he was wearing a pair of sinfully tight pale blue jeans, an equally tight white shirt, and an ugly salmon-pink jacket. It had been two weeks since he'd agreed to start eating again, and his body had started to fill out with the food and enforced exercise regime.

"Really?" he asked, wrinkling his nose as he looked at himself. "I look like a stuffed piglet. Is that what this guy is into?"

"Oh, yes. We've entertained Mr Bagshaw many times before," Lorenzo said, standing behind him and studying him critically in the mirror. "He likes his young men to be pretty, well groomed, closely shaved, and looking..."

"Like a blancmange? This isn't even a cool shade of pink – it's ugly as fuck."

"... like sweet, innocent boys," Lorenzo finished.

Alex laughed. "It's been years since I was either innocent or a boy. Who is this guy? He sounds creepy."

"He'll treat you well enough. There are plenty worse," the stylist said firmly. "Be nice to him."

"What happened to the other one?"

GHOST EYE   **43**

"What other one?" Lorenzo replied, fussing around the room, tidying up.

"The one who lived in this room and fucked this Bagshaw guy for Tyler before me. I can't be the first."

Lorenzo folded the towel he'd picked up off the bed. "He was moved to a different location. Mr Tyler has other properties and other places he does business. This is his residential London HQ, but he likes to keep different indies with different looks in various places in case he needs to parachute one of them in for a particular job."

"Like a harem?" Alex tried to adjust his clothes in a way that made them more comfortable. The skinny jeans left nothing to the imagination, and he wasn't used to the outline of his cock being so obviously visible.

"If you like. You're his star attraction now. You're beautiful and famous, so you'll be much in demand. Mr Tyler will get his money's worth out of you."

Alex made a face at himself in the mirror. "How reassuring. Do we know what Bagshaw has done for Tyler to be granted the pleasure of my company for the night?"

"I don't ask questions like that, and neither should you," Lorenzo said sharply. "I just do my job and keep my mouth shut about things that don't concern me – you'll learn to do the same."

"Easier to say when your job isn't having sex on command," Alex snapped back.

Lorenzo sighed and walked over to him. "About that, my love..." He handed Alex a little see-through bag with a couple of pills in it. "These should help if you experience any difficulties in that department."

"Never needed any help before," Alex said.

"You've always been able to choose your own partners before, sweetheart." Lorenzo patted his arm kindly.

Alex's stomach lurched. This was his first assignment, and he didn't have any idea if he'd be able to perform. He'd had zero libido for months. Maybe it'd return if he had a sexual partner, but that didn't seem likely, given the circumstances. He pocketed the pills gratefully.

"You'll do fine, lover boy," Lorenzo reassured him, brushing his

bouffant hairstyle with his fingertips. "Go get 'em, tiger." He pressed a little kiss to his cheek, and then, with one last, sad look, left the room.

Alex's stomach churned even more as his guard escorted him to the living room. He'd been forced along this path step by step, each leading inexorably to this moment, and he wasn't sure how to react. There was no way out – that much was clear – but how could he hang on to some semblance of himself when Tyler was so determined to turn him into someone else? Was this how it was for all indentured servants after losing their freedom, or was he feeling this way because he was being made to whore for his new houder?

The lights in the living room had been dimmed, music was playing softly, and Solange was standing there in a tight red dress that clung sinfully to every curve on her beautiful body.

"At least you got to wear something nice," Alex said. She gave him an understanding smile and took hold of his hand.

"You'll get through this," she said, pulling him close.

"First time is the worst, huh?" He forced a smile.

"You'll be fine." She wrapped her arms around him and danced with him slowly around the room, stroking soothing circles on his back as they swayed in time to the music.

He rested his chin on her shoulder, and the soft clouds of her hair gently brushed his cheek. He loosened up a little.

"Be brave, Alex," she whispered into his ear. "You can do this." Then, hearing footsteps and laughter in the hallway, she gave his hand a quick squeeze and drew away.

Tyler entered the room, looking relaxed in an all-black ensemble – chinos, open-necked shirt, and jacket. With him were his two "guests", both men in their forties, dressed in business suits. One had receding hair, a pudgy face, a lazy left eye, and a beer belly that hung over his waistband, while the other was tall and lean, with a wolfish quality. Neither was attractive. Alex wondered which one was his.

"Ah, here are my beautiful friends," Tyler announced, winking at Alex. "This is the lovely Solange – you've met her before, Martin, but Clive hasn't had the pleasure."

Martin was clearly the portly man. He took Solange's hand and raised it to his lips. She gave a little giggle, as if flattered by the atten-

GHOST EYE   45

tion, and it was all Alex could do not to roll his eyes. Tall thin Clive took Martin's place, his gaze travelling brazenly up Solange's body and back down again as if he couldn't believe anyone so beautiful existed. He gave her a little kiss on the cheek, and Alex saw the look of undisguised lust in his eyes. So, Solange was clearly Clive's prize for the evening, which meant his own services were reserved for Martin.

"And, of course, you must all know the new addition to the Tyler household – Alexander Lytton." Tyler put his hand on Alex's shoulder and squeezed hard, in clear warning. "We're very lucky to have such a fine young man living with us here."

"I read all about you, you poor thing," Martin exclaimed. "Thank God George scooped you up and took you in. I dread to think what could have happened if someone less understanding had bought you."

He took Alex's hand in both his chubby ones, holding on tight, never once taking his eyes off Alex's face. "Such a sweet boy, and so lost. You've been rescued, you really have," he crooned, stroking Alex's fingers.

Tyler squeezed Alex's shoulder again, and he managed to croak out a meaningless reply.

Beaming, Martin very slowly lifted Alex's hand to his lips and kissed it, lingering over the performance.

Alex barely suppressed a shudder, and Tyler dug his fingers into his shoulder hard whilst calling Clive over to be introduced. The thin man barely looked at Alex, and their introduction was brief and brusque. Clive clearly resented every second spent away from Solange.

They sat down on the sofas as a butler brought over a tray of drinks. Tyler kept the alcohol flowing and the conversation moving, flattering his guests with little compliments about their business prowess, or their golfing handicaps.

Alex felt at sea, ill-equipped to join in the chat, but that didn't seem to matter. Martin sat beside him, popping up regularly to fetch him another drink, or a footstool, or a bowl of nibbles, and repeatedly asking if he was too warm, or too cold. All Alex had to do was smile and nod – nothing else was required of him, which was a relief.

Solange laughed as Clive rested his hand on her thigh. Alex's jaw tightened; he didn't like being viewed as a piece of meat by Martin, but

he hated Clive's predatory gaze and wandering hands with Solange just as much.

Tyler noticed and leaned forward. This time, he rested his hand on the back of Alex's neck, and Alex forced himself to appear more relaxed. Tyler continued to choreograph the scene, calling for more drinks and effortlessly bringing up new subjects for discussion. Every so often, he'd draw attention to Solange's "smooth skin", or Alex's "sweet smile", to stoke up the sexual tension already escalating in the room.

Martin leaned in so close that their thighs were squashed together. Alex crossed his legs, took a gulp of his drink, and plastered on a fake smile. He'd dealt with unwanted interest before, but this was different because he wasn't allowed to object or refuse; the aim was to fire Martin's interest, not dampen it. The man's hands were wandering as much as Clive's now, gently patting his leg or stroking his hair.

He was relieved when Tyler suggested they move into the dining room. Letting the others go first, he grabbed another glass of wine from the butler's tray as they filed out of the room, jumping when he heard a hard voice in his ear.

"Take it easy with the drink," Tyler warned. "It's fine to get yourself in the mood, but if you can't perform later, then someone will suffer – I promise."

Alex put the drink back onto the tray; he didn't want to give Tyler an excuse to beat Solange again.

His houder smiled at him genially. "Good boy. See, you're learning. I can't tell you what a pleasure it is to see a Lytton whoring for me. In fact, I've always wanted my own pet Lytton, and you're perfect."

"I'm doing what I have to do," Alex snapped. "Nothing more."

"I know, but one day you'll do all this because you want to. No more frowning, fidgeting, and backchat. One day, I'll have you so well trained that you'll enjoy your work and do it willingly, with a smile on your face. Then there'll be no need for alcohol to get you through."

"That'll never happen."

"Oh, it will," Tyler purred. "I want my pet Lytton fully trained, not wild and wilful. I'll break you, Alexander, you'll see. One day, you'll come and kneel at my feet – no coercion, no threats – just a compliant

indie, begging his houder to fuck him." He ruffled Alex's voluminous hair with his hand. "You look adorable tonight, by the way." He laughed. "Ridiculous, but adorable. Who knew that salmon pink was such a good colour on you? Martin is going to love peeling you out of those clothes later. You should find his needs easy to accommodate; you might even enjoy his particular sexual fantasy."

Alex felt his throat go dry; if Tyler thought he'd enjoy bedding Martin Bagshaw, then he almost certainly wouldn't. Although Martin seemed nicer than the coldly predatory Clive, who Solange was doing her best to fend off yet also keep on the boil, at least until after they'd eaten.

He followed Tyler into the dining room, wishing the evening was over and the deed done, not hanging over him.

The meal felt like ashes in his mouth; he barely tasted it. His throat was so dry he had to keep taking sips of water to ensure the food went down, and there were times he felt like heaving it up again. Solange and Tyler kept up a light, flirtatious stream of conversation, while Martin solicitously piled his plate with food and fondled his thigh under the table.

As the meal drew to a close, his stomach began to churn again, in anticipation of what was to come. He tried to rationalise it; he'd slept with plenty of people he didn't know in clubs, had seduced strangers for the hell of it, and whored himself out for drugs. How was this any different? He traced his fingers anxiously over the pocket containing the pills Lorenzo had given him, feeling the pressure. He wasn't sure whether to take them or not. He'd never needed them before, but he wasn't sure he could perform under these circumstances. If it were just his own hide at stake, he'd resist and let Tyler beat him to a pulp, but he couldn't watch Solange being whipped again.

Tyler offered his guests illegal cigars with their liqueurs, winking conspiratorially as they lit up. They, like the indies, were all part of making these men feel special, part of Tyler's trusted little club.

The evening dragged on, a curious mixture of tedium and anxiety. Alex both longed for and dreaded the meal being over. Finally, Tyler stood up. "Well, it's been a lovely evening, but I must leave you," he said regretfully. "There's no need for you to leave just yet, though,

gentlemen. I'm sure Solange and Alex would love to spend more time with you."

It was all so smoothly done: no mention of money, of favours being repaid, or sex – just fine wine, good food, flirtatious conversation... and an expectation of more to come. Clive and Martin clearly both knew what they were being given this evening, and just as clearly were keen to take advantage of it.

Clive didn't wait long before making his move. Solange led him off to her room with a fit of false giggling that set Alex's teeth on edge.

"So, my dear boy – would you like to take me somewhere more comfortable, too?" Martin asked, brushing his arm suggestively. "You and I have really hit it off this evening, and I'd love to get to know you even better."

It was on the tip of Alex's tongue to give a sarcastic retort, but he swallowed it down. "Of course," he mumbled instead. "Um – this way."

Martin placed a hand on his arse and gave it a good grope as he followed him to the bedroom. "I knew you felt the same way," he said, closing the door behind them. "I could tell we had a special connection."

"Yeah. Right. A special connection," Alex repeated numbly. The bedroom smartwalls were glowing a seductive red, which he supposed he should have expected. There were no images displayed on them, but they radiated a sultry glow.

"Come here and sit on my lap, there's a good boy." Martin perched on the side of the bed and grabbed his arm, drawing him in close.

Alex did as instructed, feeling ridiculous.

"You're so pretty," Martin said, stroking his chest through his shirt, his fingers lingering over his nipples, tweaking them gently through the shiny fabric. "I followed your story on the news, and it broke my heart. I kept thinking – all that poor boy needs is someone to love him."

"Yeah," he mumbled incoherently, wishing they could get on with the fucking and avoid the schmaltzy talking. Martin, however, clearly needed to set the parameters of his fantasy, and Alex had an inkling of where this was headed. He wondered if he should take the pills now, and how long they took to work.

"Your father neglected you – you stole from him as a cry for help. If

you were *my* boy, I wouldn't neglect you. I'd make sure you were well looked after, in every way." Martin's hands went lower, sweeping over his belly and coming to rest on the bulge of his cock, still evident through the ultra-tight jeans. "Just a poor, misunderstood boy in need of a kind daddy."

"Yes," Alex said, feeling faintly nauseated.

"Yes, Daddy," Martin corrected, stroking his cock.

He glanced at the smartwall over Martin's shoulder and rolled his eyes at it. "Yes, Daddy," he ground out.

"That's good. Now, do you know what Daddy has for you?" Martin asked, nuzzling his neck.

He could guess, but he shook his head.

"It's a lovely present, just for you. A big lollipop for you to suck and enjoy."

"Sounds great," he muttered. "Daddy," he added when Martin pouted at him.

Martin smiled and bestowed a wet, sloppy kiss on his mouth. He stank of alcohol and tobacco, but Alex had tasted worse.

"Good boy. Why don't you take a look at Daddy's big lollipop?" he suggested.

Alex took his cue and slid off Martin's lap to kneel between his legs. "Does Daddy keep his lollipop in here?" he asked, trying not to laugh but feeling really stupid at the same time. Undoing Martin's trousers, he reached into his briefs and released his cock. It wasn't as big as promised, but he dutifully swiped his tongue over it, closing his eyes and trying to imagine he was in a club sucking off some handsome stud he'd picked up, not kneeling in front of a fat, middle-aged businessman because his houder had ordered it. He had drunk enough to take the edge off, and he'd always been good at giving head. He was good at sex, period – Tyler hadn't been wrong about that.

"That's lovely – Daddy's little boy is taking good care of Daddy," Martin sighed, stroking his hair.

Alex hoped he could suck Martin off as quickly as possible, and then it would be over and he could go to bed.

The man's crooning became more agitated as Alex sucked, and then he pulled back just before he came, purposefully shooting his load

over Alex's face and shirt. "Oh dear. Look, Daddy's got you all messed up," he said, his eyes twinkling. "Shall we get you out of these wet things?"

He undressed Alex slowly, taking his time, kissing him every so often. He seemed ridiculously excited by every new inch of flesh he uncovered, caressing Alex's nipples, chest, and belly before peeling him out of his jeans. Alex wasn't wearing any underwear, and Martin beamed as he caught sight of his flaccid penis.

"This is so pretty." He fondled it, and Alex closed his eyes and tried to get hard, but his cock failed to respond. Martin didn't seem to mind. "Let's see that beautiful bottom as well!" he exclaimed, turning Alex around. "Oh!" He sighed in pleasure. "Perfect! Such a white, perfect bottom. So smooth and silky." He stroked Alex's buttocks for several long minutes, then pressed himself up against them, his penis rubbing at the cleft between Alex's cheeks. "Daddy can't wait to be inside this precious bottom," he whispered in Alex's ear. "Are you looking forward to Daddy being inside your luscious bottom, my darling?"

"Uh, yeah. Great," Alex murmured by way of reply, wearily resigned to the fact that the blowjob wasn't going to be the only service he offered this evening. Martin clearly wanted to make good use of his time with Tyler's celebrity IS, and was working himself up to another erection.

"But first, I think we need to get you completely clean." Leading Alex into the bathroom, Martin pushed him under the shower, before taking off his own clothes and joining him there. He seemed to enjoy cleaning Alex all over, rubbing soap into him and examining every inch of him. "We must clean your dirty place, too," he murmured. "Lean forward, so Daddy can take care of it."

Alex rested his hands on the shower wall as Martin got down on his hands and knees behind him and began soaping his hole very slowly and lovingly.

"It has to be nice and clean for Daddy, so he can enjoy being in there," Martin warbled.

Alex placed his head on his hands and tried not to think about what was going to happen next. Maybe he should count himself lucky; Martin wasn't cruel or unkind – he had a suspicion that Clive was a

much nastier sexual partner. Apart from his sickly way of talking and his weird daddy fetish, Martin was treating him well.

"That's it, my little prince. Do you like me calling you that, hmm? My beautiful little prince. Talk to me. Let me hear how much you love your big, strong daddy."

Alex cleared his throat. "Uh, that feels great, Daddy," he managed.

"That's good – you're lovely and clean and open now. Do you want to feel Daddy inside you?"

"Yes please, Daddy."

Turning off the shower, Martin proceeded to pat them both dry with a towel, then led Alex back into the bedroom, gently settling him on the bed on his back, with a pillow under his bottom. Martin had a hairy chest and a big white gut, with skinny little legs underneath. He wasn't an attractive man.

A tube of lubricant and a supply of condoms were already on the bedside table. Alex closed his eyes as Martin reached for them. On several occasions when he'd slept with Neil, he'd imagined it was Hudson Brink, or some other hot celebrity; maybe he could go to that place in his head right now.

"Open your eyes for Daddy, my little prince," Martin said, stroking his cheek until he complied.

It seemed that escape was going to be denied to him. Martin was looming over him with a sickly smile on his face. After moistening Alex's hole with lube and his finger, he put the condom on with a wink. "Best to be safe, although Daddy is clean, and I'm sure his little prince is, too."

He settled between Alex's legs and pushed insistently. Alex felt tight and tense, and it took a little while for Martin to ease his way in. When he did finally gain entry, it hurt, and Alex had to bite back the hiss of pain that came to his lips, concentrating on opening up so there was less discomfort.

Martin pushed all the way in. "Such a lovely boy. There... doesn't that feel good?" He began pumping with energetic thrusts. "Now, come for Daddy, my little prince..." He wrapped his hand around Alex's cock, and Alex almost jumped out of his skin. So far, it had remained resolutely limp, and he'd thought Martin wasn't interested as long as he got

off himself, so he hadn't taken the pills. He tried desperately to think of sexually exciting situations, but he wasn't sure there was any life left in his dick.

"You must come for Daddy," Martin puffed as he thrust. "Daddy wants you to come, my darling. Daddy won't be happy if you don't come."

Alex conjured up an image of a half-naked Hudson Brink emerging from the ocean with his massive cock fully erect. He imagined lying back on the sand as Hudson kissed his chest, sucked down hard on his nipples, and then entered him swiftly with his huge dick. It worked – his own cock responded by rising half-heartedly.

"Oh, good! That's a good boy. Such a lovely little prince," Martin said encouragingly, which almost halted Alex's erection in its tracks. The older man's belly rolled majestically as he fucked, his balls slapping Alex's buttocks as he got into his stride. It was hard to hold on to the image of Hudson Brink nailing him in the sand when Martin was bobbing up and down and crooning at him, but somehow, with the help of the fantasy and Martin's relentless stroking, Alex managed to eject a small dribble of come a little while later. Martin let out such a cry of pleasure at the tiny victory that Alex almost burst out laughing. The other man's own climax took longer, and he continued to thrust away for what felt like hours before finally ejaculating with a squeal of delight.

"Such a lovely boy," he sighed. "So special." Withdrawing, he disposed of the condom and then reached for the towel he'd thrown onto the bed earlier to wipe Alex's come away. "There, there – who's my nice, clean boy, hmm?" he said, settling down beside Alex in the bed and drawing him into his arms. "Such a lovely, sweet, clean little prince..."

Alex closed his eyes as Martin murmured into his ear; he didn't feel very clean.

So that was it – his first time whoring for George Tyler, but not, he was sure, his last. He wondered if he could endure years of this. Who would he be by the end of it? Would he be able to hang on to any sense of himself, or would that be slowly chipped away in a succession of soul-destroying encounters until he didn't recognise himself?

An hour or so passed with Martin holding him tight and whispering sweet nothings. If Alex had been free, he'd have told Martin to fuck off now the sex was over – he'd never enjoyed post-coital cuddling and hated feeling smothered. He wasn't free, though, and he felt a wave of helpless frustration welling up angrily inside and then come crashing back down. He was trapped here, doomed to this life, with no prospect of release or escape. Men like Martin would slobber over him and fuck him, and he couldn't do a damn thing about it except smile and accept. For the first time in his life, he wanted to go willingly into a gym so that he could pound his fists into a punch bag and vent his anger there.

A soft knock on the door interrupted his thoughts, and he looked up to see Scarface standing there.

"I thought you might like to know that one of Mr Tyler's limousines will be here shortly to take you home, Mr Bagshaw," Scarface said politely. His gaze flickered over Alex's naked body with an expression of such intense pity that Alex suddenly understood why Scarface and Fatso hadn't risen to his barbed baiting over the past few weeks. They had understood, better than he, what he would be forced to do and what he had become – and they felt sorry for him.

Scarface closed the door, and Martin gave a regretful sigh. "It seems our time together is over. How sad – it was far too short."

Sliding out of bed, Alex turned on the light and pulled on a pair of boxers and a tee-shirt. He watched as Martin collected his clothes from where he'd left them, his big gut bouncing as he walked. There was something both pathetic and benign about him in that moment. He wasn't so bad; Alex wouldn't have chosen him, but he was harmless enough.

Martin threw his clothes onto the bed, and his wallet fell out of his trouser pocket onto the floor by Alex's bare feet. Alex picked it up to hand it back to him and a holocard dropped out. The jolt from the fall turned it on, and a small, grainy hologram flashed into life. It showed Martin with his arm around a pleasant-looking woman in her forties, while two pre-teen boys stood in front of them, smiling.

"Are they your family?" Alex asked, flicking it off and returning it to the wallet.

Martin snatched it back. "Yes," he said brusquely.

"Does your wife know you're out fucking boys when you're supposed to be on a business trip?" Alex asked, unable to stop himself.

Martin looked up sharply, but Alex stared him out. The older man crumbled and looked down, shaking his head. "No. I couldn't bear to lose her, and I would, if she knew. I don't know why I need this, but I do." He looked up again, helplessly this time. "I would never... my sons... you understand that I would never..." He looked distraught.

"Yeah," Alex said quickly. "I get it."

"You must also understand that it's only men – not boys – for me, despite... you know." Martin waved at the bed. "It's all a harmless fantasy." His podgy jowls shook as he spoke; he looked wretched.

"It's okay," Alex said softly. "I understand the difference between a sex fantasy and real life."

Martin shot him a weak smile. "You're a very kind boy; I appreciate that. Lots of people don't understand that difference." He gazed at Alex keenly. "I think you understand human frailty because of the part it's played in your downfall. You're kinder because of that."

Alex felt sorry for the man. "You do know about..." He jerked his head at the smartwall, his eyes going to the little red dot in the far top corner that indicated it was recording. Easily missed, especially if you were unfamiliar with smartwall tech, which most people still were.

"Oh yes, I know." Martin sighed. "I didn't the first time I was here, of course, but I soon found out. I fretted about it for weeks. I can't lose my wife and my boys," he said firmly, straightening his shoulders. "So now I just enjoy what's offered, because it's all I can do. I make the best of it, you see."

Alex wondered what part of his soul Martin had sold to Tyler in exchange for silence about his extramarital proclivities. His sympathy faded. Martin might not be a bad man, but he was a weak one. He might not have thought he had a choice, but he had. He still did.

Martin finished dressing and then drew Alex to him for one last kiss. "Goodbye, my sweet little prince. I do hope we meet again," he said, patting Alex's bottom affectionately. Alex was sure they would. He opened the door, and the waiting Scarface shot him another of those pitying looks before escorting Martin down the corridor towards

the lift. A few seconds later, Clive emerged from Solange's bedroom, and Fatso fell into step beside him.

Alex waited until they'd gone and then tiptoed across the hallway to Solange's room. He tapped on the door and then opened it a fraction. She was sitting on the side of the bed, naked; she stood up and reached for her dressing gown as he entered, but not before he caught sight of the bruises on her thighs and arms.

"Fucking bastard," he seethed.

"I've had worse." She knotted the white cotton gown firmly around her slender body while looking at him searchingly. "How are you, Alex? How did it go? Are you okay?"

He thought about it for a moment. "I don't have a clue," he said honestly. He sat down on the side of her bed, and she perched beside him. "How do you do it, Solange?" he asked. "How do you fake all the smiles, the small talk, and the sex? How do you fake the pleasure... just how?" He shook his head, bewildered.

"You get used to it."

"How long have you...?" He waved his hand at the bed. "I mean, how many times... for you... and likely for me?"

"I was here for a year after that time you dumped me." She shot him the faintest ghost of a smile. "I don't know how many times I entertained guests, but I'd say it was usually around twice a week – sometimes more. It's not actually that bad." She gave a little shrug. "I knew prostitutes who had it far worse back in the Quarterlands."

Alex flinched at the word "prostitutes". "At least they were their own bosses," he said. "They could choose who they slept with."

"I doubt it," she retorted. "Most of them had pretty nasty pimps, and there was a hell of a lot of trafficking – mostly French and German girls – poor cows. They were pretty much dumped in a room and raped repeatedly, and nobody cared. I know you find it hard to believe, but this was my way out. I signed up to be Tyler's whore for seven years, and there's a lump sum waiting for me when my time is up. I can go out and start my own business, leave all this behind, and make something of myself while I'm still young enough."

"Yes – *you* can," Alex said bitterly.

"I'm sorry," she said, resting her forehead against his. "I'm so sorry,

Alex. I didn't apologise before, but I am now. I got you into this, and it's wrong, and I knew that but I didn't care, because I thought – why should Alexander Lytton have everything and me nothing? Why shouldn't I help Tyler bring him down? He's just a spoilt brat who doesn't know what life is like for the rest of us."

"Well, you were right about that much at least."

"But it doesn't make what happened to you right. I don't want this for you – I'd do anything to go back and make it not happen. I'm so very sorry."

Alex drew back and kissed her forehead. "Apology accepted – now forget about it. Tyler would have found a way to have his revenge on my family and me whether you'd agreed to become his IS or not. I'm more to blame for my fate than you. We all make our own choices."

He thought of the choice he'd made to steal from his father's company – was that any better than the one she'd made to be Tyler's honey-trap courtesan? What about Martin's, to give in to Tyler's blackmail rather than risk losing his family? Martin continued to accept the offer of young men's bodies to feed his fantasies, while Tyler dangled the footage over him for whatever twisted purpose it served. Martin could have made a different choice, if he'd been brave enough. They were all making their own decisions for their own reasons; Alex couldn't condemn Solange for hers.

"Lorenzo gave me some pills earlier," he confided. "To help me perform." He gestured at his crotch. "I didn't take them, because I didn't want to admit that this is who I am now."

She made a face. "Did you manage to...?"

"Yeah – just about." He thought about it for a moment. "But I'll take them next time. There's no point fighting it – I'm Tyler's whore now."

She rested her head on his shoulder, and he wrapped his arm around her, both taking comfort from each other.

"You were right about me," he told her, kissing her hair. "I had advantages and privilege, and I squandered it all. It's not worse for me than for you just because we had different expectations of life to begin with. It shouldn't be, anyway. I *did* walk around with my eyes closed. I was too caught up in my own stupid problems, which, now I look back,

I can see were hardly problems at all. Not compared to this, anyway."
He gave a little bark of laughter. "I never thought much about what it's
like to be an IS. I used to taunt Neil about it all the time, without realising what it was like from his point of view."

"To be fair, Neil is a total dick," she said.

He laughed. "Yeah, that's true."

"You gonna be okay?" she asked softly.

He glanced at her. "No, but I'm going to try. If you can do this,
then so can I."

"It's easier for me, though," she said.

"How?"

She sighed and pressed a kiss to his cheek. "Because Tyler's not
trying to break me," she said sadly.

Chapter Four

OCTOBER 2095

Josiah

Josiah turned on the radio as a distraction during the journey. Unfortunately, his listening preference was a trashy radio talk show, and there was only one item they were discussing this morning. "This is Amanda Lewis for News-Spec, your show for discussing all the latest news and views," the presenter said excitedly. "Where the big revelation today is that Investigator Raine, the legendary indiehunter, has been granted temporary custody of the country's most infamous indentured servant, Alexander Lytton. What are we to make of this, Alan?"

Her co-host seemed equally excited by the news. "Well, Amanda, this is an extraordinary development in the search for Elliot Dacre's killer! It indicates that rather than being the prime suspect, as we all thought, Lytton appears to be helping Inquisitus with the murder investigation."

"Is there a precedent for this – transferring an indentured servant into the ownership of an individual investigator for the duration of an investigation?"

"Not that I know of, but if Elliot Dacre had no living relatives, and Lytton is central to the enquiry, it may well be that Investigator Raine made this decision to prevent the IS going into the probate system."

"In which case, I'm sure we can expect more exciting developments

soon," Amanda exclaimed. "Now, over to our listeners for their comments... First up, we have Bill in Coulsdon."

A man with an authoritative, "voice of the people" tone began speaking. "Well, it's a bloody disgrace if you ask me."

"In what way, Bill?"

"They should lock Lytton up and throw away the key. We all know he's guilty. There isn't a decent bone in his body – he's bad, through and through. I'd put money on him being the killer."

Josiah glanced at Alexander, who glanced back with a resigned shrug.

"I can't believe he hasn't been charged already." Bill's rant continued. "He must have Raine wrapped around his little finger. We all know what a con artist Lytton is."

Alexander raised an amused eyebrow.

"It's dangerous out there for all houders right now. Nobody is safe in their own home. If you employ an IS, you should hide a knife under your pillow at night."

"Thank you, Bill. Feelings are clearly running high on this topic," Alan said urbanely. "Next up, we have Sarah in East Grinstead."

"I have total faith in the indiehunter," Sarah said stoutly. "He'll defend us against ungrateful indies who should be pleased they have a roof over their heads, instead of plotting to kill people who've been kind to them. Investigator Raine is one of us. He'll make sure Lytton is brought to justice."

"How our reputations precede us, Investigator Raine," Alexander murmured.

"I don't give a shit what they say about me," Josiah said firmly.

"Let's hear now from Marnie, in Sevenoaks," Alan chirped.

"I feel sorry for Investigator Raine, but I have to wonder if he's really thinking straight," Marnie offered coyly. "I mean, that Lytton boy is very good-looking. I can see why Raine wanted to take him home—"

Josiah barked out an order to the duck to cut off the audio.

"What were you saying? Something about not giving a shit what people say about you?" Alexander said silkily.

"Shut up," Josiah growled.

. . .

As they drew closer to Lewes, Alexander fell silent. Josiah glanced at him, wondering if he was asleep. He wasn't. He was reciting something soundlessly to himself. His eyes were closed, and he was breathing deeply; this was clearly some kind of ritual – a repetitive chant designed to calm him down and keep him focused. Josiah tried to work out what the mantra was, and then he realised: Alexander was reciting the lyrics of the song that meant so much to him – the one he played every morning during his yoga practice. Josiah couldn't remember exactly how it went, but he could make out some of the words.

He skimmed the duck through the silvery strip of water leading to George Tyler's private island, then drove up an imposing tree-lined driveway to a stunning house. "We're here," he announced as he parked.

Alexander opened his eyes, and Josiah was startled by the change in him. His gaze had become as inscrutable as the day he'd been arrested, and his features were perfectly blank. All traces of the teasing man from earlier had vanished.

Josiah had wondered whether Alexander's mask was a device for hiding his guilt, but now he realised he'd got that completely wrong. The facade wasn't about hiding, but surviving; it enabled Alexander to cope with distressing situations. What the hell awaited them in this house if Alexander needed to armour up for it like this?

"Are you sure there's nothing you want to tell me about George Tyler before we walk in there?" he asked.

Alexander gave a bland smile. "Nothing at all, sir."

Josiah suppressed a sigh. However annoying Alexander could be when he was nosing around in his life and challenging him with unwelcome questions, at least *that* Alexander was real. Now, it was like talking to a brick wall.

He climbed out of the duck and strode towards the house, aware that Alexander was following silently at his heel with his head down, looking every inch the obedient servant. They were met at the door by an IS dressed in Tyler's black livery.

"Senior Investigator Raine from Inquisitus," he informed the man.

GHOST EYE
61

"My colleague, Investigator Reed, called ahead and informed Mr Tyler I was on my way." Tyler wasn't a suspect in Dacre's murder, so he'd decided not to drop in on the man unannounced as he had with Charles Lytton. Besides, he had a suspicion that Tyler was a very different kind of personality to the genial but ineffectual Charles. It wouldn't be wise to get off on the wrong foot with a man this powerful.

"I'll inform Mr Tyler that you've arrived," the IS said snootily.

They were ushered into a vast, airy hallway, with white walls and black-and-white-diamond tiling on the floor.

"Nice house. Did you spend a lot of time here when Tyler owned your contract?" Josiah asked, glancing around.

Alexander didn't answer. He was gazing serenely into the distance, his eyes glazed, his breathing shallow and fast. His hands were balled into such tight fists that his knuckles were white.

"Hey." Josiah put a hand on his shoulder, and the indie jumped. "Just take a few slow, deep breaths." He moved his fingers to Alexander's solar plexus. "Deep into here... I said *slow*... or you'll pass out."

Alexander took a few shaky but deeper breaths, until gradually his fists started to uncurl.

"I've never seen you this way – not even when you were arrested on suspicion of murder, which would upset most normal people. Why does being here have this effect on you? What did this man do to you?"

"It doesn't matter. That's not why we're here," Alexander said evasively.

Josiah knew he wouldn't get the true answer. He could sense Alexander taking reassurance from his touch, so he kept his arm wrapped around the indie's body and his hand resting on his hard, flat stomach. Slowly, Alexander relaxed against him, until Josiah thought it was safe to release him and move away.

His holopad buzzed, and he glanced at it – Elsie. He didn't want to talk to her right now, so he turned it off. After that radio show this morning, and with the press camped outside his house, he doubted she'd be the only one of his friends calling him today. "Does being here bring back memories?" he asked, still searching for the clues his IS refused to give.

Alexander glanced around the hallway. "I didn't spend much time here. Tyler has other residences."

"But you visited this place?"

"Yes." Alexander gave a thin smile. "I remember the last time I was here very well."

Before Josiah could press him for more information, Tyler's IS returned. "This way," he instructed, leading them down the hallway. They were ushered into a massive living room, decorated starkly with plain black and white furnishings, occasionally relieved by a splash of red. Every surface was highly polished, making the entire room gleam. There was a vast white leather sofa and three shiny red armchairs. Josiah found the décor overstated, but it was clearly designed to be bold and imposing.

Next to the sofa was the man himself. He strode towards them, greeting Josiah with a welcoming smile, his hand held out.

Josiah had read plenty about George Tyler over the years, but nothing prepared him for meeting the man in person. Tyler's charisma was so strong it oozed out of him, and he emitted a powerful sexual presence. This was someone serious, imposing, and fiercely intelligent. He was as different from the weak, dim Charles Lytton as it was possible to be.

Tyler was wearing a pair of black chinos and a tight-fitting black roll-neck sweater; Josiah appreciated the sharp-edged elegance of his clothing. Everything about him, from his tanned bald head and curious, dark-eyed gaze, to the way his tailored clothes accentuated the hard lines of his body, proclaimed that he viewed himself as an alpha male. He was in his late fifties, but he had the energy and appearance of a man ten years younger.

So, this was the monster Alexander dreaded so much. Only Tyler didn't act much like a monster; his handshake was firm but not crippling, and his manner warm and genial. "Good morning, Investigator Raine. I'm pleased to meet you."

"Likewise, Mr Tyler."

Tyler glanced over Josiah's shoulder and gave a beaming smile of what looked like genuine pleasure. "You've brought Alexander with you! What a nice surprise. Bloody good to see you again, son." Tyler

ignored Alexander's politely outstretched hand and drew him into a warm hug. Alexander seemed to respond in kind, putting his arms around the older man and hugging him back.

Josiah surveyed the scene impassively. Was the hug calculated, on Tyler's side, to show ostentatious warmth, and on Alexander's to display precisely the right degree of reciprocation so as not to cause offence? Or was he reading too much into it?

"It's good to see you again, too, sir," Alexander replied demurely.

"It's been a while. It's great to see you looking so well." Tyler patted Alexander's arm, smiling broadly.

"You too, sir," Alexander responded serenely, the impassive mask firmly back in place after the interlude in the hallway. Josiah was impressed by how adeptly his IS was able to hide the challenging, witty personality he only allowed him to glimpse when they were alone together.

"Funnily enough, I was just watching you on the news." Tyler jerked his head at the smartwall. "The damn media are going nuts for the latest development in the Dacre case. I presume that's why you're here?"

"You're right," Josiah said.

"So – can I offer you a drink?"

"Not for me. I don't drink," Josiah replied as Tyler walked across the room to a large, imposing bar.

"What, never?" Tyler shot him a quizzical smile. "Or just not while you're on duty?"

"It's not my thing." Josiah smiled back blandly. Tyler was sizing him up, trying to get a feel for him, and Josiah couldn't blame him for that. He was here in an official capacity, investigating a high-profile murder; a man as sharp as Tyler would obviously want to know what he was dealing with.

"And what *is* your thing?" Tyler asked with a conspiratorial wink.

"Chocolate, I'm afraid." Josiah patted his stomach ruefully, which made Tyler laugh.

"Well, I don't have any to hand right now, but I can at least give you something to sip." He gave them each a glass of sparkling water and took one for himself. "Please – sit down, both of you." He took a seat

on an armchair. Josiah sat at the far end of the giant sofa, while Alexander perched on the red leather armchair opposite.

"So, how can I help you?" Tyler asked, gazing at Josiah earnestly. "I do hope I'm not a suspect in Mr Dacre's murder." He gave a little chuckle, as if the idea was completely absurd.

"Not as far as I know." Josiah took a thoughtful sip of his drink, watching as Tyler leaned back, looking supremely confident. "It would help if I could rule you out of our inquiries, though. Do you have an alibi for the morning of Tuesday, October twenty-fifth?"

There was a flicker of something in Tyler's eyes that took Josiah by surprise. Was it... relief?

"I was in Spain, on business."

"You have witnesses?"

"Dozens," Tyler laughed. "I was the keynote speaker in a conference on floating city technology."

"Thank you. You'll have no objection to sending through the details of your participation in that event to Investigator Reed?"

"Not at all." Tyler waved his hand around expansively. "I'm curious, though... Why, exactly, would I want to murder Elliot Dacre? I barely knew the man."

"You used to be Alexander's houder; it's possible you wanted him back."

"I sold his contract for a reason. No offence, Alexander." Tyler shot the indie a rueful smile. "He was a great IS but also a very expensive one. I was overstretched financially at that point in time, so I made the reluctant decision to free up some money by selling him. I was fond of Alexander, so it wasn't a decision I made lightly."

"Did you ever regret it to the point of wanting him back?" Josiah queried smoothly.

Tyler raised a questioning eyebrow.

"Mr Dacre had a couple of offers for Alexander, and we're investigating where those came from." Josiah was happy to give away that piece of information to see where it led.

Tyler shrugged. "Not from me, Investigator Raine. I was fond of Alexander, as I said, but by the time I sold his contract he'd really

completed his purpose and therefore was no longer of much use to me."

"And what purpose was that?" Josiah took another sip of water, gazing keenly at Tyler over the rim of his glass.

"He designed our Destiny range of AVs that revolutionised the market. They were his brainchild."

"You used him to help you design this revolutionary AV, and then you sold him when you were done?" Josiah probed.

Tyler shook his head. "No. God no. It was a little more complicated than that."

"In what way?"

"It's a long story." Tyler gave a pained smile. Then he leaned forward. "Do you play golf, Investigator Raine?" he enquired unexpectedly.

"I have a working knowledge of the game. I wouldn't say that I 'play'," Josiah replied. He had little interest in golf, but he'd acquired the basics in order to obtain a witness statement during a previous case.

"Good. How about I fill you in over a round?"

"I'm not normally in the habit of pausing to play golf during a murder inquiry."

"I'm sure, but it's a glorious day, and I was looking forward to playing with one of my friends this morning. I had to cancel when your colleague called and said you were on your way. Make it up to me, Raine – we can talk just as easily outside."

Josiah was intrigued as to where this was going. He gave in gracefully and nodded his agreement.

"Excellent." Tyler stood up. "I'll go and organise some clubs."

Josiah wondered if he was arranging the game as a way of separating him from Alexander. He glanced at his IS for clues, but Alexander's face remained impassive.

He looked around the room during Tyler's absence. Everything was neat, tidy, and kept perfectly in its place – including the two indentured servants standing to attention by the door. Even Alexander had lapsed into a well-trained silence and was sitting with his back straight,

as if he were still wearing Tyler livery. There was little to see in a house this spartan, but Josiah looked anyway.

His eye was caught by the slightest glint of the sun, shining through the huge windows onto the wall in front of him. He frowned. The wall was painted white, perfectly ordinary... but... was that a faint shimmer where the light hit it? He realised, suddenly, that the wall wasn't painted at all – it was a smartwall. Smartwall tech had been around for a few years, but was still the preserve of the well off. The people who could afford this fashionable new technology usually showed off their smartwalls, setting them to display beautiful scenery, or showcasing a rotating selection of favourite family photos. However, *this* smartwall had been set to be as invisible as possible. It looked as if the wall was painted, even down to mirroring the tiny smudges, bumps, and imperfections that you'd see on any normal painted wall. Yet, the realistic effect was an illusion produced by the thin layer of electronics covering the entire wall. Josiah glanced up, to the top right-hand corner, and saw the tell-tale shimmering of pixels at the very edge of the wall – and that was when he saw the small red dot that indicated the smartwall was recording.

Now his interest was piqued. Was the smartwall set to record *everything* that happened in this room, or was it just because an investigator was visiting? If so, why did Tyler want their meeting recorded?

At that moment, Tyler returned, walking briskly. "Right – let's get going. Alexander can be your caddy – he's very good at it. I had him trained especially." He winked at Alexander and then swung back towards Josiah.

So this wasn't a ruse to separate him from his indie. Alexander took a bag of clubs from Tyler's IS and followed silently behind Josiah, shouldering it like a pro. Tyler's IS was walking just as quietly behind him. Josiah couldn't help but notice how streamlined Tyler's world was, his indies trained to fall into step with his every whim.

"It wasn't my intention to avoid your question," Tyler said as they walked to the teeing ground. "I'm happy to answer any questions you have. In respect of why I sold Alexander, there's a rather long story attached. I wasn't kidding when I said it was complicated." He grinned

and held out his hand. A club was placed into it, a tee was put in the ground, and a ball was quickly balanced on it.

"I'm impressed by your servants," Josiah said. "Were they all trained at Belvedere, like Alexander?"

Tyler gave a bark of laughter. "Fuck, no. That place is bloody expensive! Even I couldn't afford to send *all* my servants there. No, we have an in-house training programme run by my major-domo. He ensures that all my staff are equipped to do their jobs properly."

"So why send Alexander there?" Josiah asked, watching as Tyler gave a practice swing.

"He's the most expensive IS I've ever bought, so I paid for him to go to Belvedere to give him the most exclusive training possible."

"Even though you bought him to help you develop your Destiny range of AVs?" Josiah inquired blandly. "Surely, teaching him to be a caddy, or butler, or whatever they do at Belvedere, is somewhat redundant in those circumstances?"

Tyler brought his club down with a decisive swing, and the ball flew off into the distance, landing on the green a few inches from the hole.

"Good shot," Josiah said.

Tyler winked at him. "It's my course – I should be good at playing it. In answer to your question – I felt Alexander deserved the best. I'd known him for a little while before I bought his contract, and I thought he was a huge talent. He made one mistake, that's all." He glanced at Alexander, who was standing by, gazing blankly at the golf course. "I intended to keep him at that point, but let's face it, I'm old enough to be his father. I wanted to make sure he was equipped to handle his life as an IS if I should die or have to sell him – which was what happened."

Without saying a word, Alexander placed a ball on the tee and handed Josiah a club. Josiah smacked the ball with a blunt lack of finesse, in contrast to Tyler's far more elegant style. The ball landed on the green all the same, although much further from the hole than Tyler's shot. "You had Alexander's best interests at heart, then?"

"Of course." Tyler slapped Alexander's arm affectionately. "His mother and I were friends for years. I always tried to do my best for

him, as far as I could, for her sake. I knew it was what she'd have wanted. Isn't that right, Alexander?"

Alexander gave a vacant smile. "Yes, sir. Completely right."

"So, this complicated story you mentioned?" Josiah prompted.

"Yes, of course. I'll tell you while we walk." Tyler led the way across the course at a fair trot, but Josiah easily kept pace with him. "Look, I'm not from a privileged background, like Alexander. I'm a self-made man. I came from nothing and worked my arse off to get all this." Tyler waved his hand at the island, with its beautiful mansion and perfectly manicured golf course. "I'm not sure if you know this, but my father was the brains behind the first Lytton AV − the classic post-Rising duck that got the country back on its feet again. You know the design − ugly as fuck, but it did the job and got people and goods around the country."

"I'm not all that interested in ducks, to be honest," Josiah said.

Tyler gave him an incredulous look. "Green, utilitarian, no frills, but solid and reliable. That was the Lytton Classic AV − and it was my father's brainchild. He was Alexander's grandfather's IS."

"What did Alexander's grandfather bring to the table?" Josiah asked.

"Money." Tyler shrugged. "He financed it and took all the profit. Theodore Lytton never gave my father a penny of the money his design earned."

"I seem to remember reading somewhere that Lytton mortgaged his house and sold everything he owned to make his company a success," Josiah said.

Tyler glanced at him sharply. "It wasn't without risks, but once it was successful he didn't share anything with my father − and they were good friends. My father was a quiet, unassuming, gentle man − he was satisfied with what he had."

"But you weren't?"

Tyler sighed. "No, because I saw how hard he worked, and that he deserved so much more. We all lived in that fucking great house together − my mother was the housekeeper, and I grew up with Noah Lytton, Alexander's father, running up and down the long dark corridors, chasing each other, playing hide-and-seek in all those rooms.

Even back then, I knew he was the lord and master, and I was the servant's brat."

"So you were bitter?"

"Not at all." Tyler grinned. "It was the making of me. Growing up in all that luxury but never owning any of it myself gave me the drive and determination to build a business of my own. I went to Oxford with Noah – his father paid for me, because he wanted him to have a friend there."

"Someone to keep an eye on him?"

"No, just a friend. Noah didn't exactly need watching; he was always a model student."

They reached the green, where Josiah took four shots to sink his ball into the cup. Tyler only needed two.

"After university, I rejected Noah's offer to be his IS at Lytton AV and struck out on my own," Tyler explained as they walked to the next tee. "It wasn't easy, but I had a head for business and gradually built up my own company. So, when Alexander came to me with his designs for a new, high-concept kind of duck, I admit I was intrigued. I knew the family so well, and despite my feeling that they owed my father more than they'd ever given him, I was fond of them. The Lyttons and the Tylers – we have a long, complicated history."

"I'm intrigued about one thing..." Josiah watched as Tyler teed off again, hitting yet another perfect shot onto the green. "You said in your court deposition that Alexander's designs couldn't be made to work, and yet now you say you used him to develop the new Destiny range, and this time it did work. What happened?" Josiah took his own shot and sent his ball flying... straight into a bunker.

Tyler patted his arm in commiseration. "Designing ducks is hard – Alexander's designs were promising but needed considerable tweaking," he said, striding off.

"So, after his disgrace you bought his contract to finish what he'd started?" Josiah called after him.

Halting, Tyler hesitated. "No. At that stage, I still thought the designs wouldn't work."

"Then why buy him?"

Tyler sighed. "I didn't ask him to steal that money, Investigator

Raine. I had no idea he was going to do that, but I did feel sorry for him afterwards – and for his poor father. I asked myself if I'd put too much pressure on him, but I'm a businessman, and I wanted a good return for my company. I admit I felt guilty. I bought his contract partly because Lytton AV was in poor shape. It would have gone under if Alexander hadn't been sold for a good price, so I put in a very high bid. My father loved that company and poured the best years of his life into it; I didn't want it to fail." He glanced away, looking suddenly vulnerable, then pulled himself together. "I also couldn't bear the thought of him falling into the wrong hands – he was so notorious by that point, I genuinely feared for his well-being if his contract was sold to the wrong person. I wanted to make sure he was treated properly, with the dignity he deserved."

"So, it was a rare act of sentimentality from a hard-nosed businessman?"

They'd reached the bunker, and Alexander handed Josiah a club. Josiah didn't have a clue which iron he needed to hack his way out of the sand, so he was grateful that Alexander seemed to know.

"I have my weaknesses – don't we all?" Tyler shrugged. "I'm sure you do, too, Investigator Raine." He gave Josiah a knowing wink.

Josiah shot him an enigmatic smile by way of reply.

Tyler turned his attention to Alexander, who was studying his golf bag intently as he waited for Josiah to take his next shot. "Alexander – am I telling this story right? I would hate to get any of the details wrong. Please do correct me if you feel I'm being inaccurate or biased in any way."

Alexander slowly peeled his attention away and met Tyler's eye. It looked to Josiah as though some unspoken conversation was taking place between them, then Alexander shook his head. "You're telling it perfectly, sir. I don't recall it being different in any aspect."

Tyler smiled and glanced back at Josiah. "And there you have it. I hope that answers your question, Investigator Raine."

Josiah swung his club at the ball in the sandbank and managed to bludgeon it onto the green by sheer force. "Not entirely. If you felt so much compassion for Alexander, why did you sell him?"

"Like I said, I needed the money. I agonised about it for some

time, but in the end I had no choice. I explained it to Alexander, and he accepted it. I think he was even a bit excited about his new life. We both felt there were no more challenges left for him with me. I didn't just sell him to the highest bidder, though – I researched Elliot Dacre thoroughly to make sure he was a man of integrity, who would treat Alexander well. I'd met him socially a few times, and I liked him. He assured me that Alexander would be his only IS, and that he'd be looked after – to be honest, it sounded like Dacre would spoil him rotten. He was looking for a muse for his holophotography, and he sure as hell found that in Alexander. And, of course, Alexander got to mix in exciting new circles. I could barely read a news site without seeing photos of the lucky fucker and his new houder at some celebrity party."

"Idyllic," Josiah murmured as he watched the other man sink another hole.

"I was sorry to hear of Dacre's death," Tyler said in a more sombre tone. "But I can assure you that I had nothing to do with it. I did my best by Alexander and then sold his contract on as responsibly as I could. I didn't want him back."

Josiah gazed at Tyler steadily as he spoke, taking in the man's body language and the intent behind his words. Tyler spoke fluently, and there was complete sincerity in his tone. Josiah believed him when he said he'd had nothing to do with Dacre's murder. Of course, a man as wealthy and powerful as Tyler could pay someone to do his murdering for him, if he wanted, but Josiah didn't sense any kind of defensive subterfuge on the matter. Besides, it was all too messy for Tyler: the dead man being found by the cleaning lady; the antique murder weapon arriving for whatever reason soon after the event. Josiah suspected that if someone as shrewd and wealthy as Tyler ever committed a murder, it would be perfectly covered up and no clues would be left behind to incriminate him. The body and murder weapon would both disappear without a trace, and any witnesses would be paid off, threatened, or both. No, George Tyler hadn't killed Elliot Dacre – so why had Alexander brought him here? What did he expect him to find? He'd given Josiah no clues, no indication as to what the hell this was about, and had agreed with every word Tyler had said.

Josiah looked at Alexander, who gazed back at him enigmatically. Josiah had known from the outset that he'd been manipulated into coming here today, but he'd gone along with it willingly, thinking he'd learn something. What use had it been in solving Elliot Dacre's murder? Did Alexander even care about that? He said he did, but Josiah was starting to feel as if he'd wasted the day when he could have been investigating a real lead. With a surge of anger towards his IS, he sank his ball into the hole, then threw the putter back at him with enough force to indicate his displeasure. Alexander flinched.

"This way." Tyler smiled at him brightly, and as they walked to the next tee, he regaled him with a dirty story that was undeniably funny. Josiah laughed at the punchline and saw Alexander's shoulders slump.

Tyler spent the next hour wielding his charisma like a weapon. He was sexy — Josiah couldn't help but notice that — but it was subtler than that. He had no idea whether Tyler was gay or straight; although the man didn't openly flirt with him, Josiah felt himself being expertly seduced all the same. Tyler was a man of the world, full of interesting, often slightly risqué stories and amusing anecdotes. He seemed to know everyone and have been everywhere, but without ever making it seem like he was name-dropping or boasting. He treated Josiah like an old friend, creating a cradle of intimacy that didn't exist but seemed seductively within reach.

Josiah couldn't help wondering why Tyler was making such a determined effort to charm him when he clearly wasn't a serious suspect in Dacre's murder. However, he allowed himself to be charmed anyway, taking pleasure in watching an expert giving such a virtuoso performance.

"How long have you worked as an investigator?" Tyler asked.

"Too long," Josiah grunted, taking a shot.

"Must be interesting work."

"It has its moments."

"Not very well paid, I'd imagine." Tyler laughed.

"I do okay."

"I read somewhere that investigators work such long hours, and see such dark and troubling things, that it's hard for them to keep a relationship going."

GHOST EYE
73

"I wouldn't know," Josiah said stiffly.

"I read about your husband's murder," Tyler murmured. He put a hand on Josiah's arm, his brown eyes blazing with sincerity. "I'm sorry."

"It was a long time ago," Josiah replied, struck by how genuine Tyler's condolences appeared to be. Tyler squeezed his arm sympathetically. Out of the corner of his eye, he saw Alexander's shoulders hunch even more.

"Between you and me..." Tyler wrapped an arm around his shoulders and led him away from their servants. "Do you think we'll see more IS riots? I thought we'd calmed that situation down a few years ago, but now I'm not so sure."

"I have no idea," Josiah said, aware of the heat Tyler was generating, and the proximity of his lean, hard body.

"We're seeing more of this type of thing – indies killing their houders. Obviously, it worries me. You know more about it than me – you see it up close. Do you think it's an issue?" Tyler radiated concern, and Josiah felt almost flattered, being treated as an expert and confidant.

"My husband was killed by an IS on the run, so I might not be the right person to ask," he replied, smoothly sidestepping the question.

"But you've caught a few indies who killed their houders – you've made quite a name for yourself doing that... indiehunter." Tyler smiled meaningfully. "So, I wondered what your honest view of it is."

"I do my job – I didn't set out to catch indentured servants; they just happened to be involved in my investigations on a couple of high-profile occasions."

"I understand." Tyler released him with a conspiratorial wink, as if they'd shared a moment of connection.

At that moment, a helicopter flew in low overhead and landed on the helipad beside the house.

"That'll be Owen – my protégé," Tyler said, shading his eyes from the sun as he watched it land. "He's an IS I'm training up in the business. He has a bright future ahead of him – when his contract runs out, I'll consider employing him as an independent. He needs to prove himself first, but I'm giving him every chance."

They finished playing the course, which Tyler predictably won – but not without making Josiah feel he'd been on the verge of beating

him, which he hadn't. He glanced at his indie – Alexander hadn't said a word unless spoken to, and while his eyes were still vacant, his body language was dejected.

They returned to the house, and Tyler turned to the two caddies. "Take the bags back to the storeroom and then go to the kitchen for refreshments. You've both done an excellent job." He beamed, then led Josiah to the living room.

"Look, you seem like a decent man, so I feel I should tell you something about Alexander," Tyler said when they were alone. "He's a good-looking young man, as I'm sure you've noticed..." He gave a wry smile. "But please be careful. It's not just his looks that make him so bloody attractive – let's face it, he's sex on legs, and he knows it." He gave a raucous bark of laughter. "I'm fond of him, always have been, but Alexander uses sex to manipulate people. I don't think he knows he's doing it half the time – it's just who he is. He tried it on me at first. I think that's why he stole that money – because he thought he could manipulate me, and when that didn't work, he ran out of options. He's a beautiful, charming, very sexy liar. Don't get sucked in by him – and don't let him use you for his own ends."

Josiah considered that for a moment. "Thank you for the warning, but he's not my type," he said eventually.

Tyler nodded thoughtfully. "Good, good. I just thought you should know... I'd hate for him to lead you down a wrong path. I don't know what he's said about me, or his time with me, but he isn't a reliable source of information."

"He hasn't said anything about you," Josiah replied honestly. "He's been quite scrupulous on that score; he refuses to say a word about his time as your IS."

Tyler gave a satisfied smile and then glanced over Josiah's shoulder. "Ah, Owen. Good to see you! Come and meet Investigator Raine."

Josiah spun around – and came face to face with a tall, attractive man with a mop of dark hair, styled messily so that it fell endearingly over one eye. He was wearing khaki combat trousers and a tight green tee-shirt that clung to his toned body... He could have been a younger, fitter version of Peter.

At that moment Alexander returned to the room, and for a second

GHOST EYE
75

his impassive mask slipped. He looked at Owen, and then at Josiah, and deflated visibly. He seemed bone-weary, as if he'd run a marathon only to be beaten at the finish line. He moved silently to the fireplace and stood there, gazing at a spot on the floor.

"Investigator Raine – this is Owen," Tyler said, drawing the young IS towards him. Josiah shook hands with him, taking in the firmness of the handshake and the sweetness of his smile. Owen didn't have Alexander's smouldering sensuality, but he was very attractive.

"Nice to meet you, Investigator Raine," Owen greeted him, holding both Josiah's hand and their eye contact a little too long.

"Mr Tyler informs me that you're his protégé, and he's training you up for an important place in his company," Josiah said.

Owen gave an easy laugh that revealed a set of perfect white teeth. "Mr Tyler has been very kind to me; I just hope I don't let him down."

"You'd better not!" Tyler laughed. "And please, Investigator Raine – call me George." He wrapped one arm around Josiah's shoulders, the other around Owen's, and enveloped them both in a hug. "We're all friends together here, aren't we? I was lucky enough to escape that tedious trend that went on for far too long after the Rising of giving children biblical names. You weren't so fortunate, Josiah." He grinned. "Were your parents Floodites, like old man Lytton?"

"Not at all. My father was vehemently against religion – and monarchy, which I suspect was the origin of your name. I believe my mother just liked the name," Josiah said, with a smile.

Another IS entered the room bearing a tray of refreshments, which were set down on the bar. "Come on – sit down," Tyler said, drawing them both over to the sofa. Have some tea and cake – which is chocolate, by the way." He winked at Josiah.

As he sat down on the sofa, Owen sat next to him, so close that he could smell the sweet, fresh scent of his cologne.

Owen glanced sideways at him and nudged his thigh. "Forgive me if I'm a little starstruck, but I've read all about you... I'm a huge fan." Owen lowered his head as if embarrassed, and Josiah noticed how thick and dark his eyelashes were, brushing over his lightly tanned skin.

Josiah sat back and watched the various people in the room with a

detached eye. Alexander was still rooted to his spot by the fireplace, gazing fixedly at that point on the floor. Owen was talking enthusiastically about Josiah's various high-profile cases, his hand resting lightly on Josiah's thigh. Tyler was standing at the large bar, watching everything that was going on. There were only three teacups, so Alexander clearly hadn't been invited to this party. Tyler had sent him very pointedly to the kitchen for his refreshments, but Alexander had returned to the room far too quickly to have taken advantage of that offer.

"If you want to play golf here again, I'm always on the lookout for a worthy opponent," Tyler said, bringing Josiah's tea over to him, together with a slice of rich, dark, freshly baked chocolate cake.

"I'm hardly that, surely," Josiah demurred.

"You could be – you have excellent hand-eye coordination – but if you want to practise, I'm sure Owen would be happy to play with you."

"I'd love to," Owen cried, looking delighted.

"How very kind," Josiah said, noticing that Owen's hand had inched a little further up his thigh.

"You can stay over if you don't want to travel. Just give Owen a call, and the two of you can sort out a convenient time," Tyler said.

"I wouldn't want to take Owen away from his training."

"Not at all. It'd be such an honour for me, and if the boss says it's okay" – Owen grinned cheekily at Tyler – "then it's okay. Here's my nym." He reached for his holopad and sent the code over instantly. "Please call. Anytime," he said eagerly.

Josiah grunted and took a bite of the cake. It was as delicious as it looked, and he sat back and revelled in the rich flavour; good chocolate was always something to be savoured.

Owen started chatting to him excitedly about golf – and his hand resumed its place on his leg. Tyler moved towards the bar with a satisfied look on his face, pausing in front of Alexander. For a second the genial manner slipped, and he flashed a dark, knowing smile at his former indie. Alexander didn't flinch, or return the smile – he just kept on staring at the floor. Tyler followed his gaze, frowning, and then his expression darkened. Giving a startled growl, he strode away.

"Excuse me, gentlemen – I need to piss," he said, leaving the room abruptly.

The instant Tyler was gone, Alexander began to shake. He tried visibly to get himself back under control by clenching his fists tightly and taking deep breaths, but he looked as if he was going to faint.

Josiah couldn't remember the exact words of the song that Alexander played during his yoga practice, but he could remember the tune, so he began to hum it softly. Owen glanced at him, startled, but Josiah only smiled genially and hummed even louder. The sound finally permeated Alexander's panic attack and had an effect, his breathing slowing, colour returning to his skin, and his fists beginning to uncurl. By the time Tyler returned to the room a few minutes later, Alexander's impassive mask was firmly back in place.

Josiah finished his tea, ate up the last morsel of the delicious chocolate cake, and put the plate down with a happy sigh.

"Thank you. That was very good," he said. "Almost spot on, in fact."

"I thought you'd enjoy it – you said chocolate was your favourite." Tyler grinned.

"I'm not referring to the cake." Josiah pointedly removed Owen's hand from where it was now resting perilously close to his crotch. "I'm referring to the young man. He does look a lot like Peter – although far too young, much too good-looking, and ridiculously over-styled. Peter wouldn't have known good styling if it had bitten him on the arse, despite all my best efforts." Josiah stood up.

"Sorry?" Tyler looked rattled.

"I understand." Josiah inclined his head sympathetically. "You didn't have much time to prepare. After Reed called, you found out as much about me as you could before I arrived. You put a call through to wherever you keep your charming young men and instructed them to get Owen ready. No doubt someone on your staff did some research to discover what my 'type' is, and dressed and styled him accordingly. Then, when the conversation between you and I had turned serious, you went to arrange the golf and gave the order to have him helicoptered in. I'm impressed. People don't usually go to such lengths to seduce me."

Out of the corner of his eye, Josiah saw a look of surprised delight pass across Alexander's face – which he quickly suppressed.

"I think there's been a misunderstanding," Tyler said, his voice becoming flatter and harder. He looked like a deadly snake, poised to strike.

"Oh, I don't think so – although that was one of the deftest interrogations I've been party to for a long time, and I speak as a trained investigator."

Tyler feigned bafflement. "I don't follow..."

"Firstly, there was the offer of alcohol, trying to discover my particular vices. You used what you'd found out – the very delicious chocolate cake that you instructed your chef to make – to ingratiate yourself to me. Then there were the gentle questions, too harmless to be inappropriate: ascertaining my level of job satisfaction, probing whether I'm happy with my salary, and establishing my view of indies – whether I'd be amenable to fucking one, presumably." He glanced at Owen, who had gone quite pale. "You created a false sense of intimacy by telling jokes, including me in your clique, and offering me access to any of the attractive young indies you employ who take my fancy. It was all very well done. You warned me against Alexander's seductive powers, but really, he's not the expert seducer in the room – you are."

Tyler gave an amused grunt, his eyes glittering. "Well, well, this *has* become interesting. You know, I like you, Raine."

Josiah gave a hard smile. "I have no idea why."

"Because you're different. Most people are boring and easy, but you're far more interesting."

"Thank you. The one thing I can't work out is what this whole charade was all about." Josiah waved his hand around the room. "You almost certainly had nothing to do with Elliot Dacre's murder, so why go to such lengths to get me onside?"

Tyler shrugged. "It's a habit. I like to make friends and influence people. Who knows – I might need the advice of a senior investigator one day."

"You play a long game."

"I have to. You don't start out with nothing and get to where I am without learning to make friends in useful places along the way."

"You started out with nothing? I wasn't aware of that," Josiah mused.

Tyler stared at him from narrowed eyes. "I told you my story."

"And I heard it, but clearly you and I have different definitions of 'starting out with nothing'. You grew up in a big house with plenty to eat, were given a good education, and someone paid for you to attend the finest university in the land. Now, I can understand that you feel your father was exploited, and he probably was, but it seems to have upset you more than him, and not to the point where you've fought against the exploitation of indies yourself." Josiah glanced meaningfully at Owen, whose skin tone had gone from pale to ghostly. "You see, I grew up in the Quarterlands. Go take a visit sometime and then let's talk again about starting out with 'nothing'. Now, this has been interesting, but it's time for us to leave. Alexander." Josiah snapped out the name, and the IS immediately scuttled over, his head down.

Tyler stared at him coldly. "You don't want to make an enemy of me, Raine."

Josiah gazed at him, equally coldly, for a long moment. "Likewise," he said quietly. Then he strode from the room with Alexander at his heels.

Josiah didn't say a word as they left the mansion and climbed into his waiting duck. He drove off that island as fast as he could, speeding through the water to put as much distance between them and George Tyler as possible. They emerged onto solid ground on the other side, and he slammed his foot down until they were miles away. Then he pulled over and turned to his IS.

"So... that was interesting," he said.

Alexander's mask was now well and truly gone, and there was a huge smile creasing his face. "Oh my God. You were magnificent!"

Josiah grunted. "I probably shouldn't have done that, but I really hate being played. I was an idiot to show my hand so clearly, though."

"A magnificent idiot," Alexander said proudly.

Josiah shook his head. "Alexander – what the hell was that about? George Tyler didn't kill Elliot Dacre, or arrange to have him killed. So why did you take me there?"

"You said you wanted to find out about my life. It seemed a good

place to start." Alexander shrugged, turning away. Josiah put a hand under his chin and pulled him back, so he was facing him again.

"The truth," he insisted.

"The truth is that I'm a bad judge of character, and you're not. You saw my brother's weaknesses, when most people are starstruck by him."

"What has that got to do with George Tyler?"

"Nothing." Alexander winced. "It has to do with me."

"I'm lost." Josiah threw up his hands in despair.

"I like you, and God knows I want to trust you, but I don't have the best track record where trusting the right people is concerned. So, I wanted to see how you handled George Tyler. I wanted to see what you made of him, and whether you could see the truth of him, the way you did with Charles."

"You were testing me?" Josiah asked incredulously.

"Yes. You passed, if that's any consolation."

Josiah rubbed his temples wearily. "It could be – if you trust me now, and if you'll help me find Dacre's killer, because I'm sure you're the key to his murder."

"I'm not quite there yet." Alexander gave an apologetic smile. "Not even after today, although that really helped. If you knew my history, you'd understand why."

"Tyler seduced you, too, once..." Josiah said slowly.

"Yes – he *dazzled* me, like he tried to do with you today. If only he'd known how very hard you are to seduce." Alexander grinned. "I could have told him that."

"But back there you thought it'd worked – you thought I'd give up my integrity just because Tyler sweet-talked me and offered me a pretty young man to sleep with."

Alexander sighed. "Don't take it personally – it's just that I've seen it happen too often before. I thought Tyler had worked his magic on you, the way he did with me. I adored him when I first met him. He was so unlike my father; he had such drive and ambition. He made me feel like I was part of something, and that I could be his friend – and I wanted that, so much."

GHOST EYE

"That's how he works, and he's good at it – the best I've seen. You shouldn't blame yourself – it's easy to be sucked in by a man like that."

"You weren't," Alexander said quietly.

"I'm thirty-nine, and I grew up in the Quarterlands. You were barely more than a kid when Tyler sank his claws into you."

"He played me like the fool I was."

Josiah pondered that for a moment, trying to piece together the parts of this very complicated jigsaw. "I've read your file. Are you saying that you ended up as his IS because...?"

"It was a trap. He trapped me."

"You didn't steal that money?" Josiah asked eagerly. "Is that why you took me there? Do you want me to prove your innocence and get your sentence overturned?"

"No," Alexander said firmly, his jaw clenching. "I stole the money; I'm not pinning that on him. It was a trap, but I didn't have to walk into it quite as stupidly as I did."

"Alexander, I can't help you if I don't understand what you want me to do," Josiah cried in exasperation.

"I'm getting there. The trouble is, that trust I spoke of goes both ways, and you don't fully trust me yet, either."

"I'm getting there," he parroted back with a wry smile.

Alexander didn't return it. His face was deadly serious as he spoke. "None of this is what you think. In order for you to understand what's really going on here, I'll have to tell you something that will make you angry, or upset, or both, and I want you to trust me before I risk that."

"Angry?" He felt his old wariness return. "With you?"

"Possibly. I don't know." Alexander gave a despairing shake of his head. "But I can't tell you what this is about without also telling you the thing that will upset you, and right now, I don't think either of us trusts the other enough for that. I'm sorry."

"You do know that I can't just sit around waiting for this bloody trust to happen, don't you?" Josiah said. "I have a killer to catch."

"I know that."

"So, what do you suggest I do while we're both circling around each other like this?"

"Your job," Alexander said quietly. "Just do your job. That's all I ask."

Josiah let out an explosive sigh and banged his hands against the steering wheel. "This would all be so much easier if you told me what the hell is going on."

"I need to be absolutely certain that you're the man I think you are first. You're the one shot I'll ever get at this; I can't blow it. I've been waiting too long."

"Okay – but if you wait much longer I might run out of patience, and then it'll be too late."

Alexander nodded. "Understood. And Josiah?" He leaned over and pressed a gentle kiss to his cheek. It was sweet, innocent, and heartfelt, and its warmth spread through him. "Thank you," he said softly.

Chapter Five

AUGUST 2088

Alex

"Good morning, sunshine!" Lorenzo's cheerful voice trilled. Alex raised his head from the pillow blearily. The smartwall display showed that it was 5.30 a.m. As he came to, he saw that the smartwall was also displaying several familiar pictures. He blinked in surprise to find himself staring at his own duck designs. She was still beautiful. If Tyler thought these images would upset him, he was wrong: Alex loved this duck and could never grow tired of gazing at her. She might have been the ruin of him, but he could never hate her for it.

"What's going on, Lorenzo?" he asked, drinking in the sight of his designs greedily.

"Today's a big day. Mr Tyler wants you in his office at seven a.m. to start work."

"Work?" Alex queried. "I thought that's what I did for him here, in this bed, with the stupid saps he makes me fuck." In the past couple of months he'd slept with several of Tyler's "guests". It hadn't become any easier, but the format had always been the same.

"Well, today it's something different." Lorenzo grabbed the duvet and yanked it back, and cool air caressed Alex's warm, naked body. "Now get in the shower, pronto." He slapped Alex's buttocks affection-

ately. Alex gave a growl of annoyance, tore his gaze away from the designs, and slid out of bed.

After his shower, Lorenzo shaved him, and then styled his hair flat with copious amounts of gel, parting it severely down one side.

"I look like I walked out of one of those ancient movies," Alex complained. "You know, the ones from the 1940s, where everyone talked like this." He mimicked the clipped, precise tones from the period.

"It's a good look on you," Lorenzo said approvingly. "What am I saying? Everything's a good look on you."

Alex stood still as Lorenzo finished dressing him. He'd learned that the stylist was kind-hearted and good fun, but he also had a core of steel and was not to be messed with. He allowed Alex to tease him, and they could laugh together at whatever absurdity life as George Tyler's indies threw up, but at the end of the day Lorenzo had a job to do, and it was one he took very seriously. Alex could bitch and whine all he liked, but Lorenzo demanded that he hold still while being shaved and having his hair done, and that he allowed himself to be dressed with the minimum of fuss. Those were the rules, and Alex had found it better to cooperate than to be truculent. Besides, he liked Lorenzo – the guy was just doing his job, the same as everyone else around here. Making Lorenzo's life difficult wasn't going to hurt Tyler in the slightest.

It felt absurd, as a grown man, to be helped into clothes as if he was a child, but Alex obediently stepped into the plain white boxer shorts Lorenzo held out for him. They were made of expensive cotton, and felt cool and crisp against his skin. "Nothing but the best for Mr Tyler's protégé," Lorenzo said approvingly.

"Protégé!" Alex snorted. "I'm his prize whore. It's not like he's training me to take over his company."

"If we're given a part, we play it. That's part of your learning process, darling." Lorenzo gave him a peck on the cheek. "You must play the roles Mr Tyler gives to you."

"And what is this role?" Alex asked as Lorenzo held out an exquisitely tailored pale blue shirt.

"I don't know, I'm afraid. Sorry, sweetie." Lorenzo eased him into

an elegant navy-blue suit, complete with waistcoat, and then knotted a cerulean tie around his collar. A pair of fine navy-blue silk socks and shining black shoes completed the ensemble. "Perfect." The stylist smoothed his fingers over Alex's suit jacket and then took hold of his shoulders and positioned him in front of the mirror.

Alex was barely able to recognise the beautifully turned-out apparition in front of him. He looked like a businessman, but not remotely like the one he'd actually been. His appearance was more like that of an ambitious account exec at some posh New London bank.

The wet-look hair and closely shaven face gave him a sharp look, while the beautiful suit screamed ambition. He'd always hated corporate schemers like this. He rolled his eyes at his reflection, and there it was – that glimmer of his true self. Tyler could dress him any way he liked, but the real Alex Lytton was still there underneath. He hoped he'd never lose sight of him.

"So, where am I going?" he asked as Lorenzo opened the door. His guard fell into place behind him, as usual, as Lorenzo led the way down the corridor towards the lift.

"Why, Croydon, darling." Lorenzo grinned. "Where else?"

Instead of being taken down in the lift and escorted into a duck as he'd expected, Alex was taken to the very top of the building. He paused in the doorway as the lift doors opened onto the world; it was the first time he'd been outside in months. Ever since his arrival, his entire universe had consisted of the suite of rooms below, and his only companions, aside from Tyler's guests, had been Solange, Lorenzo, Mason, Chef, and his guards. It was a cool morning with a light breeze that fluttered across his face, failing to make any impression on his tightly slicked-down hair.

A helicopter was waiting on the rooftop helipad.

"This is where we part company," Lorenzo said, adjusting Alex's tie minutely. "Now, darling – be good, and I'm sure it'll be over soon."

"What's waiting for me, Lorenzo? What does he want from me this time?" Alex beseeched, feeling anxious about the change of scene.

"I don't know any details, my love. I only know he wanted you

looking sharp and business-like." Lorenzo patted him down. "Don't worry – you look amazing."

He didn't care how he looked, but he supposed that from Lorenzo's point of view it was the most important thing.

"I didn't bring any of the pills you gave me," he said.

"Well, hopefully you won't need them," Lorenzo said. "In future, remember to put them in your pocket wherever you go, just in case. Off you go now."

Scarface directed him into the helicopter, then climbed in beside him. The blades whirred, and they were whisked up into the air.

"Why are we going to Croydon?" Alex demanded. "What's there?"

"Tyler Tech HQ," Scarface replied.

Alex had never been to Tyler's business headquarters before. Any work he'd done with Tyler had been in houses, workshops, and restaurants. The helicopter quickly ate up the short distance to the fringes of New London.

Croydon had once been a downmarket commercial centre on the outskirts of London, a poor relation to Canary Wharf's gleaming towers. Now, that financial and business powerhouse lay mostly under water, and Croydon had taken over as its unlikely successor, transforming over the past decade as money from the new prosperity had come pouring in.

Alex viewed its imposing skyscrapers from a distance, the dark water lapping up high against the flood barriers showing just how close the place had come to being lost in the Rising. From this high in the air, he could see how virtually all of Old London was underwater; Croydon marked where that stopped, and suddenly there were large areas of land stretching out in front of them to the south.

Tyler's HQ was, unsurprisingly, the tallest tower in a cluster that dominated Croydon's centre. It soared high above the others, and at its very top was a massive sign: *TYLER TECH*.

Alex was excited. Outside of his work entertaining Tyler's clients, all his days for the past couple of months had been the same: tedious exercise routines in the gym, and hanging out in the living room, reading and watching movies on the smartwall. He'd spent the rest of his time chatting to Solange and Scarface. He liked it when Lorenzo

dropped by, as it livened the place up, even though he was bored witless by the constant fittings and style sessions that Lorenzo insisted upon.

He hadn't realised how much he'd missed being out in the world. Maybe this would be the start of a new chapter of his life as an IS. Maybe, just maybe, Tyler had a purpose for him other than serving as his corporate whore.

The helicopter landed on the roof of the building. Alex was escorted off and taken to a lift, which travelled down a couple of floors before opening into the heart of Tyler's business empire.

He looked around in awe at the sight that greeted him. The building hummed with industrious activity, smartwalls showed rolling news updates and views over the city outside, and everywhere he looked Tyler's staff were busy working on state-of-the-art holopads. Compared to this, Lytton AV was small fry, a little company that hadn't grown or developed in years.

He was ushered into a waiting room that was as big as his father's entire office. Scarface gestured that he should sit on a black leather sofa, then stationed himself beside it, between Alex and the nearest exit. The smartwall display told him the time was exactly 7 a.m.

George Tyler suddenly appeared in the doorway. He looked smart and business-like, in a tailored black suit, crisp black shirt, and scarlet tie. "Ah, you're here on time – good. I'm glad you're not late for your first day in the office."

"I'm going to be working here?"

"Yes, you are. Don't look so surprised. Did you think I'd spend a fortune on you just to leave you mouldering away in some penthouse tower forever? I've got big plans for you, Alexander. Come with me."

He followed Tyler into his office, which was immense and beautifully furnished. There was an entire wall of glass, with stunning views over Croydon.

"Nice view, isn't it?" Tyler grinned.

"Yeah. You seem to be addicted to big windows," Alex commented. "You've got them everywhere."

"I like natural light and wide vistas. I'm a man of vision, Alexander; it's important to me."

"I bet you also like owning the tallest, fanciest building in sight, so everyone can see how important you are," he returned snidely.

Tyler laughed. "You're right. I do. Part of running a business empire like Tyler Tech is impressing on people that I'm a man of power and influence – someone they should want to do business with. People might distrust the company, or me individually, or even my staff or my projects, but they always trust impressive surroundings."

"Maybe they see this and want a little piece of it for themselves," Alex said.

"Of course they do. It's aspirational. I don't mind that – I approve of ambition."

"Why am I here?" Alex changed the subject abruptly. "You don't need to impress me – you own me."

"That's right, I do." Tyler sat down in his huge leather desk chair and reclined, looking pleased with himself. "It still gives me a kick, every time, to know I own a Lytton. Who'd have thought it, huh? With all our family history." He shook his head, chuckling.

Alex gazed at him stonily; Tyler waved a hand. "Aw, you have no sense of occasion, Alexander. Okay – have it your way. You're here because I say so – that's your entire life in a nutshell now. However..." Tyler paused, looking thoughtful. "It's been a couple of months, and I thought it was time to broaden your experience, so you'll accompany me to my meetings today."

"Why?" Alex blurted, confused.

Tyler pursed his lips irritably. "We're back to 'because I say so', Alexander. Do keep up. You're brighter than this. I want you to watch and learn today – think you can do that?"

"Yes, I'm sure I can manage it," Alex snapped, not even bothering to keep the sarcasm out of his voice.

"Good. Now sit over there, keep still, and shut up," Tyler ordered, jerking his head at yet another vast leather sofa in the corner.

Alex did as he was told, watching in silence as Tyler recorded some memos, blasted a few hapless staff members in a group holochat, and played twenty minutes of carpet golf.

He followed when Tyler went walkabout, stopping to talk to various members of his staff along the way, sharing jokes and asking

GHOST EYE

about their families as if he really cared. Alex noticed that they all wore ID tags. He remembered his father saying that the government provided tax incentives for every IS he employed. This was to tackle the huge housing crisis and get people out of the Quarterlands and government work camps, but Alex wondered if the unintended consequence was to turn everyone into indies and reduce their rights and freedoms accordingly.

Tyler's office indies stared at Alex curiously, much to his discomfort. To them, he was probably shocking and exotic: the drug addict playboy who'd brought down his family. He'd been bored on Ghost Eye City, but now he almost wished he was back there, locked away from prying eyes. Luckily, the workers were so scared of Tyler that they didn't speak to him directly; they just looked.

Returning to his office, Tyler instructed Alex to sit again by clicking his fingers and pointing at the sofa. A short while later, two staff members entered and perched in front of his desk to discuss the budget for a project Tyler was keen to pursue. There seemed to be some kind of a cash-flow crisis that they were concerned about.

"We can't really afford it at the moment. It's not in the budget," an earnest middle-aged man said.

"You know I don't like the word 'can't', Anders," Tyler said genially.

"It's a significant investment, and you've sunk so much into the floating city project," a small, mousy-haired woman pointed out.

"We'll get a huge return on it one day." Tyler shrugged.

"Yes, but not today. Can't this new project wait?"

"No." Tyler glanced at Alex. "No, it can't."

It seemed that even Tyler's massive wealth had its limits; Alex wondered why this project was so important to him.

Tyler dismissed his employees and turned to Alex. "In business, if you're not moving forward, you're going backward," he announced. "There's no standing still."

"But if you don't have the money?" Alex asked, genuinely interested in how Tyler ran his business.

"Money." Tyler laughed. "Money attracts money, Alexander. That's something your father never learned. You have to borrow money in order to make money."

"My father hates borrowing. He likes to own everything he has, so that no bank can ever take it away from him."

"I know, and that's why he's run his company into the ground over the years. You need to speculate to accumulate – that's the oldest business wisdom in the book. Your father needed to invest, but instead he's just trundled along. He's pedestrian, uninspired. Being in business is about creativity, not caution."

Alex wanted to argue, but instead he remembered why he'd fallen under Tyler's spell in the first place. He might be a complete bastard, but nobody could deny his business acumen.

"You had vision," Tyler said, leaning back in his chair and gazing at Alex broodingly. "You could have turned that company around. You could have been a great businessman, Alexander. You still can."

He said it as if it were tantalisingly within reach, instead of the impossibility Alex knew it to be. What was going on here? Was Tyler offering him a lifeline?

"We make a great team," Tyler continued. "You and I – we're more alike than you think. There's work to be done here, and you're the one to do it, Alexander."

Alex didn't know what to make of that, but he had no chance to reply because Tyler stood up suddenly. "Lunch!" he announced, striding towards the door.

They ate together in a private dining suite a few floors down. Tyler was as amusing and entertaining as he'd been the night he'd taken Alexander to Ghost Eye for dinner and tried to impress him. Alex didn't know why, because Tyler had made it clear that Alex was nothing more than his whore.

"Your duck designs," Tyler said, leaning across the table towards him. "Wouldn't you like to see them in action? Wouldn't you like to drive around in one of those beautifully designed AVs, Alexander?"

Alex frowned. "Are you taunting me?"

"No, I mean it. Your designs are good – wouldn't you like to be part of making them happen? I don't think you ever cared about making money. I think you only ever cared about making something beautiful. Well, I'm offering you that chance."

"To be part of your team, working on my ducks?" Alex felt his

breath catch in his throat. Maybe Tyler realised he'd made a mistake in locking him up. Perhaps he realised how much more use he could be making something beautiful. Or was he being tricked again?

"You have a talent, and I want to make good use of it," Tyler said earnestly. "The Destiny AV range *will* happen; the question is whether you want to be a part of it or not."

"You told me you have engineers and designers – why do you need me?"

"It's in the name – Destiny. Your destiny, Alex, and mine. Those designs are fantastic – and I know you want to make them happen as much as I do." Tyler sat back and glanced at his watch. "We should move on. We have an important meeting to attend."

He led the way to yet another floor and another suite of plush offices – this time to a boardroom with a gleaming white table in the centre and twelve black leather chairs around it. Alex followed, still reeling from the unexpected turn the day had taken.

Tyler sat at the head of the table and gestured to Alex to sit on his right-hand side. At 2 p.m. the door opened, and a tall, silver-haired man entered the room.

"Ah, Jake – good to see you." Tyler stood up and shook hands with the man. "This is Alexander Lytton – although I'm sure he needs no introduction," he added with a grin. "His reputation precedes him. Alexander – this is Jake Harper from Parminters." Alex looked at him blankly. "The bank," Tyler explained. "It's small but exclusive – it specialises in private banking services."

Harper looked at him curiously. Alex wondered what he saw – the "bad seed" who'd ruined his family or someone to be pitied? He couldn't tell. The man was in his forties and fit, with a lean, hard body clothed in an expensive suit. He was also very handsome, with aquiline features and a square jaw. His crisp cologne teased Alex's nostrils.

They all sat down at the table, and one of Tyler's many assistants brought them coffee.

"So, I asked you here today, Jake, because—" Tyler began.

"You want money," Harper interrupted brusquely. There was nothing affable about this man. "Question is, why not go to your other financiers, George? Why come to Parminters? Could it be you're so

maxed out that they won't lend you another penny? If so, why should we?"

"You've seen the designs." Tyler clicked on his holopad, and Alex was mesmerised to see one of his own designs floating as a holoimage in front of them. "They're good."

Harper glanced across the table at Alex. "These are the Lytton designs? The ones that got him arrested?" He looked oddly interested in that fact.

"Oh yes. Alexander here has been a very bad boy. Talented and beautiful, but very naughty." Tyler grinned.

"I thought his designs were crap," Harper said dismissively.

"They're not crap!" Alex cried hotly, without meaning to, the words just coming out.

Harper raised an eyebrow. "Tyler Tech couldn't get them to work last time – what makes you think we should sink money into a second attempt?"

"They *will* work." Alex felt his hands clench into stubborn fists. "They're beautiful, and people will buy them."

Harper glanced at him coldly. "Your IS seems to be talking out of turn," he said to Tyler.

"You're right. He is." Tyler suddenly leaned over and slapped his cheek. "Sit still and shut up, boy."

Alex pressed his hand to his face in shocked surprise, the humiliation smarting more than the slap. Harper's eyes gleamed.

"You know the designs are good," Alex said to Tyler. "You know the only reason they didn't work last time was because you sabo–"

Tyler jumped to his feet. "Excuse us, Jake. I want to have a few words with this rude young man." He grabbed Alex's arm and dragged him into a small, empty room next door.

"I don't understand," Alex protested as Tyler closed the door. "I thought you wanted me involved. I thought that's why you took me in there. I thought you wanted this bank's money."

"I do." Tyler grinned. "And you're doing perfectly, Alexander. Better than I expected. I like that about you – you're a quick learner. You're doing exactly what I need to reel Harper in. I approached Parminters

because I know his tastes – particularly his liking for rebellious, hot-headed young men."

"I'm... leverage?" Alex asked, feeling his cheeks burn with humiliation. "I thought—"

"That I wanted you to work on the designs again?" Tyler laughed. "Nah. Like I said, I've got that sorted. You're here to whore the money in for me, Alex. Harper's right, I *am* overstretched. I may be one of the richest men in the country, but you borrow here, you invest there, you build this, and you sell that – and sometimes, your cash flow isn't so good, and investors won't give you more until they start to see some returns. I spent a lot on you – now you're going to give me a return on that investment by securing the finance I need to start producing the Destiny range of ducks you so kindly designed for me."

Alex stared at him helplessly, wondering how he could have allowed himself to be duped again. Maybe it had been desperation, or the blind hope that finally he could be part of making his designs happen the way he'd always wanted.

"Harper's tastes aren't pretty, but I'm sure you'll agree that's a price worth paying to get your designs made," Tyler said. "Now, go back in there and whore me my money." He grabbed Alex's arm and shoved him back into the boardroom.

Harper looked up as they entered, his eyes gleaming.

"I'm sorry, Jake, but it seems this troublesome young man has the hots for you. He knows he behaved badly, but he wanted your attention," Tyler said, throwing Alex towards him.

"Really?" Harper stood up, his gaze fixed on Alex as though he were prey.

"Yeah, but you're a good-looking guy – you must be used to that. Now, I need to make a holocall. I'll leave this badly behaved young man here for you to deal with in any way you see fit. Don't go easy on him, Jake; he doesn't deserve it."

Tyler left the room, closing the door emphatically behind him.

Harper stepped forward, gazing at Alex wolfishly. "I followed your trial," he said. "You're a disgrace. If I were your father, I'd have taken a belt to your arse years ago."

"My father wasn't like that," Alex said hoarsely, looking around desperately for a way out.

"That's why you turned out so badly. You're a brat."

"And you're a sucker," Alex retorted. "Tyler is using you. He just wants a deal."

Harper laughed. "Oh, I know that, but I'll never get offered someone like you again."

"I'm sure you can have anyone you like, looking like you do," Alex pointed out.

"I can have young men on their own terms; I want someone on mine," Harper told him sharply. "Specifically – I want you. You're quite a celebrity, and I've never fucked a celebrity before."

"Piss off," Alex said defiantly.

Harper's lips quirked appreciatively. "Oh, that's good. You press all my buttons, boy." He stood up, slowly, his eyes dark with arousal.

Alex made a run for the door and tugged on it desperately, only to find it was locked.

"There's no way out. You're Tyler's gift to me," Harper crowed. "Nobody cares what I do to you in this room."

Turning, he found Harper leaning back against the table, a cruel smile playing on his lips.

"And in return you give him the money he wants? What does that make you?" Alex asked.

"Someone who knows the value of what he's getting," Harper said dismissively. "I looked at those designs – they're good, and they'll work. Tyler wouldn't be pursuing them if he didn't believe in them. Sure, they're a punt, but he's right that it's a risk worth taking. I always intended to make him work for it, though. I wondered what he'd give me to sweeten the deal; I had no idea it would be you. Tyler has surpassed himself. There's no way I'd pass on a chance to fuck your sorry arse."

"Please... you don't have to do this," Alex begged.

"No, but I want to." Harper gazed fixedly at him. His tongue darted out and moistened his lips. "Now, get over here."

Alex didn't move, so Harper started to advance on him. Alex considered his options. Maybe he could sweet-talk the man – cajole

him into something more pleasant than he suspected Harper had in mind.

"Let's talk about this," he said as Harper drew close.

"Talk? I'd prefer to hear you scream." Harper smirked.

"You want sex. I can do that. How about I just..." Alex sank to his knees and tried to open Harper's fly, but the man shoved him away.

"I'm in charge, not you," he growled, grabbing Alex's arm.

He tried to pull away, but Harper was strong and put an arm around his neck, pushing him towards the table. He kicked back fruitlessly, missing his target. Desperate, he sank his teeth into Harper's arm, making the man yelp in pain and release him.

It wasn't a wise move. The bite made Harper angry, and he seized Alex and pushed him face down over the table. Alex struggled, but Harper was tall and fit and seemed to be made of pure steel. He was also determined. He leaned over Alex, pushing his weight on top of him, and slammed Alex's head onto the table. "The more you fight, the more turned on you make me," he hissed into Alex's ear, pressing his erection against Alex's buttocks to prove it. Then he pulled Alex up by the neck and unzipped his trousers.

Alex hung in his grasp like a kitten, unsure of what to do next. Maybe if he just let the bastard fuck him... it wouldn't be nice, but at least it'd soon be over and done with. The alternative was to fight him off, but for how long? It wasn't as if Tyler was going to let him out of this room until Harper was satisfied – and what would happen to Solange if he refused?

"I can hear the cogs turning... you're thinking too hard." Harper ran his free hand over Alex's body, caressing his chest through the expensive blue shirt. He undid his tie and drew it away. "It's too late for that. There's no escape. I'm taking what I want, whether you like it or not." He found his left nipple and pinched it hard.

Alex growled and kicked backwards, trying to break free.

"Naughty... very naughty..." Harper gathered his hands behind his back and secured them tightly with his tie. "I'm going to punish you for all the biting and kicking," he said, yanking Alex's trousers down.

Alex didn't like the sound of that. He remained torn between

complying to get it over with and fighting, both impulses warring with each other.

Harper took advantage of his indecision and grabbed his bound wrists, pushing him face down onto the table, holding him there in a vice-like grip.

Alex heard a whooshing sound and looked over his shoulder to see Harper whipping his belt out from his trousers and doubling it over.

"I want to see your bare arse," he barked, yanking Alex's boxers down to his knees. He pushed Alex's head back onto the table, angling it sideways. "This is how I want you when I beat your arse. Hold still for me."

Alex couldn't do anything but obey. His trousers were around his ankles, his boxers around his knees, his suit jacket flicked up, leaving his backside fully exposed. He squirmed, but Harper mercilessly pressed one hand into the small of his back, keeping him in place, and then drew back his other hand, which held the belt.

Alex heard a cracking sound, and then felt a wave of shocking pain. He struggled frantically to twist out of Harper's grasp, only to be pressed firmly back into place. "Please... no... fuck, that hurt... please," he begged. He wriggled, trying to get free, but it was useless.

"First, I'm going to tenderise this prime piece of arse meat, and then I'm going to fuck it hard," Harper said with relish. "Scream all you like – Tyler won't send anyone to stop me."

"He'll be recording all this. He always does," Alex panted. "He'll use it to blackmail you."

"I don't care. I've got Alexander fucking Lytton on the table, bare-arsed in front of me, and that's a once in a lifetime deal. You have no idea how often I wanked off to your pouty little face going to court each day and whining about your sad life."

"I didn't whine," Alex protested.

"Well, you can now. Whine, beg, pout, and plead with me to stop. I'll enjoy that." He drew back the belt and cracked it down on Alex's buttocks again, drawing an involuntary scream. Alex didn't want to give Harper the satisfaction, but the pain was so sharp he couldn't help himself.

Harper got into his stride, slamming the belt hard against his arse

and upper thighs over and over again, until his screams were one long shriek of pain.

He looked over at the smartwall. Was George Tyler watching this right now? Was he even enjoying it, because in his twisted mind Alex deserved it? Maybe he *did* deserve it. He'd certainly fucked up enough over the years. Maybe this was exactly what he deserved.

He blinked the sweat out of his eyes. The humiliation of being held over this table and beaten for the sake of Tyler's business empire hurt almost as badly as the physical pain. He was nothing but a piece of meat to the men who fucked him, and Tyler was making sure that message went home loud and clear. He'd been an idiot to think he could ever work on the designs again. He was an indie, a whore, nothing more. He put his head down, accepting his fate.

His arse felt raw, he was breathing in ragged gasps, and his throat ached from screaming. Sweat dripped into his eyes, blurring his vision. He felt like a landed fish, flopping pathetically with each new stroke of Harper's belt.

Then, suddenly, the beating stopped, and Harper leaned over him. "Your arse looks fantastic like this – bright red and covered in my belt marks. How does it feel?"

Alex blinked – was that a serious question? "It fucking hurts, you bastard," he croaked.

"Good. Is it really painful?" Harper took hold of his burning rear and squeezed.

"Yes. Fuck you – yes!"

"I'm glad to hear it," Harper purred. "You look even more beautiful when you're in pain, but you're still so defiant. I thought I'd beaten that out of you." Harper squeezed again, making him yelp. "How much does it hurt? Tell me."

"Please, stop... please... I'm sorry," he whimpered.

Harper squeezed even harder, making Alex scream. "I said, how much does it hurt? Answer me."

"So much... it hurts so much... please, please... stop. Please stop, sir. Please."

"That's better. I like hearing you beg – it's such a turn-on."

Alex heard the sound of a zip and then felt Harper's hard length

pressing against his backside. He squirmed sideways, but Harper pushed him back into position.

"I see you've still got some fight in you – maybe I should have beaten you for longer." He spat on his hand, and Alex felt a wet finger press against his hole. "The spit's for my comfort, not yours. Open for me."

Alex felt his hole tighten instinctively.

Harper slammed his hand down on his sore bottom. "Come on, we all know what a little slut you are. Plenty of cocks have been in here and now it's my turn. Open up for me."

He pushed his finger inside, then removed it only to immediately shove his cock into Alex's cleft.

Alex tried to relax, knowing it would make it easier, but his traumatised body wouldn't obey.

"Damn it – fuck you," Harper swore, shoving hard. He grabbed handfuls of Alex's flesh, wrenched his buttocks apart, and then thrust again, with all his force. This time he breached the tight ring of flesh, wringing a scream from Alex's lips in the process.

He closed his eyes and concentrated on breathing as Harper sank deep inside him, paused for a second, then began fucking him vigorously. The hard edge of the table was digging into the front of his thighs, his wrists were tied too tightly behind his back, making his arms ache, and he hurt more than he thought he could endure.

Harper slapped his raw, sore arse as he fucked him, and Alex's hole tightened involuntarily around Harper's cock, making the man grunt with pleasure. He fucked Alex so hard that he screamed with each savage thrust.

Looking up, Alex caught sight of his reflection in the tall glass windows opposite. His stupid hair was still slicked down, the parting still severely in place – Lorenzo had surpassed himself. The top part of his body was fully clothed, apart from the missing tie. His face was red, shiny, and wet, the sweat from his forehead mingling now with the tear tracks running down his cheeks.

He could see Harper behind him, still fully dressed, plunging into him with hard thrusts. Harper caught him looking and gave a growl of anger, shoving his head back down on the table. Alex closed his

eyes, glad to look away from the sight of himself being so abjectly debased.

Harper climaxed with a throaty shout of triumph and rested on top of him. Then he withdrew, making Alex cry out again.

Alex lay on the table, panting, hoping it was over. He could smell the sharp scent of Harper's cologne, overlaid with sweat and the musky smell of his come. He felt like throwing up.

"Very nice," Harper murmured. "It's not often a man gets to live out one of his filthiest fantasies." He caressed Alex's bottom with his fingertips, making him shudder. "It was so much better in reality than in my head." He straightened up, tucked his spent cock back into his boxers, and threaded his belt through his trousers. Then he slicked his hair down, looking as if nothing had happened. "Get up," he ordered, untying Alex's wrists.

Alex slid off the table and landed in a heap on the floor, trembling with rage and distress.

"Get dressed," Harper said curtly. "I'm sure George will be back soon."

Alex staggered to his feet and gingerly pulled his boxer shorts over his abused flesh. He could feel Harper's come dripping out of him and running down his leg. It felt disgusting. He slowly pulled up his trousers and fastened them, looking down at the ground the whole time, too humiliated to meet the other man's eye.

"Good boy," Harper purred, knotting Alex's tie back into place around his throat.

Alex stood still and let him do it, too exhausted to move. It felt like an oddly intimate act after such a violent encounter.

"That's better." Harper smoothed Alex's suit. "So respectable; nobody would know what a tasty little slut you are underneath." He pinched Alex's cheek, grinning. Alex remained frozen to the spot.

Harper drew back with a mocking smile. "Aw, what's the matter? Didn't you have a good time?"

"No, but then I'm not the first person to be fucked over by a banker, and I doubt I'll be the last," Alex snapped, the defiance making him feel a little better, if nothing else.

But Harper didn't seem stung by the comment – if anything he

looked amused. "Your smart mouth is such a turn-on. I'm so bored of boys who enjoy it," he drawled. "It's much more fun if it's real."

At that moment Tyler walked into the room, a big grin on his face.

"So, do we have a deal, Jake?" he asked genially, placing his holopad on the table, right where Alex had been lying a few minutes earlier. A contract popped up in mid-air in front of them.

"We do... subject to one minor caveat," Harper said. Tyler raised an eyebrow. "I'd like longer with Alexander next time. I don't think we dealt with his behaviour sufficiently on this occasion. So, I think an overnight stay would be best, or maybe an entire weekend."

Tyler nodded pleasantly. "I'm sure that can be arranged." He watched as Harper biosigned the contract, grinning all the while. Then Tyler escorted him to the door, making small talk while Alex stood there impotently, fists clenched by his side. He felt like a child, flushed with useless rebellion in the face of powerful adults. Tyler handed Harper over to one of his assistants, and the banker gave Alex a mocking wave and then left.

"That went well," Tyler commented, turning back to Alex. "You did good work here today. See, I knew I wouldn't regret spending all that money on you."

"He beat me like a dog and fucked me over the table like I was nothing," Alex spat.

"I know. I saw." Tyler shrugged. "I can see why so many people desire you, Alexander. There's something about you – maybe the attitude, or maybe because you're so notorious. Nobody cares about you, because they know how toxic you are. That makes it easy for them to act out whatever nasty little fantasy they have about you. You see..." He leaned in close. "You're nothing. That means you can be anything they want you to be; you don't exist outside their fantasies."

"I'm not worthless. I'm not a piece of meat," Alex said defiantly, wishing he could calm his trembling body.

"Of course not; you're worth a great deal to me. Take today – thanks to you, we've secured funding for those beautiful ducks you designed. You must be very proud. This small sacrifice on your part – some hurt pride and a sore arse – will ensure the Destiny range comes into being. I wanted you to learn something today, and I think you

GHOST EYE

have – that every achievement requires sacrifices. That's what you can take from your work here today."

He rested a hand on Alex's shoulder and escorted him to the door, where Scarface was waiting for him. "Take him home and put him to bed," Tyler ordered. "He's had rather a taxing day."

Alex positioned himself on his side on the mercifully short flight back to Ghost Eye, unable to sit comfortably on his beaten backside. Scarface didn't talk; he just sat in sympathetic silence beside him.

Alex had stiffened up so much by the time they returned to the floating city that he stumbled getting out of the helicopter, barely able to put one foot in front of the other. Without saying a word, Scarface scooped him up in his arms and carried him back to his room. It was a kind gesture, but a fittingly humiliating end to a terrible day.

The guard placed him gently on the bed in his room and pulled a blanket over his still-trembling body.

"Is he okay? What happened?" Alex heard Solange ask in the doorway.

"He'll be okay, but he needs to be on his own right now," Scarface told her, with a greater degree of insight than Alex would have expected.

The door closed, leaving him in welcome solitude. He turned his face to the wall and noticed, blankly, that it was no longer a solid colour but showed a bucolic meadow scene, complete with cows in the distance and the bobbing heads of red poppies in the foreground. He had no idea why Tyler had changed it, but it seemed incongruous given what had just happened. Was that the point? Was Tyler mocking him in some way? Or was it designed to be soothing?

He was still in shock, and it was hard to think because of the pain rolling off his backside in waves. Then he remembered that Harper had said he wanted him again – for longer next time.

Was this how Tyler intended to break him? If so, then maybe he'd succeed, because Alex didn't think he could endure that. His breath hitching in his throat, he closed his eyes to block out the cheerful meadow scene and buried his face in the pillow.

OCTOBER 2095

Josiah

They drove home in silence. Josiah was lost in thought – until he heard an unmistakeable gurgling sound coming from the direction of Alexander's stomach.

"Shit – you must be hungry." He could have kicked himself. "You haven't had lunch. I should have thought; you should have said."

"You haven't had lunch, either."

"Nah, but I did have a great big slab of a really fantastic chocolate cake." Josiah grinned. He saw a café in a parade of shops ahead and swung the duck into a parking bay across the street. "What do you want? Tea? A sandwich?"

"Both would be nice. Cheese or tuna."

Josiah glanced out of the café window as he waited in line to order. Alexander seemed unaware he was being watched as he sat in the duck. Suddenly, he smiled, and for a brief moment he looked ecstatically happy – then he flinched, as if remembering something. He wrapped his arms tightly around his body, and Josiah saw him mouthing the lines to that song again as he calmed himself. It was a rare unguarded moment.

After buying two teas and a couple of sandwiches, he carried them back towards the duck. He'd just stepped out into the road to cross the

street when he was hit by a sudden, vivid flashback. His arm jerked upwards of its own volition, and the teas almost went flying. Closing his eyes, he stood still, fighting the rising tide of memories – the scent of blood, the bright red stains on his hands and clothes, the sound of screaming...

"Hey... Josiah, are you okay?" A strong hand grasped his arm and mercifully took the tray away from his trembling fingers.

"I'm fine." Josiah blinked, clenching his teeth hard, sweat trickling down his face.

"Here – hold on to me." Alexander gripped him tightly, holding him up. Josiah had a few years and several inches on his indie, but he still felt like an infant clinging to his father as Alexander steered him safely back to the duck and helped him inside.

"Fuck!" Josiah banged the palms of his hands on the steering wheel. Alexander silently handed him his tea. He took a deep gulp, feeling the warm fluid ground him, and his vision slowly cleared, his breathing becoming calmer.

"The same nightmare as before?" Alexander queried gently.

"Yes. It's never happened during the day, though. It's usually when I'm asleep."

"Any idea what could have triggered it?" The IS glanced at him curiously.

"No. Just... I was crossing the street with a tray of cups the night Peter died, but I've done that plenty of times since without this happening. I always buy drinks for my team when we're working a case."

"Perhaps because of Owen – triggering memories of Peter?" Alexander suggested.

"I don't know." Josiah clenched his fists so hard they made his sore knuckles sting, but the pain was a blessed distraction.

"Here." Alexander passed him a sandwich, shooting him a few concerned glances as they ate. But mercifully, he said no more.

A little cluster of reporters was still gathered outside Josiah's house when they returned home.

"Get down," he ordered. Alexander swiftly ducked, just in time, as the reporters spotted the AV. Dozens of camera flashes lit the air, but they didn't get what they'd come for. Clicking open the garage door, Josiah drove swiftly inside and the doors closed behind them, shutting out the media scrum. "Fuckers," he growled.

"I thought you'd be used to them by now. They've been all over you for the past few years," Alexander said as they climbed out of the duck.

"Yeah – at Inquisitus, usually, not here." Josiah glanced at Peter's gleaming red car.

"Ah, I see. This is your home. Your sanctuary."

"Yes, but it was his home, too. It feels like they're violating him. His memory." Josiah placed a hand on the car. "This was Peter's house. It still *is* his house, more than it's ever been mine. He grew up here. Sometimes, I swear I can still hear him around the place..." He broke off, feeling stupid. "Christ, I sound like a nutter."

"No. I understand," Alexander said quietly. He touched Peter's car too, lightly brushing his fingertips along the smooth surface until he reached Josiah's hand, stopping next to it so their fingers were touching. "After my mother died, I sometimes thought I could sense her, although she was always just out of reach, as if she was in another room, or behind a curtain. I used to—" He stopped abruptly, and Josiah was surprised to see that his eyes were wet.

"I used to have her scarf," he confided. "It smelled of her, and when I inhaled, I could see her, vividly, in my mind's eye. That's one of the hardest things about being an IS – no scarf, no photos of my mother, no videos – just my memories, and you forget. You forget their faces, the details of their features... how they looked, and moved, and sounded."

"Yes." Josiah covered Alexander's hand with his own. "That's exactly it." They stood there for a moment, and then he cleared his throat. "Come on – I have work to do."

"Were you taken in by Tyler?" Alexander asked as they walked up the steps to the house. "Even for a second?"

Josiah paused. "No. Not even for a second."

"I wish I'd known."

"You should have trusted me," Josiah said meaningfully. Opening

GHOST EYE 105

the interior door, he locked it again behind Alexander once they were safely in the house.

"You have a good poker face; I thought he'd caught you in his web. I've only ever known him to win, you see," Alexander explained. "That's all I saw during my time as his indie – all the people he caught and used. He finds out what people want most, and then he creates a trap designed especially for them."

"Well, he doesn't have it in his power to give me what I want most."

"Peter? That's what you want most, isn't it? You want Peter back?"

Josiah grunted. "Yeah, and that can never happen."

"Owen..."

"Was a pale imitation." Josiah snorted derisively. "Men like Tyler always mistake style for substance, because they believe everyone thinks the same way they do. Peter wasn't a type. I fell in love with who he was, not what he looked like. Owen didn't come close."

"He sounds very special," Alexander responded softly.

"He was. I'd never met anyone like him before, and I never will again. You can't replace people with someone who looks a bit like them. It doesn't work like that."

"Elliot tried," Alexander said. Josiah stopped in the process of removing his jacket. "He even gave me his dead husband's name. He wanted me to pretend to be Chris – that's why he got upset when I forgot and called him 'sir' by mistake. I felt sorry for him, because he had to know it wasn't real."

"Maybe, but from what you've said, Elliot had the emotional depth of a potato." Josiah hung up his jacket and then jogged up the stairs.

"You're not like that. You're much better than him." Alexander stood at the bottom of the stairs, gazing up.

"Me? I'm an idiot," Josiah told him gruffly. "I like to be in control, but grief makes you realise how little control you have. You realise your love can't protect the people you care about, no matter how strong it is. Life and death are chaotic, messy – nobody controls them. Peter understood that; he was chaotic and messy, too. He took everything life threw at him in his stride. He'd have moved on by now if I'd been the one who'd died that night. He'd have known how. I don't. I'm

frozen in the same spot, holding on tight to something that's long gone." He felt his voice break and wondered where those words had come from.

"You must be so tired," Alexander said gently. "Holding on so tightly for so long. You must ache to put that burden down."

His sympathy made Josiah's eyes sting; bending his head, he struggled to regain control. When he looked up, he found Alexander still gazing at him from the foot of the stairs.

"Trouble is, I think it might be the only thing holding me together," he said. "If I let it go…"

"You're afraid you'll fall apart?" Alexander shook his head. "You won't. You might unravel a little, but you're strong. I've found the human spirit is more resilient than you could ever believe."

"You're more flexible than me. You adapted."

"Oh no." Alexander gave a little laugh. "I broke. I broke, but I survived, and once you realise you can survive that, then you can survive pretty much anything."

"I don't want to break," Josiah told him firmly.

There was a mystified expression on Alexander's face that slowly turned into one of profound sympathy. "Oh, Josiah – you don't realise, do you? You broke years ago. All you've been doing ever since is keeping yourself broken, instead of allowing yourself to heal."

Josiah gave another little grunt and turned away. "I must do some work," he said tersely. "Don't disturb me."

He took a shower to clear his head. He was still shaken by what had happened in the street, but he couldn't let that distract him now. He stood under the pounding water, trying to understand what Alexander wanted from him. The trip to Tyler's house had been enlightening, for all sorts of different reasons, but he was no further forward in solving Dacre's murder. Why had Alexander taken him there? What was this big secret that would make him angry and upset? Would it help him find Dacre's killer?

So many mysteries wrapped up in such a fascinating package, Peter's voice murmured in his ear. *No wonder he intrigues you.*

"Not helping," Josiah growled. "God, I miss you." He rested his head against the cool shower tiles. "If you were here, I could talk this through with you – although fuck knows what you'd have said if I'd brought an IS home to stay with us." He grinned.

"I'd have welcomed him. You can tell that poor bastard has been through hell."

"You'd have wanted to free him."

"Don't you?"

"Yeah." Josiah turned off the tap abruptly. "I miss Hattie, too," he added as he towelled himself dry. "All those long walks after you died, where I'd tell her about a case and go through all the details until a pattern started to emerge. She was a great help."

"You could get another dog," Peter suggested.

"She wouldn't be Hattie."

"No, she'd be a beautiful, complex, quirky character in her own right. Your heart is big enough to love more than just one man and one dog your entire life. You're allowed to be happy again, Joe."

"I'm not sure I remember how."

"My stubborn Joe." Peter sighed.

"Yeah. You know me," Josiah chuckled.

He pulled on a pair of faded blue jeans and a tee-shirt, then sat down on the bed. He turned off his holonym, so he wouldn't be disturbed, then checked in with Inquisitus. Reed had uploaded some more information, but none of it looked very promising. He had to think hard about where he went next with this investigation. So far, he'd centred his enquiries around Alexander, but was that the right approach? He'd been so sure the indie was the key to Dacre's murder, but he kept drawing blanks. Had his fascination with Alexander taken him down the wrong path?

He went over the evidence again, trying to immerse himself in the facts. He reread all the forensic reports and rummaged through Dacre's financial details, social media accounts, and press interviews. He went through everything in painstaking detail, taking it apart. Slow, methodical detective work always won out in the end. He examined Dacre's portfolio – was there something in his creative life that might have prompted his murder? A rival holophotographer? A dispute over a

piece of work? He trawled through endless exhibition catalogues and still copies of Dacre's work.

What was it about Elliot Dacre's art that had made him so successful? How much would an original Dacre holopic sell for, anyway? He glanced at the catalogue prices – they were expensive, but not exorbitant. He could afford one, if he liked that sort of thing. Would someone want a specific piece so much they'd murder for it? An exclusive Elliot Dacre original? If so, which one?

An image flashed into his mind of that holopic of Alexander, standing in the rain under a street lamp. What had been so compelling about that image that it'd stayed in his mind long after all the others had faded? Was it because it had felt so real, unlike the more posed pieces Dacre specialised in? Alexander hadn't been a blank enigma in that piece, but real flesh and blood. The image evoked strong emotions – danger, dread, distress. Had someone else been as struck by that image as him? Had they wanted it for themselves and been prepared to kill to get it? Yet both Alexander and the cleaning lady had insisted it didn't exist. Was this the secret Alexander was hiding from him? If so, why?

His neck ached, so he moved it from side to side until it clicked. He glanced at the time – it was later than he'd realised, and his rumbling stomach insisted it was time for dinner.

He slipped his holopad into his pocket and trotted down the stairs in his slippers.

"Hey." Alexander was flicking through a book; he looked up as Josiah entered the kitchen.

"Hey," Josiah replied. "What are you reading?"

"A book on Pre-R cars that I found when I was clearing up. I assume it's Peter's – I hope you don't mind?" Alexander said warily.

"No, of course not. I'm not going to go nuts on you again." Josiah gave an apologetic smile. "I thought I'd call out for some hachée – do you want some?"

"That sounds really nice," Alexander said politely. "But there's enough of last night's casserole left over for another meal. I've heated it up, and the table's set in the dining room."

"I was upstairs for hours. You should have eaten."

"I wanted to wait for you." Alexander opened the oven door and a delicious smell wafted out. "Oh, by the way, several of your girlfriends called."

Josiah frowned. "What?"

"I think you must have turned off your holonym? When you didn't answer, your calls automatically came through on your old nanopad – the one you gave to me." Placing the casserole dish on the kitchen table, Alexander began serving up.

"Damn it – I didn't think of that." Josiah ran a tired hand through his hair.

"You told me not to disturb you, so I answered the calls and took messages. Esther called but wouldn't leave a message. Then there was someone called Liz – is she the one who made the vase we were talking about this morning? You're right – she is pretty." He shot Josiah a cheeky grin. "And someone calling herself 'Big Jen', although she didn't look that big to me. And lastly an Elsie?" He looked at Josiah searchingly. "They didn't leave any messages, either. I don't think they liked me; they seemed shocked that I was answering your calls."

"They probably saw the shitstorm about us on the news and wanted to find out what the hell's going on." Josiah took out his holopad and removed the call block.

"Let's eat first – your girlfriends can wait," Alexander said, handing him a tray.

"Girlfriends!" Josiah snorted.

"Friends who are female, then; you do seem to have a lot of them." Alexander led the way into the dining room.

"I like the company of women," Josiah said, following him.

"No male friends, except for the deeply cynical and suspicious Investigator Reed?" Alexander raised an amused eyebrow.

"He's not a friend; he's a colleague," Josiah said, sitting down at the table. Alexander had a knack for making the place look homely and inviting. Lamps were lit, the house was warm, and music was softly playing in the background.

"Maybe you don't want to risk accidentally falling in love by having any male friends," Alexander said, sitting down opposite him.

"And maybe you should give yourself an hour off from psycho-analysing me and eat something."

Alexander laughed. "Sounds like a plan."

They'd just started eating when Josiah's holopad buzzed.

"One of your girlfriends again?" Alexander said cheekily.

Josiah kicked him under the table and answered the call. Esther popped up in hologram form, looking uncharacteristically flustered.

"Joe — where the hell have you been?" she demanded. "I called you hours ago."

"Sorry, Esther. Is there a problem?"

"Yes, there bloody well is. I've had George Tyler, of all people, calling me."

"Ah." Josiah glanced at Alexander, who looked suddenly terrified. "What did he want?"

"Your head on a platter. He's demanding that I fire you."

Josiah gave a little chuckle.

Esther glared at him. "What the hell did you do to piss off one of the most powerful men in the country?"

"My job," Josiah replied firmly. "It's what you pay me for."

"But George Tyler? How is he part of your investigation into Dacre's murder?"

"I don't know. Maybe he isn't." Josiah shrugged. "All I did was ask him some questions."

"They must have been some bloody annoying questions if he wants me to fire you."

"He has his own agenda, and I have no idea what it is. I asked him some routine questions to rule him out of our inquiries. I don't know why that would upset him, unless it's the fact we had the temerity to suspect him at all."

"Well? Do we?" Esther demanded. "Was he involved in Dacre's murder?"

Josiah shook his head. "I don't think so."

"So, you wasted a day questioning an innocent man who has the

power to get you fired and packed off back to the Quarterlands with your tail between your legs – fine work, Joe."

"*Are* you going to fire me?" Josiah asked.

"Of course not."

"Then he doesn't have that power. He's a citizen of this country like everyone else – why should he get special treatment? I've also questioned Dacre's cleaning lady and solicitor, and Alexander's personal trainer, brother, and father – none of them has registered a complaint."

"Okay." Esther folded her arms and glared at him. "Tell me, Joe – did you deliberately antagonise George Tyler?"

"I might have told him a few home truths," he admitted.

"I knew it." She threw her hands up in the air.

"Look, I don't go out of my way to antagonise people. I just do what's necessary to get the job done. That's why you gave me this case."

"True, but I know you. You're like a bloodhound that won't let go when you've got the scent of something – and that's not always in your best interests, or ours."

"Are you telling me to leave poor, defenceless George Tyler alone?" Josiah challenged.

"Yes. You just said he wasn't involved in Dacre's murder."

"Maybe not – but he stinks to high heaven all the same." Josiah glanced at Alexander to find him gazing back intently.

"That's not within the remit of your investigation. Stick to solving Dacre's murder."

"Is that an order?"

"Yes. No..." Her expression softened. "Look, I'm worried about you, Joe. I can only protect you so far – Tyler is a powerful man with powerful friends; he can make your life a misery if he chooses."

"I can handle George Tyler," he said confidently.

"Maybe so – but he's got friends in high places, and a man like that doesn't always play by the rules."

"I did nothing wrong today. Why should I be scared of him?"

"Don't be so naïve," she snapped. "Everyone has weak spots, Joe –

even you. It wouldn't take Tyler long to find them and use them against you." She paused and then spoke again, in a softer tone. "I think I made a mistake in asking you to take Lytton as your IS. I understand and respect your views on the issue; I should have listened to your objections."

"This has nothing to do with Alexander," he told her sharply.

"Doesn't it?" She raised an eyebrow. "I want you to come into the office tomorrow. You can update me on the case, and we can decide where to go with it next."

"Fine. I'll see you then." Josiah flicked his hand curtly over the holopad, ending the call.

"What's she like?" Alexander enquired as he picked up his fork to start eating again.

"Esther? She's my boss."

"And your friend? She likes you. She's protecting you. Do you trust her?"

"Completely. I'd trust Esther with my life."

"How did you become an investigator?" Alexander pressed. "You were in the army before, weren't you? How did you go from that to a job at Inquisitus?"

"Under false pretences, as it turns out," he replied. "Although I didn't know that until a few days ago."

"What do you mean?"

"It's a long story."

"I'd like to hear it."

Josiah gazed at him thoughtfully. Alexander had been challenging him since he'd arrived, constantly pushing boundaries, testing him, trying to work out what kind of man he was for some reason of his own. The sooner he could win Alexander's trust, the sooner he'd get the answers he needed to solve this case. He had nothing to lose by sharing some of his life story with the IS – or a highly edited version of it, at least.

"After Peter and I married, I joined the Military Police..."

Alexander sat back in his chair, listening intently.

———

GHOST EYE

It was the best time of his life – they'd finally been able to live together as a married couple, sharing a tiny square box of a house on camp. Josiah had never known this kind of stability and happiness – early-morning sex, long walks in the countryside with Peter and Hattie at weekends, and having someone to come home to every evening. He loved his job with the Military Police and thought he might have finally found his niche. He aced all his training courses and was rapidly promoted as a result.

He arrived home one evening to find a small woman in her late sixties sitting in their kitchen. Her grey curls were cut close to her head, and there was a pair of outsize spectacles perched owlishly on her nose. She was a neat, tidy kind of person, from her starched navy-blue suit down to the bright white trainers on her feet. Her cream-coloured blouse was open at the neck to reveal a plain gold cross shining on her dark brown skin.

"Hey." Peter jumped up and kissed him on the cheek, while Hattie barked and squeaked her way through her usual excited greeting, tail wagging frantically.

"Is this the Elsie I've heard so much about?" Josiah asked when Hattie finally calmed down.

"You can't possibly have heard as much about me as I have about you." Elsie ignored Josiah's outstretched hand and pulled him into a big bear hug. "As if a handshake would do!" she snorted, and he laughed and wrapped his arms around her slight body. She was a little bird of a woman, but he could sense the steel in her.

"That's better," she said. "This makes up for you two not inviting me to your wedding."

"To be fair, we didn't invite anyone." Josiah released her, and she took a step back and looked him up and down.

"So, this is the only man in the world who could make Peter Hunt settle down. You never told me he was such a big, strapping lad, Peter."

Josiah rolled his eyes, grinning at her all the same. She had such a warm, motherly air that it was impossible not to instantly like her.

"It's good to meet you at last, Elsie," Josiah said, sitting down at the kitchen table.

"I'd have come before, but I've been recovering from a bunion operation," she said, gesturing to her comfortable footwear.

"Elsie and I have been using her downtime to restructure the Kathleen Line," Peter said, handing Josiah a freshly brewed cup of tea. "The situation in Europe shows no sign of settling down, so there's no chance of me returning there anytime soon to run the convoys. I have plenty of contacts out there, though, so we've been coordinating with them, and I'm confident we'll have the Line up and running again soon."

"When were you doing all this?" Josiah demanded, stirring his tea noisily.

"While you were at work. You were busy with your new job – I didn't want to distract you," Peter said with a disarming smile.

"There's no stopping Peter Hunt when he's on a mission," Elsie laughed. "You must know that, Joe. Although..." She gave him a thoughtful look. "I reckon if anyone can 'rein' this man in, it's you, Josiah Raine."

"It's spelled differently. Like the weather with an 'e' on the end," he told her grumpily.

She gazed at him quizzically. "Is he on our side?" she asked Peter. "'Cause I'd hate someone this grouchy to be against us."

"He's definitely on our side," Peter told her firmly. "Aren't you, Joe?"

"Of course I bloody well am. But I'd appreciate you keeping me in the loop."

Peter made his "I'm in the doghouse" face for Elsie, which just annoyed Josiah even more. Peter winced at his expression and reached out to squeeze his arm gently. "Sorry, Joe, but there was nothing you could do to help, and now you're working with the MPs – well, I didn't want to put you in a difficult position."

"What does that mean?" Josiah demanded.

"It means I'm breaking a dozen different laws, and it's kind of your job to arrest people like me."

"Is that what you think of me? Christ, Peter – you know I'd never do that."

Peter exchanged glances with Elsie.

"What?" Josiah asked impatiently. He hated feeling like an outsider in his own home, with his own husband.

"Well, see, thing is, you might have to," Peter said apologetically.

Josiah went cold. "What do you mean?"

"You know how bad things are out there, son," Elsie said gently. "You're an MP – you know the rumours are all true. There's been a tsunami of escaped indies hiding out in the Quarterlands, and their houders are up in arms about it, demanding something be done."

Josiah glanced around, but they were completely alone, and Peter trusted Elsie with his life, so he did, too. He lowered his voice all the same. "We've been briefed that investigation agencies are being sent in to track the indies down and haul them back to their houders – which is pissing off the Quarterlanders no end."

"Joe grew up in the Quarterlands," Peter explained to Elsie.

"Ah," Elsie said. "Then you'll know how they feel."

"Yeah – they don't appreciate the government interference, but they don't like all those escaped indies moving in with them, either. Conditions are bad enough in the Quarters as it is, without all those extra people. They won't hand them back, though," Josiah said flatly. "There is no way any Quarterlander would cooperate with the Thorities on this."

"No, but they're angry. You know the Quarterlands better than anyone else in this room," Peter said. "You know what a powder keg they are."

"I'm friends with an investigative journalist in my church," Elsie confided. "He says there have been riots all over the country. Civil unrest everywhere."

Josiah and Peter exchanged worried glances. "It's been hushed up, but we've been briefed," Peter said. "The government's been cracking down hard, but that just makes the Quarterlanders fight back harder."

"The government!" Josiah snorted. "The government would like to clear out the Quarterlands, rip them down, and force everyone there into indentured servitude."

"That's their long-term goal," Elsie agreed. "It's why they're offering all these tax breaks to anyone hiring indies. They want to

sweep all the undesirables into the IS programme and demolish the Quarterlands, so there's nowhere left for escaped indies to hide."

"Well, fuck that," Josiah said.

"Elsie and I have been thinking... and we have a plan," Peter said tentatively. Josiah fought down his irritation that Peter had been discussing this plan with Elsie rather than him. It wasn't Elsie's fault; she and Peter had been working together on the Kathleen Line for years, so it was natural that he'd confide in her, but it hurt all the same.

"How can I help?" he asked, without hesitating.

"See – that's why I married him." Peter grinned at Elsie.

"I'm sure that's not the only reason." She gave a little wink that made Josiah blush.

"It won't be easy," Peter warned. "I'm going to ask you to do something hard, Joe – maybe the hardest thing you've ever done."

"Okay." Josiah squared his shoulders. "Tell me."

Peter went into captain mode, straight-backed and to the point. "I was called in for a briefing this morning. The police can't cope with the rioting in the Quarterlands, so the government is going to send in the army."

"Christ," Josiah said. "I knew it was on the cards, but I didn't think they'd actually do it. When?"

"Tonight. I've been put on standby from midnight to lead an assault against the rioters if the police action fails."

"Shit." Josiah hadn't been back to the Quarterlands in years, but he still thought of those who lived there as his people.

"It gets worse," Elsie said.

Peter looked Josiah straight in the eye, deadly serious. "We're not just talking about riot drones and water cannons here, Joe. They told us that if we meet any resistance, I'm to give the order to open fire."

"What the fuck...?" Josiah got up and paced around the room. "They want you to shoot British citizens? Jesus!"

"It's an object lesson," Peter explained. "A warning to the Quarterlanders to stop harbouring escaped indies."

"Hundreds could die. Thousands."

"I know," Peter said quietly.

"There are no hospitals in the Quarterlands, and no doctors apart

from a few druggies and ex-cons. If you open fire on them, they'll suffer horribly."

"I know, I know. Hey, calm down." Peter placed a hand on his chest to stop him pacing. "Of course I won't fire on them, Joe."

"But you can't disobey a direct order." Josiah suddenly realised the invidious choice his husband faced. "They'll have you for that."

"I know. That's why, if they order me to open fire, I want you to arrest me."

"What?" Josiah stared at him uncomprehendingly.

"I want to be court-martialled. Elsie has her press contact – we'll ask him to cover the trial and publicise what's really going on. We'll blow this whole thing wide open and provide a focus for rebellion."

"They'll send you to the Glasshouse," Josiah said, sitting down on a chair with a thud. "I can't be the one to put you there, Peter. You can't ask me to do that."

"I'd rather it was you, if possible – and I realise it might not work out that way. Firstly, it gains us publicity – an army officer arrested by his own husband. Secondly, I don't want you implicated, Joe. They might start sniffing around and find out what I was up to in Europe. I don't want you tainted by association. If you arrest me, you'll be showing them you don't approve of my actions. It puts you in the clear."

"I don't care about that."

"I know, but I do." Peter knelt down in front of him and put his hands on Josiah's knees. "We don't gain anything if you're locked up, too."

Josiah gazed at him miserably. "Look, Peter, I'm happy to stand side by side with you on this. I couldn't fire on the Quarters, either, if ordered, but I don't want to be the person who arrests you for refusing to do it."

"Sure, but there are other reasons why this makes sense. While I'm locked up, I'll need someone I trust on the outside. They can't stop my husband from visiting me – and you'll be my link to Elsie. I need you to be whiter than white, Joe. That's why you have to be the one who arrests me."

"You have a way of making something bloody awful sound reasonable," Josiah said helplessly. "You're a persuasive bastard, Peter Hunt."

"You're only just finding that out?" Elsie sighed. "We've all been there, Joe."

"It'll look like I betrayed you. It'll feel like that, too."

"No – you'll just be doing your job," Peter insisted. "Besides, who'll look after Hattie if you're arrested, too?"

Hattie, who was flopped out on the kitchen floor, raised an ear at the sound of her name and thumped her tail a couple of times.

"Will it work? Or will we be putting ourselves through a shitstorm for nothing?" Josiah demanded.

"I don't know." Peter shrugged. "We're hoping that the publicity will show people what's really going on, and they'll rally to our cause."

"And then what? We could end up with a situation like we saw in Europe, with the warlords and the scavs – no law and order, no real government..."

"Or this whole thing could make people understand how corrupt the IS system has become."

"You'll go to prison. Damn it, Peter – we just got to be happy," Josiah said brokenly.

Peter put a hand on his shoulder. "I know, but this is who I am, Joe. You knew that when you married me."

Josiah let out a long, shaky sigh. "Christ, I hate you."

"Yeah." Peter grinned and pressed a kiss to his lips. "And thank you."

"I didn't say yes."

"Yeah – you did." Peter stood up.

"What happens to the Kathleen Line while you're in prison?"

"Elsie will take care of it."

"With my help," Josiah said firmly.

"I'd like that, love." Elsie patted his arm.

"It'll be a relief knowing Elsie has you to lean on while I'm in jail," Peter agreed.

"Are you sure you'll go to jail and not into the IS system, Peter?" Elsie asked. "It'd break my heart if you were sentenced to indentured servitude after all the work you've done to help indies."

GHOST EYE   119

"No, it'll be the Glasshouse – military prison – for this. Refusing an order is a military crime, unlike helping indies escape," Josiah explained.

"I can argue that in my estimation the order is unlawful," Peter said. "I doubt the court will accept that, but it might provide mitigation."

"Or none of this might work, and you might end up going to prison for years on end for nothing," Josiah pointed out.

"It's possible," Peter agreed. "But I don't see what else I can do. This is a matter of conscience, Joe."

"God, I hate your bloody conscience; it'll get you killed one day."

"You're always saying that, but I'm still here." Peter ruffled his hair affectionately.

"What about the Quarterlands?" Josiah asked. "Someone will still open fire on them, even if it's not you. The army has plenty of officers who won't give a damn about firing on our own people."

"We've sent a warning," Elsie said. "We're hoping we can get the rioters to back off, but I don't think they'll listen. People are too angry."

"That's all we can do, Joe," Peter told him. "I can't control this situation – I can only refuse to be part of it."

Later, after Elsie left, Peter touched Josiah's arm gently.

"I know you're angry. Talk to me."

"I *am* angry, but not for the reasons you think. I appreciate how brave you're being – throwing away a career you love for the sake of your beliefs. What I hate, Peter, what I really bloody well hate, is that you've been doing all this in secret. You've been restructuring the Kathleen Line behind my back, and you cooked up this scheme with Elsie when you should have discussed it with me first. I'm your husband. I want to share your life, but you keep shutting me out."

Peter gave him a look that reminded him of Hattie when she'd been caught raiding the bin. "You're right. I thought I was protecting you and your shiny new career, but that's no excuse. The truth is, I've

been a lone wolf for too long; I'm not used to sharing this part of myself. I'm sorry."

"So, from now on – no more secrets?" Josiah insisted.

"No more secrets – I promise."

"Even if you think it'll piss me off, or put me in danger?"

"Even then. Hmm, you're turning me on with all this tough-guy talk, Joe." Peter angled his head for a kiss.

Josiah couldn't resist. Tangling his hands in Peter's shirt, he pulled him forward and kissed him hard.

―――――

"So, what happened?" Alexander asked, his eyes wide, looking totally engrossed.

Josiah paused to finish his dinner. He'd given Alexander the edited highlights, omitting Elsie's involvement and any mention of the Kathleen Line. He'd presented Peter as a man of principle, faced with carrying out an order he found morally repugnant, which was true.

"Did Peter receive the order to fire on the rioters? Did you arrest him?" Alexander pressed eagerly.

Josiah pushed back his plate and looked Alexander straight in the eye. "Yes – on both counts."

―――――

The riots went on for several days. Peter worked the night shifts, when the rioting was worse. He came home every morning stinking of smoke, covered in dozens of little wounds from all the missiles being thrown at them, although thankfully nothing worse.

"It's bad out there," he said tiredly. "We've used riot drones, water cannon, all the usual stuff, but there are too many of them, and more all the time as word goes round. We just put down one riot and another springs up. The police are exhausted, and we're running out of options as to how to contain the violence. We're just waiting for the order to start shooting now. I don't think it'll be long in coming."

. . .

GHOST EYE

The following evening, Josiah had the chance to see the chaos for himself as the MPs were shipped in to provide backup, because the army was stretched to the limit.

He smelled the riots long before they reached them. The acrid scent of smoke hung over everything, permeating his hair, his clothes, even his skin. The entire horizon was one giant sheet of flames, engulfing houses, shops, and offices. As they travelled closer, he could hear the screaming of the mob, see them lobbing missiles at the combined force of the army and police. The fighting had spilled out of the Quarterlands and into nearby towns, spreading like wildfire. The government had imposed a news blackout, but information was seeping out anyway. Overhead, army helicopters whirred, collecting strategic intel.

It was chaos, but Josiah fought his way through the ranks to find Peter, his face black with grime.

"Joe – what the hell are you doing here?"

"We've been brought in to help. It's all hands on deck," Josiah explained. "Now – where do you want me, sir?"

Peter shot him a grateful smile – he knew, better than anyone, just how much use Josiah could be in a pitched battle. Soon, Josiah had taken command of a small unit and launched them headfirst in an attempt to drive the rioters back into the Quarterlands.

Josiah usually loved a fight, but he hated this one. It felt wrong to be fighting their own people – *his* own people, all Quarterlanders, just like him. He could tell the army was losing the fight. They were well trained, with specialist equipment, but they weren't a match for the sheer numbers of mainly young men, but some women too, pouring out of the Quarterlands, angry and spoiling for a fight. This particular struggle had been a long time coming – years of pent-up anger at being the have-nots in a society that hated them had come to a head, and the mood was ugly.

Josiah could see which way this was going to go. The government couldn't afford to lose control of the situation – this rebellion had to be put down, by any means necessary.

He fought his way back to Peter's side. "We're losing," he growled.

"I know," Peter replied grimly. "I've just had the order." Josiah

stared at him blankly, not wanting to take in the enormity of the situation.

"Joe – did you hear me? I've been ordered to open fire – to use deadly force." His jaw tightened. "Those aren't orders I'm prepared to carry out, Staff Sergeant Raine."

Josiah stood there for a long moment.

"Joe?" Peter prompted. "It's time. I'm surrendering myself to you."

Josiah swallowed down the bile in his throat. "Very well, Captain Hunt." He took the handcuffs off his belt. "I'm placing you under arrest." He snapped the cuffs around Peter's wrists with more force than he'd intended.

Peter winced. "A bit looser, Joe?" he asked. He had such big hands that the metal cuffs were digging into his flesh.

"No special treatment, Captain Hunt," Josiah said stonily. He had to armour up, to find the strength to do this.

Josiah had never run away from a fight in his life, and it hurt to take Peter out of this one, to make him leave his unit and all his men behind. He saw faces he knew, people he'd fought alongside for years, looking angry and upset as he marched Peter out of there. He felt like the bad guy, and he wished he could explain it to them.

This is what he wants. It's all part of a bigger plan. It's his bloody idea." But all they saw was him arresting Peter and marching him away in handcuffs.

———

"It felt like a betrayal," Josiah said to Alexander. "Peter was trying to put a brave face on it, but I don't think it hit him until that moment what he was giving up. He'd been in the army for most of his adult life, and he loved it. Now his career was in ruins, and he was facing a prison sentence. I arrested him, as he'd asked me to, and took him in."

"What happened after that?" Alexander asked, clearly enthralled. "I don't remember hearing about it on the news."

"That's because it all came to nothing," Josiah replied wearily. "They put the riots down in the most brutal way – it was a massacre – but that was hushed up. The press reported only that the army had

contained the rioting with minimal casualties. People were so afraid of the breakdown of law and order that they took the government's side – they even approved of the military action."

"And what happened to Peter? Did he go to prison?"

"No. They didn't want Peter using the trial to draw attention to the fact the army had been ordered to fire on our own citizens, so they quietly discharged him." Josiah sighed. "He tried to drum up some media interest, but nobody would touch it. Everyone was too scared of the bogeymen that lurked in the Quarterlands. The riots were subdued, and all the escaped indies were found and returned to their houders. It was made very clear to the Quarterlanders that they were not to harbour them again. That made it harder for indies to escape in the years that followed, leading, in my view, to the rise in cases of houders being murdered by their servants that we've seen lately." He clasped his hands together and leaned across the table. "Desperate people with nowhere to go will lash out when they reach breaking point," he explained, looking Alexander straight in the eye.

"What happened to you after you arrested Peter?" Alexander didn't rise to the bait.

"I had a commendation placed on my file for my actions." Josiah gave a bitter snort. "I couldn't stay in the Military Police, though, not after that. I got out as soon as I could after Peter's dishonourable discharge." He sat back and took a sip of his Coke. "Dishonourable." He shook his head. "That man didn't have a dishonourable bone in his body."

Alexander was still gazing at him intently, obviously captivated by the story. Josiah cleared his throat, feeling uncomfortable with the scrutiny.

"You asked me how I joined Inquisitus – well, that's how. I sent an application to Inquisitus, because they're the best investigation agency around. I didn't realise it at the time, but Esther hired me precisely because of that commendation. She liked it, because she thought it meant I'd always put the law above everything else, even my own husband."

"She was wrong," Alexander said quietly. "You put love first, even

though it broke your heart. You're not a pragmatist, you're a romantic."

Josiah gave a dry laugh. "Are you only just figuring that out? I keep all of Peter's clothes in boxes upstairs because I can't bear to throw them out, and I haven't touched another man in the seven years since he died."

Alexander gazed at him thoughtfully. "That's quite a secret you shared with me. If it forms the basis of the trust Esther Lomax has in you, then I could tell her, and that could cause problems for you."

"I know." Josiah nodded. "But you told me earlier that you want to trust me, so I thought the best way of earning your confidence was to share something secret and personal." He leaned forward expectantly. "Now it's your turn."

Chapter Seven

AUGUST 2088

Alex

Alex dozed fitfully all night. He hurt all over, but it was a darker pain that kept waking him. So far, he'd managed to cling on to an illusion of consent in his sexual encounters with Tyler's guests. He'd convinced himself that it was no different to fucking strangers in clubs when he was drunk, or using his body to whore croc from people at university, which he'd done almost as a game.

However, being bent over a table, beaten, and forcibly fucked had stripped away that defence mechanism, revealing his position for what it truly was. He'd been raped, not just this time, but every single previous time, too, and he had to find a way to come to terms with that.

Halfway through the night, he needed the toilet. He slid out of bed, hissing with pain, and staggered into the bathroom. Leaning against the wall for support, he pissed, and then decided to try to remove his crumpled clothes, taking them off slowly, one garment at a time, shuddering as every movement sent agonising shockwaves through his body. His white boxer shorts were streaked with blood and stuck to his buttocks. He peeled them away gingerly, his breath coming in shaky gasps. He was so shattered from the effort that he had to hold on to the sink afterwards, panting.

Looking up, he caught sight of himself in the bathroom mirror. He looked terrible – the slicked-down hair from the previous day was now a mess, pointing up stiffly in many different directions, and his face was pale and pinched.

He angled his body sideways and glanced over his shoulder to see the reflection of his backside in the mirror. The marks of Harper's belt were imprinted on it in livid welts, and there were dark red and purple bruises, too.

There was also another issue – he'd been in so much pain from the beating that he'd been less aware of the damage caused by the violent penetration. Now he realised that his hole ached from where it had been pounded and torn.

He felt used and dirty, so he crawled into the shower. He leaned against the tiled wall, shaking, hoping the warm water would wash Harper's stench from his skin. The water stung his bruised flesh, but he stayed there anyway, the need to feel clean overriding the pain.

Finally, he forced himself to slather his hands in shower gel and carefully rinse out his abused hole. It hurt so much, and at first the water ran pink with blood. Seeing it, something inside him broke, and for the first time since he'd become an IS, he cried.

Sinking down on his haunches on the shower floor, he sobbed. He wept so hard his throat hurt, and he didn't stop until he was too exhausted to cry anymore. Then he crouched there for a long time, staring into space as the water continued to flow over him.

He still felt dirty. If he closed his eyes, he was immediately back in that room, being held down over the table. He could feel Harper's hands on his thighs, the warmth of his breath on the back of his neck, and the hardness of the surface beneath him.

Looking down, he could see marks on his hips where the edge of the table had dug into him, and an ugly red line around his wrists where they'd been tightly bound. He was bruised all over, including on the sides of his thighs, where he could see the imprint of Harper's fingers painted on his flesh. Nothing could wash them away. No matter how long he stood under the spray, nothing could remove the sense of shame and humiliation he was feeling right now.

Eventually, after more than an hour, he staggered out, patted

himself cautiously with a towel, and crawled back into bed. The walls had changed again and were now showing a woodland glade that was calming and restful. He gave up trying to understand Tyler's choice of décor and closed his eyes once more.

He was asleep when the door opened at 9 a.m. and a short, round man he'd never seen before entered, waking him. He was carrying a medibot.

"I'm Doctor Parker," he said. "Mr Tyler has sent me to check you over."

Alex gazed at him blankly. "Anyone would think he cared," he croaked, his voice sounding strange to his own ears. "But I guess he's just worried in case his investment loses value."

Dr Parker examined him carefully; Alex was too far gone to care about the further indignity of what that entailed. He closed his eyes and concentrated on dealing with the pain. When the doctor had finished his examination, he injected him with a combination of antibiotics and painkillers.

"You'll be fine. You need some rest, but then you'll be fit to resume your duties," he said.

"Shouldn't you tell the authorities?" Alex rasped. "What happened to me isn't legal. No IS should be whipped and raped. Don't you have a duty to report it?"

The doctor pointed to the ID tag pinned to his jacket. "I do as Mr Tyler orders," he said, although there was a trace of shame in his eyes.

Alex buried his head in his pillow. What kind of doctor ended up as an IS? Parker was either a convict, like himself, or had acquired debts he couldn't pay without selling himself. Either way, he wasn't an ally.

The medic gave him a reassuring pat on the shoulder. "Just rest. You'll feel better soon."

Alex didn't leave his room all day – he stayed in bed, gazing blankly at the wall, which was displaying an ocean view on a sunny day, the movement of the waves oddly mesmerising. Surprisingly, both Chef and Mason left him alone, which could only have been on Tyler's instructions. Trays of food were left outside his door, but he couldn't face eating.

When he didn't surface on the second day, Solange knocked on the door and tiptoed inside, with Scarface close behind.

"Come and be with us, Alex," she said. "We've made a kind of den for you in the living room."

He lifted his head to see them gazing at him sympathetically.

"It hurts to move," he admitted, feeling desperately ashamed, even though it wasn't his fault.

"I'll carry you," Scarface offered.

"I'm fine here." He buried his face back in his pillow.

Solange sat down on the bed beside him and gently stroked his hair. "Please, Alex. Let us help," she said tenderly.

Their kindness somehow penetrated the foggy haze of his depression, and he allowed Scarface to lift him off the bed and carry him into the living room, where they'd created a little bed of soft pillows and light blankets on the sofa. Scarface laid him on it carefully, and Solange spread the blankets gently over him.

She and Scarface were his constant companions for the next few days. They sat with him as he watched movies, read, and took regular naps to help his body heal. Solange chatted to him for hours on end, about anything other than what had happened to him at Tyler's office. It reminded Alex of when she'd been covered with bruises after her night with Clive: they both knew that suffering had taken place, and could guess the nature of it, but no good came from talking about it. They both had their pride.

She was curled up next to him most of the time, getting up only to fetch him cups of tea and snacks that he barely picked at. She painted her nails while telling him a story she'd heard about Mason losing his ID tag and being punished for it by the major-domo – an idea they both relished, although Alex wondered if it was true.

When Scarface was on duty, he could often be prevailed upon to gossip indiscreetly about life in the IS dormitories downstairs, and everyone he shared quarters with. Fatso liked to tell dirty jokes that nobody found very funny, but apart from that he left them alone.

Alex found himself liking Scarface more and more. He noticed also that Solange had grown close to the tall, lean man with the lugubrious face and dry sense of humour. The two of them introduced Alex to a

show they were both hooked on. Alex thought it was terrible, but he liked the in-jokes they had about it, and feeling part of their little gang as they watched it together.

"How did you become an IS?" he asked Scarface one day as they watched another episode together.

Scarface shrugged. "I was born in the Quarterlands, like Solange, but I wanted to get away; there was nothing there for me."

"Couldn't you... I don't know... find a job and move out?"

Scarface laughed. "You're so dumb it's almost cute. There *are* no jobs. Most people only want to employ indies these days, because it's cheap labour. Being a Quarterlander doesn't help; people don't like us. Some will take us on without putting a chip in our wrists, but only because they don't want the responsibility of keeping servants."

"Then how do you cope in there? How do you survive?" Alex wondered why he'd never thought about it before. His father had always been suspicious of the Quarterlands, insisting that the people who chose to live there were murderers and thieves. He'd said that the sooner the government cleaned them all out and forced them into the IS scheme, the better. For Alex, it had always been a case of out of sight, out of mind – he'd seen dramas set in the Quarterlands, but he'd never been anywhere near them himself.

"A few Quarterlanders have menial jobs, like cleaning and construction; the rest get by on the black market, but it's not easy," Scarface said. "I was tired of always struggling to find enough to eat, of just getting by instead of really living. I wanted a future; becoming an IS seemed the best way of finding one."

Alex shifted; his bottom and the backs of his thighs still hurt, but the previously intense pain had at least faded now to a dull, throbbing ache. "So what happened? How did you end up here?"

"There were all these adverts on giant screens around the area of the Quarterlands where I lived, deliberately targeting us," Scarface explained. "The government also sent in IS recruiters all the time, offering to match us with good houders. They told us we'd get a lump sum payment put into a special government account that would gather interest and be waiting for us when we finished working out our contracts. They said that it'd be enough for us to start a new life. They

showed me the figures, and it was more money than I could dream of."
His eyes gleamed hopefully. "Plus I'd get fed, housed, clothed, and
medical insurance during the term of my contract. I figured I could
give up ten years of my life, and at the end maybe have enough to rent
a little flat somewhere that wasn't the Quarterlands – a place to myself
that wasn't covered in damp and mould, and that I didn't have to share
with a dozen other people."

"Is that what the Quarterlands are like?" Alex asked, trying to
imagine such a place.

"Worse," Scarface said flatly. "As a kid it was all I knew, so it didn't
seem so bad. There were lots of other kids, and we used to run around
in a pack like a bunch of rats, having fun and causing trouble. But it's a
hard life; there's no sanitation beyond throwing your shit and piss out
of the window, and the damp gets into your whole body – your skin,
your bones, and your lungs. You never really feel dry. Diseases go
through the Quarters like wildfire, and people die all the time. As kids,
we used to jump over the bodies of people who'd passed away in the
hallways and staircases overnight... we didn't think anything of it. The
grown-ups used to do a sweep every morning and clear out the corpses,
so they didn't stink us all out."

"Where did you bury them?"

Scarface laughed. "In the water – where else?"

"You just threw the bodies away?" For some reason that shocked
Alex more than anything else Scarface had told him.

"Yeah – it's called the Quarterlands Splash. Weigh the bodies down
with whatever you've got – usually rocks or bits of debris – and throw
them out of the windows to sink in the water."

"I had no idea," Alex murmured, feeling ashamed of that fact.

"Solange is a Quarterlands girl," Scarface said proudly. "I knew that
as soon as I met her. She's one of us; we can always spot one another."

Solange looked up from where she was sitting on a beanbag, reading, and shot him an affectionate smile.

"Did you two know each other from Quarterlands days?" Alex
queried.

They exchanged glances, and then both burst out laughing.

"You do know that the Quarterlands are basically any old tall

building in a lost zone with the top sticking outta the water that can house those with nowhere better to go, right?" Scarface grinned. "We don't all know each other – Solange lived miles away from me, in a completely different Quarter. I never met her until she came here."

"Of course... I did know that. I suppose I just assumed you all... socialised or something," Alex muttered, going red.

"No, darling. It's not like that." Solange came and sat beside him and began smoothing his hair gently with her fingers, the way his mother used to when he was a child. He loved it when she did that; it was so relaxing.

"I can see why becoming an indie was a good way out for you," Alex mused.

"And I can see why it's shit for you," Scarface retorted. "You grew up in a nice, dry house, with plenty to eat. You had chances and choices. You can't ever have imagined you'd end up like this." He waved his hand at Alex's little huddle of pillows and blankets.

"I was shunted around a load of different boarding schools, but yeah, it was dry and there was food. I suppose I took it all for granted without even realising it."

"Well, at least I had my family with me and wasn't sent away anywhere," Scarface said. "And they took good care of me."

"My dad was busy with his company, and my mum was always off being glamorous. Later on, she became my brother's coach and spent all her time ferrying him around to training and practice sessions. I used to get into trouble just so I'd be suspended or expelled, and then sent home, so I could see them." That was the first time he'd admitted that, and he was surprised it was to these two people.

"There are different kinds of deprivation," Solange said. "I used to hate you and your kind. I thought you were living the high life, and had everything you wanted while I had nothing. My life wasn't great growing up, and neither was Ted's, but I realise that yours wasn't the paradise I'd always thought it was, either."

"Ted?" Alex raised an eyebrow. "Who the hell is Ted?"

"Me!" Scarface rolled his eyes.

"Sorry." Alex grinned at him. "I'm just so used to thinking of you as 'Scarface'."

"I don't reckon you thought of me as a person at all, at first anyway. Back when Tyler first brought you here, you thought you were better than the rest of us, even though you wore an ID tag and were chipped under the skin, same as us," Ted pointed out. "You had to find some way of making it seem like we were less than you, so you gave us those names."

Alex opened his mouth to deny that, and then closed it again. "Maybe you're right," he admitted. "I apologise. I was a shit; I'm surprised you were so nice to me."

"I felt sorry for you." Ted shrugged. "I've seen Tyler's boys come and go over the years, and what he makes you do is far worse than anything I've ever had to do as a security guard."

"How did you get the scar?" Alex asked. "Does being part of Tyler's security team get dangerous at times?"

"Nah." Ted grinned. "It's pretty dull most of the time."

"That's disappointing. I was imagining one of Tyler's previous 'boys' going after you with a knife in some wild escape attempt."

Ted laughed mirthlessly. "Nobody escapes from Tyler," he said. He glanced at Solange, who gazed pensively back at him.

"That's because you're so good at your job," she told him.

"It's because there's nowhere to bloody well go if you *do* get out," Ted retorted. "Tyler would tear the country apart rather than let anyone he owned get away."

"So nobody's tried?"

"Nobody would be that stupid."

Alex pondered if that was merely a myth that Tyler wanted them to believe. He'd certainly found no means of escaping, but that didn't mean it wasn't possible.

"I got the scar in a knife fight in the Quarterlands, years ago," Ted went on. "It's not even an interesting story, just a regular fight. I used to scrap all the time back then, and apart from that one occasion I was pretty good at it." He gestured to his scar. "That's why I chose security when the government sent in their IS recruiters."

Alex was fascinated by this glimpse into another world, but he was also growing tired after their long conversation. Solange's gentle

combing of his hair was soporific, and soon his eyelids drooped, and he was fast asleep.

He woke up a couple of hours later to find Solange snuggled up on Ted's lap in the armchair, his arms cradling her gently as if she were the most precious thing in the world. They were talking quietly.

Solange glanced at him and smiled. "Hey, sleeping beauty. Want to see a picture of yourself?" She held up Ted's nanopad and showed Alex a picture of himself lying fast asleep on the sofa. He was still pale, and his eyelashes looked particularly thick and long, resting on his ashen skin.

"You looked so cute that I couldn't resist," Solange exclaimed.

Alex flicked through the nanopad to find some selfies of Solange and Ted together, her arms around his neck as they both smiled at the camera. "I like this one." He showed them a photo of Solange wearing the big white tee-shirt she slept in when she wasn't entertaining guests. She wasn't wearing a scrap of makeup, and she looked wistfully beautiful as she gazed out of the window at the grey waters below.

"Hey! I don't remember this." She took back the nanopad and thumped Ted's arm. "When did you take this pic?"

"A couple of days ago," he admitted. "Sorry, Solange, but you just looked so pretty. You were so in your own head you didn't even notice me taking it."

Her expression softened, and she pressed a little kiss to his forehead. "You're forgiven, Teddy."

"Tyler allows you to have your own nanopad?" Alex asked.

"It's not mine – it's the suite security nano," Ted replied. "Whoever is on duty has to carry it at all times in case we get new instructions. All the calls are logged," he added. "In case you were thinking of contacting someone in the outside world and arranging a break-out."

Alex gave a wry grunt. "I don't know anyone in the outside world who'd take my call except possibly my brother, and there's no way he'd know how to arrange my escape. Besides, like you said, it's impossible to evade George Tyler."

At that moment, they heard Fatso in the corridor, signalling the change of shift. Solange pressed a kiss to Ted's cheek, then slid off his lap. He gave her a loving smile and left the room to do the handover.

"So, I already know Ted's got it bad," Alex commented. "But now it looks like you've got the hots for him, too."

She laughed, looking happier than he'd ever seen her. "I thought it was time I stopped falling for unobtainable men and went for a guy who's actually into me, instead."

"He's your guard."

"He's an IS, just like me," she replied staunchly. "And he sold himself to Tyler, just like me. We're not so different. I like him. He's good to me; he makes me feel special."

"I'm glad to hear it. Your last boyfriend was a bastard who didn't deserve you." Alex gave her a self-deprecating wink.

"Well, my last boyfriend also gives himself a hard time when he shouldn't." She put her arms around his neck and kissed him. "I'm happy, Alex. Ted's contract with Tyler finishes around the same time as mine, so we're talking about starting a new life together when all this is over. We'll collect our completion fees and pool them and hopefully find a flat together. Ted's still got family back in the Quarterlands who he wants to get out, so we'd work towards that."

"That happened fast."

"Not really." She shrugged. "We've spent months together cooped up in this place, so we've had plenty of time to discuss it. Ted comes into my room when he's on a night shift and I'm not working, and we talk for hours. He was so kind to me after Drummond beat me that I decided to get to know him better, and I like him. I really like him."

"Do you love him?" Alex asked softly.

She blushed. "You know, I think maybe I do. For a long time I wondered how I'd ever get you out of my system, but Ted is very different to you, and I think that's what I need."

"Good for you." He caught hold of her hand and kissed the palm. "Is Scar... I mean, is *Ted* okay with watching what you do here, given how he feels about you?"

"Ted knows what we have to do to get out of the Quarterlands. For the guys it's often security or manual labour, and for the women it's usually... this." She gave a resigned shrug. "Ted's a realist. He under-stands that I belong to Tyler, and therefore to all the men and the

occasional woman Tyler gives me to. He has to suck it up for now, but it won't last forever."

"Do you think Tyler will cause any problems for either of you because of this?" Alex jerked his head at the smartwall, which recorded every single thing they did and said.

"I don't see why." She flung back her head defiantly, making her curls dance and shimmer in the sunlight streaming through the window. "He doesn't care how I feel as long as I do my job. Nobody's said anything so far, anyway. If he wanted to stop it, he could have done by now."

Alex smiled, feeling genuinely pleased for her. "Then I wish the pair of you every happiness."

She lifted up the blanket and snuggled in beside him. He rested his head on her shoulder.

"Do you ever miss the croc, Solange?" he asked. "And the drinking, and the drugs, and the clubs?"

"Not really. It was more your scene than mine. I did croc because Tyler told me to, because it was a way of being part of your world. Why, do you?" She combed her fingers through his hair again.

"Yeah. I mean, I was never an addict, despite what the press said – I could always take it or leave it, but..."

"But?" she prompted, still stroking.

"It was an escape." He closed his eyes, remembering that mellow feeling of being on croc – how everything seemed a little bit out of focus and nothing really hurt. "I can see now that I used it to avoid feelings I didn't want to feel and situations I hated. The irony is, being here is the worst situation of all, and the feelings are worse than anything I've ever experienced, but I have no croc to get me through. I wish I'd appreciated how good life was back then, compared to how bloody awful it was going to become."

"It wouldn't have made a difference." She smoothed his hair gently away from his forehead.

"Do you believe what Ted said, that there's no way of escaping from here?" He turned his head to look at her.

She looked away sharply, gesturing with her head at the smartwall. "Don't even think about it, Alex."

"There's no drink, no drugs, and the sex isn't exactly the kind I can use as a form of escape," he said. "There are no pills I can overdose on, and I'm watched twenty-four hours a day, so I can't hang myself with one of Lorenzo's expensive belts. Chef makes sure there are no knives left unattended, so I can't slit my wrists, and the windows don't open, so I can't throw myself out. There are no ways out, Solange, and that's what I don't think I can stand."

"Those aren't ways out – they're permanent exits," she said firmly. "You have to find a way of living with it, Alex."

"I can't help it. Every time I close my eyes, I dream of being free. Do you know what I miss most?"

Solange shook her head.

"I miss being able to drive about in a duck, just me and my thoughts. I miss driving through a lost zone, with water all around, and then being out on the open road and stopping for lunch in a village somewhere. When I was a kid, after I'd been suspended or expelled from one of those god-awful schools my parents sent me to, I'd have a few precious weeks at home before they sent me somewhere else. I'd get on my motorbike and go off, all alone. I miss that."

"Well, maybe you'll have that again, one day," she told him. "You don't know what the future will bring – it might be a lot better than it seems right now."

"How do you handle it?" he asked. "You've been here, doing this, for years. How do you keep going?"

"Hope, partly," she replied, tangling one finger in her glorious hair and twisting it around and around. "Hope for the future, and for the day I'll eventually be free."

"I don't have that. I could be here for the rest of my life," he said bleakly.

"I know, which is why you have to find something else – something inside yourself, Alex. You have to dig deep and find some kind of inner strength, or Tyler will destroy you."

"Do you think he'll succeed?" he questioned anxiously.

She smiled down on him sadly. "I don't know. But what I do know is you have to find something to keep you going, or you'll fall apart. For me, it's hope. For you, it has to be something else. I hope you find it –

and if you do, promise me you'll cling on to it and let it see you through the dark days."

Alex looked up at her glumly. "I don't know what I can find that will help me do that."

She wrapped her arms around him and held him close. "Neither do I, but find something, Alex – find something, hold on to it tightly, and never let it go."

Chapter Eight

OCTOBER 2095

Josiah

"My mother once had an affair with George Tyler," Alexander said.

"What?" Josiah stared at him blankly. He hadn't been expecting that.

"I've thought about it a lot over the years. Wondering how she felt about Tyler, whether she really loved him, and whether I really knew her at all. Maybe we never really know anyone. Everyone has secrets."

"You certainly have your share."

"As do you," Alexander retorted.

Josiah glanced at him sharply. "Why are you telling me this?"

"So that you can understand my long and tortured history with Tyler."

"Does this have anything to do with Elliot Dacre's murder?"

"No. You asked me to share something personal – you didn't say it had to be about Elliot." Alexander shrugged.

"That's something personal about your mother – not you," Josiah pointed out.

"It becomes about me," Alexander said tightly. "My mother met Tyler when they were both at Oxford. I've often wondered if she regretted not marrying him then. She grew up in a government work camp, whereas my father was in line to inherit the Lytton empire. I

wonder if she genuinely fell in love with Tyler but chose my father over him because of Lytton AV. Tyler certainly thinks so."

"He feels your family cheated him out of both his father's designs *and* the woman he loved?" That explained a great deal about Tyler's seething animosity towards the Lyttons.

"Yes. I think my mother got exactly what she wanted with my father – at first, anyway. I remember her dressing up, looking glamorous. She always wore the same scent – *Winter Bloom* by LaBelle – whenever I smell it, I always think of her." He smiled wistfully.

"I think of Peter whenever I smell wet dogs," Josiah said dryly.

Alexander laughed. "I know my father always loved her – she was beautiful, dramatic, and interesting – and he was none of those things. I think she grew bored with him, and when Tyler came back into her life, she was ready for some excitement. When I was sixteen, they rekindled whatever was still simmering between them. He wanted her to leave my father, but she insisted on waiting until I was eighteen. I used to wonder why – because honestly, although she loved me, she used to swan in and out of my life while I was at boarding school. It wouldn't have made much difference to me at that point if my parents had been divorced. Then I figured it out..."

"Your brother," Josiah said.

"As always, you're one step ahead, Investigator Raine." Alexander gave an ironic nod. "Charles was showing real promise at rowing. She began managing his training, and I think that was the purpose she'd been seeking for so long. She ferried him around, took charge of his career, and organised his life – his diet, his races, even his bloody bedtime."

"I doubt he minded," Josiah commented acerbically.

Alexander gave a wry chuckle. "You're right. He didn't. He liked being taken care of and told what to do. He might have been the brawn, but she was most definitely the brains. I think she put Tyler off for so long because she wanted to make sure Charles won an Olympic gold medal first. She was a bright woman who'd led an unfulfilled life; this became her great purpose, and she threw herself into it."

"You must have felt left out," Josiah observed.

Alexander ducked his head, his eyes glittering. "I did. I tagged

along behind them whenever I could. At that point, the UK hadn't won gold at the Olympics since before the Rising. My mother knew what a huge deal it would be, and she was right. Charles became an overnight sensation when he won that medal. The morning after, everyone in Britain knew his name – and I mean *everyone*."

"I remember it well." How could he forget? Josiah thought back to that night in LKG, how he'd gone there to celebrate Charles Lytton's win and uncovered Peter's secret in the process.

"Everyone remembers it, but what they don't know is that it was her victory as much as his." Alexander looked up, his eyes glowing with an odd kind of pride in his family. "Charles might have been the one sitting in the boat, but she masterminded his triumph. I often wonder – would she have walked away from my father and started a new life with Tyler a few short months later, or was she stringing Tyler along while she decided what she really wanted? I don't know."

"She died before you could find out."

"Yes – and Tyler blamed me. He was so close to finally screwing over the Lyttons, and the way he sees it, I stole that away from him." Alexander gave a twisted little smile. "I think he probably *did* love my mother, but at least part of the attraction was that he wanted to hurt my father and stick it to the entire Lytton family in some twisted way. He wanted her to leave Dad so he could finally have his revenge for what he viewed as a lifetime of unfairness."

"You said he set a trap for you?" Josiah leaned back in his chair, enjoying this glimpse into his enigmatic indie's life.

"He did, yes, but don't feel sorry for me," Alexander responded bluntly. "I walked right into it. He tempted me, but I took the bait. He gave me some money to build the new style of duck I'd designed, but he sabotaged all my attempts to make it work. I was in a hole, so I kept digging – that's when I stole all that money from my father's company. Tyler saw to it that I was found out and arrested – and then he bought me as his IS to ruin my life the way I'd ruined his. He planned the whole thing."

"Christ, Alexander. That's so fucked up," Josiah exclaimed. "I had no idea – none of this is on record. Just the bare facts – what crime you committed, and the fact Tyler bought you." He leaned forward. "What

did he do to you? I saw you today, at his house; you were completely different to how you are with me, in private. Why? What happened to you during your time with him?"

"I was Owen," Alexander said flatly. "That was my job when I was Tyler's IS. Tyler dressed me up to fulfil the fantasies of the people he wanted onside, for whatever reason: a business deal, a favour, a bank loan. I was his celebrity whore – he kept me in a gilded cage, locked up in a tower on the floating city he helped build, and he prostituted me to anyone he wanted to buy."

"It's illegal to prostitute an IS," Josiah growled, bile rising in the back of his throat.

Alexander laughed. "Are you going to arrest him for it?"

"Is that what you want me to do? Is that why we went there today?" Josiah asked eagerly.

"No." Alexander shook his head. "You'd never pin it on him. He has far too much money, power, and influence."

"Nobody is above the law."

"We both know that's not true. He filmed me having sex with those people and used it to blackmail them. He has so many people in his pocket – judges, politicians – even investigators." Alexander gave him a pointed look.

"He doesn't bloody well have me."

"No, but I didn't know that until today." Alexander gave a wry shrug. "You must forgive my caution; Tyler gave me to men who beat me, raped me, and treated me like I was nothing. I know what he's capable of. It's made it hard for me to trust anyone, even you."

Josiah fought down a tidal wave of rage. "I can arrest him for it. Hell, I'll arrest all of them – everyone who was involved. We can find the footage, use it as evidence…"

"He'd never let you get close to finding the footage. I'm sure he's got it very well hidden, but thank you for being so ready to ruin your career for me." Alexander shot him a grateful smile.

"I don't like bullies," Josiah said tightly. "Christ!" He slammed his fist down on the table, ignoring the stab of pain from his injured knuckles. "This makes me—" He stopped abruptly, before he could say too much and let slip a part of his life he kept secret.

"Makes you...?" Alexander raised an eyebrow.

"Bloody angry." Josiah nursed his sore hand absently. "But if you don't want revenge on Tyler for what he did to you, what do you want?"

Alexander leaned forward and spoke in a tight, intense tone. "When the time comes, I want you to understand. That's all."

"When the time comes for what?" Josiah asked, bewildered.

"When the time comes for you to learn the truth, or when you work it out for yourself." Alexander grimaced. "Look, I just want you to know some of the background when that happens."

"Why not just tell me now?"

Alexander hesitated. There was an agonised look in his eyes, as if he genuinely wanted to tell Josiah what he was hiding. Then the moment passed, and he shook his head.

"I'm not ready, yet, and I don't think you are, either. Maybe I'm paranoid, but with good reason. I've carried this with me for a long time; I don't want to rush it and get it wrong. Now, why don't I clear up, while you return those calls?" Getting up, he stacked their plates onto a tray and walked towards the door.

"Why did you get into the duck with your mother and brother that day, Alexander?" Josiah asked suddenly. "You were hyped up to the gills on croc – I read the medical report – you had so much in your system that you were as high as a kite. You must have known it wasn't safe for you to be driving. Why did you do it?"

Alexander paused in the doorway for a long moment, his shoulders hunched. "I was seventeen," he replied at last, without turning back. "We all think we're immortal at that age, don't we?"

Josiah remembered getting into stupid fights as a teenager and loving every second of them, never for a moment thinking he could be seriously hurt. He gave a little grunt of acknowledgement.

"If I could go back in time, I would change everything about that day, but I can't. I have to live with that," Alexander finished quietly.

Josiah nodded, thinking about the day Peter had died and how he'd give anything to go back and change that, too.

Alexander glanced over his shoulder, shot Josiah a tight smile, and then left the room.

Sitting back in his chair again, Josiah tried to make sense of it all.

Of course, it was entirely possible that Alexander was a total drama queen, intent on creating mysteries where none existed, and yet there was something here – he was certain of it. Having met Tyler, he believed the man was capable of everything Alexander had said, and more.

He felt sorry for Alexander, trapped in such a horrendous situation. How had he survived it for so long? According to his file, he'd been George Tyler's IS for four years, and then Elliot Dacre's for three. No wonder Elliot had seemed like a better houder to Alexander, despite his predilection for displaying him at shows as if he were a pet, and the weirdness of calling him by his late husband's name. If Alexander was going to snap and kill his houder, then surely that person would be George Tyler and not the silly but relatively harmless Elliot Dacre?

The buzz of his holopad broke through his thoughts, and Liz's face popped up in the air. She was plumper these days, and her dark hair had little silver streaks at the temples, but Josiah thought that age had only increased her beauty. Her uncle had died a few years ago, and she'd hired an artistic young man to help out in the pottery. They'd fallen in love, and now Liz was the mother of three beautiful, boisterous children. Josiah was happy for her; she deserved it. She was living proof that Peter's work had been worthwhile.

"Hey – you didn't return my call," she accused.

"Sorry – busy." He smiled apologetically. "Although you did speak to me just a few days ago." She was one of a small group of his close friends who called every year on the anniversary of Peter's death.

"I can call you more than once a week, can't I?" She grinned.

"You can, but rarely do. What's going on, Liz?"

"I heard the news. Big Jen brought some newbies here today on her way to LKG, and she told me about it when she dropped them off."

"What news?" Josiah parried.

Liz rolled her eyes. "The fact that you've taken on an IS. You, of all people. I thought it must be a mistake, so I called you, and *voilà* – he answered. I almost freaked out."

"It's a work thing. I don't want him here – Esther insisted. It's for complicated reasons to do with a case I'm investigating."

"He's very good-looking. Very sexy."

"Is he? I hadn't noticed," he deadpanned.

"Hmm. Right. Honestly, if it was anyone but you, I'd worry, but I know you'd never take advantage of an indie. I almost wish you would. Seriously, Joe – Peter wouldn't want you living like this."

"Like what?" Josiah glared at her.

"Like a bloody monk. You're flesh and blood, and you deserve to be happy. It's been seven years – he'd have wanted you to find someone else."

"Liz, we've had this conversation many times before…"

"Well, if you'd listen to me, we wouldn't have to have it again."

"I'm fine," he said flatly.

"You're not. Look, I adored Peter. He was a lovely, good-hearted man, but he was also flawed and human. Don't turn him into a saint and worship at his altar for the rest of your days. He'd have hated that."

"I'm not doing that."

"Aren't you?" She put her head on one side and studied him thoughtfully. "Peter was one of the most charming men on the planet, but we both know he used that charm to get his own way. He dragged you along on a journey you weren't always comfortable with because he sweet-talked you into it. So, don't sit there and pretend he was so perfect you can never find another man to hold a candle to him."

"He was the love of my life," Josiah said tightly. "How could *any* other man come close?"

"Maybe give one a try and see?" she suggested.

"How are the newbies doing?" he asked, in a valiant attempt to change the subject.

"Scared of their own shadows, overly earnest and eager to help, but worried about doing the wrong thing – you know how newbies are. God, was I ever like that?"

"Yeah, you were," he chuckled.

"You must have wanted to slap me."

"No, you were very sweet. Which ones are they?"

"It was probably you who drove them down to Folkestone a few weeks ago: a little Chinese woman, a couple of Dutch guys, and an

older woman who talks a lot when she's nervous – it can't have been easy for you to get her out of the country."

"I remember her." Josiah grunted. "When she's really scared, she shuts up completely, which was a huge relief. I thought at one point I might have to gag her."

"I'm sure one of your cold stares would have sufficed," Liz teased. "Anyway, they're fine. They'll be with me for a few more days, and then Big Jen is coming back to pick them up and take them on to various other places." At that moment, a small child scrambled onto her lap. She hauled him up and pointed at the screen. "Say hello to Uncle Joe, Peter."

Little Peter grinned a gap-toothed smile and waved a podgy hand. He was the youngest of Liz's children, and had a mass of dark curls like his mother.

"Hey, Uncajo!"

"Ask him when he's going to visit us again, Peter," Liz said, but the little boy just laughed and slid off her lap without saying goodbye.

"Not anytime soon," Josiah told her. "Maybe in the spring."

"You could bring your new IS with you. We could release him into the wild," she said with a wink.

"He's only temporary. I don't get to keep him. Or release him," he added more sombrely. "I wish I could."

She picked up on his change of mood. "Joe – I'm sorry. He's got quite a reputation, this Alexander Lytton. I assumed you'd be glad to hand him back to Esther when your case is over, but it sounds as if there's more to it than that."

"I help transport escaped indies out of the country, Liz," he explained wearily. "I don't make them live in my house, cook my dinner, and clean my shoes."

"Is that what he's doing?" She asked, looking startled.

"Yes. I don't ask him to do it – he just does. I didn't want to bring him home, but the alternative was the probate system, and I thought he might have a lead on the case, and Esther... no, it wasn't Esther's fault, it was Peter's."

"Peter's dead, dear. You know that," Liz chided. "How can it possibly be his fault?"

"I heard his voice in my head telling me to bring this one home. I argued with him, but you know how Peter can be."

"God, yes. Bossiest man I ever met, in the nicest possible way. Well, if Peter insisted, then of course you had no choice." She smiled at him gently, and he smiled back, enjoying their banter.

Liz knew him better than anyone else in the world, except possibly Elsie. She'd been a lifeline in the dark days immediately after Peter's death, calling to talk to him every night when he'd barely been able to function. He visited her a couple of times a year, between cases, and she always wrapped him in a warm hug and was happy to reminisce long into the night.

"Where on earth are you?" She frowned, looking around suddenly.

"The dining room."

"You have a dining room?" For obvious reasons, Liz had never been to the house. Her original houder was long since dead, but she was still listed as an escaped IS and technically formed part of his estate, so she'd never be able to return to the UK. "Why have I never seen you in there before?"

"I never used it when it was just me; Alexander makes us eat in here."

"Are those some of the dreadful things I made when I first started at the pottery?" she asked, glancing over his shoulder at the row of misshapen pots. "God, they're awful."

"You were learning. You got better. The wedding vase is beautiful." Josiah picked it up from the centre of the table and held it up for her to see.

"Hmm, not bad, but I'm much better now. I should send you some of my more recent stuff. Now look, I'm worried about you – this Alexander sounds almost as bossy as Peter, with the making you eat in the dining room thing."

"He's not bossy – he's challenging. There's something he's not telling me, and it's irritating the hell out of me."

"Well, we all know how you feel about mysteries. I'm sure you'll solve this one. You always do."

"I will, and I'm fine, Liz. I'll catch the killer, and then Alexander will go into probate and be sold to a new houder."

GHOST EYE

"Poor Alexander. Can we really not save him?" she pleaded.

"No," he replied shortly. "I've got half the country's media camped outside my home right now – it's hard enough to get him out of the house without them seeing, let alone out of the country. If I help him, we can say goodbye to the Kathleen Line, and I'm not ready to sell you all out for the sake of one man. Even if by some miracle I managed to smuggle him out, he's not someone you can just lose in LKG – he's the most famous IS in Britain."

"Seems ironic. You've saved so many of us, starting with me." She gave a sad little smile. "And now you have this one living under your very own roof, and you can't lift a finger to help him. That must be hard for you."

"It is," he said gruffly. "I'm trying to figure out other ways to help him, but he's not exactly making it easy for me."

"You can be quite scary, dear."

He opened his mouth to protest, but she shot him a knowing look that made him close it again with a wry smile.

"Maybe you could try being nice to him?" she suggested.

"I've been *very* nice to him."

She raised an eyebrow.

"Okay, I've been my usual self, but he doesn't scare easily, trust me."

There was a noise in the background, and Liz's daughters appeared in the doorway, shouting something. "Sorry, there's some kind of domestic drama – I have to go. Take care of yourself, Joe, and be careful with this Alexander person. He sounds very mysterious and sexy, and those people are always the most dangerous." She gave a little wave and then disappeared.

Recalling her comment about the dining room, he smiled, remembering when Peter had first brought him here, years ago.

———

"You have a whole room just to eat in?"

"Yes, Joe." Peter leaned against the doorframe, watching him with twinkling dark eyes. "It's not unusual; lots of people do."

"I wouldn't know. I mean, I went straight from the Quarterlands to

the army." Even married quarters in the army camps only had kitchens to eat in – no separate dining rooms. "And you own this whole house? All of it?" he asked incredulously.

"Yup. It belonged to my grandmother, and she left it to me when she died. I've been renting it out all these years – I never thought I'd want to come back here. It was always her house, you see, and I didn't think I could live here without her."

"What changed?"

"I got married, was thrown out of the army, and finally decided I wanted a place to call home – then I remembered I already had one." Peter grinned at him. "Could you be happy here, Joe? Just say if not, and we'll sell it and buy a place together."

"Are you kidding? It's a bloody palace. I'd love to live here."

"Just wait until you see the bedrooms." Peter grabbed his hand and tugged him towards the stairs.

"Bedrooms? Plural? There's more than one?"

"There are three, although one of them is pretty small."

"What on earth will we do with three bedrooms?" Josiah asked as Peter dragged him up the stairs.

"Make love in every single one of them," Peter replied, pulling him into a large room and leading him over to a big double bed. "Also..." He paused in the act of unbuttoning Josiah's shirt. "I thought we might have the occasional guest... sometimes we need a safe house to park an escaped indie in for a night or two, before we can get them to the coast. Would you be okay with that?"

Josiah took hold of Peter's hands and held them. "Of course I'm okay with that. In fact, I want you to get Elsie down here sometime soon, so we can talk about how I can help out going forward."

"Really?" Peter exclaimed softly. "Really, Joe? I mean, you're applying for all these jobs with investigation agencies. Are you sure you want to be involved with something illegal?"

"Yes," Josiah said firmly. "But we must be equal partners – no hiding, and no more making decisions behind my back."

Peter's eyes were shining as he leaned forward and kissed Josiah sweetly on the lips.

GHOST EYE   149

Another buzz on his holopad interrupted him, and Big Jen's face popped up in the room.

"Evening, Sarge." She shot him a sloppy salute, even though they'd both long since left the army. She'd stumbled upon the Kathleen Line when bunking down with him and Peter after being made temporarily homeless following her army discharge. She'd demanded to be allowed to join – Big Jen loved "sticking it to the man", as she put it. She was now Josiah's most capable pair of hands – and his trusty second-in-command, given Elsie's advancing years.

"I thought it'd be you," Josiah grunted. "I've just had Liz bending my ear."

"Well, come on! This is the best gossip we've had in years." She grinned at him. "Seriously, though... you've taken an indie? You, of all people?"

"He's temporary," Josiah growled, in an exasperated tone. "Perhaps you could pass that information on, so I don't have to go through this again with anyone else."

"It's all over the news. Your indie is dead famous. Gary says you're shagging him." Gary was her on-off boyfriend of several years. Apparently, he was currently "on".

"I'm not."

"I know that," she said indignantly. "I defended your honour – I punched Gary's lights out for you."

"My hero." He rolled his eyes at her. "Where are you now?"

"Just left LKG. I'm on my way to do the pick-up from Liz – I left a handful of newbies with her who aren't cut out for LKG, so I'll be taking them to Jean-Paul. Should be back with you in a couple of weeks. Now look, I've been reading up about this Lytton bloke, and he's a nasty piece of work. Be careful – I don't want you getting hurt."

"How very touching, but I can take care of myself."

"Yeah." Big Jen grinned. "I know. Liz always thinks you need scooping up and looking after, but I know you're as tough as old boots. This could be good for you, though."

"How, exactly?" Josiah raised an eyebrow.

"Well, it helps your cover. Everyone knows you hate indies, and now they'll think you're using and abusing this one. Nobody is likely to suspect that you're the evil genius behind the biggest IS escape network in the country." She twirled an imaginary moustache.

"Piss off," he growled.

She laughed. "Understood. Speak to you soon, and don't, you know, do anything too stupid." She gave him another half-arsed salute and was gone. Josiah smiled to himself, shaking his head. He was lucky to have such good friends, and he knew it.

———

Peter soon talked his way into a job as a mechanic in a local garage. Josiah had never seen him so content. He loved working on any kind of engine, old or new, was quite the specialist in Pre-R cars, and soon had the grease engrained in his fingers to prove it.

Josiah came home one day soon after they'd moved in to find Peter in the garage, his legs poking out from beneath the wreck of an unidentifiable hunk of metal. Hattie, always Peter's faithful companion, leapt up from her rug by his side and came running over to greet him, yapping excitedly as always.

"Hello, girl. Hello! Yes, I know. Hello." Josiah rubbed her head and accepted a few wet kisses before she calmed down and returned to chewing up an old tennis ball on her rug. By that time, Peter had emerged from under the car.

"Hey." Peter came over and kissed him, too. "How did it go?"

"Careful." Josiah shoved him away, gesturing at his clean suit.

"If you get the job, you'll be able to afford a nice new one – maybe one of those fancy-arsed things you keep showing me on those stupid men's fashion sites you like so much."

"Just because you're happy hanging out in a pair of greasy old overalls doesn't mean we all are." Josiah looked Peter up and down.

"I'm just as happy out of them as in them." Peter gave him a sly wink. "Come on, Joe, put me out of my misery – how did it go?"

"I think it went well," he replied slowly. "I'll know by tomorrow if I've got the job. The woman who interviewed me, Esther Lomax, is

good – really sharp and efficient. I liked her. She seemed particularly impressed by the fact I arrested you – she asked me lots of questions about that."

"What did you say?" Peter queried cautiously, wiping his hands on a rag.

"I stuck to the party line. Said I had to do my duty and uphold the rules and regulations despite the fact you were my husband, blah blah blah."

"Good."

"She seemed surprised we're still together, but I said I'd given you another chance as the army hadn't actually sent you to prison in the end. Told her we'd decided to make a fresh start."

"Well, that's the truth. I hope she gives you the job. It's what you're good at, Joe – investigating crimes, solving mysteries, bringing the bad guys to justice. Will it be a problem for you?"

"What?" Josiah frowned.

"Working with us on the Kathleen Line whilst also working at such a prestigious investigation agency? Your weird sense of honour and all that." Peter prodded him gently on the arm.

"Inquisitus doesn't investigate escaped indies; it's too classy for that." Plenty of investigation agencies made easy money by having a division for catching runaway servants, but Inquisitus wasn't one of them – Josiah had done his homework on that. "I've asked to work in the Special Investigations Division, which focuses mainly on homicides, so hopefully there won't be any conflicts of interest."

"You'll be brilliant at this job. I know you'll get it," Peter pronounced confidently.

"I hope so. Now, I have to ask – what the hell is that?" Josiah pointed at the heap of metal Peter had been working on.

Peter laughed. "It's a Pre-R car. Quite a classic, too – a Jaguar – not many of them around these days. She was brought into the yard today – they were going to sell her as scrap, but I thought I could make her as good as new again, so I bought her."

"Why?" Josiah asked blankly. "What possible use is a Pre-R car around here? We're only a stone's throw from a massive lost zone – we need ducks to get to most places."

"You're such a philistine, Joe," Peter chided. "It's not about useful-ness – it's about the beauty of the thing."

"If you say so." Josiah rolled his eyes. "How long will it take for you to make this rust bucket actually look beautiful, though? Because right now it looks like a pile of junk to me."

"Depends on how much time I find to work on her. A year? Maybe two?" Peter grinned. "I love having a project."

At that moment, Elsie arrived for their meeting. Peter washed up, then spread several large maps on the dining room table - he never liked to use electronic devices on Kathleen Line business if he could avoid it. He and Elsie pored over them, discussing how they could expand and improve on the operation.

Josiah listened to them in silence for a few minutes and then cleared his throat. "I have some thoughts."

"You do?" Peter glanced at him in surprise.

"Yes – what you've done so far has been great, but it lacks a certain organisation and eye for detail."

"And that's what you bring?" Peter smiled.

"Yup," Josiah replied confidently. "See, the flaws in your organisa-tion are, unsurprisingly, the flaws in its leadership. It's well-meaning, but piecemeal. It relies too much on maverick individuals with a flair for improvisation" – Josiah glanced pointedly at Peter – "and good-hearted people who just want to help." He glanced at Elsie. "How do you find the escaped indies who want to be smuggled out of the coun-try, Elsie?"

"Word of mouth," she responded, shrugging. "We have been doing this for several years now, you know." She sounded a little stung by his criticism.

"I know – and it's been a fantastic achievement." Josiah shot her a mollifying smile.

"We've come a long way – we've improved hugely from the early days," Elsie said. "After Kathleen died, Peter joined the army, and I thought it'd fall apart, but I counted without this one here." She rolled her eyes at Peter, who grinned back at her.

"As if I'd let all Gran's hard work go to waste," he riposted.

"He and I coordinate the whole thing, but we've built up a little network of volunteers who help us."

"And you've done a great job," Josiah told them. "But I think we can turn it into something more structured."

"Joe is big on structure," Peter informed Elsie.

"I just think you're wasting your biggest resource," Josiah said.

"What's that?"

"All the people you've helped escape. They're out there, scattered all around the world, and I bet plenty of them would be happy to help other people in the same situation they were once in. You could contact them, find those who would be willing to be part of a chain of safe houses, and that would replace the army convoys as a way to get people around Europe."

There was silence for a moment as they both stared at him. Then Elsie turned to Peter.

"You told me he was cute, but how come you never mentioned how smart he is, too?"

Peter laughed. "He has his moments."

"Cute!" Josiah snorted. "Nobody has *ever* called me that."

"You are to me." Peter wrapped an arm around his neck and planted a big kiss on his cheek. "I should have brought you in on this ages ago, Joe."

"What about the UK side of things?" Elsie asked. "That's the hardest part of the whole operation."

"Most of the people you get out of the country have relatives here," Josiah told her. "They might be in a position to help – out of gratitude for what you've done to help the people they love. We could slowly start recruiting them – with proper checks, of course."

"If you get that job at Inquisitus, you'll have access to databases that could help us with that," Peter ventured.

"No," Josiah said flatly. "My work and the Kathleen Line must always be kept separate. I'm going to do my best for Inquisitus if I get the job, Peter. I'm not going to take their money and screw them over. Also, just so you know, I can't condone murder, whatever the circumstances. I'll help indies escape from abusive houders, but if they've killed their houder, I'll arrest them for it. Simple as that."

"Fair enough." Peter turned his attention back to the map. "Now, let's talk about your plan in more detail..."

———

There was another buzz from his holopad, and Elsie popped up, looking solemn. He clicked to accept the call, with a sigh.

"So, is it true you've got yourself an indie, Joe?" she asked.

"It's temporary!" he said, exasperated.

"It's a bad thing, Joe." She shook her head. "A very bad thing."

"Elsie, you've known me for years. Is it really likely that I'd buy myself an IS when I've spent over a decade helping to free them?"

"I'm not concerned about that; I know you'd mean him no harm." She waved her hand in the air. "But this particular indie comes with a history, and I'm worried about you, and what you could be getting yourself into."

"Nothing I can't handle," Josiah told her firmly. "Look, this is my job, Elsie, and I've always done my job to the best of my ability. That hasn't changed."

She nodded thoughtfully. "I know you're a good man. I also know that when Peter died you shut down."

"And you think that's a weakness?" Josiah trusted Elsie to always tell him the truth, as she saw it, but that didn't mean he had to agree with her.

"No, you're a strong person, Joe – the strongest I know. You could've turned your back on the Kathleen Line after Peter died – God knows, it cost you enough – but you didn't. Instead you worked even harder at it and made it even better."

"Then why do you think I'm going to turn my back on my principles now?"

"Because you've been working like a crazy man for the past seven years. The only break you give yourself is that one day of the year when you stay home on the anniversary of Peter's death and polish his car. The rest of the time you're working either at your job or for us."

"I like to keep busy. I'm still not seeing why this is a problem," he responded irritably.

"You've seen it for some time now, but you don't want to deal with it."

"Nope. Still not understanding." He shook his head stubbornly.

She sighed. "Joe, you've worked so hard, and been so good at your job, that you've got this reputation now – you're the indiehunter."

"I didn't—" he began, but she held up her hand.

"Let me finish. I know you didn't ask for that name. I know all you did was solve a couple of high-profile cases involving indentured servants. It's not your fault the press have latched on to you like this, but now you've taken on this notorious indie, it's become far more dangerous. How can we keep what we do a secret while everyone's looking at you? You're front-page news. One day, some nosy journalist is going to dig deeper than all the rest and find what you've been hiding – and then we could all go under."

"I won't let that happen," Josiah said tightly.

"You might not be able to stop it," she warned. "I had a call this morning from a woman who needs help getting a relative out. Normally, I'd ask you to do the pick-up, but I had to tell her there was nothing I could do for her."

"You could ask Jan or Derek."

"They're both in France right now, in case you forgot."

He paused and took a deep breath. "You're right, I did forget. It's been a busy few days."

"You fight for two causes, Joe," Elsie said bluntly. "You've managed that very well for a long time, but it's starting to be a problem now. You stand for a certain kind of hard justice to the people of this country, but you repeatedly break their laws. If they ever find out, they'll crucify you, son."

"It's a risk we all take," he said flatly. "Being exposed is hardly the worst thing that can happen to me."

"I know. The worst thing that could happen to you already has. That's why I don't think you're seeing this clearly."

"Peter paid for this cause with his life, and I won't let him down. I'll carry on his work, Elsie, the way I promised."

"Promises to the dead don't have to be honoured forever, sweetheart," she said gently.

Josiah heard a noise and tapped his holopad, muting her.

"I have to go, Elsie. We'll talk another time – and stop worrying."

He severed the connection and glanced up to see Alexander standing in the doorway. How long had he been there? Suddenly, he saw Elsie's point. If Alexander had heard what they were talking about, then she could have been placed in danger. He liked Alexander, but the indie had freely admitted he was playing some kind of game. Until Josiah knew what that was, how could the IS be trusted? Elsie was right – Josiah was a liability to the Kathleen Line right now, and he had to find a way to fix that.

"How long have you been skulking in the doorway?" he demanded angrily, standing up.

"I just got here. I've finished clearing up and wondered if you'd like a cup of tea," Alexander replied, looking startled by the new belligerence in Josiah's mood.

"Well, I wouldn't," he growled, striding over to the door. Alexander shrank away from him, and he remembered Liz's advice. "Sorry, I'm just tired," he said more softly.

"That's fine, sir," Alexander replied meekly.

Weirdly, Josiah found he missed the use of his first name. "Look, there's no need to call me sir; I don't mind if you call me Josiah," he said awkwardly.

"Thank you." Alexander smiled brightly. "So, have you finished calling your friends?"

"Yes." Suddenly, an idea occurred to him. "On the subject of friends, you told me yesterday that you only found a true friend after you became an IS. Well, I've interviewed your previous houder, and I've interviewed your family – but maybe I've been looking in the wrong places. Who was this friend you mentioned?"

"You think I have friends who'd kill for me?" Alexander asked incredulously.

"It would explain why you aren't cooperating."

"Yes, it would, wouldn't it?" Alexander sighed. "If only it was that simple – it'd save you a lot of time and trouble. No, Josiah, I don't have any friends who'd kill for me, and even if I did, I would never ask them to."

"I'm not saying you asked them, or even that you knew they would do such a thing. Just... maybe it's something a true friend might decide to do?"

"I have no friends like that," Alexander said, in a tone so final that Josiah knew he'd learn nothing else from him on that subject tonight.

"Fine. Will you tell me about him or her one day? This friend of yours? I'd like to know. Nothing to do with the investigation." He waved his arm in the air dismissively. "I'd just like to know who they are, and what they did for you, that you speak of them so highly."

Alexander gave the smallest flicker of a smile. "One day, yes," he said quietly. "I'd like nothing more." There was a strange intensity to his voice.

"Then I'll wait. I'm a patient man," Josiah said wearily. "Now, it's late, and I'm tired, so I'm going to bed."

Alexander placed a hand on his arm. "Um, so... I was wondering if I could sleep in your bed again tonight, Josiah?"

Josiah exhaled. "Look, Alexander..."

"Alex."

"What?"

"If we're going to talk about our names, then I prefer to be called Alex."

"Okay... Alex... look, what I said last night about not having sex with an IS still stands. You do understand that, don't you?"

"Of course. I experienced a similar issue myself once, with my father's secretary; I handled it with much less dignity than you have." Alex gave a rueful smile. "There was also Neil, but I'm not sure who was exploiting whom, there."

"Neil – the bloke you shared a flat with at university?"

"Yeah. Anyway, I wasn't planning on us having sex. I just..." Alex paused and looked down, then looked up again with such an honest expression in his eyes that Josiah knew he was seeing the real person. "It's been a strange day, seeing Tyler again after all these years, and last night was nice. You know, just being next to someone."

"Yes, it was," Josiah admitted.

"So, I wondered if we could do that again. Just that. Not sex – just keeping each other company."

Josiah knew he should say no, but when he opened his mouth, the word "yes" came out instead.

Alex gave a delighted smile. "Thank you." He pressed a kiss to Josiah's cheek and then made a run for the stairs before he could change his mind.

Josiah followed him, already regretting his impulsive decision. He suspected this was a bad idea, but Alex had already spent one night in his bed. What harm could another one do?

Heading for the bathroom, he cleaned his teeth, then climbed into bed wearing his boxers and a tee-shirt. A couple of seconds later, Alex joined him. He slid into the bed with his back to Josiah, and they both lay there stiffly until Josiah gave a little growl and put his hand over Alex's stomach, drawing him close, and then they both relaxed.

"Good night, Alex."

"Good night... Joe."

Josiah prodded him. "Only my friends call me Joe, you cheeky bastard – I give you an inch, and you take a mile, as always."

Alex laughed and melted against him.

Josiah liked how it felt to be holding a relaxed, laughing man in his arms again. It wasn't only the physical intimacy – it was the emotional warmth as well, the sense of sharing a joke, and feeling comfortable and at ease with one other. It was addictive.

A small, gnawing voice at the back of his mind wondered how he'd be able to give it up when the time came.

Chapter Nine

SEPTEMBER 2088

Alex

Tyler gave him two weeks to recover – more, Alex suspected, because he didn't want his clients to see the ugly bruises on his body than from any great concern for his welfare. Normal service resumed after that, with a succession of guests he blanked out. He performed his duties mechanically, going through the motions. At least none of them wanted to hurt him, and if they were disappointed by his listless performance, they didn't say anything.

When he wasn't working he spent a lot of time in his room, staring out of the window at the familiar vista below. Sometimes, on a bright day, the dull grey waters of the lost zone cleared a little, revealing the swirling shadows of Old London. The Rising itself had killed fewer people than might have been expected for such a cataclysmic event. The venerable old city had disappeared slowly, over several months, and people had plenty of time to get out, leaving the city intact behind them to be swallowed whole by the waters. The crisis caused by all those displaced people had been what almost caused humankind to go under. Alex spent hours gazing down from his vantage point, trying to make out the lines of the old roads and buildings of that eerie underwater city that had once been a thriving metropolis.

A couple of weeks after he resumed work, Fatso opened his bedroom door and told him his presence was required.

"Now? But Lorenzo hasn't given me an outfit to wear," he said sullenly.

"Not in the living room. Upstairs. Tyler wants to see you."

Alex felt a knot of tension forming in his stomach as he was escorted along the hallway and into the lift to the penthouse suite.

Tyler was sitting on his vast red leather sofa, sipping a glass of wine. He looked up and grinned. "Ah, there's my sulky whore. I've had complaints from my clients. They say you haven't been giving the most enthusiastic performances of late."

"Forgive me for not enjoying being raped," Alex retorted.

"Raped?" Tyler raised an eyebrow. "That's a strong word. I thought you enjoyed sex, judging by how much you've whored yourself out over the years. Who knew you actually had standards?"

"You can force me to fuck people – you can't force me to enjoy it," Alex snapped.

"I don't give a damn whether you enjoy it or not. All I care about is that my guests *think* you enjoy it. Right now, you're on autopilot, and they don't like it." Tyler gave an order, and the smartwall flared into life, bringing up a recording of one of Alex's recent sessions; he recognised the occasion from the previous week.

Alex winced at the sight of his own naked arse taking up half the opposite wall. He was staring into space, disinterestedly sucking on some bloke's cock – he couldn't even be bothered to remember the man's name. Ever since the incident with Harper, he'd found a way of distancing himself from what was happening to his body. He'd switch off and pretend it was nothing to do with him.

"Now, I could threaten to hurt Solange again, but we need to find a more permanent solution," Tyler said.

Alex felt a chill of foreboding. "Such as?"

"I need you to break, Alexander. I need you to break down to the point where you obey every single order I give you, without question. So that even if I send you the ugliest, meanest, sleaziest bastard in the world, you'll get down on your knees and suck his cock like it's the tastiest treat you've ever had."

Alex fought down the bile that rose in his throat.

Tyler fixed him with a stern glare. "I need you obedient and skilled at your work, not sulking and miserable. I need you to give people a good time, not bring them down with your sad-arsed face." He gestured at the screen just as Alex was bringing his guest to climax, before drawing back listlessly and spitting into a towel.

"You should have thought of that before you gave me to Harper," Alex retorted.

"Aw, diddums – are you still upset about that?" Tyler rolled his eyes. "Grow up, Alexander. I paid a huge amount for you, and I want my money's worth."

"Fuck you," Alex snapped.

"Hmm." Tyler surveyed him thoughtfully. "You know, the petulant princeling act gets old really fast. I think we need to work harder on breaking your spirit." He stood up, and it took all Alex's courage not to flinch as he walked over to him. "It won't be nice – for you, anyway." Tyler grinned. "But when it's done, we shouldn't have any more trouble with you."

"What are you going to do? Beat me? Rape me? No, wait – already happened. What else can you possibly do to me?"

"Oh, I've only just started. You're a privileged brat with an attitude problem – I'm sure we can find more creative ways to break you."

Tyler barked out another instruction at the smartwall, and the image on the screen instantly changed. Alex was hit by a wave of nausea as he recognised the inside of the boardroom at Tyler's HQ and saw himself running towards the door, trying to escape. Surely Tyler wouldn't make him relive that awful day again? But that was exactly what Tyler intended. Alex's knees trembled as he watched Harper hold his neck and force him towards the table.

"You know, I generally prefer the charms of the fairer sex, but I found this pretty hot." Tyler leered at him. "Sit down beside me, so we can watch it together. Don't be shy." He launched himself back down on the sofa and patted the empty seat next to him. Alex remained rooted to the spot. Tyler sighed, and Fatso came over and shoved Alex onto the sofa, where Tyler wanted him.

Onscreen, Harper forced his boxer shorts down his legs.

"Do you know which bit is my favourite?" Tyler asked.

"I really don't give a shit, you sick bastard."

"We'll watch it all the way through, and I'll tell you when we get there." Leaning back, he put his arm around Alex, holding him as if they were a couple watching a movie together during a quiet night in. "You look good like this." He nodded at the screen. Harper was pressing his hand into the small of Alex's back to hold him in place. "It's a good thing I thought to order popcorn."

He clicked his fingers, and Fatso picked up a tub from a nearby table and handed it to him. Tyler put it on his lap, took a handful, and squeezed Alex's shoulder with his other hand. "Help yourself, Alexander. Just relax and enjoy."

He threw the popcorn into his mouth and chuckled as Harper drew back his belt and slammed it down on Alex's buttocks. Alex winced at the loud, cracking sound. In an instant, he was there, back in that room, over that table, being beaten. Watching it on screen, he realised now how long it had lasted – no wonder he'd been in so much pain afterwards. Harper was hammering him with the belt while he screamed and desperately tried to squirm away, but Harper had him tied and held him firmly in place. He swallowed hard, tasting the bitterness rising again to the back of his throat.

"Now we're coming to my favourite part," Tyler said, pointing.

Alex saw himself look up and stare directly at them, his eyes full of pain.

Tyler paused the image and then studied it. "You, looking straight at the camera, knowing I'm watching you suffer... I love the expression in your eyes: so much rage, helplessness, and anguish. And then this..." He started the image again. Now, Alex's expression had changed to one of resignation, and he slowly put his head back down on the table. "I like this bit, because it's where you finally accept your punishment. You know you're a shitty little arsehole who deserves it. That's why I wanted you to watch this – so you can see yourself as I see you. So you can see what you've become."

Harper finished beating him and asked him if it hurt. Then he unzipped his trousers. Alex closed his eyes, but Tyler wasn't having

GHOST EYE   163

that – he pinched his neck hard until he opened them again to see Harper thrusting into him with grunts of pleasure.

"Hmm, now I'm turned on." Tyler put the bowl of popcorn to one side, took hold of Alex's hand, and pressed it into his crotch. He was semi-hard.

Alex pulled his hand away in disgust.

"And that, right there, is the problem," Tyler told him. "Now, I'm giving you a choice. I want you to get on your knees in front of me, right now, and give me the best blow job of your life."

"And if I refuse?"

"Then I'll do something that'll hurt far more than a few slaps with a belt and a hard arse-fucking." Tyler jerked his head at the screen. "See, the way I view it, the day you willingly suck my cock, or get on your hands and knees and hold your arse cheeks open and implore me to fuck you, is the day I've tamed you. I might have bought you, but you're not really mine until I can shag you every which way 'til Sunday, only for you to crawl to me and beg for more. That's what I want, and I'll wear you down until that's what I get. So... what's it going to be?" He gestured to his crotch again. "Are you going to suck me off, smile and enjoy it, and let me come down your throat and thank me for the honour after? Or am I going to have to slowly grind you down until you do? I don't mind, either way. Like I said, it'll be fun."

"I will never, ever willingly fuck you," Alex told him defiantly, ignoring the knot of fear in his belly. "I'll never beg for it. You can beat me all you like, but I won't do it."

"Beatings are one way of controlling people, of course," Tyler said airily. "But there are others. Okay – you're on." He held out his hand. "You and me, a fight to the finish. May the best man win."

Alex ignored him.

Tyler laughed and ruffled his hair. "Aw, poor Alexander. You have no idea what you've let yourself in for. Let's see how long it takes. Okay, we're done." He nodded at Fatso. "Take him back downstairs."

As he walked out of the door, Alex heard Harper give a throaty growl of pleasure as he climaxed.

· · ·

He was returned to the suite, where he told Solange what had happened.

"You should have just done as he asked," she said. "Just sucked him off, there and then – you could have closed your eyes and pretended he was Hudson Brink."

"I couldn't do it. He repulses me. I'd have gagged if I'd tried. Don't worry, Solange – he isn't going to make you pay for it. He said something about finding a more permanent solution and a load of crap about breaking me."

"Do you know what he has in mind?" she asked anxiously.

"No, but I figure he can't do too much to me physically if he still wants me to be attractive to his guests. I can stand anything else he does."

A few hours later, Lorenzo arrived in the suite, carrying a box. He took Alex into the bedroom and laid some towels on the bed.

"What's happening?" Alex asked.

"Take off your clothes, sweetie. We have some waxing to do," Lorenzo announced brightly.

"Waxing?" Alex began stripping off his jeans and tee-shirt.

"Orders from Mr Tyler. Apparently, he thinks you'll be more appealing to his guests if you are completely without hair save for on your head."

It wasn't nice to have every single hair below the neck forcibly pulled out by the root, but if Tyler thought this was going to do him any great psychological harm, he had another think coming. Alex endured it while Lorenzo kept up a constant stream of jokes that at least distracted him from the discomfort. It was humiliating to have all his pubic hair removed, leaving his crotch completely denuded, but he just rolled his eyes at the smartwall that was recording it. Tyler was going to have to try harder than this.

Lorenzo stripped every inch of him. Then he rubbed in aloe vera lotion, soothing all the areas of irritation. "Any redness should be gone by morning, sweetie," he said. "And then you're good to go."

"Go where?" Alex asked.

"That I don't know. You do look mighty fine, though. Like a porn star." He surveyed Alex's naked body critically.

Alex looked down – bereft of hair, his cock seemed longer, and his balls looked as if they hung lower.

"It's pretty. Cleaner. Your cock is all pink and sweet like that," Lorenzo observed.

"I feel like a prat."

"Well, get used to it. My orders are to wax you every few weeks from now on, so that you're permanently hairless."

Lorenzo returned first thing the next day, carrying a small suitcase.

"What's this?" Alex asked as the stylist placed it on the bed.

"I was given some rather special orders, so I had to go through my storage wardrobe to find something that would work for today," Lorenzo said, with a tight smile that implied Alex wasn't going to like it.

He was right. After Alex had showered and been shaved, Lorenzo styled his hair with copious amounts of product, making it look artfully tousled, as if he'd been fucked all night. Then he opened a little bag he'd brought with him.

"Eyeliner and mascara," he said.

"Really?" Alex sighed, although in his clubbing days he'd rocked a Goth look occasionally, so it didn't bother him.

When Lorenzo finished, he stepped back with a smile. "Gorgeous!" He turned Alex around, so he could look in the mirror.

Alex stared at himself in disbelief. The mascara and eyeliner had been slathered on, giving him a heavy-lidded, sultry look, while his lips were shimmering from copious applications of a pale, shiny lip gloss. "It might work in a dark club when everyone's off their heads on drugs and booze, but stone-cold sober and in broad daylight?" He grimaced.

"It's beautiful. Smoky, smouldering, sexy." Lorenzo blew a kiss at him. "Now, let's get you dressed."

He opened up the suitcase and took out a pair of tiny black leather shorts, and a black top made of loose, see-through mesh. There was a little satiny pouch of a thong, and a pair of diamante-encrusted high-heel shoes.

Alex stared at the ensemble. "No way."

"Sorry, darling – these are my orders," Lorenzo said, with an empathetic look that implied he agreed.

"So, what – Tyler is going to make me stand on a street corner touting for passing trade? These are hooker clothes, Lorenzo."

"And I'm sure you'll look beautiful in them," Lorenzo told him firmly, in his "making the best of a bad job" tone. "One more thing..." He took a little jewellery box from the suitcase and opened it to reveal two starbursts connected by a chain.

"What the hell are they?"

"For your nipples, darling. They aren't clamps – don't worry," Lorenzo added hurriedly. "They nip a bit when they go on, as they have to hug in order to stay there, but you'll soon forget you're wearing them. Now, come here, and let's get you dressed."

He beckoned, and for a second Alex baulked. "You know he's doing this to humiliate me, don't you?"

"Oh, sweetie – he's your houder. He can clothe you any way he likes; if he wants you dressed like this it's his choice, which reflects only on him, not on you."

That sounded reasonable enough, but Alex wasn't sure he'd be able to hold on to that thought while wearing this ridiculous outfit. "I look like a twink," he said.

"There's nothing wrong with that. I happen to like twinks." Lorenzo winked. "Look, there's nothing to be done but go with it, sweetheart, so come here and let me dress you."

Alex considered rebellion, but he liked Lorenzo and didn't want to get him into trouble. There was also Solange's safety to consider. He knew he was being deliberately humiliated, but he thought he could stand that better than another dose of Harper's belt.

He walked sullenly over and stood still while Lorenzo nestled his hairless cock and balls inside the satin pouch. The fabric was sensual against his bare skin, caressing it, and he knew it had been chosen deliberately to remind him that he was Tyler's whore.

The shorts were worse. They were tight, hugging his bottom obscenely and clearly showing the outline of the pouch. They reached only a few inches down his thighs, leaving his slim, smooth legs exposed. When he turned around and glanced over his shoulder, he

could see how the tiny garment hugged his arse, clinging tightly to his crease, accentuating it.

Next, Lorenzo knelt down and helped him into the shoes. He'd never tried heels before and stumbled when he walked in them.

"Sashay, darling," Lorenzo instructed. "You'll get the hang of it, with practice."

But it was impossible without his bum jerking up and down. "I look like I'm saying, 'Here, fuck my arse,' to the whole bloody world," he observed miserably.

"Well, that's how it's supposed to look, sweetie," Lorenzo said apologetically. "Now for the nipples." He opened the catch on the left nipple decoration, placed it against Alex's chest, and then fastened it. It pinched, but Lorenzo was right, the sensation soon receded. The stylist fastened the second one, then linked the silver chain between the two.

Alex looked at himself in the mirror – there was now a silver starburst attached to each of his nipples, covering each areola completely, with the pink tip of each nipple poking through.

"Now the top." Lorenzo threw it over his head and tugged it down, then arranged it to his satisfaction. The mesh top was sleeveless, displaying his waxed armpits. It was also see-through, and the weave was large enough that his decorated nipples were clearly visible, the linking chain swinging when he moved.

"Please tell me he's taking me clubbing," Alex groaned. His rebellion the previous day had centred on his joyless performance and refusal to willingly fuck his houder; this was clearly a punishment to fit the crime. He was suddenly worried that Tyler was going to take him to some kind of vile party and play a game of "hump the indie" with the guests. The timing didn't support that, though – who held that kind of a party during the day?

"I don't know where he's taking you. I just know he wanted you looking... like this." Lorenzo waved a hand. "He was very specific."

"Rent boy chic?" Alex gazed at himself pathetically in the mirror.

"Something like that. I think his actual words were that you had to look like 'a whore who's just been fucked and is desperate for more cock'."

"Congratulations on being so good at your job," Alex said morosely.

He looked in the mirror, trying to find Alex Lytton under the heavy eye makeup, hair product, and hypersexualised clothing. He couldn't lose himself now, because that was precisely what Tyler wanted. He had to find the essence of who he was and hold on to it tightly, or Tyler would win. His lips curled in disgust as he thought of his houder – and he found himself again in that gesture of mute rebellion. He wasn't this exotic, hairless creature in the mirror, with his jangling nipple jewellery, high heels, and tiny tight shorts. He was Alexander Lytton, and he'd survive whatever George Tyler threw at him.

Tottering out of his bedroom, he found Fatso waiting for him. The guard was usually an impassive presence, but this time he looked Alex up and down, several times, and then his face broke into a lewd grin. He stepped back to get a better view, then let out a long wolf whistle.

"Looks like you've done your job properly," Alex remarked bitterly to Lorenzo.

Fatso gestured that Alex should follow him, so he teetered along the hallway after him. The shoes were his size and fitted properly, but the high heels made his feet ache after only a few steps. He hoped he wouldn't have to walk far in them.

Fatso escorted him into the lift and down to the ground floor, where a limousine AV was waiting. He was pushed inside and found Tyler sitting there, reading his holopad. He put it aside as Alex tottered in and gave a delighted laugh.

"Well, aren't you a vision of beauty."

"If this is what turns you on," Alex replied with a dismissive shrug, trying to hold on to Lorenzo's words about his appearance reflecting more on Tyler than on him. "Bit obvious, though, isn't it?"

"Oh, I do hope so," Tyler purred. "That's the point. You're a whore on the inside, Alex, so I wanted the outside to match – you seem to have forgotten who you are and what your job is lately."

Fatso took his seat beside Tyler, opposite Alex, and the limo set off.

"How does it feel – not having any body hair?" Tyler taunted. "I expect it's nice and smooth, like a woman. One day I'll stroke my hands all over your smooth, hairless body, and you'll love every second of it."

GHOST EYE

"Never gonna happen, pervert," Alex drawled.

"We'll see." Tyler sat back in his seat, smiling. "So, I'm sure you're wondering where we're going at this hour of the morning, with you dressed like that."

"Not really." Alex wasn't going to give him the satisfaction.

"Well, I have a job for you." Tyler handed him the holopad. "There are some pictures on this. When the time comes, and not before, you will press this icon" – he pointed – "and display them."

"Or?" Alex demanded.

"Or I'll take a whip to sweet Solange and beat her until she's raw."

"I thought you weren't going to use her against me again," Alex protested.

"Then you thought wrong. I'm happy to use her to motivate you for now, but we need to get to the stage where your aim is to please me, not avoid pain for her. Now, do you think you can do as I've asked?" Tyler gestured at the holopad.

"I don't have much choice, do I?" Alex said sullenly.

"There's always a choice, Alexander. You're making one right now by refusing to give in to me. Any time you want me to stop today, just agree to my terms, and we can go home."

"Dream on, Tyler. It'll never happen." He sat back and stared out of the window, wondering what fresh hell his houder had in store for him.

It felt strange to be out in the world again, seeing people walking around, shopping, talking, laughing, and living their lives while he was trapped in this nightmare. The tiny shorts rode up his buttocks, but they were so tight it was useless to try and pull them down, so he sat there, feeling uncomfortable and exposed. He envied Tyler his expensively tailored suit, crisp black shirt, and scarlet tie.

He crossed his legs in an attempt to cover his bulging crotch area, only to find Fatso leering again at his slender, hairless limbs, accentuated by the high heels dangling from his feet. He uncrossed them and put his aching soles firmly on the floor.

They drove for over an hour. At first, he drank in the scenery, looking so beautiful in the crisp autumn sun. The limo effortlessly cut through several lost zones, making short work of the stretches of

water. However, as the journey continued, he started to recognise land-marks – and then a sudden, dreadful realisation dawned.

"Where are we going?" he asked in a panic.

"I thought you didn't want to know." Tyler grinned.

He craned his neck as they passed a familiar parade of shops. "I know where we are. I know this area."

"I should hope so. You were born nearby."

Alex felt a lurching sensation in the pit of his stomach. "No... don't do this, Tyler," he said urgently.

"You know what you have to do to stop it." Tyler sat back, opened his legs, and gestured to his crotch. "Willingly embrace your role, not just this once but always, and we can turn the duck around and go home."

Alex's entire body crawled with revulsion at the thought of taking Tyler's cock in his mouth and bringing the smug bastard pleasure.

"No," he snapped.

"Very well. Ah – I believe we've arrived."

The limo travelled, inexorably, down a street and drew up outside an old, familiar building. Alex's stomach lurched.

Lytton AV.

He couldn't believe Tyler would bring him here, of all places, and yet here they were. Tyler climbed out and buttoned up his suit, looking excited, full of anticipatory energy. Fatso grabbed Alex's arm and pulled him out of the AV and into the courtyard in front of the building.

"Now, I want you to remember that you are my IS, and at least pay lip service to obedience while we are here, because if you don't, Solange will suffer for it," Tyler ordered. "Walk two steps behind me at all times; do not, under any circumstances, speak unless you are spoken to; and bring forward the holopad and display the pictures upon my command. Do you understand?"

Alex stared at him in mute horror.

"Do you understand?" Tyler repeated in a harder tone.

Alex nodded, his mind racing. He couldn't put Solange in danger, but could he handle being paraded in front of his father as Tyler's

whore? He had no choice, so he had to somehow find the strength to endure it.

Tyler swept in the front entrance with Alex staggering along two steps behind, as ordered. Fatso brought up the rear.

"I'm here for my eleven a.m. meeting with Mr Lytton," Tyler announced to the receptionist on the front desk. "I represent the Magnus Association."

"Yes, sir – of course. He's expecting you, Mr Bellman," the receptionist replied, with a bright smile.

"Unfortunately, Mr Bellman is indisposed. I'm the vice-chair of Magnus, so I'll be taking his place," Tyler said. "I believe it's this way?"

He headed into the building, steamrollering his way along the corridors, making plenty of noise. Employees came out of their offices to see what was going on, and Alex wished the floor would open up as they stared at him in his rent boy chic. He hoped they wouldn't recognise him, but some of them clearly did. Indeed, word must have gone around like wildfire, because people rushed out to gawp.

Tyler took the long way around, walking through the accounts department, allowing the staff there to get a good look at him, and then along to the design studio, where Alex used to hang out as often as he could. People stared, pointed, and even laughed at his appearance, which would be out of place anywhere except the most extreme of gay clubs. He certainly didn't belong, mid-morning, in an AV factory.

Tyler smiled at them all genially, waving his hand as if he owned the place.

Alex felt himself growing redder and redder as the laughing turned to jeering and catcalls. He was an object of humiliation, as Tyler had intended, and it wasn't as if he had any friends here. He'd first been the moody son of their houder, who they'd had no choice but to treat with deference, and then he'd stolen millions from the company that fed, housed, and clothed them, robbing the very fund of money designed for that purpose. They hated him, and he could feel it with every single step he took.

They finally ended up in the reception area outside his father's office. Spencer looked up, taking in first Tyler and then Alex, dressed

in his ludicrous outfit, his face flushed with embarrassment. Spencer's mouth opened and closed like a goldfish's as he struggled to grasp the situation.

"We're from the Magnus Association – Noah is expecting us," Tyler said loudly, taking advantage of Spencer's confusion to sweep past his desk. He swung open the door to Noah's office and strode inside. Alex put his head down and followed, his entire body burning with shame.

His father got to his feet as the uninvited entourage entered. Alex shrank behind Tyler in a desperate attempt to conceal himself. All the same, he couldn't help peeping out around the side of his houder's shoulder to catch a glimpse of his father, feeling an immediate pang of homesickness. He had to fight down an urge to run to Noah and fling his arms around his neck as he'd done as a child, to hug him and never let him go. When he was small, he'd viewed his dad as strong and invincible, capable of lifting him onto his shoulders, swinging him up into trees, and hauling him out of brambles. Now he longed to return to a time when Noah had been able to solve all his problems, and he wished he could ask him to save him from Tyler. Such salvation was not in his father's power, though, and he knew it. He'd made his bed and was well and truly lying in it.

When had their relationship soured? When had the small boy who'd loved and trusted his father turned against him and found him wanting? He tried to trace the path of their estrangement in his head to make sense of it. It had crept up so slowly. At some point in his childhood, his father had taken over the business from Alex's grandfather and begun working such long hours that Alex barely saw him. Then his father had insisted on his sons being sent to boarding school, which Alex had hated. Noah wanted Charles and Alex to have the best education available, but Alex had always felt like an outsider. He'd struggled to make friends and was bullied into a constant state of misery. Noah ignored his complaints, and when Alex saw him in the holidays he couldn't connect with him anymore, too angry about being sent away to a place he hated so much.

When he was expelled the first time, Noah's anger had surprised and upset him. Their relationship became distant and strained, without either of them understanding the other's point of view, and

Alex had built up walls of rage that had never come down since. Now he wished he'd been less consumed by his own misery and more aware of the pressures on his father. That he'd tried harder to enter his father's world, to listen and learn from him, instead of being so quick to descend into sullen anger. He wondered what it had been like for his dad to watch his mum and Charles bond over Charles's rowing career and to be effectively shut out of that relationship, left only with the glowering younger son who wanted nothing to do with him. It had been expensive to nurture Charles's ambitions, and Noah, always eager to please his vivacious wife, had worked hard to afford it.

Alex also wondered now if his father had ever really wanted to join the family firm, or if he'd done so because it'd been expected of him. Noah was a practical man who enjoyed pottering around in his garden and nurturing plants in his greenhouse. He was good at repairing broken items in their rambling old house, like shelves and taps, even though they had servants to do that. Lytton AV was his birthright, but maybe he'd have been happier as a gardener or handyman. Alex's grandfather had been a sharp businessman, obsessed with making money, who expected the same to be true for his only son. Had those expectations for Noah been as damaging as Noah's expectations for Alex? Had they all failed each other, passing on a curse of misunderstanding down through the generations?

Studying his father, he was worried by what he saw. Noah had lost weight – his suit was rumpled and hung from his shoulders, and his face was gaunt, with a grey cast. Suddenly, he felt a pang of guilt for the part his behaviour must have played in Noah's state of health. He hung his head again, remaining hidden behind Tyler in the vain hope his father wouldn't see or recognise him.

"What the hell are you doing here, George?" Noah demanded.

"I'm here at your invitation, on behalf of the Magnus Association. I believe Lytton AV isn't doing so well, so you approached Magnus for some funding as all your usual sources have dried up," Tyler said smoothly.

"I have a meeting with Bellman—"

"Indisposed." Tyler waved a hand in the air. "I'm the vice-chair at Magnus, but I like to keep it quiet. Of course, Magnus is a private and

somewhat loose association of businesspeople and financiers with money to invest in the right projects, so you can understand why I like to keep my involvement under the radar."

"You're not welcome here, George," Noah told him coldly. "You know that."

"So you don't want Magnus's money?" Tyler raised an eyebrow. "As you know, our usual practice is for one of us to make a study of a company and then put forward a recommendation to our members regarding an investment package. If you refuse my visit today, Magnus won't deal with you in any capacity again; I'll make sure of that." Tyler smiled. "I suppose it depends on how much you want the money, Noah."

Alex saw the desperate look on his father's face and felt sorry for him. He knew what it was like to be hooked on the end of Tyler's line.

"You won't put forward a favourable recommendation regardless," Noah said wearily. "So there's no point me playing along with whatever game you're playing."

"I might, if you're civil to me."

"You're a competitor. I'm hardly going to share sensitive financial information with you."

"So be it." Tyler shrugged. "I'm sorry to hear your fortunes haven't improved, but when Lytton AV finally hits the wall, please do call me. I'm always interested in buying you out."

"I know you've always wanted to sit behind this desk," Noah retorted. "It's your life's ambition. Will you never give up trying, George?"

"I was more your father's natural heir than you ever were," Tyler snapped. "I got on with the old man – we were cut from the same cloth. Given the total mess you've made of running this place, I think he'd be happy to have me sitting there."

"Lytton AV isn't for sale," Noah said firmly.

"It won't be long," Tyler predicted confidently. "I hear you've already had to sell some of your IS contracts."

"We're doing fine, thank you. Now, please leave." Noah gestured towards the door. "Unless you'd prefer me to call security and have you escorted from the premises?"

GHOST EYE   175

"There's no need for that. I came here to do you a favour, but if you don't want it..." Tyler turned. Alex edged around, too, hoping desperately that he might get out of here without his father noticing his presence. "Oh, one more thing..." Tyler swung back again, and Alex's heart plummeted. "I'm curious – how is Alexander doing?"

The expression on Noah's face darkened. "I have no idea. I disowned him."

"So you didn't make any effort to request information from the court as to who his contract was sold to, or where he is? That's harsh."

"My son is dead to me," Noah said flatly. "I don't want to know where he is. He's nothing to me."

"That's a shame. Did you hear that, Alexander?" Grabbing Alex, he thrust him in front of his father's desk. "Your father doesn't care who your houder is," he said silkily.

His fingers were digging into Alex's flesh, making Alex remember his threat about Solange. "I heard him, sir," he muttered.

Noah made a startled sound and looked at him properly for the first time.

As his father's gaze raked over him, Alex could sense him searching for some hint of his son beneath the vile outfit. Feeling desperately ashamed of his appearance, he wondered what his father must be thinking as he realised that his old enemy had been the one to buy his son.

Noah took a step backwards and fell into his chair. "Alex?" he said hoarsely.

Tyler's fingers dug even deeper, indicating that he should reply.

"Yes," he said, barely able to meet his father's eye.

"I didn't want news of my purchase to be common knowledge, so I've kept him under wraps," Tyler said.

"Do you hate me that much?" Noah asked, never taking his eyes off his son. "That first you ruined him, then bought him, and then turned him into... into whatever he is now?" He waved his hand.

"Hate you? No." Tyler shook his head vehemently. "I remember our time together at Oxford and our old friendship fondly, Noah, even if you did destroy it by first stealing my girlfriend, then trying to make me your IS."

"I made mistakes," Noah said abruptly. "And you've never let me forget it."

"Yes, you made mistakes – and I forgive you. It isn't you I hate. It's Alexander."

"Why would you hate him?" Noah asked blankly.

"For the same reason you should – because he killed Izzy," Tyler said fiercely. Alex could feel the pain and rage boiling inside the man's body. He sensed Tyler struggling to keep it under control and realised that he'd never fully appreciated the passion behind Tyler's cruelty. Maybe Tyler *had* genuinely adored his mother – his feelings certainly remained fiery and undimmed, even after all these years.

"She was my wife," Noah said softly. "If anyone should hate Alex it's me, but I forgave him – for that at least."

"She was your wife, but I loved her," Tyler flung back at him. "Come on, Noah, you know that. You knew it years ago, because I spent weeks telling you how much I worshipped her, and that she was the love of my life. But the minute I introduced her to you, you wanted her for yourself. You were already going to inherit Lytton AV, which was built on my father's talent and hard work, but that wasn't enough – you had to have Izzy, too. You took everything that should have been mine, and then you had the bloody nerve to offer me a job as your fucking IS." His voice was full of a barely controlled fury that Alex knew had been decades in the making and was integral to what made George Tyler tick. He was merely a pawn in the bitter feud between Tyler and his father that stretched back to before he'd been born. "Izzy loved me, but you seduced her with your wealth, your power, and your prospects – so she left me and married you."

"I loved her, too," Noah said in a shaky voice.

"I loved her first – but you wanted her, so you had to have her, like a typical spoilt Lytton."

"No, I genuinely fell in love with her. Yes, I knew you were in love with her, and I knew I should walk away out of respect for our friendship, but I couldn't help myself. I really loved her," Noah said.

"Well, she didn't love you," Tyler continued mercilessly. "She realised she'd made a mistake, but by then she had two young sons and didn't want to abandon them. She promised me she'd leave you when

Alexander was eighteen, and she would have done so, too, if your son hadn't killed her."

Noah stared at him in shock. "Isobel wasn't going to leave me."

"Yes, she was," Tyler crowed. "She was having an affair with me. Alexander – show your father the holopad."

Alex had almost forgotten about it. He hesitated, but Tyler shoved him forward. He teetered, unsteadily, to his father's chair and clicked on the icon.

A holopic sprang up in the room. It was his mother, wearing a dressing gown, sitting on a bed in a room that was decorated in Tyler's favourite colours – red, white, and black. She was smiling as she looked at the camera, her eyes dancing.

"It's a fake," Noah cried angrily. "AI generated, no doubt."

"You can show it to your experts, but it's real. There's an authenticity logo to prove it." Tyler pointed at the truth mark on the image. "There are more. Show your father the truth, Alexander."

Alex hesitated again, unsure what else might be on the holopad. But Tyler mouthed "Solange" at him, so he did as he'd been ordered, and brought up the next holopic. It showed his mother and Tyler, walking hand in hand across the golf course at Lewes, talking to each other and laughing.

Alex felt like he was thrusting a dagger into his father's heart and twisting it with each new image, but Tyler was relentless, and Alex had no choice but to keep flicking through holopic after holopic, all damning evidence of his mother's infidelity, all truth-marked. There could be no more denials – Tyler had proved his point to both father and son.

"Please stop, Alex." His father wrapped a hand around his wrist. "Please... I don't understand what's happening here today."

"Revenge, I think," Alex said shakily.

"Not at all," Tyler rebutted smoothly. "Like I said, this isn't about you, Noah – it's about Alexander. If he'd done as I asked in the duck on the way here, none of this would be happening. He's the one to blame for this."

Alexander reeled, the holopad slipping from his fingers. Was this his fault? Should he have just got onto his knees in the duck and

agreed to Tyler's terms? He'd had no idea Tyler would go this far, or open up a wound this deep.

"Isobel is dead – let her rest in peace," Noah said hoarsely. "Would she want you doing this" – he gestured at Alex – "to her son?"

"Doing what?" Tyler queried. "I'm giving Alex the opportunity to be who he really is. Oh, you didn't know about that, either, did you? While you were paying for his education at Oxford, he was going to clubs, sleeping with men, snorting croc, and drinking himself stupid."

Alex wished he could run away and hide, but Tyler wasn't going to stop until his father knew the truth.

"That's not true," Noah snapped. "Alex was involved with a nice girl at Oxford. He wasn't on drugs during that time. I know this for a fact."

"Because you paid Neil Grant to spy on him?" Tyler raised an amused eyebrow. "Sadly, your son seduced Grant into lying to you. Alexander didn't change after killing Izzy. He wasn't so full of remorse for his crime that he turned over a new leaf. He continued taking drugs, and he whored his way through university, sleeping with anyone who'd help him score some croc."

"Alex?" Noah looked at him desperately. "This isn't true, is it?"

"Dad... I'm sorry," was all Alex could choke out.

"I've put evidence on the holopad," Tyler said helpfully. He picked it up from the floor, clicked on a different icon, and brought up a holopic of Alex dancing at a bar in Oxford with crocodile tears streaming down his cheeks. Flicking his fingers, Tyler then displayed another photo of him fucking a young man in the alleyway outside a club, then yet another of him vomiting into the gutter.

Noah gave Alex a look of utter disgust. "I was right to disown you," he said coldly. "You've brought nothing but shame and misery to your family. I wish you'd never been born."

Alex flinched at the words, and Tyler smiled. He knew that Tyler had won this round. He'd inflicted a killer blow, and Alex couldn't shout, or defend himself, or storm out, as he might have done when he was free. He couldn't do anything unless Tyler gave him permission. He hated himself and wished there was still a chance to make things right with his father, but he knew it was too late.

"Well, this has been lovely – it's been so good to clear the air and

bring everything out into the open. However, we really must be going. I'm sorry for dragging you into all this, Noah, I really am." Tyler spoke in a regretful tone, as if he actually meant it. "Alexander – with me. You can leave the holopad – Noah might like to look through those pics again at his leisure."

Alexander hesitated. He didn't want to abandon his father like this, but he didn't know what he could do or say to help. He longed to throw his arms around Noah and make it all better, but they were long past that. He stood there, agonised.

Tyler clicked his fingers. "Now, Alexander," he barked.

Noah didn't even look up as Alex followed Tyler reluctantly to the door. Alex glanced over his shoulder as he left the room, to see that his father had picked up the holopad and was staring at the pictures vacantly as they scrolled through the air in front of him.

They swept out of the building and into the waiting limousine. Tyler sat down with a smile as Alex was shoved into the seat opposite.

"That went well," Tyler said, smirking.

"You didn't have to do that to him. It was cruel," Alex croaked.

"I seem to remember you droning on not so long ago about how much you hated him, how he didn't understand you, and how he kept thwarting your ambitions. It's a bit late to play the dutiful son now." Tyler sat back, still wearing that smug smile.

Alex wanted to wrap his hands around his throat and throttle it off his face. He clenched his hands into fists and looked down at his feet.

"So, how am I doing?" Tyler asked smoothly. "Have I broken you yet?"

Alex felt a wave of rage and defiance sweeping through him. "No," he ground out, under his breath.

"I'm sorry, I didn't hear that. Speak up." Tyler put a finger under his chin and lifted his head.

"I said no, you bastard. You haven't fucking well broken me."

Tyler chuckled. "Well, it's early days. We'll get there. We have plenty of time."

They returned to Ghost Eye City in silence. Fatso was ordered to return Alex to the suite he shared with Solange, while Tyler disappeared into his own private lift. Taking off the hated high heels, Alex

walked in his bare feet, relieved to finally be able to tread without pain, Fatso escorting him along the corridor.

"That wasn't right," the guard said suddenly as they waited for the lift to arrive.

"What?" Alex asked, surprised. Fatso rarely spoke to him.

"What he did today. It wasn't right. Look, there are IS Agency inspectors. They come down and inspect all the houders signed up to the IS scheme. If you have any complaints, you're allowed to call them. They have a helpline."

"What the hell use is that when I don't have access to a holo or nanopad, and I'm guarded twenty-four hours a day?" Alex demanded. The lift arrived, and they stepped inside.

"I've got a nanopad," Fatso said quietly. "I can leave it out for a second while I take a piss. Take it and contact them; I'll leave their nym open. They'll have to send someone down to investigate, by law."

"Why are you doing this?" Alex asked suspiciously.

"I'm not," Fatso said firmly. "Tyler's suite and this lift aren't bugged, so nobody will know we had this conversation. I'll say you nicked the nanopad when I was in the bog. Minor reprimand. It's up to you, if you want to give it a try. No skin off my nose if you don't."

The lift doors opened, and Fatso strode out, silent again, as if he hadn't said a word. Alex followed, his mind buzzing with possibilities. This could be his chance. Escape might not be possible, but if the authorities realised what Tyler was doing here, if they knew he was using his indies as prostitutes, beating and abusing them, then maybe he could be brought down.

He didn't have much time to think about it, because Fatso went to the toilet almost immediately, leaving the nanopad on the kitchen counter. Alex stared at it for a second, then palmed it and ran to his room. He knew that the smartwall was monitored in real time, but unless he was seen making an obvious attempt to escape, he suspected his actions would go unnoticed. Hiding under his duvet, he clicked on the nym Fatso had left open, his heart beating fast as he waited for a response. "Come on, come on..."

A friendly-sounding woman popped up. "Hello, this is the Indentured Servant Helpline, how may I help?"

"I don't have much time," he told her. "I'm an IS, and my houder is abusive. He's had me beaten and raped."

"Please give me your name and ID number, sir," she said. He stumbled through them quickly, willing her to hurry up. "Okay, I've pulled up your details. You're registered to George Tyler – is that correct?"

"Yes."

"Thank you. We'll send an inspector down to assess the situation, sir."

"When will that be, please?" he asked. "Only, he'll probably find out I've made this call, and I don't know what he'll do to me."

"We'll contact an inspector immediately. Someone should be there within a few hours."

He thanked her, ended the call, then went into the kitchen. Fatso hadn't returned, so he discreetly placed the nanopad back on the counter, his heart still thumping in his chest. He had no idea what would happen next.

When Fatso came out of the toilet, he picked up the nanopad and pocketed it without so much as a glance in Alex's direction.

Alex couldn't believe what he'd done. He was full of jitters as he waited anxiously for the inspector to arrive. He decided to kill some time by stripping off the vile clothes he'd been forced to wear and taking a shower, scrubbing his face until all the mascara, eyeliner, and lip gloss were gone. Then he dressed in a pair of grey sweatpants and a plain white tee-shirt. When he returned to his bedroom, he stopped, aghast, at the new wall décor: instead of meadows, oceans, or forest glades, there was now a huge picture of his father displayed on the smartwall opposite his bed. He recognised it as a publicity promo for the Lytton Classic; his father was wearing a business suit, his arms crossed over his chest as he gazed sternly down on his errant son.

"Really?" Alex yelled at the smartwall. "Just how fucking low can you stoop, Tyler?"

He stomped off to the living room, but was in such a state of nervous anticipation that he couldn't sit still. Solange gave him a strange look and asked him if he was okay, but he just shook his head

and chewed on his nails. What was taking so long? What did "a few hours" mean? Three? Five? Ten?

When Fatso received a call later that evening, Alex watched him in agonised suspense.

"With me," Fatso ordered. He jerked his head. "Boss wants you again."

Alex accompanied him to the lift, his stomach knotted with anxiety. He didn't dare even look at Fatso, so he stared straight ahead, still chewing on his fingernails.

"I wanted to say thank you," he said when they were safely in the lift. "Uh…" He racked his memory for the man's real name but totally failed to find it. "Um, Fatso," he finished lamely. "Thanks."

Fatso gave a little grunt, but said nothing. He escorted Alex to Tyler's living room, where the older man was pacing around in a fury.

"I've had a call from the bloody IS Agency," he yelled as soon as he saw Alex. "Apparently, a certain Alexander Lytton has made a complaint about his treatment here, and an inspector is on the way."

Alex lifted his jaw defiantly. "I stole the suite nanopad and called them," he said, trying to word it in a way that wouldn't get Fatso into trouble.

"You shouldn't have done that," Tyler said menacingly.

"What you do here, how you operate – it's illegal," Alex flared back at him. "My father doesn't treat his indies like this—"

"That's because your father likes to play lord of the manor and have everyone fawn over him. It's also why your father is such a bloody useless businessman who doesn't make any money. ISs are cheap labour, but they don't come for free – you have to feed, clothe, and take care of them. In your father's case, he built them their own village with little toy houses, a community centre, and medical facilities. In short, your father is an idiot," Tyler said dismissively. "He wants to go to bed every night believing he's a good man – and that's his weakness. I don't give a damn about that."

"Clearly," Alex answered pointedly.

Tyler glared at him. "The one thing I learned from being shafted repeatedly by the Lyttons growing up is that you have to use people, or they'll use you. I don't employ indies out of the goodness of my

heart – they're here to serve my purpose, and they'll do exactly what I say."

"Or you'll break them?" Alex snorted.

"Precisely," Tyler snapped. "So, your inspector will be here shortly, Alexander – what do you intend to say to him?"

"The truth. I'll tell him exactly what goes on here, and how George Tyler treats his indentured servants."

"You're well fed, well clothed, and there isn't a mark on you," Tyler pointed out, waving at him. "It'll be my word against yours."

"I'll tell them what you made me do this morning. I'll show them that I'm being recorded night and day."

"A perfectly reasonable precaution to prevent a high-value IS being kidnapped, wouldn't you say?" Tyler raised an eyebrow.

Alex refused to be daunted. This might be his only chance: he had to take it. "I'll make them believe me somehow. I'll at least make them investigate, force them to write a report."

"Aw, so you're a campaigner for social justice now." Tyler sneered. "Funny, I didn't see you going on any 'Free the Indies' marches when you were a privileged young man pissing your father's money away on booze and croc."

"That's because I didn't know houders like you existed, then. I thought all indies got looked after the same way my father's are."

"You didn't care then, and you only care now because you're an IS yourself, so it's your arse on the line. If it wasn't, you'd turn your back and walk away," Tyler said with a sly grin. "You're what you always were, Alexander – a spoilt brat who only cares about himself."

"Maybe, but I'm the spoilt brat who's going to bring you down, Tyler."

"Well, it looks like you have your chance," Tyler said as the door opened and one of his indies walked in. "Let's see how you do, shall we?"

"There's a government inspector here to see you, sir," the servant told him.

"I'd better go and greet him, then. Good luck, Alexander," Tyler said with a grim smile. He left the room, and Alexander heard him greeting the inspector in the hallway outside.

"Ah, George. What's going on here, then?" a man's voice said in a jovial tone. "We've had a call. Some nonsense about a complaint. What's got young Lytton so upset?"

"I don't know – why don't you ask him?" Tyler said, leading the inspector into the room. Alexander's stomach gave a sickening lurch.

"Alexander – you remember Martin Bagshaw, don't you?" Tyler said silkily as he brought Bagshaw over to him. "You had the pleasure of entertaining him soon after you arrived. In fact, I believe he was the very first guest you entertained here."

Bagshaw grasped Alex's hand and shook it, tutting the whole time and gazing at Alex fondly. "Dear oh dear, what on earth is the matter? Complaints against George? I can't believe that. Let's sort this out, shall we, Alexander?"

Alex stared at him in shock. "You're an IS Agency inspector?"

"Yes – didn't George tell you? I've been looking after his IS account for years now. I do all his inspections and write up all the reports. If a call comes in regarding George's IS account, I'm the one they send along. If I'm not available, they send Clive. So, what's the problem?" Bagshaw asked. "You complained that George here is abusing you. In what way?"

Alex caught Tyler exchanging a quick glance with Fatso over Bagshaw's shoulder and realised how comprehensively he'd been set up. Tyler had wanted him to make the call. Tyler had facilitated it precisely because he wanted to rub his nose in the futility of his situation. He'd raised Alex's hopes on purpose, because in dashing them, that would hurt Alex even more.

"You know what happens here," Alex told Bagshaw desperately. "You've seen it. Hell, you've been a part of it. You know how Tyler treats his indies. It's against the law for him to prostitute us and use physical violence on us."

"I know nothing of the sort," Bagshaw replied. "Can you show me any evidence of this physical violence? Are you bruised or hurt anywhere?"

"Not right now, but that's irrelevant, isn't it? You're not going to do anything about Tyler's setup here, because you're part of it. Christ, how can you bear to live with yourself, Martin?"

GHOST EYE   **185**

A flicker of self-loathing appeared on Bagshaw's face.

Tyler stepped forward and wrapped an arm around the man's shoulders.

"Because he loves his sons," Tyler said pointedly. "Isn't that right, Martin?"

"I do," Bagshaw agreed sadly, sitting down on the sofa with a heavy sigh. "And I can't lose them, Alexander, you know that. You know there are certain things that if my wife saw... well, she'd divorce me and take my boys away. I can't let that happen."

"So you'll continue to let George Tyler get away with beating and prostituting his ISs to cover up your own sexual indiscretions? You're a bloody coward," Alex flung at him.

Bagshaw gave a helpless shrug. "I know. I've long ago faced up to who I am, Alexander. I'm a weak, stupid fool who made a mistake and must pay for it."

"It's not just you who's paying for it," Alex retorted. "Be brave, Martin. Step up for once. All it takes is one report – one call. You could let the IS Agency know what's really going on here."

"I love my family; I can't lose them." Martin stretched out his arms helplessly. "Did I think, as a little boy, that I'd grow up to be a coward and an idiot? No. Nobody does, but we're none of us the great men we imagined we'd be. Look at you – you stole millions of pounds from your own father."

"And I'm paying for that every single day," Alex said tightly.

"Which is precisely as it should be," Bagshaw told him righteously. "You were sold into servitude as a punishment – it's not supposed to be a holiday."

"It's one thing to lose your freedom, and another to be whored out to perverts like you for the sake of George Tyler's business empire," Alex yelled.

Bagshaw stood up. "There's nothing more to be done here," he said primly, glancing at Tyler. "I'll report that I found conditions here to be excellent, as usual, and the complaint was made by a well-known troublemaker, seeking attention. Given the young man's notoriety, that won't be hard to believe."

"Thank you, Martin." Tyler walked him towards the door. "I'm

sorry you had to make this journey for nothing, but I tell you what, why don't you come for a proper visit sometime soon? You can stay for the weekend. Alexander will be happy to keep you entertained for a couple of days. Then you can really enjoy your time with him, just the two of you, away from prying eyes. Let me know if there's anything in particular you'd like to see him wearing next time, or any little extras we can lay on to help you enjoy your fantasies more. I'm sure it can be arranged." He cast a vicious smile in Alex's direction.

"Martin – please!" Alex called out desperately.

Bagshaw hesitated and glanced back.

"It's not too late – your choices aren't set in stone. You can still be a good man and do the right thing."

Bagshaw shook his head. "I'm sorry, Alexander, I really am. Now, be a good boy for your houder, and I'll come and visit you again soon."

Tyler ushered Bagshaw out of the door and then returned with a broad smile on his face. "Broken yet?"

"Fuck you!" Alex roared. "You set this whole thing up. All that fake anger that I'd stolen Fatso's nanopad to call the IS helpline when you knew about it all along – and you knew they'd send Bagshaw."

"Well, of course." Tyler shrugged. "I did tell you this was a fight, and I don't pull my punches. I *will* win, which means I won't stop until I've broken you."

Fatso gave a grunt of satisfaction; Alex turned on him. "And you – you saw what he did this morning, but you still went along with his sick game. What the hell is wrong with you?"

Fatso shrugged. "What's my name?" he asked.

"What?" Alex stared at him.

"You see me every day, and you can't even be bothered to remember my name. Why should I care about you, when you don't give a fuck about me?"

"You're my guard," Alex said, shaking his head in confusion. "I didn't think you'd want to be my friend." But he was realising he'd made too many wrong assumptions. At school, older boys who looked like Fatso had bullied him, and nobody had ever wanted to be his friend. Now he could see that because he wasn't used to anyone caring about him, he'd made it look as if he didn't care about others. He'd

always lacked the skill of making easy friendships that his brother had. He'd envied Charles his ready smile and happy personality that drew people to him.

Tyler laughed. "Poor Alexander. Outplayed again. You'll have to do better than this to stand any chance of beating me."

"How can I?" he cried helplessly. "You hold all the cards. How can I win?"

"Well, any time you want to give up, you know what you have to do." Tyler stood there expectantly.

Alex felt a wave of impotent fury sweep through him. He would *not* give in and crawl to Tyler on his hands and knees. He couldn't. He'd rather kill himself.

Something inside him snapped. He grabbed the holopad on the coffee table and threw it at the large bar area in the corner of the room. It shattered, slamming into bottles and sending shards of glass flying. Running around the room like a demon, he yelled at the top of his voice, destroying anything he could lay his hands on. Glasses, coffee tables, vases, chairs... they all went flying. He shouted and roared as he kicked and threw, like a child having a temper tantrum, unable to contain the anger inside. He was hyperventilating, lost in his own rage, and couldn't stop himself. Fatso moved towards him, but Tyler gestured him back. He seemed intrigued, leaning against the wall and watching as Alex rampaged around like a man possessed.

Alex wasn't sure how long his fit of insanity lasted, but it seemed like forever until it blew itself out. Then he stood in the centre of the carnage he'd created, panting heavily, unsure what to do next or what the repercussions for his outburst might be.

Tyler ventured towards him cautiously, as if he were a wild animal. He flinched, expecting a blow. But instead, bizarrely and unexpectedly, Tyler put his arms around him. Alex struggled against him, but Tyler hugged him even more tightly until all his anger vanished, leaving him limp and completely drained. Then he started shaking, his legs like jelly, and it was all he could do to stand upright as his knees nearly buckled beneath him.

"My poor, dear Alexander. You must be exhausted," Tyler said. "Here, come and sit down..." He nodded to Fatso, who stepped

forward and righted the sofa Alex had knocked over in his rage. Tyler gently guided Alex towards it, eased him down, then sat next to him. Putting his arm around Alex again, he held him. "There, there. Poor boy. Being broken isn't easy, but we'll get you there. You're doing very well. We'll break your spirit in no time."

Alex hated himself for wanting to cling to Tyler's firm body and cry into his expensive shirt. He tried to be strong, but his emotions took over, and he wept on Tyler's chest, holding on tight to the very person who was causing him so much pain. Tyler stroked his hair and rubbed his back, comforting him as if he were a kindly friend and not his most bitter enemy.

Finally, he stopped sobbing and sat there, utterly numb.

"There, that's better," Tyler said gently. "Good boy." He took a handkerchief from his trouser pocket and gently wiped Alex's tear-stained face. "You know, I think you're finally learning that your actions have consequences. As long as you keep holding out on me, the more painful and upsetting those consequences will be."

"I'll never do what you want," Alex said, in a dull, toneless voice he barely recognised as his own. "Never. You can rape me if you like – you've made it clear I can't stop you – but I won't ask you to fuck me. I won't beg. I won't ever willingly suck your dick or go to your bed."

"Don't think about that now. The time will come, soon enough, and then you'll wonder why you ever resisted." Tyler hugged him closer. Alex slumped against him, too spent to resist. "Now, as a reward, let's watch something together, shall we? I know – let's watch one of my favourites. You'll enjoy this one."

Tyler gave a command to the smartwall, and it began playing a recording. Alex was so out of it that it took him a few moments to register what it was. When he realised, he thought he should be shocked, except he wasn't sure anything Tyler did could ever shock him again.

He was watching himself, cowering in the shower on the night following his encounter with Jake Harper, sobbing his eyes out.

"You're so nearly there," Tyler said in an encouraging tone. "I thought I might have broken you at that point, but you're stronger than I realised. We're getting there, though."

Alex watched himself keening under the shower spray and wasn't sure he could go on. "I loved her, too. I miss her, too. I didn't kill her – it was an accident," he said.

"An accident?" Tyler mocked. "Is that what you tell yourself? Was it an accident that you got into the duck that day, high on croc? Was it an accident that you drove when you could hardly see straight? As I told you, actions have consequences, Alexander."

"I'm sorry. I don't know what you want me to say." Alex buried his face in his hands.

Tyler tangled his fingers in Alex's hair and pulled his head up, so he was forced to watch himself crying on the screen. "I don't want you to say anything; I want you to watch. You see, that pain you're in there, on that screen, is how I've felt every single waking moment since you killed her. It wasn't an accident. You could have told her you'd taken croc and weren't fit to drive, but you didn't – and so you killed the only woman I've ever loved. I want you to feel just a little of the agony I feel every day, and I won't stop until you realise what a worthless little nobody you are. I'm going to strip away everything that makes you feel good about yourself and make you pay for the suffering you've caused to everyone around you – and you know what?"

Alex made no reply, so Tyler jerked sharply on his hair. "What?" Alex whimpered pathetically.

"You'll thank me for it in the end," Tyler told him. "You'll be a much nicer person, you'll be happy in your work here, and you won't cause any trouble for anyone ever again." He rested his head against Alex's. "I know you loved her too, Alexander, but she was the absolute love of my life, and you have to pay for killing her. You do see that, don't you?"

Alex stared at himself sobbing his heart out on the screen. "Yes, sir," he said quietly. "I see it. I have to pay."

"Good." Tyler gave him another hug. "We're getting there. Soon, Alexander – soon."

Chapter Ten

OCTOBER 2095

Josiah

He walked down the street, carrying a cardboard tray containing five cups of hot tea. There was a red car across the road. He stepped off the kerb towards it... and then hesitated. Something bad waited for him there. He tried to stop, to turn away, but his feet ignored him. They carried on walking, inexorably, taking him to his dreadful fate. He shouted in frustration, willing them to stop ... and then five cups of tea arced into the air. He felt warm liquid splash his arms and chest, and when he looked down, he saw that it was blood, staining his purple sweater with vivid crimson streaks.

He woke with a start. For a second, it was the same as always – he was alone and gasping for air – and then suddenly, unexpectedly, it was different. A pair of warm arms encircled him, comforting him.

"Hey, it's okay. You're okay," a gentle voice murmured.

He blinked rapidly, several times, still breathing hard.

Alex was holding him close and rubbing soothing circles on his back.

"It's okay. Just a nightmare," Josiah said, relaxing. He rested his chin on Alex's shoulder.

"The same nightmare?" Alex asked softly.

"Yes," he said gruffly into Alex's neck.

"Peter?"

"Yes. It's always the same. It's the night he died, and I'm walking across the street towards the car. I wake up screaming before I get there."

"Because you know what's waiting for you, or because you don't want to face it?"

Josiah thought about it for a moment. "Both. As I'm walking, I sometimes tell myself that this time it could turn out differently, but it never does. It can't."

"Do you ever think about the night he died?" Alex asked quietly. "I mean, really think about it? Instead of finding ways to avoid it?"

Josiah drew back and gazed at him. In the dark, he could only make out the light gleam of Alex's curious eyes and the shape of his head, his hair tousled from sleep. "No," he answered stiffly. "I prefer to remember happier moments from my life with Peter, not that one."

"Maybe that's why it haunts you?" Alex suggested. "Because you block it out? Maybe you've given it too much power."

"It was the worst night of my life. I don't want to think about it," Josiah said wearily.

"I just thought it might help if you allowed yourself to remember it, instead of suppressing it."

"I can't change what happened – why wallow in it?"

"I understand." Alex brushed his hand through Josiah's hair. "Are you feeling better now?"

"I'm fine." Josiah knew it was completely inappropriate for him to have allowed Alex to first sleep in his bed, and now to comfort him like this. Elsie, Big Jen, and Liz would be horrified if they knew – as would Esther. He pulled away. "What time is it?"

"Around three, I think." Alex glanced at the clock on the bedside table. "Yes, just gone three. Plenty of time for more sleep."

Josiah grunted and rolled onto his back. He stared at the ceiling, keeping stiffly to his side of the bed. Seconds later, Alex slid over and rested his head on his shoulder. He knew he should shrug the IS off, but instead he wrapped an arm around him and pulled him close. Maybe Alex was right. Maybe he should allow himself to remember it properly instead of always pushing the memory away.

He steeled himself and then closed his eyes and allowed his mind to return to that night, a little over seven years ago...

———

"Not that I don't appreciate you going all kinky on me, but this isn't the way to the bedroom," Josiah pointed out as Peter guided him along the hallway. He'd arrived home from work ten minutes before, and now his eyes were obscured by the soft cashmere scarf he'd given Peter for Christmas the previous year.

"No, it isn't," Peter replied, sounding like an excited schoolboy. Josiah could feel the nervous energy radiating from him.

"Well, I hope the payoff will be just as good as if we *were* in the bedroom."

"Oh yeah." Peter was positively purring. "It will."

Josiah heard a door opening, and then Peter guided him down the small flight of steps into the garage.

"Is it a present of some kind?" Josiah asked.

"It's not your birthday for ages."

"You don't have to wait until my birthday. You could get me a surprise present just for being such a nice husband."

"Hah!" Peter said. There was a pause, and then, "I could, actually. I'm not very good at thinking of stuff like that. You're the nice husband; I'm the crap one."

"I wouldn't say that. You have your moments." Josiah grinned beneath the makeshift blindfold.

"Okay, ready?"

Josiah felt himself being moved into position, and then Peter undid the scarf and whisked it away with a big "Ta-dah!"

Josiah found himself standing in front of the Pre-R car Peter had been working on for so long that sometimes he'd joked he felt like a "car widower". "What am I looking at?" He frowned.

"This. It. Her! She's done!" Peter waved a hand at the gleaming red Jaguar.

He'd been slowly and lovingly restoring her to a pristine state over the past two years, but the changes had been so incremental Josiah

couldn't see anything different about her now. She'd long since ceased to be a pile of old metal taking up space in the garage, Peter having restored her so she looked far more like a car and less like a big metal blob. He'd spent the last few months polishing her daily, until the scent of car wax permeated every article of his clothing, his hair, the garage, and most of the house, too. But even so, the car didn't actually work, because Peter had become stuck trying to get hold of some part – Josiah hadn't been paying attention to its name.

"Done? As in...?" He raised an eyebrow.

"Driveable. She goes," Peter said excitedly. "I've restored her to her original condition – she's as good now as the day her first owner drove her off the garage forecourt in 1999."

"Before the waters rose and the world changed," Josiah said. Maybe that was why Peter had poured so much of his love into this car. She was a symbol of a better time, a glamorous era when people drove beautiful, sleek vehicles, not clunky ducks. It was a time Peter had heard about from his grandmother and associated with all that was good, and kind, and free – in stark comparison to the world now. Josiah suspected that if they could go back in time, Peter would find much to be dissatisfied with, but the fantasy was compelling all the same. Walking around the car, he listened as Peter pointed out all its best features.

"And this, here..." Peter lifted the bonnet and pointed at some inner workings of the engine. "I thought I'd never get hold of the part I needed, but then this guy came into the garage, and I got talking to him, and he knew someone who knew someone..."

Josiah zoned out, just enjoying Peter's babbling enthusiasm – he positively glowed when talking about his beloved car.

"It's a huge achievement," Josiah said when his husband paused for breath. "I'm proud of you. Well done."

Peter looked as if he'd explode with joy. He launched into what would, undoubtedly, have been another incomprehensible description of engine components if Josiah hadn't grabbed him, lifted him onto the highly polished bonnet, and kissed him to within an inch of his life.

"Mmmm..." Peter sighed.

Josiah drew back. "Something this beautiful should be properly

christened, shouldn't she?" he suggested with a wicked grin. "I might not be wearing leathers this time but... remember Geneva?"

Peter's eyes lit up. "Here? Now?"

"Here. Now. On top of all this smooth, shiny red metal." Josiah traced a finger over the car.

"Yes... God, yes," Peter agreed enthusiastically.

Josiah peeled Peter out of his trousers and boxer shorts and threw them onto the garage floor. Then he glanced around. "Please tell me you have something here that we can use, so I don't have to ruin the moment by traipsing upstairs for the lube – and don't bloody well suggest engine grease."

"Vaseline – over there," Peter said, pointing at the garage shelves, which groaned under the weight of a vast array of tools, paints, brushes, and other detritus. Peter was a terrible hoarder, and his collection seemed to grow daily.

"What the hell do you need Vaseline in here for?" Josiah asked, grabbing it off the shelf.

"Prevents battery corrosion – smear it on the terminals," Peter said with a grin.

Josiah was soon buried deep in his husband. Peter looked debauched, with his head flung back and his bare arse sliding up and down on the smooth surface of the Jaguar. It was the most beautiful thing he'd ever seen.

He hoped the neighbours couldn't hear as Peter roared his way to an explosive orgasm. Josiah came with less fanfare. Then he leaned forward and, resting his hands on the bonnet, kissed Peter lovingly on the lips before withdrawing, reluctantly, from the sweet warmth of his body.

"I should buy you that present," Peter said, gazing up at him, sex-stupid and sated. "You are a very, very nice husband."

"You're not too bad, yourself." Josiah grinned. Picking up Peter's clothes, he threw them at him. "But you might need to polish the car again. She definitely received a good christening."

Sliding off the bonnet, Peter got dressed, then grabbed a cloth and polished until the Jaguar was as good as new again.

Josiah watched with a benign smile on his face, wondering how

anyone could love an inanimate object as much as Peter loved this old car.

"So, want to go for a ride?" Peter asked.

"I thought we just did." Josiah winked.

"Ha-ha. No, a real ride – out on the street."

"I don't think we have time." Josiah glanced at his watch. "We're doing the pick-up at eight. We'll have to leave soon."

"I know – um..." Peter grimaced. "I told Elsie we'd do it in the car."

"You did what?" Josiah glared at him. Life with Peter was never dull, but he wished his husband's impulsive behaviour was less risky.

"I wanted to take her out for a spin." Peter grinned. "Come on, Joe – where's your sense of adventure? It'll be fun."

"Yeah, because going to pick up a bunch of escaped indies in one of the most conspicuous vehicles in the country is a really good idea. I'm going to call Elsie and tell her we're going in the duck, as usual." Josiah reached for his nanopad.

"It's too late," Peter interrupted. "She's already told the indies to look for a red Pre-R car parked on Station Road in West Wickham at eight p.m."

Josiah could have thumped him. "Peter, this is stupid. We can go out in the car any time. We're collecting escaped indies – if someone sees them getting into this, they'll remember it."

"It also helps them identify which car to get into," Peter retorted. "Last time, we told them to look for a grey duck, and that poor woman got into the wrong AV. That's just as dangerous. The driver could have reported her."

"No, this is far more dangerous," Josiah argued. "Oh, what am I saying? That's part of the thrill for you, isn't it?"

"I'd never put you in more danger than necessary to get the job done," Peter said, looking suddenly serious. "Look, Joe – this is a quick job – just a pick-up and drop-off at Jan's place. There are no lost zones to cross – we can do the entire thing on roads, so there's no need to be in a duck. I'm not a complete idiot – I checked." He gave an appeasing little smile. "C'mon – we'll be home by eleven, no harm done."

"Fine," Josiah said grudgingly. "But next time, talk to me first before making this kind of decision. We agreed on that, remember?"

Peter was much better at including him in his decisions these days, but sometimes he still forgot. It wasn't easy for him to curb his naturally spontaneous behaviour for long enough to run an idea past Josiah. However, they'd found a way to mostly meet in the middle; Josiah had learned not to sweat the small stuff, while Peter had learned to share the big stuff. But problems still sometimes arose over grey areas in between, like this.

"Sorry, but seriously, it'll be fine. Changing vehicles every so often is a good idea, in case anyone is on to us," Peter said.

This seemed like a flimsy justification to Josiah. "If you say so." He stomped back up the garage steps.

"Where are you going?"

He glanced back down to where Peter was standing beside the Jaguar, his mop of dark hair still mussed up from their love-making, and gestured at his rumpled trousers. "To change."

———

That was the last time they'd made love. Josiah could still remember how sexy Peter had looked as he lay, panting and happy, over the bonnet of his beloved car. If he'd known those were to be his last few hours alive, Josiah was sure that was how he'd have chosen to spend them.

Moving carefully away from Alex so as not to wake him, he slid out of the bed and headed to the en-suite bathroom, where he sloshed cold water on his face.

"Coward," he told his reflection in the mirror. "You're afraid of getting to the bad part."

He dried his face and then paused in the doorway to gaze at Alex, lying in the bed. It had been seven years since he'd shared that bed with Peter, and he'd felt nothing for anyone else in all that time... until now. It was a bitter irony that this man was the ultimate in unobtainable. Josiah didn't have the millions required to buy him, and it was impossible to rescue him without exposing the Kathleen Line. It would do him no good to fall for Alex – it was as hopeless as wanting Peter back, because he couldn't have either of them.

Returning to the bed, he slipped in beside his IS. Alex mumbled something sleepily, then turned over and rested his hand on his chest. Josiah wrapped his arms around him, and Alex nestled into him like a sleeping cat. He buried his face in the crook of Alex's neck and inhaled the scent of his hair. Then he closed his eyes again.

He returned to the garage to find Peter polishing a non-existent smear off the Jaguar's door.

"Ready?" Peter asked excitedly, glancing up.

Josiah had changed into a pair of smart blue jeans, a soft purple sweater, and a navy-blue sports coat.

"Mmm, you look good in that," Peter said, reaching out to give him a placatory kiss.

"You're only saying that because I'm in a bad mood," he snorted.

"Yeah – but you do look good." Peter winked as they got into the car. He turned on the engine, and the Jaguar purred into life. "Doesn't she sound great?" he enthused as Josiah luxuriated in the soft black leather seats. "They're heated," he said proudly, pressing a switch.

A few seconds later, Josiah felt a gentle warmth start to radiate through his back and bottom.

"They really knew how to design objects of beauty in the Pre-R," Peter said, clicking the garage door open. "We seem to have lost that art these days."

"Someone should design a duck that looks and sounds like this," Josiah said as Peter edged the car slowly out of the garage.

"Maybe, now that more people can afford them, they will." Peter shrugged. "I read somewhere that Tyler Tech has some new design in the works that might be a game-changer."

"As long as they get me to where I want to go without drowning me in a lost zone, I don't really care how they look," Josiah said. "But I appreciate the comfort – this feels nice."

Peter gave a chuckle of glee that Josiah was joining him in the car worship.

The car was smoother on the road than a duck, so Josiah sat back

in his heated seat, enjoying the ride. It was a blustery autumn evening, with wet brown leaves falling around them, squally winds, and occasional downpours of rain. He noticed a few heads turning to look at the Jaguar. "Only you could possibly think it was a good idea to go on a secret mission in a vehicle this distinctive," he grumbled.

"Are we back to that again? I'm sorry," Peter said, not sounding it. "You have to admit that she glides along smoothly, though."

"Yeah, she does," he agreed grudgingly.

They reached Station Road, but the street was lined with more ducks than usual. Peter found a parking spot, but had to angle the Jag to cross the path of oncoming traffic. This pick-up point had been chosen randomly, as they all were, never being decided upon until the day to avoid being predictable. Josiah made a mental note not to use it again. He glanced at his watch: 7.45 p.m. They always tried to arrive a little early. Escaped indies were understandably nervous, and if their rescuers were even only a few minutes late, it greatly increased their anxiety.

"So, who are we waiting for?" Peter asked, pulling on the handbrake.

Josiah fished his nanopad out of his pocket and glanced at the message from Elsie. "Three men: Matthew, Lars, and Ben."

It still astonished Josiah how many indies reached out to the network on the strength of word of mouth. He and Peter made regular pick-ups, usually two or three times a week. Sometimes, they took their escapees all the way to the coast themselves, and sometimes they placed them in a safe house overnight and one of their volunteers took over. It would be impossible for him and Peter to deal with them all. Luckily, the police, investigation agencies, and freelance bounty hunters were all in competition with each other for the rewards many houders offered for the safe return of their indies, so they didn't share information. Enough escapees were still rounded up and returned to their houders that the relatively small amount that the Kathleen Line managed to rescue was hidden.

Sometimes, Josiah wondered how long they could get away with it. He knew they risked being sold into servitude themselves, if caught. Peter had a plan to make the most of the publicity if that

happened, but it was small comfort. Josiah tried not to think about it.

"Matthew, Lars, and Ben. Any intel?" Peter asked.

"Not much," Josiah replied, scanning Elsie's notes for more information. "Lars worked for a cleaning company – apparently they were crammed in, ten to a small room, lying on the floor – no mattresses and just one blanket and pillow each. They got sent out to clean sixteen hours a day, seven days a week, with no breaks, and were fed the absolute minimum."

"Modern-day workhouse," Peter murmured. "That's all it is."

"Lars escaped a few months ago and has been trying to get out of the country ever since. He nearly got caught at the port in Folkestone a few weeks ago, so he's a bit jumpy. He met some other escapees when he was down there, and one of them passed on Elsie's number. Elsie said he sounded agitated – he was sure a bounty hunter or IA was after him."

"Seems unlikely," Peter said. "They usually only go after high-value escapees, and working in a cleaning company hardly makes Lars that. I suspect the reward for his return is minimal – the company can probably pick up another IS cheaper than getting him back."

"Yeah, usual escapee paranoia probably," Josiah said. They'd seen it plenty of times before – most of their indies were jumpy, forever looking over their shoulders. It was understandable.

"What about Matthew and Ben? Anything on them?" Peter asked.

"Ben – not much. Quiet and scared, according to Elsie. He escaped from a factory about a week ago. Matthew – cultured voice, had a long story about how he became an IS that Elsie suspects was bullshit. Escaped a month ago and has been on the run ever since."

"So, one's paranoid, one's petrified, and one's a phoney." Peter grinned. "Sounds like a fairly typical batch."

"Yeah. Poor bastards." Josiah grunted. He glanced at his watch. "Eight p.m. They should be here soon. In fact, I think we have one coming our way."

He pointed at a hooded figure walking quickly up the street. The man glanced around furtively as he got close, and then opened the back passenger door and slid inside.

"Am I in the right place? Elsie sent me," he said anxiously.

"You are. I'm Peter, and this is Joe. What's your name?" Peter asked cheerily. He was much better at putting people at their ease, so he always did the "first contact" bit.

"Ben," the man said, although Josiah had already figured that out simply by how scared he looked. "Uh, Smith – Ben Smith," their new escapee added. He had several days' growth of beard on his face, just visible above the scarf wrapped around his neck and lower jaw, and his hoodie was at least three sizes too big for him – probably stolen. He leaned into the corner of the car in the seat directly behind Josiah's, making himself as small as possible, his hands sunk deep into his pockets.

"We're waiting for two more – Lars and Matthew – and then we'll set off, Ben," Peter explained. "We'll be taking you to a safe house overnight, and then we'll get you to the coast and out of the country. By this time tomorrow you'll be in France – and free."

"Thanks," Ben muttered. He put his head down and pressed himself even more tightly into the corner. Like Peter had said – petrified.

Josiah cleared his throat and turned in his seat, trying to think of something to put the terrified man at ease.

"We've got a change of clothes for you at the safe house," was all he could think of – practical and pertinent. "Something clean and dry. Good food waiting there, too."

Ben gave a furtive nod and then disappeared back into his hoodie, like a turtle.

Josiah sighed and gave up.

A few seconds later, a giant loomed into view. Josiah was a big man, but their next escapee had a good three inches on him; huge and gangling, he had brown hair and a straggly ginger beard. He jogged the last few paces to the car, opened the door, and hunching, peered in. Unlike Ben, he didn't immediately get in as Elsie had instructed.

"Who are you?" the giant demanded. "If you're from an IA, then I warn you, I'm armed." He stuck his fingers into his jacket pocket in such a poor impression of a gun that Josiah almost laughed.

"You must be Lars," Peter said gently. "It's okay – you're safe. We're

not an investigation agency – Elsie sent us to help you escape. I'm Peter, and this is my husband, Josiah." He jerked his thumb in Josiah's direction.

Lars stood there for a moment, hopping from one foot to the other uncertainly.

"It's okay, Lars. You're safe. We're here to help," Peter said softly. "Aren't we, Joe?"

"Yeah – get in, Lars. This is Ben – he just arrived. We're just waiting for one more person – someone called Matthew – and then we can set off," Josiah said, wishing he had Peter's knack for sounding soothing instead of brisk.

Finally, Lars manoeuvred himself onto the back seat, and the rank smell of his body odour immediately assaulted them. Josiah exchanged a little grimace with Peter; it was common for escapees to smell if they'd been on the run for any period of time.

"Bit wet and cold tonight," Peter said. "But you'll soon warm up now you're in the car. When Matthew turns up, we'll get you to a safe house where you can have a bath and a change of clothes." He shot Josiah a little wink.

Lars blew on his fingers, his eyes darting and his knees bouncing up and down with nervous energy.

"Yup, definitely paranoid," Josiah muttered under his breath. Peter mouthed "Shh" at him, and poked his thigh firmly with his finger. "So, are you guys all right?" he asked the men sat in the back brightly. "Any injuries we should know about? We've got a sympathetic doctor on call if anyone needs medical attention, but we need to know about it now, so we can arrange it."

Ben shook his head, causing his hood to fall even further over his downcast eyes.

"We should leave now. I think I was followed," Lars said urgently.

"What makes you say that, Lars?" Josiah queried, turning again in his seat to look at the big man. Lars might be paranoid, but that didn't mean his fears were unfounded.

"Investigation Agency, or bounty hunter – I'm not sure which. I was followed for two miles yesterday but managed to lose them."

"Do you have any reason to suspect an IA is on your trail?" Josiah

probed. "By law, they have to identify themselves and ask to see some ID – they can't just follow you around for hours on end."

"A bounty hunter, then. Everyone knows they act outside the law," Lars said, looking out of the windows wildly.

"No offence, but bounty hunters only go after high-value escaped indies; a cleaning company IS isn't likely to attract them," Josiah said drily. "Ben – where did you escape from?"

Ben looked like a frightened rabbit at being asked a direct question; he mumbled something about a factory into his scarf.

"How much longer must we wait?" Lars demanded. "We must go now." He waved his hands in the air. Ben shrank back as far away from Lars's manic energy as possible.

"It's only 8.10," Peter said patiently. "We always wait for half an hour. It's not always easy for our escapees to get to us on time. Some of you don't have money for transport and have to walk to the rendezvous point. You're scared and alone, so we take that into account and give you some leeway."

"Half an hour is too long," Lars complained.

"Well, that's how long we're going to wait," Josiah said firmly, glaring at the man.

"How about some music?" Peter suggested, trying to calm the situation. He shot Josiah a warning look and pressed a button on the car's dashboard. "This will interest you – it's a CD player, so it's perfectly in period for a Pre-R car."

"The music isn't, though." Josiah snorted as the familiar sounds of one of Peter's favourite artists crooned at them. "Peter's a fan of New Wave Emo music," he told their passengers, "which seems to mean sad young people with raspy voices singing daft songs with incomprehensible lyrics that sound like they mean something but don't."

Peter laughed.

In his wing mirror, Josiah saw Ben peek out from under his hood to gaze at them, apparently startled by their old-married-couple schtick. But he and Peter did this all the time. Their light banter was normal for them, but must have sounded incongruous to Ben, who was probably lost in the worry and drama of his escape. Lars was still looking out of the windows, rocking manically.

GHOST EYE

"Joe, on the other hand, is a fan of Pre-R rock, when men were men and liked to form bands with bonkers names, throw electronic goods out of hotel windows, and sing about important man stuff," Peter joked. It was an old argument, and one they got into frequently and with relish.

"At least Pre-R rock is more in keeping with the Pre-R car," Josiah pointed out. "How did you even get this modern trash onto a CD?"

"Pre-R burner tech." Peter shrugged. "Not very hard to find."

"Oh, God." Josiah sighed as the familiar sultry tones of a rising star going only by the name of Ashton blared out sonorously.

Old dreams fade slow
You once said that you'd never let go
Sweet words, wide smiles
You always said that you'd stay awhile

"Oh no, I'm so bloody sad, please let me drone on about how sad I am," Josiah mocked, in tune.

"It doesn't go like that," Peter reprimanded, turning up the volume as the chorus started.

They said you'd been a sinner
They said you'd been a saint
I didn't want either
Just wanted it to be fate

"What's it about?" Josiah demanded. "It's all just sad words about nothing."

"Nonsense, it's a song about love, and yearning, and... stuff," Peter said.

"And stuff?" Josiah made a face.

"You know – stuff." Peter waved his hand in the air, grinning.

Josiah turned around in his seat. "So – how about a vote?" he asked. "Anyone want something less pretentious? Something with a beat, perhaps? Maybe The Beatles? Or Queen?"

Ben shrugged and crossed his arms over his chest, hugging himself

tightly, but Lars looked calmer, so Josiah thought the banter had defused that situation at least.

"I'm the driver," Peter said firmly. "And the driver always gets to choose the music."

"Yes, Captain." Josiah tipped him a salute, as he always did when Peter pulled rank.

Peter laughed and sang along to the next verse.

Fever – rages on, making small talk was never much fun.
Voices – too loud, skin on skin speaking words unsung.

"God, it's awful," Josiah sighed as the chorus repeated.

"Hey – how about you go and get us something to drink while we're waiting?" Peter suggested. "I'll have a tea." They always parked near a café, so they could buy hot drinks and food for the escapees, some of whom hadn't eaten in days.

"Good idea. What do you guys want? Ben? Lars?" Josiah asked, pulling out his wallet to check he had enough cash cards. He never used his bank account, so these kinds of transactions couldn't be traced later. Lars just stared at him, but Ben whispered "tea" into his scarf. "Anything to eat?" Josiah pressed. Ben shook his head, while Lars ignored him completely. "Okay – five teas, then. We'll assume our missing Matthew will also fancy a cuppa when he shows up," he said cheerfully, getting out of the car. "Hopefully this horrible song will be over by the time I get back." He grinned at Peter.

"Hah. Just for that, I'm going to play it again," Peter laughed. Josiah made a face at him and left, with Ashton's sad voice serenading him as he walked away.

Never heard the branches of the tree against my window
Scratching on, and on, and on...
Never felt the cold of winter creeping in
Snow on the sheets where you left me.

Much to his annoyance, he found himself humming the mournful melody as he waited for his tea order. He laughed, thinking how badly

Peter would mock him if he were still humming it when he returned to the car. He took the tea – five warm cups tucked into a cardboard tray – and left the café.

It had started raining again. He paused on the kerb and pulled up his jacket collar with his free hand to ward off the damp. He stepped off the kerb and began crossing the road. Halfway across, a piercing scream rang out, and the car rocked. His arm jerked in surprise, and the five cups of tea went flying upwards.

He never saw where they landed. He was sprinting across the road and wrenching open the rear passenger door, where he found a wild struggle going on in the back seat. Lars was wielding a long sharp knife, and Ben was fighting to take it from him. Lars pushed Ben away and lunged towards Peter. Ben slung a clumsy punch that deflected his aim – but not for long. Lars raised the knife again, aiming for Peter's neck. Josiah threw himself into the car and grabbed Lars's wrist, holding it tight.

"Drop it," he ordered. Lars struggled, trying to pull his arm free. "Peter – help me! Get out and pull him out of the car," he yelled, sinking his fingers even harder into Lars's wrist. He twisted Lars's hand, so the man had no choice but to drop the weapon.

Lars lashed out with his free hand to deliver a stinging blow to Josiah's jaw. "You're a fucking investigator! I saw your badge in your wallet. You're going to hand us in and claim the reward," he yelled.

"Peter – get him out of the car," Josiah shouted again, punching Lars repeatedly. Peter made no reply. Ben scrambled out past Josiah, ran around to the other side of the car, and yanked the door open. Josiah pushed, and Ben pulled, and between them they managed to force Lars out onto the pavement. Lars lay there, panting, and then got to his feet and stumbled off down the dark street.

Josiah turned to Peter. "What the hell just happened? Why didn't you help?" he yelled. Then he stopped. Peter was sitting in the driver's seat, his hands pressed against his neck, an expression of surprise on his face.

"I..." He looked down at the stream of bright red blood gushing out over the car seat. "Joe... I think he got me."

"Lars went for him," Ben gabbled as Josiah ran around to the other

side of the car. "He suddenly lunged forward and stabbed Peter in the neck. I didn't even see he had a knife until then. I grabbed his arm and pulled him back before he could stab Peter again, and then you got here... Is he okay? Is Peter okay?"

"Christ!" Josiah pulled open the driver's door, and Peter fell sideways against him. He sat down on the pavement and gathered Peter in his arms, trying to assess the damage. Pulling Peter's hands away, he saw the deep wound in his neck, pumping out blood.

"Call an ambulance," he shouted, putting his hands over the wound and pressing down hard. Ben looked at him helplessly. His scarf had been torn off in the struggle, his hood was thrown back, and in the glow of the streetlight Josiah could see that he was very young. He looked like a frightened child, but to his credit, he didn't run. He pulled a nanopad out of his pocket.

"Joe." Peter raised a bloodstained hand to touch Josiah's face. "Sorry," he said. "Didn't see the knife."

"Don't talk, Peter. Help's on the way. You're going to be fine," Josiah told him frantically.

"Fight," Peter said, a little smile on his lips. "Just like the old days, huh, Joe? Scavs."

"Shh, you idiot. Just shh."

"Cold," Peter muttered.

Josiah pulled him closer, holding him tight to try and warm him. "Gonna be okay," Peter told him. "S'okay, Joe. S'all gonna be okay."

"Yes, it's going to be fine," Josiah told him desperately.

"Don't go after him, Joe," Peter whispered. "Lars... Let him go."

"He fucking stabbed you."

"Not his fault. Promise me, Joe."

"Shut up, Peter."

Ben crouched down in front of him. "The ambulance is on its way. What do you want me to do now?"

"Go," Josiah told him firmly.

"But..." Ben looked at him helplessly. It was raining hard now, and his dark hair was plastered to his head, his clothes sodden.

"The paramedics will be here soon – and so will the police. They'll question you. Save yourself. Go!" Josiah ordered.

GHOST EYE   207

Ben got to his feet, then hesitated. "I'm sorry," he said. "I didn't see the knife... It all happened so fast... I'm so sorry."

There was a noise from the direction of the café, and then a group of people started crossing the road towards them. Ben glanced at them, and then back at Josiah and Peter, lying on the pavement. Then, with one more desolate "sorry", he turned and ran.

"Joe," Peter whispered. The flow of blood seemed to be slowing, which Josiah thought was a good thing – until he realised it was because Peter's heart was failing. "Promise me, Joe. No revenge. Keep saving them. Promise." Peter stroked his face feebly.

"You'll be up and about in no time – we'll save them together," Josiah soothed.

"Promise," Peter gasped. His hand fell away from Josiah's face. "Promise." His lips made the word, but no sound came from them.

"I promise," Josiah told him, holding him tight. "Don't go, Peter. Stay with me. Please don't leave me." He could feel Peter's heart slowing under his fingertips – beat, pause... beat. Beat... pause... beat... pause... pause... Josiah waited for the next beat, but it didn't come.

"Peter!" he screamed, patting his husband's face frantically. Peter's eyes were still open, but they were empty, and his face was deathly white. Suddenly, the world around him came back into focus in excruciating detail. He was sitting on the pavement, holding Peter's lifeless body in his arms. A little crowd from the café had formed around them, and he could hear the sound of sirens in the distance.

His purple sweater was covered in blood, as was the driver's seat of the Jaguar, and the pavement, and his hands. The car door was open, and Peter's stupid emo music was still playing as if the most terrible thing in the world hadn't just happened.

The rain was pouring down in earnest now, washing streaks of red water into the gutter – and Peter, who had spent his life helping others, was lying dead in his arms, killed by one of the people he'd been trying to save.

Josiah felt as if his heart had been ripped from his body. He threw back his head and howled like a wounded animal, holding Peter tight against his chest and rocking back and forth as he screamed out his pain.

Josiah sat up in bed, unable to bear it. Alex was sprawled out beside him, fast asleep. Josiah rolled out of the bed, breathing hard. He didn't know what he was doing, just that he had to escape the pain, to do something – anything – to stop it hurting.

He ran out of the bedroom, down the stairs, and unlocked the garage door with trembling fingers. Snapping on the light, he paused at the top of the steps, gazing at the red car. Then he ran towards it, wanting to punch it, to vent all his sadness, fury, and grief upon it, but the car hadn't killed Peter – he had. He'd killed him by carrying his ID card with him that fateful night. By opening his wallet to check he had cash cards. By letting Lars see he worked for an investigation agency. By being stupid and careless, despite all the times he'd warned Peter about the very same thing. He sank down beside the Jaguar, shaking.

From a great distance he heard the sound of a door opening, and then hurried footsteps.

"Hey." Alex knelt down in front of him. "What's going on, Joe?"

"I did as you suggested. Let's just say it didn't help," Josiah said hoarsely.

"Shit. When I told you that you should face the memory, I didn't mean on your own. I thought I'd be there with you, talking it through," Alex responded softly. He wrapped his arms around Josiah and held him.

Josiah was glad of his warmth, because he was shaking in earnest now. "Sorry... used to doing things alone," he muttered.

Alex pulled his head up to face him and looked at him searchingly. "What do you remember?" he asked.

"All of it," Josiah said through chattering teeth.

Alex sank back on his heels and gazed at him. "Do you want to talk about it? It might help."

Josiah shook his head. "Want to. Can't," he refused, because he couldn't tell Alex about that terrible night without revealing the existence of the Kathleen Line and his part in it.

Alex nodded slowly. "Okay. I understand."

Josiah's entire body was now trembling violently. Alex pulled him

close and rocked him in his arms as if he were a child. Josiah buried his face in the hollow of Alex's neck, remembering how he'd cradled Peter in the same way, willing his husband to come back and still be alive. He let out a guttural sob that felt as if it had been wrenched from the pit of his stomach. He bit back another sob, trying desperately not to fall apart in front of his IS.

Alex had other ideas. "Let it out," he insisted. "You've been holding on to it for such a long time, Joe. It's time to let it out, so you can start to heal. Peter wouldn't want you to still feel so bad after all this time."

"Can't," Josiah said through gritted teeth.

Alex took hold of his face and looked into his eyes. "Have you ever cried?" he questioned. "Have you ever let yourself cry for him, in all this time?"

Josiah shook his head mutely. He'd howled into the rain like a wolf that night, but he hadn't cried. He'd forced his emotions down, frozen in that moment of time, and locked them away.

"You should," Alex chided softly.

"Hurts too much," Josiah rasped, wrapping his arms around his body.

"Not as much as gripping on to it for all these years does. I've got you, Joe. I'll keep you safe." Alex tightened his embrace around Josiah, holding him within the protective circle of his arms. "Just let it go," he urged. "Let *him* go. Set him free. Set yourself free. Let Peter go."

Alexander's soft, insistent words broke something deep inside him and another great, wrenching sob wracked his body. This time, he couldn't hold back; he gave a wild, keening cry, then another, and another. Then he sobbed in earnest, weeping for the man he'd lost, and all they could have done and achieved together. He cried for the sheer unnecessary waste of a life, sacrificed on the blade of a misunderstanding, and he cried for the loss of a truly good person who'd been making a genuine difference. He cried so hard that his entire body heaved – and through it all, Alex was with him, holding him tight, taking every ounce of his pain and comforting him through it.

Finally, his grief was spent, and he had no more tears left to shed. He sat beside the car, utterly exhausted, with Alex rocking him gently.

He should have felt embarrassed, falling apart like this in front of his indie, but he didn't.

"Come on. You're freezing. Let's go back to bed," Alex said.

Pulling Josiah to his feet, he slung an arm around his shoulders and helped him up the stairs to the bedroom. Guiding Josiah onto the bed, he climbed in beside him and pulled the duvet over them both. Then he wrapped his arms around Josiah again, keeping him safe, as he'd promised.

Josiah was aware of a strange sense of peace. The pain in his heart was gone, leaving him empty. His body felt light, released from the aching heaviness that had weighed him down for so many years. He was no longer a slave to the tragedy that had defined him for so long. He'd been set free – yet the man beside him, who had helped to free him, was the one person he could never release in return.

Somewhere, at the dim, weary edge of his consciousness, there was a new set of questions:

Who was he now, and where did he go from here?

Chapter Eleven

SEPTEMBER 2088

Alex

Tyler sent Alex back to his room in the middle of the night. The picture of his father had, at least, disappeared, and the walls were now a plain plum colour. He shut the door and sat on his bed in the dark, fully clothed, trying to process the appalling events of the day.

He was still there the next morning when there was a soft, apologetic knock on the door. Solange poked her head around it.

"Hey." She tiptoed into the room. "You didn't go to bed last night?"

"No." Wrapping his arms around his body, he stared into space. She sat down beside him and rested her head on his shoulder.

"Ted told me what happened yesterday; Mick filled him in during handover."

Alex frowned. "Who's Mick?"

She made a face. "Fatso. Ted calls him 'Big Mick'. In fact, that's what pretty much everyone calls him, except you."

"He's a bastard."

"He's got his story, same as everyone. You could try being friends with people, Alex, instead of creating new enemies."

He looked down at her helplessly. "I've never had any friends, Solange. Even at school – I didn't fit in, and nobody seemed to like me. Sometimes, the other kids pretended they liked me because I was

Charles's brother, or because my family had money, but I could always see through them. Then, later, people said they liked me because they wanted to fuck me, but nobody ever really liked me for me."

"You *are* a bit of a weirdo," Solange told him affectionately. "I think that because of your wealth, and Charles's fame, and because you're so beautiful, people always assume you're arrogant, when actually you're just shy and a bit lost in your own little world."

"Croc helped. It made it easier for me to talk to people at school. It's also why I got expelled so much." Alex shot her a wry smile. "That and being a smart-arse; I can't seem to stop myself."

"You can be very sweet, too," she said, poking him in the ribs.

"I don't feel it. I'm sarcastic and moody. Nobody wants to know that guy."

"I do." She kissed the side of his face.

"You're the only real friend I've ever had," he told her, gently stroking her hand. "Not when we were out there, in the world, because that wasn't real, for you or for me – but in here, like this, you are. In here, I know you don't want me for my looks, or money, or status, and you don't like me only because Tyler ordered you to. You really do like me."

"Of course I like you." She snuggled up against him. "Ted does, too. You *can* make friends, Alex. I judge you by how you've behaved towards me through all this. You could have hated me – maybe you should have – but you stepped in when Drummond was beating me, and you've gone out of your way to protect me ever since. You're a good person – very loyal and kind – but you don't let people get close enough to see that."

"Fatso... Mick... was pissed off with me because I didn't know his name yesterday."

"He sees you as the spoilt rich kid who needs to be brought down, like the media says, and like Tyler says, too. Most people don't look deeper."

"He's my guard. I didn't exactly think he'd want to be my friend. Maybe I *was* rude towards him, but I'm angry about being here."

"I understand that, but you do put up a lot of barriers, and most people won't bother to look beneath them. They'll take you at face

value. You're kind of notorious – everyone thinks they know you, but nobody actually does. But I think you prefer it that way." He glanced at her in surprise. "You prefer people hating you for who they think you are, rather than letting them in and running the risk they'll hate you for who you really are," she said.

"Maybe." He put an arm around her and hugged her close. Then he gazed down on her, bleakly. "What am I going to do, Solange?"

"I don't know." She hugged him back.

"I've been thinking about it all night. I can't keep going like this. I have to find a way to survive, but Tyler holds all the cards, and I hold none. I'm powerless."

"Yesterday sounded awful. I wasn't sure if you'd want to talk about it," she said softly.

"I don't." He shook his head vehemently. "But Tyler wants to break me, and he will." That realisation made his voice catch in his throat. "He will. He's got me on the ropes, and he knows it. I think..." He paused and hung his head, feeling ashamed. "I think I have to give in, Solange. I have to give him what he wants."

She drew back. "You're going to let him break you?"

"No – I have to give in before it gets that far. He's told me repeatedly that I have to beg him to fuck me. I said it'd never happen, but I have to do it. I have to..." He trailed off miserably. "Shit, I'm not even sure I can go through with it without retching. Solange – you've slept with him, haven't you?"

She nodded. "When he first bought my contract. He wanted to make sure I'd be able to do the job properly – with you, and with his clients."

"So tell me what I need to know about pleasing him. I'll do it, if it keeps him from going after my father again, or you... or me." He gave a pained shrug. "It's only sex, after all. I can do that. He's right – it's the one thing I've always been good at."

"You found him attractive once," she suggested. "Can't you draw on that?"

"No. Just the thought of sleeping with him makes me feel sick," Alex responded bluntly. "But it's the only way I can think of to stop this becoming even worse. So, I need to know how to turn him on. Is

he even into men? Is he bisexual? I've always had a weird vibe off him, even before he bought me, but I wasn't sure what it was. It was a mixed message – as if he wanted to fuck me but he didn't actually desire me."

"I don't think a person's sex is what turns him on, to be honest. I think it's something else."

"What?"

"Power," she said crisply. "Sex as power – that interests him. He uses sex to control and exploit people. We see him do it all the time." She glanced at the smartwall, which they both knew was recording everything they said.

"That doesn't sound good for me," Alex sighed.

"No." She shook her head sympathetically. "It's weird. I think maybe, with someone he loved – with your mum perhaps" – she shot him an apologetic smile – "he could be tender and loving. I think he could, because he does throw himself into his passions, whether it's business or hurting you. But when you take love out of the equation, then I don't think sex interests him much. Power is his aphrodisiac, and it doesn't matter if you're male or female. He might even get a kick out of fucking a man, because it would make him feel even more powerful and in control."

"Right." Alex slid off the bed and headed towards the bathroom.

"What are you going to do?"

"Give him what he wants." He shot her a defeated smile.

Alex took a long shower, letting the warm water pound away at his weary body. He washed his hair and dried it. He couldn't shave himself, because only Lorenzo was allowed to do that, but he slapped some cologne onto his neck and then looked in his wardrobe. There was nothing inside that he'd have chosen for himself, but he tried to pick out something that would appeal to Tyler. He went for a pair of smart black jeans and a plain red cotton shirt, knowing how much Tyler liked stark colours. The shirt was tight over his chest, the buttons straining, which Lorenzo had told him was the way it was supposed to look; Alex found it both ridiculous and uncomfortable.

He studied himself in the mirror, searching for some trace of the real him in the sad reflection gazing back. Finally, he caught a glimmer of himself in the determined set of his shoulders. At least this time he was the one making the decisions. Tyler might have forced him into it, but he was the one making the choice to go to the man he loathed and offer himself up to be fucked.

Even so, his skin crawled at the idea of having to give pleasure to a man he despised.

"It's only sex," he told his reflection. "You can do sex. You've been doing sex for years without caring who it's with. You can do this. You can. You really can."

The words sounded hollow, but he tried to take comfort from them all the same. "Just sex, just sex, just sex," he repeated to himself as he walked to the door.

Fatso – Mick – was back on duty. Alex smiled at him. "I'd like to see Mr Tyler, please, Mick," he said in a small, quiet voice.

Mick gave a little grunt. He put in the call, then jerked his head at Alex and led the way to the lift.

Alex tried to keep calm on the short journey up to Tyler's suite. He fiddled with his too-tight shirt and muttered "just sex" under his breath. He could do this. He had to.

Tyler was sitting on the big sofa in his living room, reading his holopad. He was dressed only in a plain black silk dressing gown and a pair of black leather slippers. He glanced up as Alex walked in, looked him up and down, and then broke into a wolfish grin.

"Very nice." He waved a hand at Alex's outfit. "You've clearly given it some thought."

"I have, thank you," Alex said politely.

"Am I to take it from your appearance that you've had a change of attitude?"

"Yes." Alex nodded firmly.

"And?" Tyler put his holopad aside.

Alex walked slowly over to stand in front of him. He took a deep breath; now the moment was here, he wasn't sure where to start.

"Anytime today." Tyler tapped his fingers on the arm of the sofa.

"Right. Okay. Well... uh, I'm here to ask you if..." Alex tried to think of a way of saying it that didn't sound stupid.

"I'm a busy man, Alexander."

"Yes, I know. So, you wanted me to..." Alex paused again.

"To?" Tyler raised an eyebrow.

"To, um, ask you to fuck me, and I'm here to do that," Alex said, feeling himself blush to the roots of his hair.

"This *is* good, considering you said just a few short hours ago, and I quote: 'Never gonna happen, pervert.'"

"Well, I've had time to reconsider."

"Okay, go ahead, then." Tyler sat back expectantly, arms crossed over his chest.

Alex frowned. "What?"

"Go ahead – ask. You just said you were here to ask me, but you haven't actually done it yet."

Alex took another deep breath, trying to steady himself. Of course Tyler was going to turn this into a power game; Solange had been right about that. All he had to do was get through this. *It's just sex...*

"Please, will you fuck me, sir?" he said through gritted teeth.

"Hmm, it doesn't sound like a very enticing invitation, delivered like that," Tyler replied. "Try again – and at least *try* and sound as if you mean it."

Alex tried again. "I'd love it if you fucked me," he said in what he hoped was a sultry tone, doing his best to put some enthusiasm into it.

"Better, but I still don't believe you," Tyler laughed. "I think you're just saying it – and I want you to mean it."

"I don't know how to do that."

"Really? You've seduced enough people in your time – I'd have thought you'd be an old hand at it." Tyler winked at him. "Go on – try again. How would you like me to fuck you? Up the arse? In your mouth?"

"Any way you like," Alex replied, with a shrug. "Um, I mean, you're in charge, sir. I'm yours to do whatever you like with."

Tyler sighed and twirled his finger in the air. "I know that. I want details, Alexander. I want you to look and sound sexy, and I want to believe you really desire whatever it is you're offering."

GHOST EYE

Alex tried to think back to his many so-called "seductions", but mainly recalled a series of croc'ed up encounters in clubs. "Um," he said again, floundering.

Tyler rolled his eyes. "Well, firstly – get on your knees in front of me," he instructed.

Alex steeled himself and then knelt.

"That's better. I like you like that." Tyler grinned. "Now – try again."

"I'd like you to fuck me," Alex said, putting as much emotion into it as he could.

"With what?" Tyler asked, picking up his mug of coffee from the side table and taking a sip. "Elaborate, Alexander. What would you like me to fuck you with? My big fat cock maybe?"

"Yes, sir. Please fuck me with your big fat cock," Alex repeated dutifully.

"Where?" Tyler asked.

"Here – on the sofa?" Alex suggested.

Tyler sighed again. "No, what part of your body would you like me to fuck with my big fat cock?"

Alex considered taking Tyler's cock in his mouth, but he honestly thought he'd gag on it. He didn't like the idea of taking it up his arse, either, but at least he wouldn't have to do anything except lie there.

"Please, fuck me up the arse with your big fat cock," he responded.

"Would you like that?" Tyler took another sip of his coffee.

"Yes."

"Take off your clothes and say it again, then," Tyler ordered.

Alex blushed even harder, but he removed his clothes as ordered. Tyler had already viewed the footage of him having sex with various clients, so it wasn't as if he had anything to hide. Finally, naked, he sank down on his knees in front of Tyler again.

"Please fuck me up the arse with your big fat cock, sir," he croaked pathetically.

"Why?" Tyler asked.

"Uh..." Alex floundered. "Because you want to? Because I want you to?"

"For what reason?"

"To... come?" Alex suggested, confused.

Tyler roared with laughter. "Young people – it's always about the end result, not the journey. No, Alexander, I want to know *why* you want me to fuck your sweet arse. I want you to tell me how it'll make you feel, and what pleasures you anticipate. Maybe throw in some references to what a horny little whore you are and how you can't wait to be filled by a real man's cock. Something like that."

Alex stared at him, feeling an old sense of petulance rising up inside.

"Well?" Tyler asked. "Running out of steam? Not as up for it as you thought? I sense resistance."

"No, I'm just not used to sounding like I'm in a really bad porn flick," he snapped. "All this shit about how horny I am for your big fat real man's cock." He bit on his lip to shut himself up, too late, and flinched in anticipation of a blow, but Tyler simply gave a smug smirk.

"Oh dear, and you were doing so well." He put his cup of coffee back on the side table. "Come here." He beckoned, and Alex shuffled over to him on his hands and knees. "As tempting as your clumsy attempt at seduction was, Alexander, I'm going to have to decline. See, I don't want your grudging acquiescence – I want you to capitulate, totally and completely. I want it so that taking my cock is your one aim and all-consuming passion. So that you can think of nothing you'd like better in the whole world than to feel me fucking your tight little arsehole. I want you to beg, plead, and whimper for my touch. Only then will I deign to fuck you – and afterwards, you'll be so grateful you'll cry your slutty little heart out and beg me to do it all over again."

Alex sat back on his heels, feeling stupid, small, and very naked. Solange was right – Tyler got off on the power, not the sex, and while he was very good at sex, that was almost irrelevant right now. Tyler wanted nothing less than his most abject humiliation and surrender, and he wasn't going to stop until he got it.

"Now, in order to convince me, I want you to follow a simple order. Think you can do that?" Tyler asked.

Alex nodded mutely.

"Good. So, when I click my fingers and say your name, I want you to get down on your hands and knees, crawl towards me, and convince

me that you're my horny little whore who's desperate for me to fuck you. Understood?"

"Yes, sir," Alex said.

"Remember – wherever and whenever I click my fingers at you – that's your cue to crawl up to me and beg to be fucked. Got it?"

"Yes, sir."

"Then we're done for now. Piss off." Tyler picked up his holopad and returned to his reading, ignoring Alex altogether.

Alex's entire body burned with humiliation as he pulled his clothes back on, but Tyler carried on sipping his coffee and reading his holopad without giving him another glance.

Solange was waiting for him in their suite, but he just shook his head at her mutely. He returned to his room, threw himself on the bed, and stared up at the ceiling miserably. Somehow, he had to lose every shred of himself in order to convince Tyler that he wanted to be fucked by him, even though they both knew it wasn't true. Even though he'd spent all his servitude trying to hold on to his identity, Tyler wasn't going to stop until he'd annihilated his sense of self completely.

He was well and truly out of his depth pitted against such a master manipulator, and he didn't know what to do next. He despaired of ever being able to give Tyler what he wanted – and was terrified of what would happen if he didn't.

He had an unexpected respite for a couple of weeks as Tyler went away on business, and he was kept busy entertaining the usual steady stream of "guests", managing to do his job with a reasonable facsimile of enthusiasm – enough to fool them and Tyler's cameras at least – or so he hoped.

In private, it was a different story, as he became more withdrawn. He felt as if he were splitting into two: the charming, obliging prostitute who took Tyler's clients to his bed and gave them a good time, and the melancholy recluse who spent most of his time in his bedroom, trying to conjure up some way out of this nightmare. He knew Solange and Ted were both worried about him, but as his personality fractured

and his depression deepened, he felt less and less able to communicate with them.

Upon Tyler's return, he and Solange were called to a meeting a few floors below. He'd never been that far downstairs before, and wondered what could possibly be happening as they filed into a huge ballroom filled with Tyler's staff. Drummond was standing at the front, on a podium, his cold gaze raking around the room, watching for any sign of disorder. Alex spotted several familiar faces – Chef, Lorenzo, Mason – and a crowd of other people he'd never met, all of them wearing the black Tyler livery and ID tags.

When they were all gathered, Tyler swept in. Silence fell immediately as he made his way to the podium – his indentured servants were well trained.

"As some of you know, Tyler Tech will be hosting a conference on floating city technology next weekend," he announced. "I can think of nowhere more appropriate to hold it than right here – on the UK's very first floating city."

He paused, and Drummond led a round of sycophantic applause.

"We have over three hundred delegates attending, from all over the world, the most important of whom will be accommodated here, at Vertex Tower. You all have your jobs to do, and you know what those are, but first and foremost we must make our guests feel welcome, and show them a good time. The conference will last for three days, and there will be a full programme of events. Alexander and Solange..." He glanced at them. "Lorenzo will introduce you to some key people; you will make them especially welcome. Mr Drummond will brief the security team on their responsibilities during the conference." He nodded at the burly men bunched together at one side – Alex noticed Ted and Mick amongst them.

"We will have our usual team of outside caterers – Benitos. They will work with my own chefs for the entire weekend to provide delicious food, as well as supplying the extra catering staff required for such a large event. I expect the conference to run like clockwork. Preparation is key – so you will all spend the next week ensuring that

GHOST EYE 221

every detail is worked out, and that everyone knows what's expected of them. This conference is the cornerstone of my ambitions. It will greatly affect my reputation and ability to do business, so anyone who falls short of my expectations, or affects the smooth running of the event, will be severely punished. Any questions should be directed to Mr Drummond."

He nodded that he was done, and Drummond stepped forward to lead another round of applause. The doors opened, and they were about to file out when Tyler clapped his hands.

"One last thing... I believe one of you has something he wishes to ask me. Alexander?" He clicked his fingers.

Alex felt a cold chill run down his spine. He stood, rooted to the spot, as everyone turned to stare at him.

"Well, Alexander? Nothing to say? Don't you remember the instruction I gave you?" Tyler clicked his fingers again.

Alex stared at him in mute desperation. Tyler smiled back. They stood with their gazes locked in a silent battle of wills that stretched on for what felt like an eternity.

Alex considered his options. If he did nothing, Tyler would no doubt find some particularly nasty form of revenge, and his life would become even worse than it already was. Who might be caught in the crossfire this time? Possibly Solange, or his father again, or maybe Tyler would find some way to harm Charles...

"Yes, sir – I do have something to say," he replied quickly, before he lost his nerve. He began walking towards the podium, but Tyler cleared his throat, held up his hand, and clicked his fingers once more.

"I think you're forgetting something," he said, pointing at the floor.

Alex flushed to the roots of his hair as he got down on his hands and knees and crawled the rest of the way to the podium. The crowd parted in front of him, and a startled buzz went around the room. He wished he could disappear into the highly polished wood and cease to exist.

He stopped in front of the podium, kneeling directly in front of Tyler, and looked up at him.

"Well?" Tyler asked. "What do you want to ask me, Alexander?"

He swallowed hard and put his head down. "Please, sir... will you

fuck me up the arse with your big fat cock?" he muttered in the direction of the floor.

"Why?" Tyler asked.

"Because I'm a horny little whore who wants to be fucked by a real man, sir," he mumbled.

"Very good – but nobody heard you. You'll have to speak up," Tyler ordered. "Turn around and face them, so they can all hear what you have to say."

Aware of more than a hundred pairs of eyes on him, he shuffled around on his knees so that he was facing the audience. He lifted his head and spoke in a louder voice.

"I'm a horny little whore who wants to be fucked up the arse by a real man, sir," he said, unable to keep the quiver out of his voice. "Please fuck me with your big fat cock, sir."

Some of those assembled were clearly embarrassed, but others burst out laughing. The security team all high-fived and gave a little cheer, except for Ted, who crossed his arms over his chest and looked straight ahead, his face expressionless. Lorenzo was looking down at the ground, his lips pursed, and Solange was staring at him from glassy eyes, her mouth shaped in a silent little "no".

Tyler seemed to be considering his offer. Alex trembled at the thought that he might take him up on it and fuck him right here and now, in front of all these people.

"You're a little overdressed for sex, don't you think?" Tyler pronounced, after a long pause.

Alex gazed up at him in silent desperation.

"Why don't you show all these good people that you really mean it by taking off your clothes. Then I'll let you know my answer."

The room went quiet as Alex fought an internal battle with himself. Solange pressed her hand over her mouth as she watched in horrified silence. Lorenzo, who was standing next to her, put his arm around her. It was Ted, of all people, who gave him the strength to carry on. Instead of looking away in embarrassment, Ted met his gaze, unflinching, and gave him a little nod, as if to say, "We're with you, mate." Somehow, that gave Alex the courage he needed to unbutton his shirt. He slid it off his shoulders and placed it miserably on the

GHOST EYE

floor, then looked up at Tyler beseechingly. Tyler raised an eyebrow, and Alex knew he wasn't going to be let off the hook.

He kicked off his shoes and peeled off his socks, then with trembling hands he removed his jeans, placing them carefully on top of his shirt. Someone in the audience let out a wolf whistle, and he froze, but once again Ted came to his rescue; he gave another little nod, much fiercer this time, willing him on.

He closed his eyes for a second, then quickly, before his bravery deserted him, hooked his fingers into the waistband of his boxer shorts and took them off. He knelt down again, acutely aware of his nakedness in front of this ballroom full of people, and looked up at Tyler.

"Please fuck my arse with your big fat cock, sir," he said, in as loud and steady a voice as he could muster.

Tyler's gaze raked over him, and he grinned, clearly delighted with the fresh humiliation he'd heaped upon his IS.

"You're such a little slut, begging to be fucked," Tyler gloated. "Unfortunately, I don't want you today. Maybe another time, if you keep asking so nicely." He winked, then swept out of the room.

An excited buzz of chatter broke out immediately. Within seconds, Lorenzo, Solange, and Ted were by his side. Ted and Solange stood in front of him, shielding him from the room, while Lorenzo helped him back into his clothes. The sting of Tyler's humiliation went deep, but Alex was warmed by the knowledge that for the first time in his life, in the midst of all this adversity, he had somehow made some genuine friends.

Solange held his hand as they were escorted back to the suite, glaring defiantly at anyone who dared to smirk at him. When they were alone, she took his face in her hands, her eyes shining with tears.

"I didn't know he'd go this far. I had no idea... Oh, Alex." She kissed his forehead.

He held onto her for a moment and then pulled away. "I think I need some time by myself," he said. She nodded, tears falling down her cheeks – but then grabbed his hand as he tried to leave.

"Alex, I'm worried we're losing you. I mean, what's the difference between you acting as if you're broken, and Tyler actually breaking you? Because what I saw back there..."

"Was me doing what I have to do, if nobody else is to get hurt," Alex told her firmly. "Not you, or my father, or my brother, or anyone else."

"Except you."

"I don't think I matter anymore," he said quietly, pulling his hand away.

The next week was spent preparing for Tyler's conference. Lorenzo was in overdrive, bringing in new outfits for both Alex and Solange and insisting on several tedious fittings to decide which ones he liked best for which occasion.

"There's the banquet on the first night, of course – to welcome everyone to the event. Alex – this lovely tuxedo will look beautiful on you, and for Solange, I think the red satin... or maybe the green silk," Lorenzo mused, holding up two dresses. "There's also the meet-and-greet cocktails on the first day, the private lunch for special guests on the second, and all the coffee sessions during the conference where you'll have to mingle and make small talk – elegant but workaday, I think." He selected various garments and experimented with different hairstyles until Alex wanted to scream.

Once Lorenzo had resolved their images, he sat them down in the living room for a day of learning about who their main targets were, bringing up their photos on his holopad.

"Alex – one of your main priorities is this man." Lorenzo pointed to a holopic of a grey-haired, middle-aged man with no fashion sense wearing a dull tie. "His name is Eric Latham, and Tyler wants him in his pocket. He's married to a woman, but has been known to frequent gay saunas, seeking out pretty young men. He'll want oral, probably."

"Giving or receiving?" Alex asked, unfazed now by talking openly about this particular aspect of his job.

"No idea. Play it by ear. Another priority is this lady – Rebecca Lang. She's never been married, and frankly, we think she might be a virgin."

"Really?" Alex gazed at her holopic, hovering in the air in front of

them. Rebecca Lang was a very large woman in her mid-thirties, quite plain, but with a sweet smile and gentle brown eyes.

"Yes, body issues, self-esteem, that kind of thing." Lorenzo waved a casual hand in the air. "Very bright and superb at her job, but petrified of sex. Keen on romance novels, though. Reads them all the time." Alex didn't ask how Lorenzo knew all this – Tyler obviously had a whole team of ISs whose sole job it was to research this kind of information. They no doubt trawled through people's social media accounts to find out what they liked to buy and followed them around to see where they liked to go. It was precisely what Tyler had done to him, after all. "So, sweep her off her feet," Lorenzo instructed. "Make her feel like a princess."

"And take her virginity?" Alex asked, feeling sorry for poor Rebecca Lang, who had no idea what awaited her at the upcoming conference.

Lorenzo shrugged. "I don't suppose anyone pays her much attention; she'll probably be delighted by a real-life romantic encounter with a handsome young man, rather than just reading about them."

"It won't be real, though," Alex said stubbornly. It was one thing to offer people sex, but this was the first time he'd been asked to deliver romance. He was appalled by the idea of fooling this woman, leading her along, and then offering her up for Tyler's blackmail on a platter.

"No, but it's your job to make it feel real." Lorenzo sighed. "Your orders are to spend day one on Rebecca. You'll target her at the meet-and-greet on the Friday afternoon, then seduce her at the banquet in the evening and persuade her into a sexual encounter. You must bring her up to your room, so the sex can be properly recorded. Save Latham for day two. He's a keen swimmer and will rise early to fit in a swim in the downstairs pool before he attends the morning conference sessions. You need to get Rebecca out of your room early, so that you can be down at the pool in your very tight speedos, flirting with him, at seven a.m. on Saturday morning. Mick will accompany you everywhere and show you where all these places are on the day. Again, you'll need to persuade Latham back to your room for a sexual encounter, because there are no smartwalls in the pool. Now, Solange..."

Alex drifted off, wondering how much this three-day conference

was going to ruin the lives of the unsuspecting Rebecca Lang and Eric Latham.

However, he actually enjoyed one of the preparation days, when Tyler's senior technical indie gave them a lecture on the engineering principles underlying the floating city project. He loved hearing about the design and development phases, and took copious notes.

"You'll be talking to lots of people who do this stuff for a living," the tech indie explained. "You must be able to hold a conversation with them and sound as if you understand the topic. You don't have to be an expert – you just have to know enough to make small talk."

There was that phrase again – "small talk". Alex had never been at ease in large social gatherings without the aid of drugs or drink – neither of which would be available to him. After the floating city lecture, he turned to Solange and asked her advice on how to chat to strangers.

"It's easy – you just smile and ask them questions about themselves – nothing too personal – and flatter them. Always remember to flatter them," she advised. "Try to get them onto a subject they're passionate about, and agree with them as much as possible. Feign an interest, even if it's the most boring topic on earth. If someone loves fishing, say you've always been fascinated about what type of fish it's most challenging to catch, for example, and then sit back and let them explain it to you."

"So basically, the art of small talk is lying your arse off," Alex said.

She grinned. "If you like, yeah. You can do it, Alex – you're very intelligent and well read – you can easily engage people in conversation about a topic they love. Just don't..." She bit her lip.

"Don't?" He raised an eyebrow.

"Well, don't be sarcastic," she said. "You can be quite cutting, especially with people who aren't as bright as you are, which is most people. Also, the sullen, moody thing is only attractive when you're off your head on croc in a student bar – it won't go down so well with Tyler's delegates."

He nodded. At school, he'd learned to deliver cutting put-downs – often, it was his only defence against the bigger, stronger boys who'd bullied him. He hadn't been able to compete physically, but he'd always

GHOST EYE

been able to deliver verbal smackdowns that helped restore some of his damaged self-esteem. Now, it seemed that surly defence mechanism was more of a hindrance than a help. He had to find a way to exchange superficial inanities in as charming a manner as possible instead.

The first day of the conference dawned on a cloudy October day. Lorenzo dressed him in a navy-blue three-piece business suit, red shirt, and navy-blue tie, with a red handkerchief sticking out of his breast pocket.

"Very handsome – every inch the dashing romantic hero Rebecca longs for," Lorenzo told him approvingly.

Alex forced down his rising sense of guilt about seducing her. What choice did he have?

It was late afternoon. The guests had been arriving all day, and cocktails were being served in one of the larger conference suites. Big Mick escorted them there, and Solange immediately set off after her prescribed target. Alex quickly found Rebecca, wearing a big black dress and a set of pearls, standing to one side, looking a little lost.

"Hey..." He smiled at her. She looked startled to be noticed. "Every-one's making small talk, and I'm crap at it," he told her.

"God! Me too." She gave a little laugh, and he grabbed a glass of wine off a passing waiter's tray and handed it to her.

"Dutch courage?" he suggested.

She took it with a grateful smile. He snaffled a glass of fizzy water for himself – Drummond would descend if he dared to touch any alcohol.

Rebecca was sweet and shy, and Alex hated what he was about to do to her. Remembering Solange's instructions, he chatted to her about her job, complimented her on her dress, and managed to keep the conversation going for a full hour until it was time for the delegates to leave.

"Will you be at the banquet tonight?" he asked.

She looked startled all over again. "Yes. It took me ages to find something to wear. I've got something I think will do, but I suspect I look awful in it..." She trailed off with a wince.

"I'm sure you'll look beautiful," he assured her. "Would you mind if I sit next to you this evening? I've enjoyed talking to you so much."

"Really? Well, okay. I mean, of course!"

He smiled and shook her hand as she left, holding it a little too long and complimenting her soft, pale skin until she blushed.

"Christ, that was awful," he confided to Solange when they returned to their suite to get changed for the evening event. "She was so nice. I need a shower. I feel dirty."

"Will you be able to do it?" Solange asked. "Seduce her, I mean? Have sex with her?"

He paused on his way to the door. "I don't know. I suppose so. I don't really have a choice, do I?" He was about to leave when he turned back. "You don't suppose Tyler will do the clicky finger thing again in front of all these people, do you?" he asked anxiously. "I keep waiting for it now, and I'm on edge all the time whenever I see him. I'm scared that one day he'll ask me to do something and I won't have the courage. I don't know what'll happen if I refuse – or who he'll choose to hurt next time."

Solange gazed at him miserably. "I don't know, Alex, but I don't think he'll click his fingers at you in front of all his honoured guests. It's not something he'd want the wider world to know about, so you're safe for the duration of the conference, at least."

"Unlike poor Rebecca," Alex murmured as he left the room.

A couple of hours later he stood in front of the mirror, freshly shaven and wearing a brand-new tux. It had an elegant, expensive cut, and was finished off with a white shirt, black silk bow tie, and red cummerbund. His ID tag was hidden by the high cut of the shirt collar. He'd been told not to deny he was an IS if asked, but not to volunteer the information either – he was simply to say that he worked for Tyler Tech, on George Tyler's personal staff. He was to introduce himself as Alex, and if he was recognised as Alexander Lytton, he was to nod politely and change the subject. He had put on weight since his trial, and he was much more muscular after months of healthy meals and enforced exercise. So far, nobody had asked if Alex was Alexander

Lytton, but he had noticed a few people staring at him intently, as if they weren't quite sure.

"Exquisite, if I do say so myself," Lorenzo said, brushing a non-existent piece of lint off Alex's shoulder.

He studied himself in the mirror, performing his usual trick of finding some trace of himself in his reflection. He discovered it in the cynical tilt of his head as he grimaced. He thought of Rebecca, and how he was going to take her virginity and break her heart, and suddenly wished he couldn't see anything of himself in the mirror. He didn't want to be this person.

The banquet started with a drinks reception in the ballroom. Lorenzo had settled on the green dress for Solange, who seemed uncharacteristically nervous as Mick escorted them down to the ballroom. It gradually started to fill up with delegates; Alex stood by the bar with a glass of champagne, ready to greet Rebecca when she arrived. He was surprised when Solange suddenly grasped him by the arm and steered him to one side, behind a huge potted palm.

"We can talk here. Tyler only uses the top few floors of the building for his own people. He rents the rest out as a conference facility with hotel rooms, so he hasn't installed smartwall cameras down here," she told him in a hushed, urgent tone.

"Uh, okay," Alex responded blankly.

"There are some regular CCTV cameras, but they aren't pointed this way, and I know where they all are." She nodded at the far wall.

"Right. What's going on, Solange?"

"I know a way for you to escape," she said unexpectedly.

Alex blinked. "What?"

She dug her fingers into his arm. "Look, I know a way, but it has to be now, tonight, if you want to do it."

"I don't... What?" he said again.

"Listen – about eighteen months ago, during the year you dumped me, Tyler had me working on a regular basis with this guy called Adam who he was trying to butter up. Adam fell in love with me and wanted to buy my contract. Tyler refused, so Adam asked me to escape." She spoke in rapid undertones, glancing around the room and smiling pleasantly at anyone who walked by.

Over in the distance, Alex could see Mick talking to one of the other security guards who was working the event. "How?" he asked. "How is it even possible?"

"I've always had a lot more freedom than Tyler's given you," she explained. "He didn't even have me microchipped back then, because he didn't want you knowing I was his IS. He arranged for me and Adam to meet in hotel rooms and restaurants, so we were able to talk freely. Adam gave me a burner nanopad and some cash cards, and we arranged a date for me to escape. He told me he'd get me out of the country and then join me, so that we could be together."

"But you didn't go?"

"No. I was too scared." She made a face. "Also, I didn't love Adam, and I didn't want to tie myself to him out of gratitude. I went into my IS contract with Tyler with my eyes open – I knew what I was getting into. I decided I'd prefer to work out my contract than run away and live in fear of Tyler's retribution for the rest of my life. So I stayed – but I kept the nanopad and money. I managed to smuggle them back into my room and hide them there, and that's where they've been ever since – until this evening." She opened her sequinned evening bag, and Alex caught a glimpse of the nanopad and several cash cards. She closed the bag again, quickly. "You can have them and use them to get away," she told him.

"How?" he demanded. "I'm chipped, in case you've forgotten." He pointed at the flashing red light pulsing in his wrist. "If I cut it out, Tyler's security team will be on me immediately. I'd never get out of the building."

"The microchip only sends an alarm if it's exposed to the air for more than thirty seconds," she told him.

"So?"

"So we cut it out of your wrist and put it in mine."

"How the hell do we do that?" he hissed.

"I've got a razor in here." She patted her bag. "We can go into the disabled toilet down the hallway, lock ourselves in, and do it. I've brought a plaster to put over the wound afterwards, and this bracelet that I asked Lorenzo to let me wear..." She pointed at the thick gold bangle on her wrist. "It'll cover the plaster. Nobody will know. I can

give you an hour's head start. Then I'll remove the chip and the alarm will go off. Any longer, and I risk getting caught."

"No. It'll place you in too much danger. Tyler will go nuts." Alex shook his head vehemently. "If he finds out you helped me..."

"He won't. I'll flush your chip down the toilet in an hour's time. That's when the alarm will go off, but they'll think you did it, working alone. Before that, the chip will show you spent the evening in the ballroom, which is exactly where they're expecting you to be."

"What if Mick notices I'm missing?"

"I don't think he will. He's not looking for any trouble, and there are a lot of people here. If he asks where you are, I'll say I saw you in a corner with one of your targets, or that you're in the toilet."

Alex thought about it for a moment, his heart thumping loudly in his chest, and then he shook his head again. "No, I can't do it. I can't leave you here with Tyler."

"It's my choice. I had my chance – this is yours," she told him staunchly.

"Why?" He stared at her helplessly.

"Because I can't bear to watch what he's doing to you." Her voice hitched as she spoke. "He will break you one day, Alex. His mind is set on it, and I've never known George Tyler to not get what he's determined to have. Not once. The only time it happened was, I suspect, with your mother, which is why he hates you so much."

"Why now, if you've known of a way out all this time?"

"This conference is the first opportunity I've had to get you out of the range of Tyler's smartwalls. I've been thinking about it since he made you beg and crawl on your hands and knees in front of us all. I wasn't sure if I'd go through with it, but I can't stand by and watch him break you, Alex – not if there's another way. I helped get you into this mess in the first place, and I'd do anything to get you out of it. Please, let me help you."

Out of the corner of his eye, Alex saw Rebecca enter the room wearing a salmon-pink dress that did little to flatter her figure. She was looking around eagerly, searching for him, and he thought of what the evening held if he turned down Solange's offer. He'd seduce a sweet woman who'd done nothing to hurt anyone, and then Tyler would hold

the evidence over her in the nastiest possible way. Alex could only imagine how mortifying it would be for someone with her body issues to be blackmailed with pictures of her own nakedness during sex, to say nothing of her sense of betrayal at believing he genuinely wanted her when he was simply luring her into a trap.

What else lay before him here, locked up in George Tyler's ivory tower, but the promise of more betrayals, more people being blackmailed, and more humiliation? He was already living in dread of the next time Tyler clicked his fingers and called his name.

Escape sounded dangerous but exciting. For the first time in months, he actually had a choice again – but was he brave enough to take it?

"Yes," he said to Solange. "I want to do it." At least out there, on the run, there was the chance of something better. In here, as Tyler's IS, his future was bleak.

She nodded sharply. "Okay. I'm going to go to the disabled toilet down the hallway. Join me there in a few minutes, and we'll do it."

She let go of his arm and disappeared into the crowd without a backward glance. The whole exchange had been brief, but Alex knew it could change his life forever.

The next few minutes seemed to last for hours, as he attempted to evade Rebecca Lang while edging his way quietly towards the door. He was almost there when he felt a hand on his arm. His stomach did a sickening flip as he turned to see Rebecca smiling at him uncertainly.

"Hello again. Um... I probably misunderstood earlier... but you said you wanted to sit next to me at dinner?" she said, blushing furiously.

"What?" He glanced anxiously towards the door.

"Oh, I did misunderstand. I'm so sorry!" She looked utterly mortified. "Of course someone as gorgeous as you wouldn't be interested in someone like me. I feel so embarrassed."

"Listen." Alex leaned forward. "You are the most beautiful woman in this room tonight, Rebecca. You have nothing to feel embarrassed about. I would be honoured to sit next to you at dinner, but I'm feeling a little unwell. Will you excuse me?"

"Of course. I'm so sorry. You do look a little pale," she exclaimed.

At that moment, the compere announced that they should take

GHOST EYE   233

their seats for dinner. Alex glanced at the door again. His window of
opportunity was vanishing fast, but if he didn't sleep with Rebecca
tonight, then no doubt Tyler would find another way of blackmailing
her. Recklessly, he took hold of her arm and whispered in her ear.

"Tyler is setting you up," he said urgently. "He wants to blackmail
you. Be careful. He's a shark, and you're too nice – don't let him sink
his teeth into you." He pressed a kiss to her startled cheek, then
turned and walked away as fast as he could.

His heart was thumping wildly as he left the ballroom, trying to
walk as nonchalantly as possible. He found the disabled toilet along
the hallway and knocked on the door. Solange opened it, and he
slipped inside.

"What kept you?" she hissed.

"Rebecca." He made a face. "Poor thing. I had to warn her about
Tyler. I hope she stays out of his clutches."

"You have other things to worry about now," Solange chided. She
handed him the nanopad and cash cards with shaking fingers.

"Here." She pointed to a map on the nanopad. "This shows where
all the CCTV cameras are in the building. I took the info off Ted's
holopad – he doesn't know I'm doing this. Avoid the cameras as much
as possible, and act as if you know where you're going. Nobody will
stop you if you stroll around like you own the place. Only Mick knows
you're not allowed to be walking around freely, and he's in the ballroom. Go out this way." She pointed on the map. "Go downstairs and
out through the catering area. You might want to steal something to
put over your tux, or throw it away – it's kind of distinctive. You need
to get as far away from here as quickly as possible. Tyler's men will be
after you as soon as they know you're gone, and while I'm hoping I can
buy you an hour, you might not have that long."

Alex stood there, chewing on his lip uncertainly. "I don't know
where to go," he admitted. "I can't go to my father's house, and I don't
have any friends who'd harbour me."

"You have to get out of the country ASAP," she urged. "That's what
Adam was going to do for me. There's a number programmed into the
nanopad that you can call once you're out. Whoever answers will be
able to help."

Alex nodded, trying to muster his courage. "Okay." He took a deep breath. "Okay," he repeated.

"When you get out of the building, cross the road and walk until you reach the bus stop. Bus ducks leave Ghost Eye every ten minutes. You need to get off the city as soon as possible and put as much distance between yourself and Tyler's security team as you can."

"Yes. I understand."

Solange took the razor out of her bag. "Ready? We have to do this quickly, or the whole plan will go wrong, and Tyler will know you're trying to escape."

"Ready." Alex held out his wrist, and she pressed her fingers over each side of the chip and then sliced the skin over it, making him wince. A large red droplet of blood welled up in the wound, but the chip slipped out easily. He held it, still winking, in his hand, while Solange, inhaling sharply, made a small cut in her own wrist. Then Alex pushed the pulsing chip under her skin, and she covered it with the sticking plaster to keep it in place.

He wrapped his handkerchief around his own wrist to stop the bleeding, and they both stood there for a moment, on tenterhooks, as they waited to see if the chip would keep working. After an agonising wait, Alex placed his fingers on Solange's wrist and felt the device still pulsing beneath the plaster.

"That must be more than thirty seconds," Solange said.

"It is." Alex glanced at his watch. "It worked."

"Then go. You need every single second you've got left."

"Yes." He swept her up in a hug and kissed her cheek. "Oh, shit. I just realised – I might never see you again."

"I hope so." She caressed his cheek. "I really hope we never meet again, Alex. I hope you escape and have a long, happy life far away from here."

"And you. I hope you and Ted are able to leave Tyler one day, and find a flat, and get married, and have babies, or whatever it is you want to do." He swallowed down a lump in his throat. "Thank you, Solange."

"Go!" she ordered.

He pulled away and wrenched the door open.

"Act normally," she hissed. "Remember what I said."

He took a deep breath to collect himself, and then sauntered out of the toilet and along the corridor, trying to act nonchalantly. He passed little gaggles of people from the conference on his way, and did his best to smile at them as if he were allowed to be out here, wandering around by himself. He paused at the end of the corridor to glance at the map, then navigated his way down the back stairs, away from the CCTV cameras.

He exited through the catering area, where dozens of Benitos staff were bustling around in the kitchens. Nobody paid him any attention. Alex saw a navy-blue hooded sweatshirt with the Benitos logo etched onto the left breast slung over the back of one of the chairs, and with a surreptitious glance around to make sure its owner wasn't nearby, he grabbed it. On his way out he saw a scarf abandoned on a table, so he grabbed that, too.

He put the hoodie on over his tux. It was three sizes too big for him, but that worked to his advantage, hiding his tuxedo. He pulled the hood over his eyes so it obscured his face, and then sauntered out of the back tradesmen's entrance. There were dozens of people coming and going, so nobody paid him any attention.

It was dark outside, and the cold air hit him the minute he left the building. He pulled off his bow tie and shoved it into his pocket, then did up the hoodie to the neck, completely obscuring what he was wearing beneath. Finally, he wrapped the stolen scarf around the hood so that it obscured most of his face and kept out the wind, then he put his head down and ran down the road to the bus stop.

He only had to wait five minutes for the next bus, but every second seemed like a lifetime. He could see Vertex Tower across the street, rising up taller than all the other buildings on Ghost Eye, its lights blazing, and he hopped from one foot to the other, feeling so scared he wanted to throw up. Finally, after what felt like an eternity, the bus duck arrived. He paid the fare with one of the cash cards and took his seat by a window.

He felt ridiculously conspicuous, so he pulled the scarf even more tightly over his face, wondering what was happening back in the ballroom, and if his escape had been noticed yet. The bus hit the water and began chugging across it. He turned to get one last glimpse of the

floating city that had been his prison for the past few months. Ghost Eye was an oasis of lights in the dark, but they soon faded from view as the bus hit a patch of land and drove away.

They travelled slowly across various lost zones for a couple of hours, stopping at several little island drop-offs, before coming to a halt at a terminal in Streatham.

"Final stop," the driver called, turning off the lights.

Alex got off and stood on the dark street, wondering what to do next. It was late, and there would be no more buses tonight. He decided to find somewhere to hunker down for the night, so he followed a sign to Streatham Common, which sounded like a good place to hide. This turned out not to be the case – what had once been common land, a rough area of grassland where people walked their dogs, had been filled with cube dwellings of the kind hastily constructed during the Rising. There was nowhere to hide here.

Walking up a long, sloping hill beside the cubes, he found a small park which was all that was left of the common, and there, at the very top, was a café, surrounded by a low wooden fence. It was closed for the night, but there were several wooden picnic tables on the forecourt. It was surrounded by large trees, which screened it from the road; this might do. He climbed over the fence, crawled under one of the tables, and sat there with his knees drawn up to his chest and his arms wrapped around them. It was cold and dark, there was a bitter wind, and he suddenly felt very alone.

He remembered the nanopad, and took it out of his pocket. There was only the one nym programmed into it, and no name. He clicked on the number, and it began to ring.

"Come on, come on," he whispered, blowing onto his fingers and wishing he'd stolen some gloves as well as the hoodie and scarf. Nobody answered. He wondered if the nym was still in use. Solange had kept the nanopad for eighteen months; maybe the person the nym belonged to wasn't around anymore, and he was all alone out here.

Then, suddenly, a woman's voice answered, sounding blessedly warm and motherly in the dark night.

"Hello, this is Elsie. What can I do for you?"

"Elsie, I need help. A friend told me to call you. I just ran away

from my houder," Alex said rapidly, wondering if he sounded as pathetic as he felt.

"Well, you've come to the right place, sweetheart," she said comfortingly. "Whereabouts are you right now?"

"Streatham," he said. "I'm hiding. Um, under a picnic table."

"Okay, my love. Do you have any money?"

"Yeah. A bit."

"Right. Well, we can get you out of the country, but the earliest pick-up I can offer you is Monday week."

"Is there nothing sooner?" he asked miserably, wondering what the hell he was going to do for over a week.

"I'm sorry, sweetie – we're full up until then. Look, stay strong. Will your money stretch far enough to feed you for the next ten days?"

"I think so."

"Lie low, don't act suspiciously, and keep out of sight as much as possible. I need you to make your way to West Wickham – can you do that? It's not too far from where you are now. That's where the pick-up will take place."

"I'll get there," he said.

"Good. I'll call you again on the day to tell you where and when. Is this the right nym to call?"

"Yes."

"Now, what's your name, sweetie, so I can put you on our list?"

He hesitated. He was the most famous IS in the land, and Tyler would pay bounty hunters a fortune to bring him back. Also, he knew nothing about this Elsie woman, and whether she'd sell him out if she knew the price he could command. He didn't trust her with his name.

"Sweetie?" she prompted. "I need your name."

Alex panicked, his mind going completely blank. He looked down and saw the logo of the catering company on his hoodie: Benitos. "Ben," he told her. "My name is Ben."

Chapter Twelve

OCTOBER 2095

Josiah

When Josiah woke the next morning, the bed was empty. He heard Alex's special song playing in the spare bedroom, and the little thuds that indicated he was performing his yoga practice.

Josiah smiled, enjoying the sound. It felt good to be sharing the house with a man again. He stretched, surprised by how good he felt. His mind was clear, and he had an old energy back that he'd almost forgotten he'd ever possessed.

He took a long, hot shower, and rested his head against the wall, wallowing in the sensation of the water beating down on his shoulders.

"Hippo," a familiar, dry voice murmured in his ear.

"You're still here, then?" Josiah grinned. "Thought you might have gone, after last night."

"I'll go when you let me go," Peter said.

"I'll miss you," Josiah said. His hand went instinctively to the ring he wore on the chain around his neck.

"'Til death do us part," Peter intoned gently.

Josiah left the shower and glanced at his reflection in the bathroom mirror as he dried himself. He still appeared tired, with dark smudges under his eyes, but he felt more relaxed than he had in years. Last night's catharsis had changed him – his face had lost the gaunt,

haunted expression it had held for so long. He looked younger and brighter.

He dressed in a pair of houndstooth-check trousers and a crisp white shirt, teaming them with a tie in the same shade of ice blue as his eyes. Then he pulled on his polished black shoes and grabbed his suit jacket.

He jogged down the stairs to the living room and flicked aside the curtain to see that the media were still camped outside. He wished they'd become bored and given up, but he knew they'd stay until they got what they wanted.

He strode into the kitchen, rolling his shirt sleeves up to the elbows as he walked, then tied a red-checked apron around his waist and began making breakfast, whistling as he worked.

The toast was buttered, the juice poured, and the tea brewing in the pot by the time Alex poked his head around the door twenty minutes later. He was wearing grey sweatpants and a white tee-shirt, and his hair was an unruly mess from where he'd presumably been standing on his head, or whatever he did during his morning yoga sessions.

"I thought I'd leave you to have a lie-in, but you're up... and making breakfast?" Alex queried, looking surprised.

"Yup. I thought it was my turn to cook. My eggs aren't as nice as yours, but they're not bad."

"I'll risk them." Alex grinned. "So, you're dressed in a suit — it's Saturday, so I wasn't sure..."

"I don't take days off this early in a homicide case," Josiah explained. "C'mon — it's ready. Let's go eat." He tousled Alex's untidy hair, then picked up the tray and walked into the other room.

"We're eating in the dining room?" Alex asked, following him.

"Yup — you like eating in here, don't you?" Josiah placed the plates of food on the table he'd laid earlier.

"I do, but why are you doing all this?" Alex asked, sitting down.

Josiah threw him a napkin. "Last night..." He exhaled a deep breath. "Well, you did something nice for me last night, and I wanted to return the favour."

"I wasn't sure if you'd want to talk about it." Alex took a sip of his juice.

"I feel I should," Josiah admitted. "I've never fallen apart like that, and I never thought I would, especially not in front of another person. I hope it didn't freak you out too much."

"Of course not." Alex smiled. "Did last night give you any clues as to why that nightmare has been coming back so often lately?"

Frowning, Josiah began cutting into his fried egg so that the yolk could soak into the toast.

"It's just... you said a couple of times that it's been worse lately, and I wondered why. Do you think something triggered it?" Alex took a sip of orange juice, gazing at him curiously over the rim of his glass.

"Maybe it was just time to confront it," Josiah said with a shrug. "I buried it for too long. Then there was the anniversary of Peter's death – maybe that triggered something. You know, Peter only got to drive the car that one time. He spent two years restoring her from a heap of junk into something beautiful, and then he died the first time he took her out."

"They said on the news that Peter was killed by an escaped IS wanting to steal the car?" Alex prompted, still looking at him curiously.

"Yeah." Josiah nodded. That had been what he'd told Esther when she performed the investigation, because he couldn't tell her the truth. "I went to buy us something to drink from a café, and when I came back Peter was struggling with this guy who was trying to take the car. I fought him off, and he ran away, but not before stabbing Peter in the neck." He hated having to edit the truth after Alex's kindness in the night, but he had to protect the Kathleen Line.

He'd gone to the hospital in the ambulance with Peter's body, covered in Peter's blood, and then he'd called Elsie. He still remembered the unholy wail that came out of the nanopad when he'd told her what had happened. She'd rushed to the hospital immediately, and he had to accompany her to the mortuary, because she'd refused to believe Peter was dead until she saw his body for herself.

Elsie took Peter's white face between her hands and gazed at him, her eyes full of tears. Josiah leaned back against the mortuary wall and watched. He felt as if he were far away, observing her from a great distance. There was a relief to be had in detachment. A respite. He had to keep his feelings under control, because if he gave in to the darkness raging inside, he didn't know what he'd do.

He remembered the burnt ground around Rosengarten... and he knew exactly why Peter had made him promise not to seek revenge. All he wanted right now was to go out there, track down Lars, put his hands around the man's throat, and squeeze until he was dead. Yet with his last breath Peter had made him promise not to take that path. Josiah didn't know if that was a promise he could keep, but how could he break a promise made to a dying man?

"Why?" Elsie said hoarsely, stroking Peter's bloodstained hair. "Why did this happen? Why, Joe?"

He shook his head, feeling completely numb. "I don't know."

"We were trying to help. Why would Lars attack Peter? Why?"

"He was scared, paranoid – there was something not right about him, in the head. He saw my Inquisitus ID when I opened my wallet and thought it was a trap. I don't know what happened after I left the car, but Ben said he lunged forward and knifed Peter in the neck without warning. I assume he intended to steal the car and get away. He thought we were going to return him to his houder and claim the reward, but I doubt there ever was one." Josiah had been through it a hundred times already, but he still couldn't believe it had actually happened.

"Lars was jumpy, but I didn't think he was a killer. He pretended he had a gun at the beginning, and that should have set off alarm bells, but we didn't take him seriously. We didn't even consider that he might have a knife."

"What happened to the others – Matthew and Ben?" she asked.

"Matthew never showed up. He was the one we were waiting for. Ben... he was just a kid, and so scared. He wasn't much of a fighter." Josiah recalled the clumsy punch Ben had thrown at Lars. "But he was brave. He was holding on to Lars's arm when I got there, trying to stop

him stabbing Peter again. He called for the ambulance as Peter was dying... and then I told him to run."

"He might try and call me," Elsie said.

"He might, but we can't help him now."

She looked up, her eyes swimming with tears. "Why?"

"We'll be under too much scrutiny – we can't risk it. If Ben calls you again, you have to tell him he's on his own. We can't help."

"Scrutiny?" she asked absently, still stroking Peter's hair.

Josiah could see she hadn't grasped the full implications of what they were facing. She could only think about Peter. But they had no time to fall apart right now – the living still needed their protection.

"Look, there are things we must discuss... details," he continued in his brisk work tone. It was far easier to be an investigator than a grieving husband; he didn't know how to play that role. "There will be an investigation. They'll want to know who killed Peter."

She looked up, her face ashen. "You can't tell them the truth."

"No, of course not. I'm going to call Esther in a minute, but we need to get our stories straight before I do."

"What will you say?"

"I'll tell her that Peter and I were coming to visit you, and that we stopped to buy drinks on the way... damn it," he snapped suddenly.

"What?"

"Five cups. I bought five cups of tea at the café – she'll check that and want to know why. Who were the others for?"

"Me?" Elsie suggested. "Tell her you were bringing tea for me and two mutual friends. I'll call Jan and Derek and tell them, so they'll provide the right alibi when she contacts them."

"Seems odd, but maybe you love the tea from that place so much that you insist we always bring you some when we visit?"

"That's right. That's it." She nodded.

"And while I was getting the tea, Lars was walking past – he saw the car – you can't exactly miss it – and he decided to steal it. He opened the door and stabbed Peter, and that's when I returned with the tea. There was a struggle, and he ran off..."

"Yes. That's what happened." She nodded again.

"That's not what happened." He gazed at Peter's dead body, lying on the mortuary table between them.

"No, but it's what we have to say. Yes, Josiah?" She moved around to his side of the table, took his head in her hands, and looked at him. "Josiah?"

He struggled with the darkness stirring within, trying to gain control of himself. "Esther will go after Lars, and I know her – she'll catch him. Then he'll tell her the truth about what we were all doing there, and she'll have no choice but to arrest me, too," he told her despairingly. The darkness reached up inside, hungrily, sensing an opportunity to be released and have its moment. "I have to go after Lars," he said coldly. "I have to get to him before she does. I have to take care of it. Of him."

Elsie gazed at him, still holding his face between her hands. "You have two choices, Josiah. You can either find Lars and we take him out of the country so he cannot speak of our secret, or you find him and you kill him."

"Take him out of the country?" Josiah hissed. "After he butchered Peter? What the hell do you think I am, Elsie? Some kind of saint?"

"No. I know what you want to do. I know what every aching bone in your body is screaming for. You want to go out there, find him, and kill him with your bare hands. That's what you want to do, Joe. You want to kill him and take your revenge."

"Yes." He held her gaze unflinchingly. "That's exactly what I want to do."

"It won't bring Peter back."

"No, but it'll be justice."

"Ah, justice. You and your justice." She shook her head wearily.

"What does that mean?" he demanded.

She stroked his cheeks gently. "You believe in Josiah's Justice – that killers must be caught, and escaped indies must be freed, and that it's your job to do both without either getting in the way of the other. It's very black and white."

"I have to have a code to live by, Elsie. I have to make sense of it in my own mind."

"You just said Lars wasn't right in the head. He was probably badly

treated as an IS. Is it right to take his life for cracking under the strain of an unjust system?"

"I have to draw my line somewhere," he said firmly.

"And where will you draw it this time?"

"Where I always have. I might not uphold every law of the land, but I've never tolerated murder, no matter who commits it – or why."

"Usually, you uphold the law by arresting people and handing them over to the courts, for a judge and jury to decide their fate. You can't do that this time without placing us all in danger. It's a different thing to dispense justice yourself – to take a life with your own hands."

He pushed her away. "I'm a soldier, Elsie. I've taken lives before."

"In cold blood?"

"You think I can't do it?"

"Oh, I know you can do it." She gave a sad smile. "But I don't know what it'll do to you. Who will you become if you give in to all the hatred and anger inside you right now?"

"I don't care," he said stubbornly.

"I know, but I do – and Peter would, too. Peter wouldn't ask you to kill for him, Joe."

It was as if she knew about the promise Peter had extracted from him.

"What's it to be, Joe?" Elsie pressed.

Josiah knew he had to take action one way or another. If he didn't, he would lose not only his husband but also the Kathleen Line, Elsie, his friends, his job, his freedom – his whole way of life – on this one terrible night.

Surely Peter couldn't have meant for him to have to escort his killer to freedom, and yet... Even as he struggled with himself, he knew that Peter had understood exactly what he was doing when he'd asked him to make that promise. Peter knew Josiah's dark side better than anyone. He knew that if Josiah went down that path he might never return. Peter's last act had been to protect his husband.

"I can't do it, Elsie," he raged. "I can't get Lars out of the country. I just can't."

"Then you must kill him." She patted his shoulder gently and

GHOST EYE

returned to Peter's body. "Goodbye, Peter. I'm so sorry. You were the best man I ever knew – you didn't deserve this." She planted a kiss on Peter's cold, unmoving face. "Good luck, Josiah. I hope you win the battle you're fighting right now." She kissed his cheek, too, then left him in the mortuary, all alone with Peter's body – and a promise he didn't want to keep.

———

"What happened to the man who killed Peter?" Alex asked. "Lars something? Did you go after him?"

"Lars Driessen – and yes, I did," Josiah said brusquely. "I thought you knew all this – I thought you'd read all those stupid articles they write about me every time I'm assigned to a high-profile case."

"I have." Alex shot him a speculative look. "They say Esther found Driessen's body washed up on the edge of a lost zone near the crime scene a week after Peter was killed. His DNA proved his identity – he was on the IS database, and his fingerprints were all over the knife they took from the car."

"That's right." Josiah nodded.

"So, how did he die?"

"He drowned."

"I read that," Alex said, still gazing at him searchingly. "It's in all the articles. They always say that nobody knows how he drowned, though."

"And the implication is always that I tracked him down, held his head under the water, and killed him with my bare hands," Josiah growled.

Alex put down his knife and fork. "Did you?" he asked quietly. "Nobody would blame you if you did."

"No, I didn't," Josiah said brusquely.

He'd gone looking, intending to find Driessen and kill him, but the indie's body had turned up before he had had a chance to find him. "It's possible he simply lost his footing in the dark in his panic after killing Peter – he wasn't exactly the sanest individual in the world. Or maybe he deliberately committed suicide when he realised what he'd

done, and what he faced if he was caught. Maybe he threw himself into the water. I don't know."

"But you wanted to," Alex said. "You wanted to kill him, didn't you?"

"Yes," Josiah replied honestly. "I wanted to. And I might have, if he hadn't killed himself."

"Do you think you could have done it, if it had come to it?"

Josiah remembered his promise to Peter. Could he have done it? Or would he have pulled back from the darkness at the last moment and taken Lars to safety instead? He shook his head. "We'll never know."

"You lost a good person, an innocent man, someone you loved – he was killed right in front of you. Of course you wanted to bring the man who did it to justice, but you were denied that."

"Well, Lars Driessen paid with his life, even though he didn't die with my hands around his throat."

"But all those feelings of revenge, that desire for justice, that need to avenge the person you'd lost – they had nowhere to go. You never had closure."

Josiah looked up, feeling winded. "No."

"No wonder it's taken you so long to let it go." Alex reached across the table and placed his hand over Josiah's.

"I swear it's like you've reached into my soul and seen a part of me I've never shown to anyone in my life before – except Peter," he said, bemused. "How do you do that? How do you know me so well?"

Alex gazed at him for a long time, an agonised hesitation in his eyes, and then he shrugged. "Like I said, I've read the articles – and there have been plenty of them. People are fascinated by you. A runaway IS kills your husband in an unprovoked attack and then turns up dead in mysterious circumstances a week later. You might not have killed Lars Driessen, but you've been given all the credit. People would have rooted for you if you *had* been the killer."

"Maybe it was a good thing I didn't get to Lars before he drowned," Josiah muttered.

Alex gave him a questioning look.

"Who would I be if I'd found him and killed him? Could I have stayed in my job? What kind of a hypocrite arrests people for murder

when he's a murderer himself? Peter's dying wish was for me not to seek my revenge. He made me promise. He knew what was inside me, and where I'd end up if I took that path. If I'd killed Lars Driessen, I think I'd have disappeared forever into the dark, and I know that's the last thing Peter would have wanted."

"Instead, you've remained forever poised on the brink, wondering which way you'd have jumped." Alex moved his thumb over the grazes on Josiah's knuckles. "A legend was born that night: the indiehunter. Nobody could blame you for hating indies after that, and doing your best to catch every single one who crossed your path."

"But that's not what happened." Josiah withdrew his hand. "That's the convenient narrative peddled by the media and social media, and you, of all people, know how easily that gets out of hand. I didn't kill Driessen, and I didn't turn into some demented indiehunter out of grief over Peter." On the contrary: he'd thrown himself into developing the Kathleen Line as soon as it was safe to start up again. He'd made it bigger, stronger, and safer than ever over the past seven years, devoting every second of his spare time to it.

"Yet you've pursued several indies," Alex pointed out.

"Only ones who've committed murder, or have information on who did. I don't go around hunting them for the sake of it," he snapped. "I'm not a bounty hunter."

Alex smiled at his tone. "God, it must have driven you nuts to be given that name. How you must have hated it all these years, walking about with that hanging around your neck when you were just trying to be a good investigator."

"I've arrested far more free people than indies in my career, but the press aren't interested in that." Josiah sighed. He finished the last mouthful of his breakfast and pushed his plate away.

"So the great indiehunter is a fake." Alex grinned.

"Of course he is. I never wanted the stupid name. Is the black sheep of the Lytton family a fake, too?" he threw back.

"Nobody is ever completely black or white – even George Tyler." Alex shook his head. "Shades of grey. Nuance. Context. They make all the difference."

"Yes, they do." Josiah stood up. "Look, I want to say thank you for

last night. You were kind to me when I needed it most, and you helped me get through something I found very hard to face."

"You don't need to thank me."

"Yes, I do," Josiah said firmly. "And I want to repay you by believing in you. I believe you're not the evil Alex Lytton from the news site articles, media reports, and radio talk shows. I believe you're acting from good motives right now, even if you won't explain to me what those are. Now, I'd like you to go upstairs and put on one of the suits we brought back from Dacre's house."

Alex looked up at him in surprise. "Of course. May I ask why?"

"Like I said – I believe in you, and I'm going to prove it to you. Yesterday, you said you wanted to trust me – today I'm going to show you that you can."

Alex came down the stairs half an hour later, showered, shaved, and dressed in the kind of elegant navy-blue suit Josiah approved of, complete with pale blue shirt and silver tie.

"Will this do for whatever you have in mind?" he asked, twirling for Josiah's scrutiny.

Josiah cleared his throat – there was something about a well-dressed man that always appealed to him. "Oh, yeah. You'll do," he said with a grin. He put his hands on Alex's shoulders and looked him in the eye. "I'm about to put my career on the line for you, so I need to know the answer to one important question, and I need you to be completely honest with me."

Alex gave him a startled look. "Okay," he said cautiously.

"Answer me truthfully – did you have anything to do with Elliot Dacre's murder?" Alex opened his mouth to reply, but Josiah shook his head, stopping him. "I know you have some information pertinent to the investigation that you're deliberately withholding, but I'm not asking about that. What I want to know is if you were involved in his murder in any way: if you knew it would happen; if you handled the murder weapon at any time; if you know who killed him; if you tried to cover it up; or if you killed him yourself. All I want is an answer to those questions – yes or no. I will believe

you and do my best to help you, whatever that answer is. I promise."

Alex looked him straight in the eye, his grey eyes radiating sincerity. "No," he said fiercely. "I had nothing to do with Elliot's murder. I don't know who killed him, and I didn't know it was going to happen. I didn't handle the murder weapon, and I didn't cover anything up. I wasn't involved. I promise you that, Josiah."

"Thank you, Alex. I believe you. Now, it's time to go to work."

Alex started walking towards the door to the garage, but Josiah pulled him back. "We're not going that way," he said, heading towards the front door.

"We're not?" Alex followed on behind. "Oh, shit," he said as Josiah paused by the door, his hand poised.

"Ready?" Josiah grinned at him.

"No," Alex retorted. "But let's do it anyway."

Josiah opened the door, and a dozen cameras immediately flashed in the grey morning light. Reporters scrambled over his front garden, several broadcast cameras swung in his direction, and a host of microphones were pushed under his nose.

"Investigator Raine – what's happening? Can you tell us any more about Elliot Dacre's murder? Do you have a suspect? Is Alexander Lytton a suspect? Why is Dacre's IS living with you?"

The barrage of questions came in an overwhelming wave, but Josiah didn't waver. He put his hand on Alex's shoulder to give him the strength and courage to face it, too. With his free hand, he reached for a microphone. Then he glared at the reporters until they fell silent.

"Investigations into Elliot Dacre's murder are continuing. However, we are, at this stage, able to rule out Alexander Lytton as a suspect. Mr Lytton is innocent of Elliot Dacre's murder. I repeat – Alexander Lytton is not a suspect. He did not murder Elliot Dacre, and he was not involved, in any way."

Pandemonium broke out. Josiah glanced at Alex to see him looking at him with a wide, startled smile. He held up his hand for quiet. "Mr Lytton has been assigned to my custody by Esther Lomax, the head of the Inquisitus Agency, for his own personal safety, and because we require his help in our investigation. He will be staying with me for the

duration of the case. I will not be taking questions. That is all. Thank you."

He turned firmly on his heel and guided Alex back into the house, slamming the door shut behind them.

"Fuck," Alex said. Then he flung his arms around Josiah's neck. "Thank you," he murmured into his cheek. "Thank you for believing in me."

"Whatever it is you're not telling me – I trust that you have good reason, and that you will, and soon," Josiah replied. "But for now, I can wait."

Alex drew back, his eyes gleaming with tears. He wiped them away with the back of his hand. "Sorry. It's just that nobody has believed in me for a very long time, maybe never. It means a lot to me."

At that moment, Josiah's holopad buzzed. He gave a grimace as Esther's face popped up. He'd barely answered it when she gave it to him with both barrels.

"Your unauthorised announcement is on every screen, holofeed, radio station, and news site right now," she told him in a grim voice. "You'd better have a really good explanation for this, Joe, or I'll have your balls."

He winced. "Understood, Esther."

"Now, get your arse into my office, pronto – we need to talk."

Chapter Thirteen

OCTOBER 2088

Alex

Alex was woken in the early hours of the morning by the sound of helicopters circling overhead. He felt stiff and cold – the hoodie hadn't been thick enough to keep out the chill of the October night, even with the added layer of his tuxedo jacket beneath. He glanced up, blearily, to see bright lights above. Another helicopter was whirring in the distance, and he could see a third heading south.

He hunkered down under the table, keeping completely still, his heart pounding. The helicopters surely belonged to Tyler and were out looking for him – why else would they be circling over the common? As soon as he'd realised Alex was missing, Tyler must have mobilised his security teams; if anyone had the money and power to arrange for search helicopters in the middle of the night, it was George Tyler. By now, he must know that Alex had taken a bus duck off the floating city, and there was probably also CCTV footage of him getting off at the Streatham terminal. Tyler's men would have easily seen through his disguise of a hoodie and scarf.

The helicopter's blades were now whirring so loudly overhead that Alex wondered if he'd been seen. He braced himself for the possibility that it would land on the common and disgorge a team of guards to haul him back to Ghost Eye.

He realised that he'd been a complete idiot. He shouldn't have taken refuge here overnight; he should have put as much distance as possible between himself and Streatham. He'd been stupid, and he deserved to be captured within a few ignominious hours of his escape. How had they tracked him here? Was it possible his ID tag had a tracker in it? Maybe an unsophisticated one, that gave a general location, rather than a specific one. He'd never given that any thought – he'd just assumed the microchip was the only way Tyler had to keep tabs on him. Alex immediately removed the ID tag and threw it into a nearby bush. There was something symbolic about getting rid of it. He'd already carved the microchip out of his flesh, and now he'd thrown away the other hated symbol of his servitude. He was free, and he intended to stay that way. He had to get his act together, stop being an idiot, and start thinking with his brain instead of his fear.

After a few minutes, the helicopter moved off towards some nearby houses. As soon as it left, he slid out from under the picnic table and ran down the opposite side of the hill. He passed a closed iron gate with a sign saying *The Rookery*, leading to an area of what looked like mainly tangled undergrowth, and paused. The noise of the helicopter grew louder in the distance – this was no time for hesitation. He quickly scrambled over the gate and ran into the dark bushes. Then he threw himself down and wriggled as far as he could beneath the thicket.

There was no way he could be seen here. He wrapped his arms around his body and tried to work out a plan. Tyler's men would surely also be combing the streets in AVs, but their search would be hampered by the dark. When morning came, it would be a different story.

What resources did Tyler have at his disposal? Alex had been so focused on getting away that he hadn't thought about what Tyler might do next. Leaving aside Tyler's very personal hatred of him, nobody paid a hundred and sixty million quid for an IS and then sat back and let him get away. Tyler would throw everything he had at finding him and dragging him back. His name and face were probably already all over the news by now; he'd be on every screen in the country by breakfast,

and then what chance did he stand of avoiding capture for over a week?

He decided to go to West Wickham as soon as the helicopters went away. He wouldn't use public transport, both to avoid their internal CCTV and also because people sitting on buses and trains would have plenty of time to stare at him and wonder where they'd seen his face. It made more sense to walk – people rarely looked at anyone walking along the street unless they were behaving suspiciously. He'd keep his head down and hope nobody noticed him.

The helicopters continued circling all night. Then, at around 4 a.m., Alex heard voices. Suddenly, two men with torches appeared, moving slowly through the Rookery gardens. He froze into a tiny ball in the bushes, barely breathing. The men came closer, and closer still, so near now that he could hear their muttered curses as they beat the undergrowth with sticks. If they'd had dogs he'd have been caught, but they didn't; maybe even George Tyler couldn't summon search dogs in the middle of the night on short notice. One of the sticks landed next to his shoe, but he remained frozen to the spot. The beam of a torch passed a fraction to his right and then moved on down the hill.

There was no more searching. The helicopter hovered overhead for a long time and then whirred away. He remained huddled in the bushes for the next hour, until finally he felt safe enough to move. Slowly, he uncurled his aching body enough to peek out. The gardens were eerily quiet, and there was no sign of his pursuers on the nearby street, either.

At first light, he scrambled out of the undergrowth and pulled himself over the railings, suddenly glad of Mason's stringent exercise regime. He clambered out just as two SUAVs drew up next to the café on top of the hill. Several big men wearing the black Tyler livery and ID tags jumped out... and with them were four large dogs. They disappeared into the Rookery gardens. He ran off down the street as fast as he could.

As he pushed himself to get as far away from The Rookery as possible, every so often, a black SUAV with Tyler's logo on the side came by. He spent a couple of hours evading them by hiding out in people's gardens and down alleyways. Finally, Streatham started to stir, and the

streets became busier, making him less conspicuous. He found a busy main road and, wrapping his scarf tightly around his face, put his head down and began walking. He pulled up a map on his nanopad and was relieved to find that West Wickham was only a few miles away.

He was soon lost in the Saturday morning swell of people out walking dogs and families going about their business. He felt as if every person was looking at him, despite his best efforts to be inconspicuous, and jumped at every loud noise and speeding duck. He wondered how people managed to stay sane during months on the run – he was a nervous wreck after just a few hours.

Just before noon, he stopped at a grungy-looking café and ordered a hot tea and full English breakfast. There was a screen in the corner, tuned to a news site; he watched it avidly for over an hour as he shovelled the food into his mouth, but there was nothing about him. Yet his notoriety would surely make his escape headline news – it made no sense.

Why hadn't Tyler alerted the police and hired a national investigation agency to find him? All the bounty hunters in the land would drop everything and head this way if Tyler offered a generous reward for his safe return – and yet Tyler had kept his escape secret. Why?

Could it be that the great George Tyler didn't want the world knowing that he'd been outwitted by an indie? Or... no, it had to be more than simply pride. Was it because Tyler didn't want the world knowing that Alex was *his* indie? Possibly, although enough people had now seen him wearing a Tyler ID tag that it was surely only a matter of time before it leaked out anyway.

Maybe it was more pragmatic than that. Maybe it was because if the spotlight was turned on Tyler's treatment of his indentured servants, then all kinds of unpleasant facts might come out. He might have a lot of blackmail material on a lot of different people, but he didn't control every single person in the land. Martin Bagshaw must have a boss... and once people started asking awkward questions, it could escalate. Surely the last thing Tyler wanted was anyone digging around in his setup, considering what it was built on. That had to explain it.

Besides, Tyler didn't need investigation agencies and bounty

GHOST EYE 255

hunters to recover one scared IS: he had his own people for that. Tyler knew he'd made a run for it, but he didn't know he had the nanopad, cash cards, and the fact he'd been able to contact a rescue organisation. Tyler probably calculated that it would be easy to find his escaped IS before too long, without anyone knowing he'd been missing in the first place.

Alex was determined to prove him wrong. He might not be a match for George Tyler's wealth and cunning, but he was smart. Tyler would be expecting him to make for the coast or an airport, not to hang around in this area for very long. All Alex had to do was get to West Wickham and then lie low for ten days. He could do that.

He left the café and continued walking. It didn't take him long to reach his destination. He scoped it out for a few hours, then went to a nearby park and sat on a bench until darkness fell, when he crawled into the undergrowth to sleep.

The park was small – it had clearly once been much bigger, but as was the way with most of the old green spaces, hundreds of cubes had been built on it during the Rising, leaving behind a patch of grassland with some shrubs and trees and a tiny pond. There was also a dirty, smelly toilet, but at least it provided drinking water and a place to relieve himself. The weather was dank, with strong winds and squally rain showers, and he felt bitterly cold.

He spent his days walking around the suburb until he knew it like the back of his hand. He hid in the park every night, staying out of sight as much as he could. He bought a supply of food from a nearby convenience store and ate it on benches, watching small children with their parents feeding the ducks on the pond.

Helicopters circled overhead regularly, and on a couple of occasions a black SUAV with the Tyler livery on the side passed by, but he always managed to evade them. Early on Tuesday morning, a Tyler security team did a sweep of his park; he only just got out in time, sheltering in a nearby shop until they left.

Every day seemed to last an eternity, and he lurched constantly between boredom and fear. He was anxious in case Tyler's men returned, and yet also teetered on the brink of tedium as each long hour ran into the next. His nerves were frayed, and although his

stomach griped constantly, he struggled to eat. The slightest thing startled him, and sleep was hard to come by in the cold, wet bushes. After several days of living on the edge, he felt physically and mentally run down. The damp had seeped into his chest, he had a permanent headache, and he was desperately tired. He wished he could switch off, for just a moment, as the hypervigilance was exhausting.

He often thought about Solange. He hoped Tyler didn't know about the part she'd played in his escape. Sometimes he thought about Elsie. She'd had such a warm, kind voice – it was all he could do not to call her again just to hear it, he felt so alone.

Where would Elsie's escape route take him? Most of Northern Europe had been a warzone since the Rising; he'd heard all kinds of horror stories about warlords, scavengers, and people living in vast, lawless cities made of rafts and boats. He was both scared and excited at the prospect of going there. At least in that chaotic world he'd be almost impossible to find. Then he could leave the nightmare of being George Tyler's whore and whipping boy behind.

He tried not to think about what Tyler would do to him if he caught him, but in the darkest hours of the night he couldn't help it. He flinched at the thought of a week spent locked up with Jake Harper. What would be left of him after such an ordeal? Or worse, being locked up in Tyler's own personal suite, humiliated and punished every second of the day, with no end in sight.

Would he ever see his brother or father again, or were they lost to him forever? He longed to see his father, in particular. He wanted to tell him how sorry he was for what had happened that day in his office, and to explain his part in it. Noah had looked at him with such contempt when he'd said that he wished he'd never been born. That hurt the most. Maybe it was best if he never saw him again, but Charles... His heart ached at the thought of never having another chance to see his beloved big brother.

Finally, the excruciatingly long ten days came to an end. On the morning of Monday 25th, he hunkered down on a park bench in the rain, turned on the nanopad, and waited for it to buzz. Finally, just after 2 p.m., he received the call, his cold, stiff fingers fumbling to answer it.

"Ben, honey, it's Elsie." Her voice was as warm and comforting as he remembered it, her nano set to voice only, which he supposed was a wise precaution, although he longed to see her face. "Are you in West Wickham, like I told you?"

"Yes, I am. I'm sitting in a park," he said stupidly.

"Okay, sweetie. Now listen – you need to go to Station Road at eight p.m. There's a little parade of shops there, near the leisure centre; our car will be parked there – you won't be able to miss it." She gave a throaty chuckle. "It's a red Pre-R Jaguar. Really old, though she's polished up nice and shiny. You'll be meeting two of our people – Peter and Joe. They'll get you to a safe house tonight, and then we'll get you out of the country tomorrow. Do you understand all of that?"

"Station Road. Eight p.m. Red Jaguar," he repeated.

"That's right. Just go straight up to the car and get in – don't hang around outside it, looking suspicious."

"No. Fine," Alex said tightly.

"Don't sound so scared, Ben honey. Peter and Joe are nice people – I've known Peter since he was a little kid, and he'll take good care of you. Joe's his husband, but don't worry, he's not quite as scary as he seems when you first meet him."

"Okay." Alex hung on to the nanopad tightly, not wanting her to go. "Can you really get me out of the country?" he asked pathetically.

She gave another of those warm, throaty chuckles. "Of course. That's what we do. Don't you worry – another few hours, and you'll be wrapped up warm in our safe house – and within a few days you'll be starting a new life, far away from here."

"Okay." He nodded vigorously, even though she couldn't see him.

"Where did you escape from, Ben?" she asked.

"Umm..." He cast around for a plausible story and then drew on what he knew best. "A factory," he said, thinking of Lytton AV.

"Did they treat you badly?" she asked sympathetically.

"Yes." He couldn't think of anything else to say. He desperately wanted to keep talking to her, but hated lying to her when she was so nice.

"Well, you're safe now. You be at Station Road tonight, okay?"

"Yes."

"Good boy. Now, I've gotta go. We've got other people to help. You take care now, sweetie."

"Yes. Bye," he mumbled.

He felt a pang of guilt. Should he have told her who he was? Should he have warned her to tell Peter and Joe to take extra care, because Tyler's men were on the prowl, looking for him? He was placing them in danger by keeping it quiet. Presumably, that came with the territory, but it bothered him all the same. He didn't want anyone being put at risk because of him. He'd hurt too many people in his life already. Could he trust them, though?

Elsie had put him on the spot when she'd asked him where he'd escaped from; he had to think up more of a back story, because he was likely to be asked again. He also needed a surname. He thought about it for a while, and settled on Smith. Ben Smith. It was the blandest name he could think of, unlikely to draw anyone's attention.

The day wore on, and as dusk fell, Alex visited the unpleasant park toilet one last time, to get ready. He hadn't washed properly in over a week, and his clothes were damp and muddy from sleeping in undergrowth. Gazing at himself in the cracked toilet mirror, he struggled to find some trace of himself. George Tyler's over-styled IS was gone, and in his place was someone very different. His face looked gaunt, his hair lank, and his chin was covered in a thick layer of dark brown stubble. His eyes were sunken and haunted. Nobody would recognise him now. However, he found himself in the determined gleam of his eyes and the firm set of his jaw. He was going to do this. Alexander Lytton was his past – the future belonged to Ben Smith.

At 7 p.m., he made his way to Station Road. He walked along it until he saw the parade of shops Elsie had mentioned. It was too early for the red car to be there, so he ducked out of sight down an alleyway and waited, keeping an eye out for Tyler's black SUVs. He hadn't seen any for a couple of days now, but he was always on the alert. It would be a horrible irony if one showed up now, when he was on the brink of freedom.

At 7.45 p.m., his stomach did a little flip when he saw a red car driving slowly down the street, clearly looking for a parking place. Eventually, it pulled across the oncoming traffic and steered into a

space on the other side of the road, opposite a café. Alex watched it for fifteen minutes, just to be sure, and then he made his move. Pulling his hood down over his eyes and wrapping his scarf around his face, he left the alley, his heart pounding. He crossed the road with a casualness he didn't feel and carried on walking down the street towards the red car, glancing over his shoulder a couple of times as he went.

He'd never seen such a beautiful Pre-R vehicle up close before. In other circumstances he'd have stopped to admire it, but now wasn't the time. He could make out two people inside – both were big, solid men, one blond, the other dark. His stomach churned anxiously as he put his hand on the door handle and opened it. It felt weird, climbing into someone's car without knowing them, but he slid onto the back seat.

"Am I in the right place?" he enquired anxiously. "Elsie sent me."

The dark-haired man in the driving seat turned around and smiled. He had the sort of face you trusted instantly – kind, with bright, twin-kling brown eyes, full of good-natured humour. Was he Peter or Joe? Alex decided he had to be Peter, because Elsie had said Joe was scary, and this man wasn't.

"You are. I'm Peter, and this is Joe." Peter jerked his head at his companion. "What's your name?"

"Ben," Alex said into his scarf. He slid across the seat and pressed himself into the far corner, trying to be as invisible as possible in case one of his rescuers recognised him. "Uh, Smith – Ben Smith," he added. He hadn't managed to get a good look at Joe, because he was in the seat directly in front of him and hadn't said anything yet, but Alex could see he was taller than Peter, with broad shoulders and short, spiky blond hair.

"We're waiting for two more – Lars and Matthew – and then we'll set off, Ben," Peter told him, glancing at him over his shoulder. "We'll be taking you to a safe house overnight, and then we'll get you to the coast and out of the country. By this time tomorrow you'll be in France – and free."

"Thanks," Alex muttered, putting his head down. He felt bad about deceiving this cheerful man with the kind smile, but he'd come this far and it made no sense to tell them his true identity now. Maybe he'd come clean later, at the safe house, if he could get Peter on his own. He

trusted Peter instinctively and was positive he wouldn't betray him. He didn't know about Joe – he couldn't get a read on him yet.

As if he'd read his mind, Joe suddenly turned and looked directly at him. Alex's heart skipped a beat. He was an imposing man, with a strong jaw, flat nose, and piercing blue eyes. He was wearing a purple sweater and a brown coat, looking very stylish, in contrast to Peter's more casual appearance. He was probably in his early thirties, which, Alex estimated, made him several years younger than Peter.

"We've got a change of clothes for you at the safe house," Joe said gruffly. "Something clean and dry. Good food waiting there, too."

Alex sensed immediately that Joe was a darker personality than Peter. He wouldn't take any bullshit. While Peter might be sympathetic to learning his true identity, Joe would be angry at being deceived. There was an edge of danger to him – as if he'd make a good friend but a dangerous enemy. Feeling an unexpected tingling sensation in his belly, Alex realised, with surprise, that he found Joe attractive.

Not daring to do more than nod in response, he retreated into the safety of his hood. Joe gazed at him for a couple more seconds with those piercing blue eyes, and then he gave a sigh, turning to face the front again.

Alex was relieved to be spared further scrutiny. A few seconds later, the door behind Peter was suddenly wrenched open, and a huge man with a long, straggly beard peered inside. Joe might have a dangerous aura, but at least it was coupled with a sense of tightly leashed control. This newcomer was threatening in a different way. His eyes were wild and darted around constantly, and he stank. Alex shrank away, both from the smell and from his odd body language.

"Who are you?" the newcomer demanded. "If you're from an IA, then I warn you, I'm armed."

Alex gripped the door handle in alarm when he saw what looked like the outline of a gun in the man's pocket, but neither Joe nor Peter seemed fazed.

"You must be Lars," Peter said in a calm voice. "It's okay – you're safe. We're not from an investigation agency – Elsie sent us to help you escape. I'm Peter, and this is my husband, Josiah." He jerked his thumb in Joe's direction.

GHOST EYE

Alex had forgotten that they were married. He felt a sudden knot of envy form in his stomach.

"It's okay, Lars. You're safe. We're here to help – aren't we, Joe?" Peter said, nudging his husband with his elbow.

"Yeah – get in, Lars. This is Ben – he just arrived. We're just waiting for one more person – Matthew – and then we can set off," Joe explained.

Lars lowered his big body into the back seat of the car, and Alex manoeuvred himself even further into the corner, trying to take up as little space as possible. He didn't like Lars; maybe living on the edge for the past ten days had heightened his sense of threat, but he felt sure that Lars was both unpredictable and unstable. He wrapped his scarf across his nose to block out the smell, wondering how Peter and Joe could stand it, but then he supposed he didn't smell too good right now, either.

"Bit wet and cold tonight, but you'll soon warm up now you're in the car," Peter said. "When Matthew turns up, we'll get you to a safe house where you can have a bath and a change of clothes."

That sounded good. Alex loved the thought of luxuriating in warm, soapy water after days walking the streets and nights sleeping in bushes. Peter asked if they had any medical needs, and Alex shook his head, hoping Matthew would arrive soon, so they could set off.

"We should leave. I think I was followed," Lars said unexpectedly.

"What makes you say that, Lars?" Joe turned again in his seat.

Alex studied the big blond man, trying to work out why he felt so drawn to him. Peter was a good man – he'd make you smile and do his best for you – but Joe would protect you, and right now Alex felt in desperate need of that.

"Investigation Agency, or a bounty hunter – I'm not sure which," Lars said. "I was followed for two miles yesterday but managed to lose them."

Joe pointed out, in reasonable if brusque tones, that IA investigators had to identify themselves if they suspected you were an escaped indie – he seemed very knowledgeable on the subject.

"A bounty hunter, then. Everyone knows they act outside the law!" Lars looked frantically out of the windows, his eyes darting wildly.

Alex wondered how long he'd been on the run. His own paranoia had increased exponentially in just over a week, so if Lars had escaped some time ago it might explain his craziness.

"No offence, but bounty hunters only go after high-value escaped indies, so a cleaning company IS isn't likely to attract them," Joe said in a matter-of-fact tone. "Ben – where did you escape from?"

Alex froze. Did Joe suspect him of being a "high-value escaped indie"? Had those sharp blue eyes somehow guessed his secret? He remembered the back story he'd rehearsed and mumbled "factory" into his scarf. Joe seemed satisfied with that.

"How much longer must we wait?" Lars complained loudly. "We must go now."

Alex agreed, but he didn't like the way Lars was waving his arms around aggressively. Peter explained that they'd be here until 8.30 p.m., but Lars wasn't having any of it.

"That's too long," he argued. "We must go now."

Joe swivelled in his seat to glare at Lars, and Alex felt a sudden coldness permeate the car. Elsie was right – Joe *was* scary.

"Well, that's how long we're going to wait," Joe stated, in a tone that brooked no disagreement. Alex wouldn't have dared, and Lars didn't, either. He sat back in his seat.

"How about some music?" Peter suggested, clearly to lighten the mood. "This will interest you – it's a CD player, so it's perfectly in period for a Pre-R car."

Alex was interested, but Joe clearly wasn't. He snorted at his husband's choice of music.

"Peter's a fan of New Wave Emo Rock," Joe said in a wry tone. "Which as far as I can see means sad young people with raspy voices singing daft songs with incomprehensible lyrics that sound like they mean something but don't."

Peter laughed, and Alex sensed that this was an ongoing argument between them. He was struck by how relaxed and normal they were during this most abnormal of situations. What would it be like to have someone in your life like Joe? Someone who knew you inside out, who teased you and made you laugh like Peter was laughing now. Peter bantered back about Joe's love of Pre-R rock, and Alex was transfixed.

GHOST EYE

Maybe, one day, Ben Smith could have a relationship like this, even if Alexander Lytton never could.

A song by an artist called Ashton started playing. Joe mocked it, making up new lyrics to go with the mournful tune.

"Oh no, I'm so bloody sad, please let me drone on about how sad I am," he sang. Peter grinned and turned up the volume to drown him out. They argued about the meaning of the song for a little while, and then Joe turned to look at Alex and Lars.

"So – how about a vote?" he asked. "Anyone here want something less pretentious? Something with a beat, perhaps? Maybe The Beatles? Or Queen?"

Alex shrugged, not wanting to draw attention to himself, although he sided with Joe on this one. He loved Pre-R rock and thought the New Wave Emo stuff was crap.

"I'm the driver," Peter said. "And the driver always gets to choose the music."

"Yes, Captain." Joe saluted him.

Alex wondered if that was a pet name, or whether Peter had once been in the military. If anyone had been in the armed forces, he'd have thought it would be Joe, with his straight back and sense of tightly leashed strength. Peter didn't look like the type who obeyed orders and shined his shoes until he could see his face in them.

Peter and Joe chatted away, still teasing one another, and then Peter suggested that Joe buy them some drinks from a café over the road.

"Good idea. What do you guys want – Ben? Lars?" Joe questioned. He pulled out his wallet.

Alex asked for a tea – anything hot would be welcome after days eating out of packets in the park.

"Anything to eat?" Joe pressed, glancing inside his wallet.

Alex shook his head. Beside him, he felt Lars suddenly tense up.

"Okay – five teas, then. We'll assume our missing Matthew will also fancy a cuppa when he shows up," Joe said. He climbed out of the car, still complaining about the terrible choice of music as he left.

When he'd gone, Lars poked Alex in the ribs.

"He's an investigator," he hissed in an undertone. In the front,

Peter was singing along to the song and performing a little drum solo, beating his hands on the steering wheel in time to the music.

"What?" Alex frowned.

"That one." Lars pointed out of the car at Joe's retreating back. "He works for an IA – I saw his ID card in his wallet. This is a trap." That agitated look was back in his eyes.

"I don't think it is," Alex said, thinking he'd trust Peter and Joe over crazy Lars any day. "Which agency was on the ID? Not all agencies hunt escaped indies – they specialise in different things."

"Inquisitus," Lars said.

Alex relaxed. "It's fine – I've heard of them. They specialise in big cases and homicides, not escaped indies. They're one of the classier outfits."

"They're gonna drag us back to our houders and claim the reward," Lars hissed, his eyes flickering wildly as he looked out of the window at Joe and then back at Peter.

"No, they aren't. They're taking us to a safe house, and then they'll get us out of the country," Alex insisted.

"I nearly got caught a few weeks ago, at a port. Investigators and bounty hunters all around," Lars said. "Let's take the car and make our own escape."

"What? No!"

"We could throw this one out and get away before the other one comes back," Lars said, gesturing at Peter.

"No," Alex repeated emphatically. "We don't need a car – we need a way out of the country, and that's what Joe and Peter are offering us."

Lars suddenly stared over his shoulder, through the side window. Alex followed his gaze to see Joe emerging from the café carrying a cardboard tray with five cups of tea.

"There's no time," Lars said, reaching into his inside coat pocket. Alex saw a flash of silver, and then Lars lunged forward and stabbed a knife deep into Peter's neck. It all happened so fast. Peter let out a piercing scream and pressed his hand to his neck in surprise. Lars raised the weapon, ready to stab Peter again, but Alex threw himself forward and grabbed his arm. Lars was bigger than him, and strong, but Alex held on with all his might.

He was dimly aware of the car door being wrenched open. Lars pulled his arm free and shoved him away to make another lunge at Peter. Alex threw a punch to deflect him, but it only knocked Lars off course for a split second, and then he tried again. At that moment, Joe threw himself into the car, grabbed Lars's wrist, and forced him to drop the weapon. Lars punched Joe hard, but Joe seemed to be made of granite and didn't even flinch.

Joe yelled to Peter for help in getting Lars out of the car, not knowing he'd been stabbed – so Alex sprang into action. He pushed past Joe and scrambled out of the car, then ran around to the other side, wrenching open the back passenger door. He threw himself back inside to grab Lars's arm and pull him out, while Joe punched him out from the inside. Lars landed in a heap in the pavement, knocking Alex over in the process – then scrambled to his feet and ran off down the street. Joe whirled back towards Peter, and Alex saw the horrified expression on his face as he realised his husband had been stabbed.

"Lars went for him," Alex explained desperately, using the open car door to pull himself to his feet. "He stabbed Peter in the neck. I didn't even see he had a knife until then. I grabbed his arm and pulled him back before he could stab Peter again, and then you got here. Is he okay? Is Peter okay?"

Joe ran around to the driver's door and yanked it open like a man possessed. Peter lurched sideways onto him, and Joe sank down beside the car, easing his husband gently onto his lap. There was blood... so much blood... spurting from the wound in Peter's neck, covering his clothes and the interior of the car, and staining Joe's purple sweater red. Alex realised by the sheer amount of blood that the knife had sliced into Peter's carotid artery.

"Call an ambulance!" Joe yelled.

Alex stood there helplessly, trying to take it all in. It had all happened so fast – one minute he was dreaming of a hot bath and nice meal in a safe house, and the next there was a fight, and a knife, and all that blood. He got control of himself. Peter was one of the good guys, and he had to stay and help, in any way he could. His own dramas were irrelevant right now. If Tyler caught up with him, then so be it; Peter

needed his help. Fumbling for his nanopad, he called the emergency services and asked for an ambulance.

"We're opposite the shops on Station Road in West Wickham. Please hurry," he begged.

"Can you give us your name?" the call handler asked.

"Please – just get here quickly. He's dying!" Alex looked down at where Peter was lying on Joe's lap. Joe had his hand pressed desperately to the stab wound, but blood was still pumping out around the sides of his fingers.

Alex crouched down in front of Joe. "The ambulance is on its way. What do you want me to do now?" he asked.

Joe glanced up at him. "Go!" he ordered.

"But..." Where? Alex wondered. This had been his only plan – where the hell could he go?

"The paramedics will be here soon – and so will the police. They'll question you. Save yourself. Go," Joe insisted.

Alex knew he was right. He couldn't be here when the emergency services arrived. He got to his feet and then hesitated, hating to leave like this with Peter's life hanging in the balance.

"I'm so sorry," he said. "I couldn't stop him. I didn't see the knife... It all happened so fast..."

There was a noise from the café across the street. He looked up to see the door opening and people spilling out. He was running out of time. If he waited much longer, it'd be too late.

Peter's breathing was coming in ragged gasps. Joe was looking down on his husband as if his heart had been ripped out and shredded right in front of him.

Alex barely knew these men, but their lives had become inextricably entwined with his in the space of less than an hour. He felt a deep pity for what Joe was facing. Peter was special – Alex had felt that from the moment they first met. No wonder Joe loved him so much. "Sorry," he said again, knowing how inadequate the word was. Then there was nothing else for him to do but turn and run. He took off in the opposite direction to Lars, not wanting to bump into the deranged lunatic again.

He was halfway down the street when he heard a bloodcurdling

sound that stopped him in his tracks. It took him a second to realise what it was. Then he knew. That wild howling was the sound of a man in utter desolation, and he knew in that instant that Peter was dead. He could feel every atom of Joe's grief in that unnatural, keening cry, and the hair on the back of his neck stood on end as it echoed down the street behind him.

He wanted to go back and offer useless words of comfort, but there was nothing he could do. There was nothing here for him now. He didn't know where he was going, or what he was going to do next, but he did know he had to get as far away from here as possible.

So he ran.

Chapter Fourteen

OCTOBER 2095

Josiah

Josiah's thoughts reeled back to Ben Smith as he drove to work with Alex by his side. Had Ben got away, or had he been captured and hauled back to the factory he'd escaped from? If so, what fate had awaited him there? In the immediate aftermath of Peter's death, he'd been too grief-stricken to spare much thought for Ben, but there had been many times over the years since when he'd wondered what had become of him.

Ben had been petrified. It'd been clear he wasn't cut out for a life on the run, so Josiah hoped he'd found a way out of the country. To be so close to freedom, only to have it snatched away – that had to be tough.

It had taken the Kathleen Line a while to regroup after Peter's death. Josiah had put operations on hold until he and Elsie felt able to resume. After that, they'd taken much more care. Whereas Peter had been casual about allowing indies to stay over in their house on occasion, Josiah refused to allow it going forward, not wanting an IS under his roof ever again, or to put his volunteers in danger, either. He set up safe houses for that specific purpose. He introduced new safety protocols: nobody did a pick-up alone, or was left alone with escaped indies; stun guns were routinely taken on all pick-ups; and escapees were

checked for weapons before they were admitted to a safe house. He also gave training to his volunteers on how to spot and deal with potentially dangerous indies.

Lars was long dead, and Matthew had never shown up, but Josiah still wondered where Ben was now. Was he alive? Did he blame Josiah for sending him away that night? If his life as an IS had been as much of a misery as Josiah suspected, then maybe he'd spent the last seven years hating him for being sent away. Maybe he was out there, leading a desperate existence as someone's IS, hating him to this day.

Ben was the only other witness to the events of that night. He was the only one who could testify that Josiah had lied to Esther and her investigation team about what had really happened. If he'd been captured, he hadn't talked, because Josiah hadn't received the knock on the door that he'd been half expecting since he'd joined the Kathleen Line.

Even though it was seven years ago, he felt he was still linked to Ben Smith by their shared experience that night. He hoped the terrified young man was now living a happy life abroad, free from abuse and fear.

"Hey," Alex said, jolting him out of his thoughts. "You're quiet."

"Just thinking." Josiah shrugged.

"About anything in particular?"

"No – just someone I knew once. I was wondering how he's doing."

"You should call him and find out," Alex suggested.

"Yeah, I should," Josiah said absently, wishing it was possible. Elsie had called Ben's nano as soon as Inquisitus had wrapped up its investigation, but the nym was out of service. "It's been on my conscience."

"Is he someone special?"

"Yes. I didn't know him for very long, but let's just say he made an impact."

"Then I hope you get the chance to speak to him one day," Alex said, with a sideways glance at him. Then he changed the subject. "So – Esther sounded pretty pissed off. Are you worried about your job?"

"No." Josiah shook his head resolutely. "I can handle Esther. She's firm but fair. She might be angry, but I'll survive."

· · ·

The usual media scrum was waiting for them when they arrived at Inquisitus. After Josiah's announcement earlier they were buzzing, clearly wanting more. He steered Alex through the crowd, using the bulk of his body to bulldoze them through.

Once inside, he went straight to the SID to find Reed talking to Sofie Baumann. She glanced at him coldly.

"I see you've decided this particular IS isn't guilty, Investigator Raine," she said. "Maybe you should revise your mantra about how 'it's always the serf or the spouse'."

"It's not my mantra," he snapped.

"It might as well be. If you went into cases with an open mind, instead of automatically assuming the indie is guilty, then you wouldn't have to make any more humiliating climbdowns like you did this morning," she told him tartly.

"I don't believe it *was* a humiliating climbdown," Alex interjected, taking Josiah by surprise. "Investigator Raine has been nothing but fair to me, Doctor Baumann; I have no complaints about either his treatment of me or the way he's conducting his investigation."

She opened her mouth in surprise, then closed it again. After another withering look in Josiah's direction, she left.

"You'll ruin my reputation as a hard-arsed bastard," Josiah said with a grin.

"I doubt that's possible," Alex replied, grinning back.

"I must have missed something," Reed interrupted, glaring at them both. "When, exactly, did we decide that Lytton is innocent?" He swept a hand over his holopad and pointed at all the files that pinged up in mid-air with giant red question marks over them. "As far as I can see, he's still our prime suspect, sir, unless you have some new information to the contrary."

"No, I don't," Josiah admitted.

"Then, what – you take Lytton home with you for a few nights and now he's innocent? That's bloody good mojo you've got, Lytton," Reed accused. "If there was one investigator in the country who it's impossible to fool, I'd have said it's Josiah Raine, but it looks like you've managed it."

"Hey!" Josiah turned on Reed angrily. "I'm in charge of this investi-

gation, and I made a judgement call. I believe Alex is innocent, and I'm happy to put my reputation on the line for him. Apart from anything else, I don't appreciate the media hanging around outside my house. My announcement was partly designed to call them off."

"Yeah? And how's that working out for you?" Reed asked sarcastically.

At that moment Esther arrived. "Ah – you're here – good. Why did you bring the IS with you?" She glanced at Alex.

"Because I'm increasingly uncomfortable with leaving him in my house with a bunch of news crews camped out front. Being a houder comes with certain obligations – I'm responsible for his personal safety and welfare now, and that's a responsibility I take seriously. So, I would prefer to have him with me, where I can keep an eye on him."

She gave a grudging grunt. "Well, he can stay here for now, but you're coming with me." She pointed her wheelchair in the direction of the lift.

"He's coming with us. There's nothing you have to say to me that you can't say in front of him," Josiah grated.

She paused for a moment, studying him, and then she shot a shrewd glare at Alex. He gave her his standard vacant smile in return.

"Hmm. Okay – if you want your IS to hear your boss giving you a bloody good bollocking, then be my guest."

They followed her into the lift and up to her office in silence. The minute her office door was closed behind them, she started talking.

"Joe, I've known you for ten years, and you've never let me down. I'd like to think you have a good reason for what you did earlier, but right now I don't know what the hell it can be."

"Esther, you've always trusted me to handle the press in any way I see fit," Josiah replied as calmly as he could, gesturing to Alex to sit at the table in the corner of the room.

"Usually, the way you see fit is something I approve of, but not today. Why did you do it, Joe? You've placed us in a very difficult position."

"Only if you think Alex is guilty of Dacre's murder."

"Alex?" She raised an eyebrow at the shortened name. "I warned you about getting too close to him, Joe. I told you he's a charming

manipulator who uses people to get what he wants." She shot Alex a sharp look.

Josiah glanced at Alex, and saw it was wasted on him; his expressionless mask was firmly in place. "You also said you didn't think he was guilty," he pointed out to Esther.

"I didn't – I don't – but we don't have the evidence to support that stance. You made it sound like Inquisitus is convinced of his innocence, and I don't believe we are, yet."

"I am," Josiah said tightly.

"On what grounds? Do you have another suspect?"

"Not yet, but I'm working on it."

"Joe..." She exhaled. "This isn't like you. You don't make rash decisions based on nothing."

"Not based on nothing."

"On a feeling, then?" she challenged. "Didn't we discuss this already? Since when do you do anything based on feelings?"

"I used to," he retorted. "When you first knew me. It was only after Peter died that I stopped, and that was only because I didn't feel anything very much for years. I had to rely on the cold, hard facts instead."

"You said they never let you down."

"They don't – but they haven't always helped me, either."

"So, what's changed?" she demanded. "Something has. You look different." She waved her hand at him. "What is it, Joe? You look..." She paused, studying him intently.

"Like I don't have a stick stuck up my arse anymore?"

"I was going to say younger."

"That's because I faced up to something I should have dealt with a long time ago."

"Christ, you didn't..." She looked at Alex and then back at him.

"No," he responded curtly. "I didn't fuck him."

"That's not what I—"

"Yes, it is." He glared at her. "Look, I've been a robot since Peter died. I've made a virtue out of not relying on anything as vague as a hunch, but the truth is I didn't have them anymore. I always used to

have a nose for something being off, but I lost that after Peter died, so I had to make up for it in other ways."

"What are you saying? Now you've woken up and can smell the roses again? What are you? Sleeping bloody Beauty?"

"No – I'm back to being the Josiah Raine you hired ten years ago, and he was a bloody good investigator."

"And what caused this transformation?" She glanced at Alex.

"I don't know – maybe I was just ready. It's been a long time." Josiah sighed. "Look, Esther, I've worked my arse off for Inquisitus for the past ten years. I worked day and night on all the cases you threw my way and helped you turn this Agency into the most famous in the country."

"I'm not saying you're not good at your job. I'm questioning your judgement in this particular instance."

"Well, don't. I've more than earned your trust over the years, surely?"

She studied him for a long moment, her shrewd brown eyes boring into him. Finally, she sighed. "I'd like to trust you, Joe, but I'm not sure where you're going with this. What was yesterday's excursion to see George Tyler about, for example?"

"Just following one of my hunches, the way I used to. I'm sure Alex is integral to solving Dacre's murder; I wanted to make sure that Tyler, as his former houder, wasn't interested in getting him back."

"By killing Dacre?" She raised a disbelieving eyebrow.

"We know Dacre had two offers for Alex, both of which he turned down. It's not such a stretch to think that one of them might have come from Tyler."

"That's why you went to see Tyler?"

"Yes."

"And?"

Josiah sighed. "He probably wasn't involved in Dacre's murder, but he's guilty of something. Alex has given me some information about how Tyler operates that makes me think we should investigate him."

"You want to go after one of the most powerful men in the country on the word of an IS – and one with an appalling reputation?" She pursed her lips. "And for what? What's Tyler guilty of, exactly?"

"Prostitution of his servants and blackmail of his business associates for starters, but I'm sure there's more. Much more."

"Do you have any evidence?" she demanded.

"No."

"Then absolutely not."

"I've met the guy – he's a bastard."

"Maybe, but that's not illegal," she shot back.

He rocked back on his heels, and out of the corner of his eye he saw Alex watching him curiously.

"Look, Joe, if you go after Tyler, you'd better have more on him than the accusations of one untrustworthy IS, or it'll end badly for you – Tyler will see to that. And..." Esther hesitated, glancing at Alex again. "We all have things to hide. Things we'd prefer not to get out."

"You think Tyler could blackmail me, too?" he responded incredulously.

"I'm saying... think about it," she said softly. "The entire country already suspects you killed Lars Driessen – it wouldn't take much to convince a jury that you did, and that I covered it up for you during the official investigation."

"That isn't what happened."

"I know – I'm just saying it could be painted that way. There were other anomalies I didn't look into too deeply, but a less sympathetic investigator might if the case were reopened." Her eyes went back to Alex, clearly worried about whether they should be having such a frank conversation in front of him.

"Such as?" Josiah asked icily, daring her into it.

"Such as the fact you bought five cups of tea that night, although you said that only you and Peter were in the car."

"We were taking them to a friend."

"Who lived a thirty-minute drive away. I'm sure she was looking forward to several cups of lukewarm tea," Esther said drily. "And why she couldn't make her own is beyond me. Then there was the untraceable nanopad. We never found out who called for the ambulance that night."

"I told you, it was just some kid passing by."

"Who just happened to have a burner nanopad, a nym that couldn't be traced, and then conveniently disappeared?"

"I don't know who he was," Josiah said quietly. "Maybe he didn't want to be involved any further."

"Maybe." She shrugged. "I didn't ask too many questions because we had our killer beyond any reasonable doubt, and you were so devastated by Peter's death. I thought it was an invasion of your privacy, and I didn't like to dwell too much on what you and Peter liked to get up to in your private lives. If you wanted to meet up with other men, for example..."

"Is that what you think?" Josiah stared at her. "That we were arranging to hold an orgy with three other guys that night? Christ, Esther, that's insane. Peter and I didn't have that kind of marriage. Apart from anything else, I'm not the sharing kind."

"Okay, but the questions remain, and it wouldn't take a man like George Tyler long to identify that moment in your life as a potential area of weakness."

He was silent, his chest heaving as he took in what she was saying.

"Find Elliot Dacre's killer and let's see where we go from there," she told him, in a gentler tone. "Then, if you can bring me more on George Tyler – something meaty enough to warrant opening that particular can of worms – I'll see what I can do. Just be careful, because if we get this wrong, it could bring Inquisitus down."

"Okay." He nodded. "Fine. Let's do that." Turning, he strode towards the door.

"Joe." She called him back. "This old Josiah Raine I'm getting back – is he going to be as good as the one I've been working with for the past few years?"

He grinned at her. "Better. Much better, because now I'm working at full strength, so you get an investigator with an eye for detail who has a feeling for a case, too. I'll bring you Elliot Dacre's killer, Esther, and I'll land you a big fish as well, if you let me. Trust me. I've never let you down yet, have I?"

"No," she admitted quietly. "Okay, Joe – I'll trust you."

"Good." He jerked his head at Alex. "Then let's get to work."

Alex fell into step beside him with a shit-eating grin on his face.

"What?" Josiah demanded as they strode into the lift.

"Just you. Being all... you. I love it." Alex laughed.

Josiah felt a wave of exhilarating energy sweep through him. "Me too," he exclaimed.

He strode into the SID with Alex at his heels, feeling as if he could conquer the world. He threw himself down in his chair, whistling loudly, and put his feet up on the desk.

Reed stared at him. "Who are you, and what did you do with my boss?"

"I'm still here, just mixing things up a little." He stretched his arms over his head and glanced around. "Alex – pull up a chair and sit there," he suggested, pointing to the far end of his desk. "Reed – did you look into any correspondence Dacre had on who wanted to buy Alex?"

He noticed Alex pause momentarily as he reached for the chair, and then collect himself and continue as if nothing had happened. He was sure Alex knew the identity of at least one of the people who'd wanted to buy his contract. Why keep it a secret? Who was he protecting – and why?

"I've been trawling through all the data for the past two days, but nothing so far," Reed replied.

"Okay – keep looking," Josiah instructed. "Have you found any info on the tracking chip from the envelope containing the gun?"

"Yeah, but the sender gave a fake address, which isn't exactly a surprise." Reed shrugged.

"Where was it posted?"

"A drone station in East New London. I'm checking their CCTV coverage right now."

"What about prints? Did we get any off the envelope?"

"Nope." Reed shook his head. "It's clean – just like everything else. No prints on anything."

"What about the door-to-doors? Anything?"

"Not so far, but it's taking time to gather all the footage from people's smart systems."

At that moment a member of security arrived, accompanied by a man in his fifties wearing a rumpled grey suit. He had a comb-over, a

droopy grey moustache, and a paunch – and he was bristling with outrage.

"I'm here to see Investigator Raine," he said loudly. "I called Director Lomax, and she said to come into the office and make my complaint directly to you, as you're leading the investigation."

"Really – and you are?" Josiah asked.

"Jeffrey Mead. I was a good friend of Elliot's, and I'm the executor of his will. I saw you on the news this morning, and I don't take kindly to you appropriating my dear friend's indentured servant for yourself in this high-handed fashion. I'm here to demand that you hand Chris over to me, so I can organise the reading of Elliot's will and the proper handling and disposal of his estate."

"Yeah, that's not going to happen," Josiah said, standing up. He saw Alex looking warily at Mead and was instantly certain they knew each other. "*Alex* is staying with me until we catch whoever killed Dacre."

"You have no right—"

"I'm leading a murder investigation; I have every right, Mr Mead."

"Don't try and pull rank with me. I know precisely what the rules and regulations are in cases like this – I happen to be an investigator myself."

"Is that so? What agency do you work for?" Josiah asked coolly.

"Results Incorporated," Mead replied, puffing himself up importantly.

It was all Josiah could do not to laugh in the man's face. Results Inc was a small-time agency dealing with minor drug crimes, petty theft, and fraud. It also had a sideline in tracking down escaped indies, which was enough to make him dislike Jeffrey Mead by itself.

"Just because some investigators enjoy a certain celebrity status, doesn't mean they can use said status to bend the rules," Mead said primly.

Josiah gave a dangerous smile. He was relishing the chance to do battle with this idiot, but he saw a troubled look pass across Alex's face. "This is clearly a serious complaint," he said silkily to Mead. "Shall we take this conversation to one of our interview suites?"

"I think we should," Mead retorted. "I would like Director Lomax to hear what I have to say as well."

"Fine. Reed – buzz her," Josiah ordered. "And keep looking at that CCTV footage while I'm gone."

"Yes, sir."

"And keep an eye on Alex. You know, in case he tries to abscond." He shot Alex a teasing smile.

Reed gave him a sour look and a grunt by way of reply.

Josiah led the way to the interview suite. Esther arrived a few seconds later. They both sat facing Mead at the interview table.

"What precisely is the nature of your complaint?" Josiah asked.

"As I said, I'm the executor of Elliot Dacre's estate, and I have serious concerns about your conduct in this case. By law, Christopher should have been released into my custody—"

"No, that's incorrect," Esther said firmly. "Alexander Lytton is part of Mr Dacre's estate. If he'd been released anywhere it would have been to a probate holding camp until such time as the estate is wound up – and that wouldn't happen until our investigation was complete."

"Well, that's as may be, but as the executor, I feel Elliot would have wanted Chris to live with me," Mead blustered.

"I've seen Dacre's will, I've spoken to his solicitor, and I've looked through his bank records," Josiah informed him bluntly. "Dacre was heavily in debt when he died, and despite all the lavish bequests and grand gestures he made in his will, the reality is he's got nothing to leave to anyone. Once everything has been sold and all his debts are paid, I'll be surprised if there's a hundred quid left over. So basically, you're the executor of bugger all."

Mead glared at him. "Regardless, I should have been consulted."

"Technically speaking – no." Esther gave a tight smile. "As the IA leading the investigation, we may choose to consult with you on matters pertaining to Mr Dacre's estate, but you have no right to a consultation. You also have no legal right to be granted custody of any of his possessions if we wish to retain them for the purpose of the investigation."

"Why do you want Lytton, anyway?" Josiah demanded.

"Chris was Elliot's pride and joy – his most treasured possession. I know Elliot would have wanted me to take care of him, that's all," Mead said.

"Well, you can't have him." Josiah stood up. "Are we done?"

"Not quite, Investigator Raine." Mead glared at him sulkily. "I thought that as you made that statement today about Christopher's innocence, you should be aware of a conversation I had with him not so long ago."

"Really?" Josiah sat back down with a sigh. "What conversation is that?"

"Well, as I said, I'm an investigator with a leading IA."

"You said you were an investigator, yes." Josiah nodded. "Mr Mead works for Results Inc," he told Esther.

"Right." She gave a knowing smile. "So, what was this conversation about, Mr Mead?"

"I'm telling you about it because, as a fellow investigator, I was shocked by the indiehunter's announcement this morning. Far be it from me to cast aspersions on a fellow professional's work" – he shot Josiah a vicious look – "but I did think it was strange that he would rule anyone out of the inquiry at this stage."

"You don't know what stage our inquiry is at," Josiah said flatly.

"No, indeed, but you have yet to charge anyone, I believe." Mead smiled smugly. "Now, I don't know if this is relevant, but Elliot and I were close, and I was invited to all his parties. I met Hudson Brink, Jon Mayberry, Jana Stanner, Godiva, and all the other celebrities Elliot was friends with." He puffed out his chest again proudly.

"Really." Josiah imbued the word with as much icy contempt as he could muster.

"Yes, and of course I knew Chris well. He was always so charming and full of fun at Elliot's parties, but a very different person in private."

"In what way?" Esther asked.

"Well, I remember on one occasion he asked me a lot of questions about my work. He's got quite a sharp brain, that one – not at all what I expected having seen him dance around half-naked at Elliot's parties."

"What kind of questions?" Esther leaned forward, frowning.

"I thought it was odd at the time, but when Elliot was murdered it all slotted into place – which is why I was so surprised by Raine's big

announcement that Chris couldn't possibly be the killer." He smiled vindictively at Josiah.

"What were the questions?" Esther repeated.

"He wanted to know about the process by which investigations are assigned and handled. He had many questions about how it all worked – intelligent questions, too. One thing in particular struck me, because it seemed important to him. He wanted to know how investigations were set in motion – who would be contacted, what the chain of command would be, how it all worked."

"Maybe he was just showing an interest in what you do," Esther suggested.

"Maybe, but listen to this." Mead leaned forward eagerly. "He was specifically asking about murder investigations, Director Lomax." He sat back with a gleeful smile on his face. "Strange, don't you think? He asks how murder investigations work, and then Elliot turns up murdered? Coincidence? I don't think so. Maybe that announcement you made this morning was premature, Raine." He shot a look of triumph at Josiah.

Esther glanced at Josiah sideways. He paused for a long moment, like a snake contemplating its prey, then went on the attack. "Mr Mead... how did a lowly investigator like yourself become friends with a top celebrity holophotographer?" he enquired.

"I don't see how that's relevant," Mead snapped. "And I dislike your use of the word 'lowly'."

"Ah, but we're all lowly, aren't we?" Josiah said smoothly. "Us investigators. It's not a very glamorous job, is it? We certainly tend not to have friends who move in celebrity circles. How did you meet Dacre? What was the basis of your friendship?"

"We go back a few years. We had a lot in common."

"You still haven't said how you met."

"I can't remember."

"I think you remember." Josiah gave a tight smile and clasped his hands together on the table in front of him. "I suspect the police were given a tip-off about the illegal drugs Dacre peddled at his parties – in addition to croc, he also provided cocaine, heroin, crystal meth, and sable to his party guests. He always made sure that any

drugs his celebrity friends wanted were on hand, courtesy of the dealers he had on call. The police passed the tip-off to Results Inc, you were assigned to the case, and you soon found out that Dacre was guilty. It would have been inconvenient for him if he'd been charged, and embarrassing for his celebrity friends to be named in court depositions. I'm sure he'd have done anything to protect them."

"What are you saying? Are you accusing me of something?" Mead erupted.

"Yes," Josiah said bluntly. "I think that instead of turning in the results of your investigation, you went to Dacre and offered to submit a false report, and continue submitting false reports, as long as he invited you to his parties, let you meet his celebrities – and sleep with his very attractive IS."

"That's a lie." Mead looked affronted in the way that only the truly guilty ever looked, in Josiah's experience.

"Shall we call Alex in and ask him if he ever slept with you?" he asked, his flesh crawling at the thought of this sleazy bastard laying his fat paws on Alex.

"I'm not saying I didn't sleep with him," Mead said quickly. "Elliot was kind enough to share, and Chris was always up for a good time. It doesn't prove I covered up anything on Elliot's behalf."

"A good time?" Josiah snorted. "Look at you, Mead. Normally, you wouldn't stand a chance of attracting a beautiful young man like Alexander Lytton, and there's no way he'd consider a night with you to be a 'good time'. He slept with you because Dacre told him to, because he was the price for your silence. I already know Dacre gave Alex to other men in his circle. He liked to act the jealous lover – it turned him on – but he also liked to watch."

"Lies!" Mead crossed his arms over his chest. "I came here to share valuable information with colleagues, and you've made up all these slurs about me. It's most unprofessional."

"The reason you want to take Alex home with you is because you're worried what he might tell us about your friendship with Dacre. You want to silence him, basically. If you really thought he was guilty of murdering his houder, I doubt you'd be so keen."

Mead didn't have an answer to that. He just sat there, arms crossed over his chest, glowering.

Josiah smiled. "You can leave, Mr Mead. We won't be releasing Alex into your custody."

"He asked about you, too, you know," Mead said unexpectedly.

Josiah raised an eyebrow.

"It was around that time you were on the news night and day because of that case involving the celebrity chef and the escaped indie - or maybe it was one of your other high profile cases. I don't recall. You do seem to love a celebrity murder, and they all blend into each other after awhile," he sneered.

"Anyway, I thought Christopher might have a bit of a crush on you – you were quite the pin-up, forever popping up onscreen being all gruff and macho in your fancy suits." Mead sounded like a bitter old queen who couldn't get the pretty boys to sleep with him and resented any other gay man he thought was competition. No wonder he'd resorted to blackmail to get his hands on Alex. "He wanted to know if I'd ever come across you professionally, what I thought of you, and what you were like in person."

"And what did you tell him?"

"The truth – that some investigators love chasing the limelight and showing off instead of getting on with their jobs." Mead sneered.

Josiah gave a little grunt of amusement. "I think we're done here, Mead, don't you?"

"Fine." Mead stood up. "Uh... will you...?" He cast a worried glance at Esther.

"Be reporting you to your agency for investigation?" She raised an eyebrow. "I'll let you know. Good day, Mr Mead."

She opened the door, gestured to security to escort him out, and then turned back to Josiah.

"What a nasty piece of work," she said. "Well done for seeing through him, Joe. However, what he said about Alex is worrying."

"I'm sure there's an explanation," Josiah said firmly.

"Maybe, but you have to admit it's another black mark against Lytton."

He nodded. "I agree, it's damaging – if it's true – but I stand by

what I said earlier. Give me time, Esther, and I'll crack this case. I've got Reed looking into a new area of possibility right now."

"Good. Show me."

She followed him down to the SID, where Reed was running through CCTV footage of the drone station on the smartwall. Alex was seated where Josiah had left him, that blank, inscrutable mask back on his face. Josiah wished he knew what the IS was hiding. He wasn't happy about what he'd learned from Mead, but he refused to believe that this man, who'd comforted him so gently during his breakdown in the night, had lied to him. Alex was innocent, and he intended to prove it.

"How are we doing?" he asked Reed.

"Well... I found this." Reed pointed at the smartwall. "It's the drone pick-up point the parcel containing the gun was sent from – not great quality, because they're a small outfit, but I found this." He froze the grainy footage as a woman placed a small parcel in the pick-up locker. "The parcel is the correct size to be the one containing the gun," he said. "We haven't found any images that are as close a match as this."

"Can you get a decent frame of her?" Josiah asked, leaning in close to study her. She looked young and slim, but her anorak hood obscured her hair and part of her face.

"I can get my team to work on it," Reed said.

"Good – do that. Let's see if we can track her down. She's wearing gloves, which she obviously would if she wanted to hide her prints," Josiah said, still studying the image. "Good work, Cam. I love it when we get a break like this." He rubbed his hands together. "This is good. Just like old times."

"What's got into him, Director Lomax?" Reed asked, shaking his head. "I've never seen him like this before."

"I have." Esther shot him a wry smile and reached out to touch his arm. "It's good to have you back, Joe. I'd forgotten... It's been a long time."

"It's good to be back." He sat down at his desk, feeling peckish. His hand went to his jacket pocket before he realised he'd forgotten to refill his chocolate stash and bring it with him this morning... so

he was surprised when his hand closed around the little silver box. He drew it out and opened it, finding two dark chocolates nestled inside. He glanced at Alex, who said nothing but gave him the most serene of smiles. Smiling back, he placed a chocolate caramel in his mouth, taking a moment to tune out and savour the rich, smooth taste.

Reed's team sent back a tidied-up version of the image an hour later. Reed set off with it immediately to doorstep the area and see if they could trace their mystery poster.

When they were alone, Josiah glanced at his IS. "Do you recognise this woman?" he asked, pointing at the cleaned-up still.

Alex gazed at the image on the smartwall closely, then shook his head. "I've never seen her before."

"You're sure?"

"Absolutely. I don't know her," Alex said decisively.

"Fine. You definitely recognised Jeffrey Mead earlier, though."

"Yes."

"What do you think of him?"

Alex made a face. "He's a parasite. He leeched off Elliot, so I assumed he had something on him – probably relating to drugs – which explained why Elliot kept him around."

"That's pretty much what I thought."

"They became friends, though – they were close enough that Elliot made him the executor of his will." Alex grimaced. "Although, Elliot didn't have many friends, really. He had a lot of fake ones – all those people at his parties – but not many who I'd call real friends. Maybe Mead was as good as it got for Elliot."

"It seems that way. Did you sleep with Mead?" Josiah asked.

"Yes," Alex replied unflinchingly. "Several times. Elliot insisted."

"Mead said you once asked him some questions about homicide investigation procedures." Josiah gazed steadily at Alex.

Alex met his gaze unblinkingly. "I probably did. I tried to make conversation, to be sociable and interesting to those I was supposed to entertain. It was part of my Belvedere training."

"Mead doesn't work homicides."

Alex shrugged. "I didn't know that then."

GHOST EYE 285

Josiah sat back in his chair, studying him thoughtfully. "He also said you asked him a lot of questions about me."

Alex grinned. "I expect I did. I told you, I've read a lot of articles about you. Indies tend to take an interest in someone called the 'indiehunter' – and you were all over the news at the time."

As always, he had an answer for everything and always sounded so plausible. Yet Josiah never felt he was getting the whole truth. He decided to let it go – for now.

"Lunch?" he suggested, glancing at his watch. "I could order hachée?"

"Or we could have a sandwich," Alex countered.

"Fine." Josiah was amused by the many ways Alex found to avoid eating hachée. On his first night at his house, Alex had professed to love the stuff, but Josiah was rapidly coming to the conclusion that was a lie. How many more lies was Alex telling?

Josiah bought them each a sandwich from the canteen, then turned his attention to examining Dacre's holochat history in search of clues.

It revealed him to be every inch the gossipy, overgrown child that the investigation had so far revealed, but he couldn't find a trace of any offers to buy Alex. "You must be bored," he said after a couple of hours, glancing up from his work to find his IS drawing on a piece of paper.

"I'm fine," Alex said with a smile.

Turning the paper around, Josiah gazed at the drawings. They were deft, elegant pictures by someone with clear talent. He suddenly remembered something Noah Lytton had said about how he hoped that Alex could still see beauty in the world.

"They're good," he said, wondering what it was like for an artist to be denied an opportunity to draw and paint. For years, Alex had been used by his houders as some kind of bartering chip, his attractive body always offered up as the prize, as if that was the sum of the man and all his other skills were irrelevant. "Here." He handed Alex a cashcard. "Buy yourself some proper art materials. Get them delivered to the house this evening."

Alex gave him a startled look. "Do you mean it?"

"Yes. Spend whatever you like. Just buy whatever you need to

create whatever it is you want to create." Josiah waved a vague hand in the air.

Alex shot him a smile that was so completely heartfelt it took his breath away. He reddened and turned back to his work.

Reed called at 7 p.m., looking cold and miserable. "No luck so far," he said. "I've shown the pic around, but nobody recognises her."

"Fine. Call it off for now and go back tomorrow morning," Josiah instructed.

"Okay. Thanks," Reed said gratefully. "Sarah promised me macaroni cheese this evening, so I don't want to miss that – it's my favourite."

"Sounds good." Josiah moved his neck to one side until it made a satisfying crack. "I'm going to head off, too. We'll start again tomorrow. And Cam? Good work today."

Reed gave a surprised smile at the unexpected praise; Josiah grinned back and ended the call.

"Let's go home," he said to Alex, getting up and reaching for his jacket. "What's your favourite food?" he asked as they walked. "And don't say hachée, because I won't believe you."

"Fish and chips."

"Then let's get some on the way home."

"Great. You know, I was thinking..." Alex paused, and Josiah stopped to look at him.

"Yes?"

"That thing... the thing I said I had to tell you..."

"The thing that will make me angry, or upset, or both?" Josiah asked.

"Yes." Alex nodded slowly. "That thing."

"Well?"

Alex took a deep breath. "I'll tell you tonight," he said. "After dinner."

Chapter Fifteen

OCTOBER 2088

Alex

Running blindly through the night, Alex was hardly aware of where he was going. He heard the sound of sirens blaring out behind him but didn't pause to look back. He came to a stop alongside some railings and doubled over, struggling to breathe. Taking several deep, panting breaths, he vomited convulsively, throwing up everything in his stomach, and continued retching long after it was empty, bringing up only bile.

Finally, he stood up and looked around, wondering where he was... and realised he was standing outside the park that had been his home for the past ten days. Somehow, in his confused state his feet had carried him here, to a place he associated with sanctuary. Relieved, he hauled himself over the railings and stumbled towards his old, familiar hiding place in the bushes.

He lay there for hours, gazing up at the cloudy night sky, still reeling from what had happened. All he could hear was Joe, yelling at him to go as he clutched Peter's bloodied body in his arms, and then the sound of his inhuman howl, replaying on a never-ending loop.

He didn't sleep; he couldn't. He was in shock. He wrapped his arms around his body and spent the entire night shaking. At first, all he could think about was the horror of Peter's murder, but as dawn's first

pale light began to filter through the trees, he realised he needed a plan. He had very little money left, and he doubted the credit on his nanopad would last much longer, even if he knew anyone to contact.

That reminded him – he pulled the nanopad out of his pocket and made sure it was switched off, to retain the charge for as long as possible. He desperately wanted to call Elsie and ask her whether somehow it was possible that Peter had made it, even though he knew in his heart that he was dead. But there was nothing he could say to Elsie to comfort her about the loss of her friend, and no message he could pass on to Joe that would help. He wondered where Lars was and how long he'd survive once Joe caught up with him. Joe was a dangerous man who'd lost the love of his life – Alex was sure he'd go after Lars and exact vengeance.

Alex felt inextricably linked to the man he'd met only briefly, forever tied to him by the sheer magnitude of what they'd gone through. They'd fought off Lars together, tried to save Peter together, and shared one short, horrific moment in time. It'd created a connection between them. He wondered if, maybe, in a few days, he could call Elsie and ask if there was any chance of Joe's help, but then realised how incredibly selfish it would be to make them worry about his welfare right now given their terrible loss.

No – he was on his own. He had to find his own way out of the country. He decided to make for the coast; he'd heard of sympathetic sea captains who smuggled escaped indies across the Channel. He had no idea how one found such people, or what they wanted in payment, but that was his only hope now.

As soon as it was fully light, he scrambled out of the bushes and left the park for the final time. He didn't have enough money for a coach fare, and he was wary of the CCTV cameras fitted on every mode of public transport, so he decided to walk to the coast. He spent most of what was left of his money on a meagre supply of food, ate a dismal breakfast by the duck pond, and then began walking. He wasn't sorry to leave West Wickham; he'd spent a miserable week here and one horrific night. It didn't hold any good memories.

He walked all day, wishing he had proper walking boots instead of the fancy brogues that Lorenzo had chosen to complete his evening

wear all those days ago. His months spent in Vertex Tower seemed as if they belonged to a different life now – so much had happened since. He couldn't stop thinking about Peter, or block out the sound of Joe's howling in his head, so he found a café with a big screen and went inside, spending the last of his money on a cup of tea so he could sit and watch the news and be warm for a while.

The news feed cycled for a few minutes, and then a picture of Peter came onscreen. Alex sat up and paid attention.

"Residents of West Wickham are still reeling from a brutal murder in Station Road last night," the newsreader announced. "Ex-army officer Captain Peter Hunt was stabbed to death as he sat in his distinctive Pre-R red Jaguar." So Peter *had* been military – that made sense of Joe's use of his old title, and the ironic salute. "The motive behind the killing appears to be the theft of the vintage vehicle," the newsreader continued. That took him by surprise. He hadn't given any thought as to how Joe would cover up the real reason they were in Station Road last night. He pitied the grief-stricken man having to think up a good lie at such a terrible time.

A photo of a big man with neat brown hair parted in the middle was displayed onscreen, and for a moment Alex struggled to recognise him as the wild-eyed, bushy-bearded IS he'd met the night before.

"Escaped Indentured Servant Lars Driessen is being sought by Inquisitus Investigation Agency in connection with the killing," the newsreader said. "Esther Lomax, director of Inquisitus, gave a press conference earlier today."

A fierce-looking woman in a wheelchair appeared onscreen. She had short silvery-brown hair and sharp brown eyes.

"Lars Driessen is a very dangerous, desperate, and unpredictable man. If you see him, do not approach him – I repeat, do *not* approach him. Instead, contact us immediately." Then the news item cut away to her answering questions.

"Is it true that the victim's husband is an Inquisitus investigator?" a reporter demanded.

She nodded. "Peter Hunt was married to one of our investigators, Josiah Raine, who was with him last night at the time of the murder. Obviously, Josiah is on compassionate leave and is not working on this

case. I'm taking charge of the investigation myself. We have the murder weapon, and Josiah has given us a full account of what happened. We're not seeking anyone else in connection with this tragic incident."

Alex leaned forward as the news report segued to a shot of Joe coming out of a house. He was wearing a pair of dark jeans and a navy-blue sweater, and there was a black dog trotting along beside him, shooting him uncertain glances. He clearly hadn't slept – there were dark circles under his eyes, and his face was pinched with grief. He didn't make a statement to the press, despite them clamouring for his attention. Alex didn't blame him. The last thing Joe must have wanted was all those cameras outside his house at such a terrible time.

"Meanwhile, investigators are combing the crime scene for forensic evidence." A shot of Station Road came up, focusing, with unnecessary zeal, on the blood stains on the pavement. The reporter interviewed a young woman who'd been a witness.

"I was talking with friends in the café over the road when we were aware of a fight going on in the fancy car. I saw this young guy running off... I don't know if he was the one who killed that poor man..." She pointed down the street in the direction Alex had run the previous night. "I could see the body by the car – there was a lot of blood – and then the ambulance came, but we could all see it was too late."

"Inquisitus would like to talk to a witness who was first on the scene, and who called the ambulance," the reporter continued. "He's described as being around five-foot-ten, white, of slender build, and wearing a hooded sweatshirt and dark trousers. If you have any information as to his whereabouts, please contact our hotline nym."

"Shit," Alex muttered under his breath. It was bad enough that George Tyler was chasing him, but now a big IA was after him, too.

Suddenly, he was aware that the nanopad in his pocket was a liability. If he turned it on, they might try and call him... or they might be able to trace his location and find him. He jumped up in a panic and ran out of the café, then sprinted to a nearby lost zone and threw the nanopad into the water, watching sadly as his last lifeline sank. Now all of Solange's escape kit was gone – no Elsie, no nanopad, and no money. He was well and truly on his own.

He continued his dull plod towards the coast, taking a long, circuitous route that kept him off the main roads and out of sight of people or CCTV as much as possible. He slept in a church graveyard next to a moss-covered tombstone, in bushes, and in AV parks, all the time wishing he could have escaped during the summer instead of what was turning out to be a windy, rainy autumn. His clothes never fully dried out, leaving him permanently damp, and he knew he smelled. Soon, he'd probably smell as vile as Lars had.

The longer he kept walking and sleeping rough, the dirtier he became and the more conspicuous he was. He hadn't seen any of Tyler's black SUAVs in a while, but after a few days of walking, he worried it was so obvious he was an escaped IS that he'd be picked up by any passing bounty hunter wanting to make a quick buck. It'd be like Christmas come early for them when they turned him in, found out who he really was, and claimed Tyler's inevitably handsome reward for his return. Of course, Tyler had so far kept news of his escape quiet, and would no doubt wish to keep news of his return equally quiet – a large payout to any bounty hunter who returned him would secure their silence.

He ran out of food and struggled to keep going on an empty belly. He stopped for the night in some bushes behind a pub, and ventured out after closing time to rummage through their bins for something to calm the insistent gnawing in his stomach. He found half a roll and swallowed it down without tasting it. Then he filled up an empty water bottle from an outside tap intended for dogs and crawled into a nearby ditch to spend the night. Despite what his life had become, he didn't regret escaping; he'd rather starve to death than spend another second back at Tyler's Mind-Fuck Tower.

He set off again at dawn, feeling light-headed from hunger. He was making slow progress now that he was running on empty, and his belly rumbled incessantly. All he could think about was food. He stopped at a food van in a lay-by, enticed by the delicious smell of sausages and onions. Maybe someone would drop something, or he could beg for leftovers. He had no money, but he was prepared to give a blow job in return for something to eat – if he could find anyone who wanted such a service from a lank-haired, unwashed vagrant.

There was a queue for the food; it was clearly a well-known pitstop as lorry AVs kept swinging in and out again. He hung around for a while, the smell of the food making his belly cramp until he thought he'd pass out. The woman serving gave him a disapproving glare.

"If you're not buying, piss off," she snapped. "We don't want any trouble."

He wondered how many escaped indies came down this road on their way to the coast. There were probably bounty hunters hanging around as well, so he shouldn't linger. "Sorry," he said pathetically, slinking away. He had walked to the edge of the lay-by when a lorry pulled up beside him, and a man leaned out of the driver's window.

"I saw you back there – you hungry?" he asked, holding up a hot dog covered in tomato ketchup. "I bought this for you."

The lorry driver was middle-aged, with short grey hair and a beer belly. It crossed Alex's mind that he could be a bounty hunter, so he hesitated.

"Here." The driver leaned out of the window and handed him the hot dog. Alex couldn't resist – he took it and crammed it into his mouth. "Where are you going?" the man asked in a soft, lilting Welsh accent.

"The coast," Alex mumbled between bites.

"Well, the coast is a big place – anywhere specific?"

"I don't really care." Alex finished the hot dog and wiped ketchup off his chin with the back of his hand and licked it, so as not to waste a single drop. The relentless gnawing in his stomach subsided a fraction as the food hit, and he felt it warming him inside, but he was still hungry.

The man gazed at him thoughtfully. "I'm going that way. Want a lift?"

Alex chewed on his lip, torn between wanting to accept and worrying it was a trap.

"My name's Barnabas Bates," the man said, "but my friends call me Barney. Here's my ID." He waved a nanocard displaying the name *BB Trucking and Haulage*. "Come on, you look like shit. Get in and rest your feet for a bit." The man jerked his head at the passenger door.

Alex took his life in his hands and decided to take him up on the

offer. Climbing into the rig, he sat down beside what he hoped was his guardian angel and not someone out to make a fast buck by selling him to the nearest bounty hunter when they reached the coast. "My name's... John," Alex said, deciding he couldn't reuse Ben Smith in the circumstances. "John Brown."

"Sure it is," Barney said with a grin. "Here. Have mine as well." He handed Alex another hot dog.

Alex took it gratefully. Now the edge had been taken off his hunger, he was able to eat more slowly and actually taste this one. It was divine; he could see why this was such a popular pitstop for lorry drivers.

"Take a kip if you want, Johnny," Barney said. "You look knackered."

He started the engine, and Alex knew it was his last chance to scramble out of the cab and get away, but he was too tired. Leaning back, he closed his eyes, and the rocking motion of the lorry, combined with his own exhaustion, sent him immediately to sleep. He woke up with a start a few hours later to find that it was dark, and the lorry was stationary in an AV park. "Where are we?" he asked anxiously.

"Near Swanage," Barney replied.

"So far?" Alex looked around for a sign or some clue as to where they were, to make sure Barney wasn't lying to him, but there wasn't one.

"Well, you were asleep, and you didn't seem to care where on the coast I took you, so I brought you here."

"Where is here?" Alex felt a chill of foreboding as he looked around the shadowy AV park.

"It's a place I use – off the beaten track, but cheap. They serve decent grub, and there's a shower you can use; no offence, son, but you need a good wash."

Alex stared out into the night uncertainly.

"Don't worry – I'm not a bounty hunter. That's what you're worried about, isn't it?" Barney gave him a shrewd look. "You're an escaped IS, aren't you?"

"Are you going to turn me in?" Alex asked anxiously.

Barney shook his head. "Nah. You're safe with me. Relax. My son used to ride with me, back in the day. I've still got some of his clothes. I got them out while you were sleeping. There's also soap, a razor, toothbrush, toothpaste, deodorant – everything you need." He handed Alex a bag. "You might as well trust me, Johnny; you've got nobody else."

That was certainly true. Alex took the bag and jumped out of the lorry, deciding to go along with this for now. He followed Barney across the AV park to a shower block.

"Okay – you go in and get clean, and I'll be waiting for you over in the café." Barney jerked his head at a squat building nearby. "This place has the best fish and chips in England – I'll order you some. See you in a bit."

"I can't pay you," Alex blurted.

"Yeah, I kind of worked that out, son." Barney rolled his eyes.

"I mean... I could pay you with something else." Alex gestured at Barney's crotch. "If you wanted that. Um, I mean, if that's why you're helping me," he added, feeling very bad at this.

Barney looked furious.

Alex took a step back.

Barney held up his hands, making a visible effort to calm down. "Look, Johnny, I don't know what kind of life you've been leading that you think that's why I'm helping you, but I don't want any of that. Now, take a shower, get cleaned up, and come join me for fish and chips – then we can talk properly."

Alex nodded and went into the bathroom. It was basic, but clean, and it felt so good to peel off his damp, dirty clothes and step under the warm water. He soaped himself all over, washing off days of dirt, then relaxed under the warm spray. He could have stood there for hours, allowing the water to pound into his tired shoulders, but eventually he stepped out and dried himself. It felt wonderful to shave, brush his teeth, and feel clean again. His hair had grown out of the style Lorenzo preferred for it and had started to curl, and his cheeks were sunken where he'd lost weight, but he looked surprisingly good, considering. He pulled on the red-checked lumberjack shirt and faded blue jeans Barney had given him. Barney's son was clearly bigger than

him, but he didn't care – he was just glad to be wearing clean, dry clothes.

He pulled the belt tight around his waist to keep the jeans up and shouldered himself into the thick woollen jacket Barney had provided, wondering why he was being so kind. He mulled over Barney's anger at his clumsy offer of a blow job. Had he become so jaded that he expected everyone to have an ulterior motive? His stint as George Tyler's whore had made him believe that sex was a currency in everyday use and his only value in the world. He hoped he was wrong, and that Barney Bates was genuinely a Good Samaritan. He liked the man. He liked the way he called him Johnny even though he'd introduced himself as John, and how roughly kind he was.

He rammed the old black peaked cap he'd found in the bundle of clothes onto his head. Packing up his old clothes, he put them in the bag, unsure if Barney was loaning him the new garments or if he'd have to return them, and then he went to the café. It was a clean, homespun kind of place – nothing fancy. There was a pool table in the corner and a big screen behind the bar area.

"I ordered you a Coke," Barney said, beckoning him over. "Food should be here soon." He looked Alex up and down as he took his seat. "Well, don't you scrub up well. What were you before you ran away – a model?" He grinned and took a sip of his drink.

"More like a rent boy," Alex said, pulling the cap down over his eyes, hoping his looks didn't render him too conspicuous.

"Yeah, well, I figured." Barney shrugged. "Fucking IS system. Fucking hate it. Legalised slavery is all it is."

A waitress brought over two plates piled high with food and set them down in front of them.

"Best fish and chips in the country. Tuck in, son," Barney told him.

Alex took a bite and then looked up, smiling.

"See – I told ya," Barney said with a laugh. "Good stuff, yeah?"

"Oh, yeah," Alex agreed, because nothing he'd eaten in his life before had tasted this good. He devoured the meal – the two hot dogs he'd eaten earlier were now a distant memory, and he was starving again. He finished the food and then pushed away the plate with a sigh. "You're right – best fish and chips in the country," he said happily.

Barney was only halfway through his meal; he looked up with a grin.

"Thank you for the clothes. I wasn't sure..." Alex gestured at the bag filled with his old stuff.

"You can keep 'em," Barney said with a grunt. "Throw those others away. They reek."

"Thank you. Are you sure your son won't mind?"

Barney grunted again. "He won't mind. I haven't seen him in two years; he's not coming back anytime soon."

"Where is he?" Alex asked quietly, sensing a story.

"Up north somewhere, working in construction." Barney shrugged. "His houder says I'm not allowed to contact him."

"He's an IS?" Alex realised he should have seen that coming.

"Yeah." Barney's expression hardened. "I wanted him to go into haulage, same as me. I probably pushed him too hard. Me and his mum split up when he was just a kid, and I wasn't around for him as much as I should've been – I can see that now."

"So he sold himself as an IS?" Alex pressed, frowning.

Barney shook his head. "Nah. He fell in with some bad kids, got into trouble with the law, and was sold to pay for the damage he caused. Five-year sentence – and under those new rules they brought in a few years back, it's up to his houder if I get to write to him, or see him, or even speak to him on nanochat." Barney shook his head. "I don't know what ruddy genius thought that law up, but it breaks my heart that I can't even bloody well tell him I still love him, and that I'll be here, waiting for him, when he's released."

"I'm so sorry," Alex said softly.

"I know the boy screwed up, but he's my son." Barney sighed. "I used to be one of the 'sell 'em off and let 'em rot' brigade, in the old days, but now I think the system stinks."

"That's why you helped me."

Barney nodded and skewered a chip with his fork. "I saw you and thought of Robbie – if he ever ran away and was starving, I hope someone'd stop and help him."

"Thank you," Alex told him. "I appreciate it more than I can say."

Barney shrugged. "Your dad would do the same."

"I don't know." Alex hunched his shoulders miserably. "My dad was pretty angry with me when I last saw him."

"Yeah, I could have kicked Robbie's arse for the shit he pulled, the stupid idiot," Barney growled. "But he's my son, and I love him. Your dad feels the same way, trust me."

"I'm not sure he does."

"He does," Barney said confidently. "Give him time. He hasn't stopped loving you – he's your dad."

"I wish it were that simple," Alex said, wrapping his arms around his body and hugging himself.

"It is. Look, I don't know your story, son, and I don't wanna know. I don't know how you wound up an IS, or why you're running away. I ain't asking. I just figured you need to get away, and I know a bloke with a boat in Swanage. I just called him, and he said if I can get you there by first tide in the morning, he'll take you to Le Havre. No idea what you'll do when you get there, but at least you'll be out of the country."

"You'd do that for me?" Alex asked incredulously.

"Yeah." Barney finished his food and sat back, patting his ample belly happily. "Well, that was bloody good."

"It was," Alex agreed. "Fish and chips is now officially my favourite food."

"Mine too." Barney glanced over Alex's shoulder. "I see that poor bastard turned up dead," he said, jerking his head at the screen behind the bar.

Alex swivelled in his chair to see a photo of Lars. "The escaped IS who killed the guy with the fancy car?" he said, his heart skipping a beat.

"Yeah. Heard it on the radio earlier while you were asleep. His body washed up in a lost zone a few hours ago. Poor fucker. They're probably pinning it on him just because he's an escaped indie." Barney lifted his drink and gestured to the screen with it. "I wouldn't be surprised if the husband was the real killer, not the IS." He nodded at the screen again, which was showing a picture of Joe entering the Inquisitus building. He was dressed in a suit this time, but his face was frozen in an expression of numb grief. Alex barely recognised him. Was

this really the man he'd met a few nights ago, who'd laughed as he teased his husband about his taste in music? He looked like a hollow shell now.

"You okay, Johnny?" Barney asked.

"Yeah. Just..." Alex shook his head, unable to tear his gaze from the screen.

"I know. This country's going to the dogs. You're better off out of it, even if you *are* going to a bloody war zone." Barney waved his drink at the screen in disgust. "The IS system is getting out of hand. It never used to work this way. It kinda made sense to me when I was a kid – we used to treat indies properly back then. Nowadays, it's just an excuse for cheap labour, to save money on prisons, and to get poor people outta the Quarterlands and where the government can keep an eye on 'em. Why the fuck are we putting microchips in people and making 'em wear those stupid ID tags? That's only happened in the last twenty years. Before then, we didn't bother with any of that crap. You helped people out by letting 'em live in your house and do some work for you in exchange, 'cause they didn't have nothing, and we all had to pull together. Now, we're richer than we were back then, but we treat 'em worse. Somewhere along the way, the whole damn system got twisted into the fuck-up it is today."

"Most people don't see it that way," Alex said. "Most people don't care."

"When it doesn't affect you, then I guess you don't." Barney grunted. "I never did, until Robbie..." He trailed off moodily. "Anyway, you don't wanna hear me rant. It's late – let's kip down in the lorry tonight, and then I'll take you to Swanage first thing tomorrow."

A few hours later, Barney drew up at the seafront, and they both jumped down from the truck. "My friend's boat is that one – the *Mary-Anne*." He pointed to a rugged old vessel at the far end of the dock. "He'll be along in an hour, but he won't wait as he needs to catch the tide, so be ready. Sorry to drop you and run, but I gotta get this load down to Penzance by noon to meet my deadline." He jerked his head at the lorry.

"Please – that's absolutely fine. You've done so much for me."

"His name's Paul Andrews, and he'll want paying." Barney pulled

out a handful of cash cards and stuffed them into Alex's pocket. "You give him these – it's what I agreed with him last night."

Alex swallowed hard, feeling humbled beyond belief by Barney's kindness. It was clear the lorry driver wasn't a wealthy man, but he was prepared to give him a big wad of cash cards to help him get away.

"Thank you," he said. He threw himself forward and wrapped his arms around Barney.

The man gave a grunt of surprise and then hugged him back. "Wish I could have a few hours with my boy again, same way I did with you," he choked into Alex's hair. Drawing back, he cleared his throat. "You take care, Johnny. You get out and go live someplace else. This country's a shithole these days." He climbed back into his cab, and, with a little wave, he drove off.

Alex stood there, watching him go, feeling an acute sense of loneliness and loss. He'd known Barney Bates for less than twenty-four hours, but he'd been a good friend.

It was cold on the seafront, and as Paul Andrews wouldn't be arriving for a little while he decided to kill time by buying a cup of tea in a nearby café.

He sat nursing the tea, feeling a cautious sense of hope stirring inside. He hadn't seen any of Tyler's SUAVs or helicopters around, and in a few hours he'd be in France, swallowed up in the chaos there but out of reach of the British legal system. He'd face a whole new set of challenges when he arrived, but at least he'd be free. Hopefully, he could find a job, however menial, and work to get by until he figured out what to do next.

The waitress turned on the radio and a song by Ashton blared out. Alex was glad it wasn't the one that had been playing in the car that night. He wondered how Joe was doing. He couldn't imagine ever having a love as strong as Joe and Peter had shared. Love was something other people did; it had always eluded him. He could see now that he'd been lost in self-loathing for so long that he'd never felt that anyone could love him. He'd used croc, alcohol, and casual sex as anaesthetics, so he didn't have to face up to the choices he'd made. Alex Lytton was a screw-up, but maybe there was a chance for John Brown in France. Maybe there he could learn to love himself, and find

someone who could love him back. He wanted someone like Joe in his life – teasing him out of his bad moods, making him laugh, and sharing a life together. Joe wouldn't take any shit from him the way Solange had. If Joe had a streak of darkness in him, then Alex, of all people, could identify with that.

He shook his head, silently mocking himself. Poor Peter had only been dead a few days, and he was sitting here fantasising about the grieving man he'd left behind. It was unlikely he'd ever see Joe again, and even if he did, he doubted Joe would want him around as a daily reminder of the terrible night his husband was murdered.

A news jingle played on the radio. Alex listened intently, wondering if there would be more information on Lars.

"Investigators carrying out a post-mortem on the body of Lars Driessen, the escaped IS responsible for the murder of Captain Peter Hunt, have announced the cause of death as drowning. It's believed that Driessen fell into the lost zone close to where the murder took place when fleeing the crime scene. There were no signs of a struggle, and nobody is being sought in connection with his death."

Alex wondered if Joe had killed Driessen, and his boss at Inquisitus was covering for him – although Director Lomax hadn't looked like the kind of person who'd agree to something like that.

"The Home Secretary has reassured the public that this was a one-off incident, and is not indicative of a crisis in the IS system, which is robust and still offers the best chance of a good life to the poor and dispossessed."

Alex snorted into his tea.

"In other news, Noah Lytton, the CEO of Lytton AV and father of Olympic hero Charles Lytton, was rushed to St Catherine's hospital in Sevenoaks last night after suffering a suspected stroke. A hospital spokesman said he's in a serious condition, and the next forty-eight hours are critical. Sources close to the family say that Noah Lytton never recovered from the loss of his wife in an AV accident six years ago, and that he's been in poor health since his youngest son was sentenced into indentured servitude earlier this year. Lytton AV is one of the most famous companies in the UK, a star of the post-Rising years, although its fortunes have declined in recent times."

Alex sat frozen to his seat in shock. At first, he'd thought the news was a Tyler trick to entice him into the open and trap him, but then he heard Charles's soft, unmistakeable voice, talking to reporters.

"We don't know how bad it is yet... the doctors are still running tests. I've been with him all night. I'm going home for a bit now, but I'll be back later. He's in good hands. We're all hoping he'll pull through." Charles's voice broke a little at the end.

There was no way George Tyler could have involved Charles and his father in such an elaborate ruse, to say nothing of the hospital. The news report had to be true.

He sat in stunned silence, staring out of the window at the boats bobbing up and down on the sea until he saw a man walk up to the *Mary-Anne*, glance around, and then jump onto the craft.

Standing up, Alex walked out of the café mechanically. He had to catch the boat... Paul Andrews wouldn't wait for him. He had to go over there, give Andrews the cash cards Barney had stuffed in his pocket, and set out for his new life in France.

His feet stopped moving, and he stood, hesitating, on the quayside. Barney's words echoed in his mind: *Wish I could have a few hours with my boy again, same way I did with you.*

If his father died, then his last words to Alex would be the bitter, angry ones he'd spoken in his office that day, wishing Alex had never been born. He didn't think he could bear that.

He hasn't stopped loving you – he's your dad.

He wanted to believe that was true. He watched as Paul Andrews moved around his boat, getting it ready to sail. He could go over there, leave it all behind. He'd never see his father again, but at least he'd get away from Tyler. He was an escaped IS – how could he enter the hospital without being caught? There was no way he could go back to being Tyler's IS again. He couldn't stand it. He'd rather die. His feet started moving once more towards the *Mary-Anne*. He was almost there when they stopped again.

Supposing he was letting his father down yet again by running out on him when he was on his deathbed? How many times could he let the man down and still be able to live with himself? Could he really

start a new life in France knowing he'd run out on his father when he was so desperately ill?

He was suddenly six years old, stuck up an old plum tree in the garden.

"I'll catch you, Alex. Come on – jump!" his father shouted, standing below, laughing.

"Are you sure you'll catch me?" Alex yelled down uncertainly. "You won't drop me?"

"Of course not, silly. Just jump!"

And he had. He'd closed his eyes and thrown himself into the air... and had landed, safe and sound, in his father's arms.

"See, I told you I'd catch you." Noah lifted Alex up onto his shoulders, still laughing.

Alex realised he was walking rapidly away from the boat. He had the money Barney had given him. He could catch a coach to Sevenoaks, find a way to sneak into the hospital, speak to his father, and tell him he loved him. If his father was dying, he owed Noah that. Hopefully, he could sneak out again afterwards and make his way back down here. At least he knew Paul Andrews had a boat and would take him to France. He could find a job, earn enough for the fare.

He had to do this. He had to see his father. He had to at least try.

Chapter Sixteen

OCTOBER 2095

Josiah

Josiah stopped for fish and chips on the way home at an old, traditional place near his house. It was pouring with rain when he left the chip shop, so he covered his head with his coat and ran back to the duck.

He threw himself inside and dumped the bag of food onto Alex's lap. They grinned at each other in anticipation as the delicious smell wafted from the bag.

It was such a simple thing, to buy a takeaway one evening after work and share it with an attractive man... He hadn't realised how much he'd missed it. He'd forgotten what this was like.

———

Elsie left the hospital just before Esther arrived. Josiah had a long conversation with his boss, talking her through his edited version of what had happened in cold, brisk tones. Fortunately, she didn't try to put her arms around him, or offer up meaningless platitudes; she understood him too well for that. He had lost his soulmate and life partner – nothing she said could make that better. All she could do was her job.

"I *will* find Peter's killer," she told him in a low, determined voice.

"If I have to take apart the whole damn country to do it." Maybe she would. Or maybe Josiah would get there first. He hadn't decided yet.

"We've already lifted the prints off the knife and found a match on the IS database, so I can give you a name," she said. "He's called Lars Driessen. He can't have gone far. I will track him down and get justice for Peter, if it's the last thing I do." He realised it was the only comfort she could give, and the only comfort she knew he'd accept.

After she'd left, he went to stand next to Peter's body. Instead of grief, he felt a surge of anger. "I told you your big, stupid heart would get you killed one day. All this time, I thought we'd get arrested by bounty hunters, or an IA on the make, or taken down in a fight trying to get a bunch of indies out of the country. Instead, it was this. This! Fuck you, Peter! Why couldn't you have been an ordinary person, just living your life – doing a normal job, working on stupid old cars in your spare time, walking the dog – and being alive. Being alive." He turned away and slammed his fist into the wall.

"You wouldn't have fallen in love with me if I'd been ordinary," a voice murmured.

He whirled around, but Peter's body was still lying on the mortuary slab, unmoving. He must have imagined that dry voice, whispering in his ear. He walked back to take one last look at his dead husband.

"I know. Nobody could ever call you ordinary. I was looking for a cause to fight without even knowing it, and you gave me one. Your cause became our cause, and now it's my cause. I won't let you down."

He took Peter's hand and held it against his cheek. There would be no more caresses, no kisses, no touching, and teasing, and loving – it was all gone. His fingers closed around Peter's wedding ring. It was his last link to Peter, a reminder of the vows they'd made, and before that it had belonged to his father. He couldn't leave it behind. He tugged it from his husband's finger and repeated the vow he'd once made.

"With this ring, I thee worship," he said, placing the ring in his inside jacket pocket. He would always wear it next to his heart. He wouldn't give it away a second time. "I'll never let you go, Peter. Not ever. There will be nobody else – how could there be? Who could ever compare to you?" He pressed a final kiss to Peter's forehead and then left the room.

When he arrived home, Hattie came running to greet him, her tail wagging enthusiastically. Despite her warm presence, the house felt cold and empty. She jumped up at him and buried her nose in his sweater. She smelled the blood, nosing at it intently. He didn't know what dogs understood, or if she could smell that it belonged to Peter. She looked up at him with big brown eyes, and then wandered over to the door and waited expectantly for Peter. She was Peter's dog – he'd rescued her, and she'd lived with him her entire life. She'd happily accepted Josiah into their lives, but he wasn't Peter. Josiah realised that she'd lost the love of her life, too.

"Sorry, old girl, but he's not coming home," he told her, and that was when it hit. This was it – a lifetime of Peter never coming home again. His legs wouldn't hold him up anymore, and he sank to the floor. Hattie ran over to him with a questioning whine. He put his arms around her and buried his face in her fur.

"It's just you and me now, Hattie," he mumbled. "I'm sorry, I know I'm a poor substitute for him. I'm so sorry, old girl – I let you down. He's gone."

She whined again and nuzzled his neck, and he held her tight, breathing in the scent of her thick dark fur.

———

The shower had turned into a full-blown storm by the time they reached the house, with thunder, lightning, and pounding rain. Josiah paused the duck on the driveway to click open the garage door. His announcement about Alex earlier had done the trick, and the news crews had disappeared. The bad weather had probably helped disperse them, too.

"My art supplies." Alex pointed to a box hidden behind the wheelie bin on the front drive. He dumped the bag of fish and chips on Josiah's lap and dashed out to retrieve it. Josiah steered the duck into the garage and climbed out, carrying their dinner with him. Walking to the open garage door to wait for Alex, he paused next to Hattie's collar and lead, hanging in their usual place on a hook on the wall next to Peter's car. She'd died peacefully a couple of years ago. He'd returned

to the house after that final visit to the vet and hung up the lead and collar one last time. That was where they'd remained ever since, waiting for a dog who, like the man before her, would never return home.

Alex ran into the garage with the box, chattering about his art supplies. Josiah smiled as he followed him up the stairs to the house. He had a bag of warm fish and chips in his hand, and someone to share them with. The house didn't feel cold or empty anymore.

Alex took his damp parcel through to the dining room and placed it on the table. Taking off his suit jacket, he slung it over the back of a chair and then impatiently tore open the box. Josiah grabbed bits and pieces from the kitchen and carried them through to the dining room to join him. He laid the table, pushing Liz's vase to the far end to make room for the ketchup, vinegar, salt, pepper, plates, and cutlery for their meal.

"This stuff is amazing. I read about it a while back, but never thought I'd be able to try it," Alex said, holding up a bottle of some unidentifiable liquid.

"Is that paint?" Josiah asked.

"No – lacquer. I got different colours. And some resin. There's paint, too... and brushes, and paper, and a ton of other stuff. I hope I didn't spend too much..." He prattled on.

"It's fine. I make a good salary and don't have much to spend it on," Josiah said with a shrug.

"Except fancy clothes. Do you ever dress down? Even when you're wearing jeans and a tee-shirt you look hot." Alex winked.

"Hot? Really?" Josiah rolled his eyes.

"Yeah. Trust me – I was struck by the hotness the very first time I saw you."

"The first time you saw me, I knocked you down and arrested you on suspicion of murder. You have some weird priorities if what you noticed was my supposed hotness," Josiah teased.

"Hmm." Alex gazed at him for a moment and then turned away.

Josiah was aware that the atmosphere in the room had changed, but he had no idea why. Taking off his own suit jacket, he hung it on the back of his chair. "C'mon – let's eat before it gets cold. Put the box

down – you can finish checking it out later." He served a portion of fish and chips on each plate, then made a chip butty with two slices of soft white bread covered with a thick layer of butter. He took a bite and let out a happy sigh.

"That looks good," Alex said. "Judging by those orgasmic noises you're making, anyway."

"Hah! Trust me – that's not what my orgasm noises sound like," Josiah said, and then wished he hadn't. The trouble with feeling the warmth of human companionship after all this time was that it made their situation seem normal. It was as if their mild flirtation might develop into a full-blown relationship, but, of course, that simply couldn't happen. Alex was his IS, and he was no Elliot Dacre, seeking to replace a lost love by forcing an indie to occupy that space in his life.

Alex devoured his own plate of food enthusiastically. Between the box of art supplies and the fish and chips, he looked like a kid on Christmas morning. "This is delicious," he proclaimed through a mouthful of food.

"Yup. It's the best fish and chips in England."

"Well, second best," Alex said softly.

"Second?" Josiah queried lightly.

Alex nodded silently, his expression changing. He didn't elaborate, but instead said quietly, "You know, when I was young, I thought happiness lay in the big, important stuff. Impressing my father, and being as good as my famous brother. I thought I could find it by designing the next big thing in ducks, by forging my path in the world, and having people look up to me and admire me."

"That was before you were sentenced to be an IS?" Josiah was intrigued by his change of mood.

"Yes. After that, for a long time I thought I could never be happy again. I had to learn to change my perspective and look at the world differently."

"That can't have been easy."

"It wasn't. As a child, I could spend hours looking at a butterfly's wings, learning how they worked, and studying the colours and patterns so I could draw them. After I became an IS, I had to learn to

find happiness in the small things again and forget about the big things."

"Your father said something to me the other day," Josiah recalled. Alex went very still.

"I asked him if you were capable of killing anyone, and he told me that the only way he could imagine you turning into a killer was if you weren't able to see the beauty in the world anymore, the way you once did, as a child."

Alex's eyes were suddenly wet.

Josiah realised that he hadn't appreciated the great love that existed in that relationship. He'd been blinded by the bare facts of what Alex had done to his father, and Noah Lytton's angry words in response, disowning his son. He hadn't seen what lay beneath all that – a bond that had once been strong but had become twisted somewhere along the way. Yet the love remained, beneath the bitterness, anger, and harsh words – he'd seen it in Noah Lytton's eyes, and he was seeing it now, in Alex's.

"Did he really look okay when you saw him?" Alex asked. "Was he well?"

"He was fine. He's suffered a couple of strokes and doesn't walk very well, but he's still strong mentally."

"I knew about the strokes," Alex confessed, wiping the back of his hand over his eyes.

Josiah handed his handkerchief silently across the table.

Alex took it gratefully, pressed it to his eyes, then buried his face in it for a second. When he looked up again, the tears were gone. "It's too quiet – we need music," he said brightly. "I made a playlist while you were working today; I hope you like it." He instructed the room speakers to play, then took off his tie and undid the top button of his shirt collar. Unbuttoning his cuffs, he rolled the sleeves up to his elbows with tense, jerky movements.

Josiah studied him curiously, seeing a nervous energy in all the frenetic activity.

"You should take off your tie." Alex gestured. "Relax. Chill out."

"Uh... okay." Josiah removed it and undid the top button of his shirt, too, feeling that everything had gone a bit weird. "So, you like

The Beatles, huh?" he asked, recognising the familiar intro to one of his favourite songs.

"Yes – and so do you, don't you?" Alex looked straight at him.

Immediately, Josiah sensed there was something behind the question that he didn't understand.

"Yeah – I love their stuff – and Queen and Led Zeppelin, too. I'm a huge fan of Pre-R rock. How did you guess?"

Alex took a bite of his fish and waved the question away with his hand.

There was another strangely charged silence while they finished their meal, and then Alex sat back and cleared his throat.

Josiah gazed at him expectantly. Alex had said he was going to tell him the big secret tonight – one of them, at least, because he was sure the IS had several. Was that why he looked so nervous?

"I deserved my sentence," Alex said, unexpectedly.

"Okay." Josiah sat back, too, wondering where this was going.

"I stole from my father's company. It was a stupid, terrible thing to do, and I deserved to be punished."

"Okay," Josiah said again. "Why are you telling me this again now?"

"In case you thought... in case I'd led you to believe that I was in any way innocent, or a victim. I wasn't. I did something bad, and I paid for it – by God, I paid for it. I was twenty-three, and in many ways young for my age, and completely out of my depth with a man like Tyler. I didn't know what to do, or how to fight back, and honestly, I'm not sure I had many options, looking back. I can be moody and selfish, but I'm not Machiavellian, ruthless, or even particularly cunning. I'm..."

"The boy who could stare at butterflies for hours on end," Josiah put in softly.

Alex smiled. "Yes, if you like. I was an artist, a mixed-up kid, and someone who made a huge mistake. I deserved to pay for that mistake, Joe, but I didn't deserve what Tyler did to me. I told you he had me raped in the most brutal way, and beaten until I was raw, and that he filmed it, but I didn't tell you that he made me sit with him and watch it back after."

"Christ!" Josiah felt his gut clench angrily.

"He wanted to break me," Alex said flatly. "He told me so, repeatedly. That was his aim – to break me."

"And he succeeded?"

Alex shook his head. "How could he? I was already broken."

Josiah frowned. "The duck accident with your mother and brother...?"

"Yes." Alex shrugged. "All he could do was break me further, which he did, but I was already damaged goods when he got his hands on me."

"Christ, Alex – I don't know what to say."

"I'm not telling you this because I want your sympathy," Alex retorted sharply. "I'm telling you because I need you to understand."

"Understand what?" Josiah asked. "That George Tyler is a bastard? I already know that. That he's been getting away with mistreating his indies for far too long? I know that, too – and I promise you that once I've caught Dacre's killer, I will convince Esther to go after Tyler next. We'll find some evidence from somewhere."

"Thank you, but again – that's not why I'm telling you this."

"Then why...?"

"Because this is going to get really personal really fast, and I don't know what's going to happen after that, so I want to give you some facts to hang on to before we get to the point where you stop listening to me."

"You're not making any sense," Josiah replied helplessly.

"It will all make sense soon enough. Before then... honestly, I just want to enjoy this some more. This... you... me..." Alex waved his hand at the remains of their meal and then at the box of art supplies in the corner. "This is the best day I've had in a very long time – I can't even remember a day that was as good as this. Maybe there wasn't one. Maybe this is the best day of my life so far, and I want to thank you for that. I want to thank you for believing in me, as well... for what you said to the press, for defending me to Reed, for going up against Esther for me, for including me in your work like I have a valid opinion, and I matter. For telling Jeffrey Mead where to go, for noticing I was bored, for buying me what's in that box, and for asking me what

my favourite food is and then fetching it for me. Thank you," he said sincerely, his eyes shining brightly. "Thank you so much."

"It seems little enough," Josiah murmured, a lump forming in his throat.

"Not to me. It's everything to me. Being here, with you, like this – it's something I've dreamed about for a very long time, but the reality is so much better."

"I don't see how, when we only met a few days ago. Maybe you mean you dreamed about doing something like this with someone like me," Josiah said, frowning. He could understand that – Alex had led such a lonely life as an IS, catering to the whims of evil or capricious houders. No wonder he'd fantasised about something as normal as having a nice dinner with someone who was kind to him.

"You see, I never believed what the papers said about you, but I had to be sure," Alex continued. "You became the great indiehunter, after all. How was I to know if what happened to Peter hadn't changed you?"

"It did," Josiah admitted gruffly.

"Yes – but not in the way the press thought. Now..." Alex stood up. "Let's dance."

"What?" Josiah stared at him.

"One dance – because I want to know what that's like before it all goes to hell." He held out his hand.

"Alex, what on earth are you talking about?"

"Just one dance." Alex grinned as the jangling chords of a familiar Beatles song started playing. "C'mon – it's 'Love Me Do' – what could be more appropriate?"

He took hold of Josiah's hand and pulled him out of his seat. Josiah went willingly, wondering where the hell this was going.

Alex twisted in time to the beat, throwing himself around energetically.

Josiah chuckled and joined in; he hadn't danced in years, and it felt good to let himself go. He clasped Alex's hand tightly and rested a hand on his hip as they rocked it out together, grinning at each other manically. Alex did some fancy moves, and Josiah mimicked them

mercilessly, which made Alex laugh so much he almost fell over. Josiah caught him, and Alex pressed in close and leaned up.

They stared at each other for a moment, and then Josiah dipped his head and their lips met. His body flooded with warmth as they kissed – a sweet, long, tender kiss that thawed out whatever was left of the ice inside his heart. He knew Elsie, Esther, Reed, and so many other people would be horrified if they ever found out. They would say it was wrong, but it felt so right.

Alex drew back and placed his finger over Josiah's mouth.

"Hold that thought," he said softly as the song changed.

Josiah froze as Ashton's voice began to warble sadly around the room.

Old dreams fade slow
You once said that you'd never let go
Sweet words, wide smiles
You always said that you'd stay awhile

"I hate this song," Josiah snapped. He'd avoided it since that night. Once, he'd heard it playing in a shop and had walked out – only to find blood on the palms of his hands when he got home where the nails of his clenched fists had dug into his skin.

"Yes, and I know why," Alex said. "You hate it because it was playing in the car on the night Peter was killed."

Josiah went cold. "How do you know that? I never told anyone. Nobody knows that."

"Only the four people who were there, and two of them are dead," Alex said softly. "The other two are in this room right now."

Josiah's stomach lurched sickeningly. "What?" he rasped.

Alex held his gaze intently. "I escaped once," he said. "It was so bad at Tyler's that I escaped. I ran away, and called a number I was given, and spoke to a nice lady called Elsie. I lied to her about my name because I was so afraid. I said I was called Ben."

"Ben?" Josiah stood, frozen to the spot, in shock. "You're... Ben?"

"Yes. That's why I wanted you to understand how bad things were for me at Tyler's. That's why I ran away, and that's why I was there that

night – with you, and Peter, and Lars, in that car, waiting for Matthew, who never showed up."

The room whirled around Josiah, because at its centre, standing in front of him, was Ben... Alex... Ben.

"The holopic..." Josiah said. "The holopic I thought I saw in Elliot's house... the one of you standing under the street lamp, in the rain... it wasn't a holopic at all." He had a sudden flashback to that night, to staring up at Ben and telling him to call an ambulance. Ben had stood there in the pouring rain, framed by the streetlight, his face crumpled in anguish.

"No – it was a memory," Alex said softly. "You knew, somehow, that it was me – or at least your subconscious did when you met me again. You just didn't know what it meant, and you confused it with Elliot's holopics of me."

"That's why I've been having the nightmares," Josiah said slowly, finally making sense of the past few days. "That's why it's been so vivid again, after all these years. I didn't know why. I thought I was going mad, but it was all because of you."

"I'm sorry," Alex said.

The room was swirling. When the ground lurched beneath him, Josiah staggered. Alex darted forward and grabbed his arm, guiding him into the nearest chair. So many different emotions assaulted him at the same time that he didn't know what he was feeling, just that it hurt. A scab had been wrenched off an old wound just as it was starting to heal.

"All this time... you had this secret. All this time – living in my house, sleeping in my bed, telling me to relive my memories of that night... all this time, you knew what happened, because you were there," he growled accusingly.

"At first, I thought you might remember." Alex was talking fast now. "When you jumped out in front of me at Elliot's, and I fell down – I couldn't believe it was you. I was sure you must know who I was. I thought maybe that was why you were there, that you'd been looking for me. But then you said Elliot had been murdered, and I realised it wasn't about me at all. I kept expecting you to remember – when we

walked by Peter's car in the garage the first time, I thought that might jog your memory."

Alex crouched down in front of him and put his hands on his knees. "Then I realised you'd blocked out the details of that night. Even if you hadn't, why would you focus on Ben Smith, the bit-part player in the greatest tragedy of your life, rather than on your dying husband? It was seven years ago, after all... I was younger, I had a scruffy beard, and the only time you got a good look at me was in that split second after the fight, when my scarf had come loose, my hood had fallen back, and I was standing under the street lamp in the rain... and I'm certain you had other things on your mind at that moment than looking very closely at me."

"I didn't know you, but you knew me," Josiah said, his hands clenching into fists. "All this time, from the very beginning – from the moment I arrested you – you knew me. Why didn't you say something?" he demanded hoarsely. "All the days you've lived here... knowing what you know... and you never said a word."

"When was I supposed to bring it up?" Alex queried quietly. "After you first arrested me? 'Oh, hello, Joe – remember that night you were helping escaped indies and your husband was killed? Well, I was there, too.' I was hardly going to mention it in front of your work colleagues and get you into trouble. Then, the more I got to know the real you, and how troubled you are, the more I realised what an effect it would have on you – and the harder it became."

That song – that god-awful song – was still playing, jangling discordantly on Josiah's nerves, but the noise in his head was even worse. So many different memories were swirling around in his skull as he tried to make sense of it all. He was back in the car with this man – *this* man – by his side, fighting to get the knife away from Lars. He was sitting on the pavement with Peter's body in his arms, and Ben – *not* Ben – Alex – was standing under a street light in the rain, looking down on him with a combination of terror and sadness in his eyes.

"So you said nothing? You just watched me falling apart in front of you. You knew why, but you didn't say a word." Josiah's confused emotions coalesced into rage. Knocking Alex's hands away, he jumped

up from his chair and sank his fingers deep into the other man's shoulders.

"I didn't know if I could trust you," Alex yelped, his face twisting in pain. "How could I know? I didn't know if losing Peter had turned you into the robotic, indie-hating machine the press said you were."

That night – that terrible night – everything always came back to that night.

"I thought I'd watch you," Alex said softly. "I thought I'd see for myself if I could trust you enough to tell you, or if you'd turned against indies because of Peter."

"You sent me to Tyler's house..."

"To see if he could fool you, and buy you, the way he buys everyone. You passed that test, Joe – you passed it with flying colours. Then, I overheard you talking to Elsie last night, and I realised you were still you inside, despite all that's happened. You still rescue people, Joe; you're still the good man I always hoped you were. You've helped desperate people like me to escape from a living hell. The press doesn't know the price you paid for your kindness, but I do."

"Why not tell me last night?" Josiah demanded. "Why continue this charade all day today, too?"

"You needed last night. You needed it for you – I wasn't going to make it about me. You were so sad... you've been locked up in this terrible grief for so long. I wanted to help you, Joe, not make things worse."

"This morning, then...?"

"When? During the little press conference you gave, or at work, with all your colleagues there? None of them knows about your sideline in helping indies escape, do they? Esther doesn't – that was clear from your conversation with her today."

As Ashton's song reached its mournful crescendo, Josiah released Alex, dropping him onto the floor abruptly, as if he was too hot to hold. He walked away and paced the room restlessly, like an injured bear.

Alex got to his feet, rubbing his shoulders gingerly. "I'm sorry, Joe. I'm sorry for what happened that night. I'm sorry I couldn't stop Lars. All these years, I've wanted to tell you that. I didn't see he had a knife

at first. I managed to prevent him stabbing Peter a second time, and then you were there, and we stopped him together, only to find it was too late. I'm so, so sorry. I've wanted to tell you that for such a long time."

"Shut up," Josiah said, still pacing. He didn't know how to make sense of this, or what to feel about it. It was too shocking, too much, on top of everything else. He felt as if he was going to explode.

"Joe, please..." Alex stepped in front of him, blocking his way.

Josiah grabbed him, intending to shove him aside, but twisted his hand in the front of his shirt instead, holding him there. He raised his fist, wanting to bury it in solid flesh, to find the release he always sought when his emotions overwhelmed him.

"You promised me you'd never hit me, and I know you never will," Alex said softly. "I trust you, Joe."

He stared at him, his fist still poised, ready to strike.

Alex stared back, his gaze never faltering.

Josiah dropped his fist, pulled Alex towards him, and kissed him hard. Alex kissed him back, just as hard. Now, Josiah embraced him blindly, lost to everything but the feel of Alex's lips under his, his tongue in his mouth, and Alex's hard body pressed up against his own.

He wasn't thinking anymore; he was running on pure emotion. He tore open Alex's shirt and ripped it off his body. Then he reached for Alex's trousers, only to find his fingers were shaking too much.

"Shh," Alex murmured soothingly. "I'll take care of this. Let me..." He undid his trousers and pushed them onto the floor, along with his boxer shorts. Then he stood there: naked, beautiful, and utterly irresistible.

His skin was smooth and porcelain white, his cock hard and inviting. It had been so many years since Josiah had held a nude man in his arms, and he ached with longing. "I can't. It's wrong..." he said, his entire body shaking.

"No. It's what I want, and it's what you need – so very much," Alex told him resolutely. "Shh... it's okay." He stroked Josiah's trembling body to calm him. "Look at me. It's okay. Yes?" He took Josiah's face in his hands, and Josiah was dimly aware of a pair of grey eyes gazing at him intently. "Yes?" Alex repeated.

"Yes," Josiah replied numbly. "Oh, God, yes." He pulled Alex close, caressing his waist, his back, and his beautiful buttocks. Alex's skin was warm, his body firm, and his mouth yielding under his frantic kisses. He took Alex's buttocks in his hands and revelled in the sensation of holding all that delicious flesh. "Dear God... I want you so much," he breathed hoarsely into Alex's hair.

"Have me. Here. Now." Alex unzipped Josiah's trousers and wrapped his hand around his semi-hard cock.

Josiah gasped as the sensation awakened old instincts that he thought he'd banished years ago. He drew back with a growl. He had to be inside Alex; he needed to be buried to the hilt inside him, and to fuck him hard. No, it was more than a need – it was a necessity. All his years of self-imposed celibacy demanded release.

He swung his arm across the dining table to clear it. Plates and cutlery went flying; he heard them smashing onto the floor, but he didn't care. He was lost to everything as he grabbed Alex and pushed him onto the tabletop.

Alex pulled him in close, wrapping his legs around him, and Josiah bent to lick Alex's bare chest, and the pale skin that was stretched sleek and smooth over hard, toned muscles. He sucked down on one of Alex's nipples, and Alex gasped. Holding Alex down, Josiah moved to the other nipple, suckling it, loving how Alex mewled and moaned. He explored further, moving his mouth down, trailing wet kisses and little love bites wherever he went. There wasn't a single hair on Alex's body – not his chest, his armpits, or even his crotch. He was smooth, and exotic, and Josiah had to have him – now. Some distant memory stirred, and he raised his head and looked around.

"Lube...condom..." he said. He couldn't bear the thought of going upstairs and searching for them, even if by some remote chance he still had such items in the house.

Alex pointed to his discarded trousers on the floor. "Pocket," he said throatily.

Josiah stared at him, befuddled. "Why...?"

"A precaution from my time with Elliot. I kept a supply in most of my pockets."

Josiah reached into the trousers and yanked the items out, peeled

the condom onto his hard cock, squirted lube onto his fingers, and then turned back.

Alex welcomed him, opening his legs wide and wrapping them around his waist again.

He slid a finger into Alex's hole, and Alex moaned, opening up wide and allowing him to add another finger. Alex threw back his head, panting and gasping; he looked so beautiful that Josiah couldn't wait. He pushed Alex's legs further apart, grabbed his buttocks, pulled them open, and nudged his eager cock into Alex's hole.

Alex looked up at him with a grin, encouraging him in, so he pushed, gasping at the half-forgotten sensation as his cock was enveloped in all that beautiful, tight warmth. Alex pulled him in even further, wrapping his legs so tightly around his waist that he fell forward onto the table. He braced his hands on either side of Alex's head and kissed him again. His cock was buried deep in Alex's body, his tongue deep in his mouth, and nothing had felt so good in a very long time.

The sounds, scents, and sensations of sex unleashed something deep inside, and he screamed as he gave a thrust – then another, and another. Then he was lost, possessed, deranged even, as he fucked Alex hard on the table. Alex gazed up at him, taking everything he could throw at him. It was so exhilarating knowing Alex wanted this, too, that he could take it this hard, this furious, and this fast. Their gazes locked, neither of them able to look away as they shared the most intense white-knuckle ride of their lives.

Josiah could hear the harsh sound of his own breathing, but he couldn't feel it – he could only feel his cock buried inside Alex, thrusting into him over and over again. Every so often he leaned down and kissed Alex hard on the mouth, and every time Alex kissed him back with the same strength.

Their bodies were joined in the desperate coupling, fuelling a need in them both that he wasn't sure could ever be sated. He had to consume Alex, experience every single part of him, and he knew that Alex felt the same way.

Reaching down, he took Alex's cock in his lube-slicked hand. Alex cried out and bucked into him. Josiah milked him hard, sliding his

hand up and down in time to his own deep thrusts. It seemed to go on forever... the thrusting, the sliding, the kissing... and then Alex screamed even louder as he came over Josiah's hand, although even in his moment of orgasm he didn't look away. Their gazes remained locked together as Josiah thrust even faster, feeling his own pleasure reaching a climax.

All the years fell away. He howled as he came, feeling the catharsis and the sheer sense of release after so long. He howled for the past, for what he'd lost, and for all the sad, missing years in between – and for what he'd now found. He howled until he thought his ribs would break, and this time, he wasn't alone with a dead body in the rain. He was with a warm, living person, who was gazing up at him with passion and affection.

Then it was over. Bending his exhausted body over Alex, he rested his forehead against his. Alex wrapped his arms around him, hugging him close, and Josiah nestled his face in his neck and kissed him there: sweet, soft, gentle kisses now that the urgent need had gone. "Are you okay? Did I hurt you?" he asked.

"No... it was good... so good," Alex panted, taking hold of Josiah's head and gazing at him. "Look at me – I'm okay."

Josiah nodded numbly. He kissed Alex on the lips again, loving how he pushed up against him and opened his mouth so they could explore each other with their tongues. It was a moment of such beautiful intimacy that he didn't want to let it go. He wanted to stay like this forever, pressed deep inside Alex's body and leaning over him, kissing him deeply and tenderly.

Still fully clothed, while Alex was completely naked, Josiah realised he had a new need now. He wanted to explore Alex, to discover every secret his body held, to uncover each of them with his fingers, and tongue, and cock, until this elusive, maddening mystery of a man gave up everything to him.

He didn't know what the future held for them – the investigator and the temporary IS he couldn't afford to buy. He just knew they had now, and he wanted to savour every moment.

"I'm not done. I need more," he said, drawing back. "Let's go upstairs."

He pulled out and removed the condom, throwing it impatiently on the floor to be worried about later, tucked his cock back into his trousers, then gently helped Alex off the table. Alex fell against him, his knees giving way, but Josiah caught him and swung him up into his arms. Alex wasn't light, but Josiah was strong, so he decided to carry him up the stairs. Alex smiled and rested his head on his shoulder.

Josiah paused in the dining room doorway, his arms full of a naked, exhausted Alex, and glanced back. The room was a mess, the floor littered with plates and cutlery and stained with smears of ketchup and little rivers of Coke... and there, by the box of art supplies in the corner, was the vase that Liz had made for him and Peter as a wedding gift.

It had shattered into several large pieces and was lying broken on the floor.

Chapter Seventeen

NOVEMBER 2088

Alex

Alex bought a ticket to Sevenoaks, and then sat at the coach station feeling ridiculously conspicuous, even though his cap was drawn down over his eyes.

He felt guilty for using the money Barney had given him for something other than its intended purpose. Paul Andrews would probably call Barney and ask where his passenger was, and then Barney would think Alex had scammed him. Yet Alex was sure that if that kind man knew the truth, he'd approve of what Alex was doing. Barney, of all people, would understand why he had to visit his father at a time like this.

He spent the journey in an agony of nerves, wondering what he'd do when he got to the hospital. He had no idea where his father's room was, and the press would be camped outside so he'd have to avoid them, to say nothing of the possibility of Tyler's men lurking there, too.

He knew Noah had been taken to Queen Catherine Hospital, which was where the paramedics had taken him and Charles after the duck accident. He hated the place. He remembered sitting on a bed in the A&E department as they'd sewed up the deep gash in his thigh. The large amount of croc in his system had made him feel mellow and

disconnected, but his grief had been sharp and all-consuming – the tears rolling uncontrollably down his face had been a combination of the two.

The doctor finished stitching his thigh and then left him alone in the little curtained cubicle. He gazed blankly into space, the tears running down his cheeks unchecked. They'd given him painkillers, but the wound on his thigh still throbbed. The nurses had also treated various other cuts and bruises that he hadn't even noticed, but he'd suffered no major injuries – how was that even possible? The duck was a mangled mess – how had he survived? Charles was being worked on somewhere else, and his mother's body had been loaded into the ambulance with a blanket covering her face. He couldn't stop thinking about that. Surely none of this was real? He must be trapped in a nightmare, because this couldn't possibly be happening. When he'd had bad dreams as a child, his father had made the monsters go away. He longed for his father now, to make all this go away.

The cubicle curtain was whisked to one side, and Noah appeared. He looked as if he'd aged ten years overnight.

"Alex... thank God! Alex." Noah put his arms around him, enveloping him in a warm hug.

Alex clung on to his father's shirt. "Sorry, sorry, sorry," he wept into his father's chest, suddenly feeling very small and very young.

"Shh...it's okay, Alex, I'm here. You're okay. Shh." His father kissed his hair and rocked him until his sobs finally stopped. Then he pulled back.

"Mum..."

"Yes, I know. They told me," Noah said softly, his eyes bright with his own tears.

"And Charles...? He's badly hurt... he said he couldn't feel his legs..."

"They're working on him, but..." His father swallowed hard. "His spine was crushed. They've told me he probably won't walk again."

Alex wasn't surprised. He'd sat with Charles as they waited for the

ambulance, and his brother had told him he had no feeling from the waist down.

"There's a policewoman here to see you. You have to give a statement," his father told him.

"Now?"

"Yes. Don't be afraid – just tell her exactly what happened."

The policewoman was calm and matter of fact. "We have to record the conversation. Regulations," she said apologetically, putting her nanopad on the bedside table. "Now, Alex – if you could just tell me what happened, in your own words."

Alex looked at his father for guidance; Noah sat down on the bed and put his arm around him.

"It's okay. Just tell her the truth."

"I don't know what happened, exactly... We'd just stopped at a pub for lunch. We were happy. We were driving along... talking and laughing, and then there was this bang... I didn't see anything... I didn't see it, whatever we hit. I didn't see it." He shook his head miserably. "Then the duck flew over and over before slamming into a tree. Mum and Charles must have been thrown out when it was tumbling, but I wasn't."

"And you were driving the vehicle at the time of the accident?"

"Yes. Yes, I was driving."

"I have to ask... did you drink anything at the pub?" the policewoman asked, gazing at him keenly.

"No." He shook his head. "I had a Coke."

"Did you take anything else that might have affected your driving?" she pressed.

His stomach lurched. "Yes. I... took some croc. Crocodile Tears. I took some when we stopped at the pub."

His father drew back.

Alex couldn't meet Noah's eye and kept his head down as he answered the rest of the policewoman's questions.

"We'll have to take a blood sample," she said. "It's mandatory after a fatal duck accident, and croc doesn't show up in a breath test anyway."

"Of course," his father said quietly.

"I'll go and organise it," she said, leaving the room.

"How much croc did you take, Alex?" his father demanded when they were alone.

Alex shook his head slowly, still unable to look up and meet Noah's eye. "I don't know... a lot."

"I don't understand," Noah said, bewildered. "Why would your mother have let you drive when you were as high as a kite?"

"She didn't know." He wrapped his arms around his body for comfort. "I went into the pub toilet and took the croc just before we left. She didn't know I'd taken it. The tears don't start until later."

"Christ!" His father turned away. "I thought you weren't doing croc anymore. You promised me..."

"I'm sorry, Dad," Alex said again, pathetically. "I'm so sorry."

"Sorry won't bring your mother back," his father said tightly.

Alex looked up and recoiled from what he saw. His father was glaring at him as if he were a stranger. "I don't think you understand. This isn't getting expelled from school, or some stupid scrape of the kind you get yourself into every other week. Your mother is dead, and your brother will never walk again... Oh, Christ." He pushed a shaky hand through his hair. "Christ, what have you done, Alex? What have you done?"

———

Queen Catherine Hospital – the scene of the worst day of his life – was the last place he wanted to go to, but the one place he absolutely had to be right now. He pulled his cap down low over his face as he jumped off the coach in Sevenoaks. Then he walked to the hospital, taking various back roads to keep out of sight.

Queen Catherine was a large, modern facility, built many decades after the Rising, comprising just one huge main building. Alex entered the grounds easily enough, but felt his gut churn at the familiar sight of several media AVs parked outside the main entrance, just as they had been six years ago. His family, as always, provided good value for the country's press.

He put his head down and walked quickly down one of the many

small streets that linked the hospital's various AV parks. Jogging to the end, he was about to step out onto the road when a black SUAV passed by in front of him. He took a few paces back, hiding behind a wall, then peered around the corner. The SUAV cruised slowly away, clearly on the lookout.

He considered running back to Swanage, finding Paul Andrews, and fleeing to France, but then reminded himself that he had come this far, and he desperately wanted to see his father. Of course Tyler's men were here looking for him – it was obvious he might make an attempt to visit Noah. Tyler might not have set this trap himself, but he would take full advantage of his father's illness in order to catch Alex.

He couldn't use the hospital's main entrance because of the press, but there had to be another way in.

––––––

Alex looked out of the hospital window at the crowd of well-wishers, paparazzi, and television crews below.

"Why don't they go away?" he asked, glancing back at his brother.

Charles looked pale and fragile; he was still trying to come to terms with the severity of his injuries. Their father was sitting in a chair beside him, and a nurse was busy entering his latest stats on her nanopad.

"It's been two weeks – nothing interesting is happening here. They should just piss off," Alex muttered.

"Your brother is a national hero," his father snapped. "That's why they're here. They're keeping a vigil because the nation loves him."

"I don't think it's very loving to camp outside his hospital room day and night, hoping to get a picture of him."

"What you think isn't important," his father said in a withering tone.

Alex tried not to care about the coldness in Noah's voice, or the anger in his eyes. How long would his father look at him like this, his gaze loaded with all that blame?

"Hey, don't argue," Charles beseeched, with a ghost of his old, sweet-natured smile.

"That's right. We must keep our patient nice and calm," the nurse said soothingly. She had kind brown eyes and a sympathetic smile.

"Don't worry about the press, Alex," Charles murmured, but then he would say that – he'd always loved the attention of the world's media, while Alex was starting to discover how much he hated it.

"That's easy for you to say – you don't have to push your way through them every day," Alex snapped.

"How dare you!" His father shook his finger angrily at him. "Your brother worked bloody hard for years to achieve his success. He made his country proud and gave the entire nation something to celebrate after decades of misery – but you, what have you ever done? Nothing except getting yourself expelled from three different schools and taking so many drugs you can't see straight."

Alex shrank back against the window, afraid of his father's anger. He'd endured three post-expulsion interviews in Noah's study at The Orchard in the past. Noah had sighed, sternly told him how disappointed he was, and extracted Alex's promises to do better in future – but Alex had never seen him this furious before.

"I'm sorry," he said. "I'm just scared of them." He jerked his head at the window. He didn't say it, because he didn't want to upset his brother, but the crowd had jeered at him when he pushed his way through to visit. They'd called him names, hating him for what had happened to Charles, their shining golden boy. Noah was right – Charles was a national hero. What did that make him? The national villain? He was seventeen years old, he'd just lost his mother, his brother was likely to be in a wheelchair for the rest of his life, and his father hated him. He felt so alone.

"There's a way out via the staff accommodation," the nurse said. "I'm sure we could smuggle you out through there, so you don't have to face them."

"Really?" Alex brightened. "I'd like that. Where is it?"

"I can show you."

"No." His father put a heavy hand on his shoulder. "Lyttons don't skulk in the shadows. Alex will go out there and face the press, and

he'll stand tall while he does it. He made a mistake, and he'll take responsibility for that mistake and accept all that comes with it. Won't you, Alex?"

Alex glanced at his father glumly. Was this the way back into his father's heart? If he went out there and faced that baying mob, day in, day out, would his father's look of disgust finally turn into one of pride – or at least acceptance?

"Okay," he muttered, biting back a sullen retort. He didn't want to run the gauntlet of an angry crowd ever again. He didn't want to have to win back his father's love. He wanted it to be his again, for free, the way it used to be.

Noah turned back to Charles, smiling at him lovingly. Alex felt a jealous knot form in his belly. When the nurse touched his arm and jerked her head, he followed her out of the room.

"I'll show you anyway – in case you change your mind," she said, with a pitying look. "It's down here."

She led him along a corridor and down a couple of flights of stairs to a doorway. "Go through there – you need a biokey to open it, but people come and go all the time so just tag along with someone passing through. Walk through the block – it has a side exit into the grounds, and nobody is likely to see you. You can come in the same way in the morning, as well."

"Thank you," he said in a heartfelt tone.

She smiled and patted his arm. "I've got a son around your age – I know you look all grown up, but you're still a kid inside – and your mum just died. It's vile what the press are doing to you. I know how much you must be missing her, but you've been in to visit your brother every day. Something bad happened to you, but that doesn't make you a bad person, Alex."

He lowered his head, blinking rapidly. She patted his arm again and then left.

He didn't use her escape route. He steeled himself every day to step out of the hospital's main entrance in front of the mob and take it on the chin. He was jeered and taunted each morning when he arrived, and each evening when he left, but he held his head high and took it. He was a Lytton, after all.

Alex made his way to the staff accommodation unit and hung around outside until a gaggle of people arrived at the door. He tagged along behind them as they entered and then jogged down a hallway and through another door to the main body of the hospital.

He had no idea which room his father was in, so he went to the hospital shop and bought the biggest bunch of flowers he could find. Then he went to the nearest ward.

"Flowers for Noah Lytton," he said, hiding his face behind them.

"He's not on this ward. You need the Prince Louis Ward on the second floor," a nurse told him, barely looking up.

He used the empty stairwell to reach the second floor, rather than the busy lift. He knew this hospital like the back of his hand. Charles had been here for months, and he'd spent every day with him, bringing in his schoolwork so he could sit at the foot of Charles's bed and study.

He paused on the stairs and glanced out of the window to see another black SUAV slowly patrolling the hospital grounds below. Tyler's men would be difficult to evade, but he'd come this far. If he could stay one step ahead, he might get away with this.

He made it to the second floor and along the hallway to the nurse's station.

"Delivery of flowers for Noah Lytton," he told the nurse on duty.

"I'll take them," she said brusquely. He reluctantly relinquished them, but stayed to watch her taking them into a room further along the hallway with the number 14 on the door.

Ducking into a nearby toilet, he waited a few minutes, and then slipped out again. The nurse he'd given the flowers to was talking to someone, and it was easy enough to walk past her without being seen. He paused outside room fourteen for a second, looking around, then opened the door and stepped inside.

He saw his father lying in a bed, and the flowers he'd delivered in a big plastic jug on a nearby table. He tiptoed over, his heart skipping a beat as he looked down at his father's grey, haggard face. Noah's eyes were closed; he hadn't yet regained consciousness. He didn't look like the man Alex had grown up with, or even like the man he'd seen a few

weeks ago at Lytton AV. He looked shrunken, frail, and greatly diminished. There was a cannula in his hand, attached to an IV line.

Alex sat down on the bed and took hold of Noah's hand. "Hi, Dad – it's Alex," he whispered, squeezing gently. His father didn't respond. "I'm so sorry you're ill," he continued. "I wanted to come and visit you, to say, um... well, that I love you. I'm not sure it's what you want to hear, but I had to tell you in case I don't get a chance again."

He blinked a few times, and then continued.

"I know I fucked up, and I'm sorrier than you can ever know. I'm not going to ask you to forgive me – I can't forgive myself, so I'm not asking you to try. I just wanted you to know that I love you. I've always loved you, even when I was being a shit, and getting expelled, and causing trouble for you. I think maybe that was the problem." He paused, struggling to understand his complex relationship with this man lying on the bed. "Mum and Charles had each other, so you and I were sort of landed with each other, weren't we? I think you felt as left out as I did, although you handled it better." He gave a wry smile. "I wanted to be part of their gang, doing the big, important thing – going to regattas, winning medals, getting all that kudos – but I wasn't part of their club, and neither were you. I'm sorry I didn't try to connect with you more, instead of making your life difficult. Honestly, I think all I ever really wanted was your attention – any attention – however negative." He stroked his father's hand with his thumb.

The blinds were drawn and the room dim, giving it an air of the confessional, making it easier to talk. He tuned in to the hypnotic sound of his father's breathing, watching his chest rise and fall.

"You were right about George Tyler," he said, with a bitter laugh. "He's evil. He made me show you those images – I didn't want to do it. I didn't know about him and Mum until it was too late. I don't know what she was thinking, falling for a man like that, but he can be so very charming when he wants something. I was sucked in, so I suppose I can understand why she was, too."

Noah's breathing didn't falter. His chest still rose and fell slowly, sonorously.

"I'm sorry if I'm the reason you're here," Alex told him, still stroking his hand gently. "If I could go back and do things differently,

then I would. I know I was a shit when I worked at Lytton AV, but I wanted you to see me again, really see me, the way you did when I was a kid. After the accident, you stopped seeing who I was – I just became a walking disappointment. I understand why you felt that way, but you don't know how much it hurt. I was a pain in the arse – I know that. I thought that if I could prove myself at work and show you how good I was, then you'd love me again, but I went about it the wrong way. You made me do all those other things instead of designing, but I couldn't make you proud of me, because I wasn't good at any of that stuff."

He raised his father's hand to his lips and kissed it.

"You're a good man, Dad. You deserved better. We were happy once – I'm not sure where it all went wrong. Maybe after Granddad fell ill, and you had to take over the business. You were so short-tempered with us all after that. I don't think you even like Lytton AV, really. I think it's been this bloody awful albatross around your neck. You'd probably have been happier doing something else. It was this gigantic birthright you inherited, but I don't think it was you, really."

He paused, suddenly seeing their entire family dynamic clearly.

"Running the company made you irritable, and you pushed us away. Mum threw herself into training Charles, but things weren't right between you and her, so she was probably easy pickings for Tyler when he came back into her life. You were busy with the business, so you didn't have time for me. The day she died, I was so happy to be with her and Charles, sharing some of their magic. They were on such a high after Charles won the gold medal – it was like nothing could touch them or bring them down. We were laughing so much – and then the crash happened."

He leaned over and gently smoothed his father's grey hair away from his forehead. "Tyler set me up. He wanted revenge on me for Mum's death, and for every bad thing he felt our family did to his. You were right about him all along; I wish I'd listened. I was an idiot. I wish you could save me, like when I was a little kid. I wish you could make everything all better, but instead you're lying here, in this bed, and I'm on the run. I'm glad I escaped from Tyler, because otherwise I'd be sitting in his tower, fretting about you, and he'd be holding it over me to torment me. At least this way I've been able to see you and tell you

all this stuff, whatever happens next. I don't know if you can hear me, but at least I've said it to you."

He wiped his sleeve over his wet eyes, then glanced towards the door. "I should be going now. I've pushed my luck far enough as it is. I just had to see you."

He stood up, leaned over the bed, and kissed his father's cheek. "I love you, Dad. I can't believe that that was ever hard to say – it seems so easy now. I love you. Please get better."

He was about to pull away when his father's eyelids fluttered open.

"Alex...?" One side of his mouth formed the word, but the sound came out slurred.

"Yes, it's me. I'm here. Don't talk." He put a gentle finger over his father's lips. Noah's face was screwed up in confused anguish, so Alex stroked his hair again to calm him. "You're in pain. I should get someone." He looked towards the door, reluctant to leave. "I have to go. I wish I didn't, but I do. I hope you heard some of what I said. I hope you know that I love you, and that I'm sorry – for everything."

His father said something that he couldn't make out, so he bent his head to Noah's lips. The words were so indistinct that he wasn't sure if his father was saying "I love you", "I heard you", or "I hate you".

"It's okay. Whatever you think and feel about me – it's okay. I've never stopped loving you. I never will. Now, I have to go. Goodbye, Dad."

He kissed his father's cheek again, then went to the door. He glanced back to see his father looking at him, his eyes gleaming in the dark room. The machine above Noah's head began to beep aggressively, and he made a moaning sound. Alex knew he couldn't wait any longer – he had to get help. He left the room and walked back out to the nurse's station.

"The patient in room fourteen – Noah Lytton – he's just woken up, and he's in a lot of pain," he told the startled nurse. Then he walked off quickly in the direction of the stairs. He heard a commotion behind him, and the sound of footsteps, and then someone shouting, "Hey, you. Stop!"

He glanced behind him to see a security guard in hot pursuit, so he took off, running as fast as he could, his shoes slithering on the tiled

floor. He ran down the stairs, two at a time, and then out into another hallway, and along what felt like a series of never-ending corridors. He came to the staff accommodation block just as a girl was letting herself in with a biokey. He pushed his way past her, ignoring her startled cry, then glanced over his shoulder again to see that the security guard was still chasing him. He ran through the housing block, out of the door, through the grounds, and out onto the street... straight into the path of a black SUAV. The vehicle came to a screeching halt, only narrowly avoiding hitting him. He took off in the opposite direction, running as fast as he could. The SUAV made a sharp turn to follow him, but he slipped down a side street and into a little alleyway behind some shops until he was out of sight. Climbing a wall, he landed in the back garden of a pub; ignoring the startled glances of the people sitting at picnic tables drinking, he sprinted out of a gate and down another side street. He looked over his shoulder repeatedly to see if either Tyler's men or the security guard from the hospital were following him, but nobody was in pursuit.

He heaved a sigh of relief as he realised that he'd evaded them all and took a moment to lean against the wall and get his breath back. Then he continued on down the street at a slower pace. There was another turning ahead. As he rounded the corner, he took one last look behind him to make sure he wasn't being followed... and disappeared into darkness.

A hood was thrown over his head. His arms were grabbed and his hands fastened roughly behind his back, and then he was bundled bodily into a vehicle and slung onto the floor. Someone got in behind him, the door was slammed shut, and they took off at high speed.

He felt someone leaning over him, and he cowered back against a seat, bracing himself. Then the hood was whisked away, and he was staring up into a familiar face.

"Hello, Alex." Big Mick grinned. "Nice to have you back. Mr Tyler will be pleased – he's missed you ever so much. I reckon he's a got a very special welcome home party planned for you, don't you?"

Chapter Eighteen

OCTOBER 2095

Josiah

Josiah carried Alex up the stairs to the bathroom and deposited him carefully on the wicker chair in the corner. "I thought we could take a shower – get cleaned up," he said.

"Together?" Alex asked hopefully.

"I sure as hell hope so. I...uh, I want to show you that I'm not always like I was downstairs." Josiah grimaced.

"I like who you were downstairs."

"Well, good then," he responded, feeling suddenly shy. It had been easy enough earlier, when he'd been in the grip of all those violent emotions, but now he wasn't so sure of himself. He crouched down in front of Alex and gently caressed his face.

"I can hardly believe it was you that night. You have no idea how many times I've thought about you, talked about you with Elsie, and worried about you. I prayed that you'd got away."

"I almost did," Alex said, with a rueful smile. "I was so close, but Tyler caught me."

"I'm sorry. We tried calling you, but I'm guessing you'd disposed of the nanopad by then."

"Yeah. I thought as I'd used it to call the ambulance that Inquisitus might be able to trace it."

"They attempted to," Josiah said. "I wasn't allowed to take part in the investigation, but Esther threw some crumbs my way. She told me they'd had no luck tracing your nanopad. I had to pretend to be disappointed, but I was secretly relieved."

"I threw it into a lost zone."

"That was a wise move, but you must have felt so cut off and alone."

"I was terrified," Alex admitted.

"One more casualty of that terrible night." Josiah leaned forward and kissed him gently. "Ben..." He shook his head in disbelief. "After all these years, to find you again... and in these circumstances."

"I thought about you, too, all the time." Alex rested his hands on Josiah's chest. "I read everything I could find about you. I worried about how you were doing without Peter. I could see you two had something special, even though I'd only seen you for such a short time – it was obvious. I was even jealous." He stopped short, and bit his lip.

"Jealous?" Josiah frowned.

Alex nodded. "When I told you the other night that I once met a remarkable man who made me feel something, but the timing was all wrong..."

"That was me?" Josiah asked, astonished.

"Yes. From the moment I met you in the car, I felt this instant attraction. You seemed so strong and self-assured, and I was so lost and frightened. I loved how you and Peter talked to each other, how you made each other laugh, your easy intimacy. I wanted what you had with Peter. Then he was killed, and I wished I could be with you, to help you in some way, but it was impossible. Of course, it was all a fantasy – I didn't actually know you. I've only really come to know you during these past few days."

"Ah – and how did I measure up?" Josiah questioned ruefully. "You must be disappointed. You expected the knight in shining armour of your fantasy, but found a sad basket case instead. Not the kind of man you were hoping for, huh?"

"Better," Alex said firmly. "Much better – because you're real, and because I knew why you were falling apart, and because it finally gave me a chance to help you, the way I wanted to all those years ago." He

gently clasped Josiah's face between his hands. "I've wanted you for so long, but I didn't believe it might actually happen." He leaned forward and kissed him on the lips. Josiah leaned into the sweetness of the kiss.

"Now, how about that shower?" Alex suggested, with a grin.

"I think we both need it." Josiah got to his feet and started unbuttoning his shirt, feeling self-conscious again.

"Stop," Alex said. He got up and held on to the sink for a moment before his legs started working again. Then he leaned over and batted Josiah's fingers away. "Let me," he said. "You've seen me butt naked — it's my turn now."

Alex undressed him slowly, opening his shirt one button at a time, pausing between each one to kiss the newly exposed flesh. The fourth button revealed the chain holding his wedding ring; Alex stopped and looked up questioningly.

Josiah expected to feel a pang of guilt, but he didn't. "It's okay," he said softly. "Peter would approve, I think."

Alex gently touched the ring with his fingers. "You always wear it?"

"Yes. Since that night. It used to belong to my father — I wore it around my neck for years before I gave it to Peter."

Alex smiled and kissed it. Then he pulled Josiah's shirt away and let it drop to the floor, before brushing his fingertips over his bare chest, tracing the outlines of his muscles and ribs, bending to kiss and nuzzle where the mood took him.

Josiah gazed at Alex from heavy-lidded eyes, lost in the quietly charged atmosphere between them. He longed to feel Alex's bare skin pressed against his own, but Alex was taking his time, clearly savouring every moment of undressing him. Josiah wanted to give him that, so he stood still, breathing heavily, feeling his arousal start to build again.

Alex helped him out of his socks and shoes, then slowly unzipped his trousers and slid them down his legs, along with his boxers. Finally, he was naked, too. Josiah was vain enough to suck in his stomach, which made Alex laugh.

"Too much chocolate," Josiah said ruefully, because although he was in good shape, his belly wasn't as washboard flat as it had once been.

"Skinny wouldn't suit you," Alex said, then he proceeded to circle him, kissing and caressing as he went.

Josiah gasped as he felt Alex's hands caressing his buttocks, and then the warm press of his lips upon them.

Alex lingered there, kissing and stroking, then returned to stand in front of him.

"My turn now," Josiah said. He pulled Alex in close, so that their naked bodies were pressed up against each other, skin on skin. He'd been longing for this, and it didn't disappoint. He slid his hands down Alex's back, caressing him lightly with his fingertips, and then cupped his buttocks in his hands and squeezed them. Alex seemed to enjoy this – he moaned and pressed up hard against him – yet suddenly, it occurred to Josiah that Alex might simply be giving him what he wanted. He thought of all the men Alex had been forced to sleep with, and it gave him pause.

"Do you really want this?" he asked, cupping Alex's jaw between his hands and gazing into his clear grey eyes. "Or are you just trying to please me?"

"Oh, I definitely want to please you," Alex purred.

"Stop it. I need to know. Is this to get me onside, so I'll agree to whatever plan you've been cooking up in that clever brain of yours?" Josiah demanded. "If you want something from me, then just ask – you don't have to seduce me into it."

"No," Alex said firmly. "I wouldn't use you like that, Joe."

"You've tried before," Josiah reminded him. "The first night you were here – you attempted to seduce me then."

A shadow passed across Alex's face. "Yes," he said honestly. Josiah drew away.

"Please understand – I had to give my houders what they wanted in order to survive," Alex told him, grasping his hand and pulling him back. "I thought – hoped – you'd be better than the others, but I didn't know for sure. A lot can happen in seven years, and an IS had killed your husband. You don't understand what it's like, being passed on to a new houder and wondering how to be as pleasing as possible, so they won't beat you."

"I do understand that. It's just that it's been so long for me, and it's too important. I don't want to hurt you, but I don't want to be hurt,

either. I haven't slept with many men; before Peter, there were only a handful."

Alex's eyes clouded over. "I have, though. I've slept with more people than I can even remember, and that's why this is important to me, too, in a different way." He rested his hands on Josiah's hips and stroked his thumbs over his skin. "You see, I haven't slept with anyone by my own choice in years. I was told who to have sex with, and it was my job to give them a good time. If I didn't, then I was punished. You're the first person in ages that I'm choosing. Me. I'm doing the choosing, and I'm choosing you, because I can, and because I want to." He was trembling as he said that. "I want you, Joe. My choice, my desire – mine – for the first time in a very long time. Don't doubt me, Joe."

Josiah pulled him close to calm him. "I don't. I just have to be sure it's what you really want, because the last thing I want is to exploit you. People have been doing that for too long, and I won't be one of them. Downstairs, I was upset and confused. I hope I didn't cross a line."

"You didn't take advantage of me downstairs. I enjoyed every second."

"And now...?" Josiah asked anxiously. "I want you, Alex, but I don't want to be played. I want the real you."

Alex gave him a look that was so honest it took his breath away. "You have me," he said. "Oh God, you have the real me. I promise you that."

"Good. Because I like him, this real Alex. I like him very much. You never, ever have to hide him from me again."

Alex swallowed hard, then drew back.

"You're right to push me on this. You're right to demand my honesty. I should have known that this could never be casual for you. That's not who you are. So... as we're being honest, I'd like something from you, too."

"Tell me. If I can do it, I will."

Alex looked down, flushing. Josiah wondered what he could possibly want that would make him so shy.

When Alex looked up, there was a defiant expression in his eyes. "I want you to really see me for me," he admitted, as if he were asking for something shameful. "I don't want to be looked at as a body to be fucked, or someone to be owned and possessed. I don't want to be someone's grubby little fantasy, but, just as importantly, I also don't want you looking at me as a damaged, fragile flower, some sad boy for you to fix. I'm not asking you to be in love with me, Joe, but I *am* asking you to see me as someone real, not an object, or a fantasy, but a fucked-up man with a fucked-up life who is laying himself bare. If you can do that, then I promise you'll get the real me. No tricks, no hiding, no bullshit. Just me."

"Good," Josiah said tightly. "I can see through bullshit."

"I know that." Alex gave a wry grunt. "God knows, if I know anything about you, it's that."

Josiah reached out and pulled him close. "Come here then, beautiful."

Alex pressed his hands to Josiah's chest to make him pause. "Please... don't. My looks have been a curse all my life," he said wearily. "Even before I became an IS, people projected their fantasies onto me. Hardly anyone ever saw me for who I really am. I might as well have been invisible. I certainly felt that way."

"You aren't invisible to me," Josiah told him, taking Alex's face between his hands now and gazing at him intently. "I called you beautiful because that's how I see you. Not your body, or your face, pretty though they are... but you. Nobody ever called Peter beautiful, but I thought he was the most gorgeous man in the world. Objectively, you're stunning – you know that, and you've suffered for it. That's not what I'm talking about. I'm talking about the man inside – the one who's been so kind to me these past few days while I've been slowly falling apart. Him. He's beautiful."

Alex stared back at him. "That might be the nicest thing anyone has ever said to me," he said. "But when you look at me, you see all the men who've laid their hands on me before you, and you don't like it." He drew away from Josiah's hold. "I saw how you looked when I said I'd slept with Jeffrey Mead. It makes you angry, but I can't change my past. I've slept with a lot of people, Joe – even before I became an IS. I'm not like you. I used sex the same way you use your fists." He took

hold of Josiah's right hand and ran his thumb over the bruised skin. "To avoid feeling anything that hurt too much."

"You're right. I was jealous," Josiah admitted. "I was jealous of Mead getting his slimy paws on you."

"Don't turn me into a possession," Alex said sharply. "Don't make me into something that's yours, that you own, and that others can or can't touch depending on your whim. Don't do that to me, Joe. I mean, we both know it's the truth – you do own me. You can fuck me any way you like, as often as you like, for as long as you like, and I can't stop you, or report you, or complain about it – but I'm asking you to make love to me as if I'm free – as if I'm Peter, or some guy you picked up in a bar."

"I would never treat you like that," Josiah assured him. "I like to take the initiative in the bedroom, but I would never use you, Alex. I'm honoured that you're letting me see you this way. I much prefer it to that blank mask you wear. I hate that damn expression so much. Now – will you see me, too?"

"I've always seen you. You're exactly who I first thought you were, back in that car. I knew you liked tea, and Pre-R rock, and nice clothes." Alex grinned. "I didn't know then that you had a thing for expensive chocolate, or using your fists to deal with your feelings when you're hurting, but when I did, none of it took me by surprise." He raised Josiah's hand to his lips and bestowed a little kiss on his knuckles.

"Okay, but there's one more thing I need to know, if we're really being honest with each other," Josiah said.

Alex nodded eagerly. "Anything."

"It's crucial that you tell the truth about this, Alex," Josiah warned.

"I will – I swear," Alex said solemnly.

"Okay, then. I need to know – just how much do you hate hachée?" Josiah demanded, grinning.

Alex let out a bark of surprised laughter. "Can't stand the stuff," he admitted.

Josiah threw back his head and laughed. He wrapped his arms around Alex and hugged him against his chest, and they held on to each other, both laughing their heads off.

"Dear God, I've missed this so much," Josiah said. "All the little things – someone to eat fish and chips with, to hold in bed, and to laugh with. Thank you for reminding me what it's like." Leaning down, he captured Alex's mouth in his own, kissing him soundly. It felt real, and honest, and true. Alex grasped the back of his neck and kissed him back, just as passionately.

Between kisses, they gravitated slowly towards the shower. Josiah turned on the water and led Alex under the warm spray. Lathering his hands with soap, he placed them gently on Alex's body and, finding the bruises on Alex's shoulders from where he'd grasped him earlier, dropped an apologetic kiss on each one. "Sorry," he murmured. Then he discovered a couple more on Alex's thighs from where he'd held him down as he fucked him, so he knelt down and kissed those, too. While he was there, he found an old, deep scar, a couple of inches long; he stroked it with his fingertips and then looked up questioningly.

"From the duck accident," Alex told him.

He kissed that, too, knowing that the scar went far deeper than the mark on Alex's skin.

He spent a long time on his knees, kissing and caressing. Alex's cock was hard again now, straining upwards, but Josiah didn't touch it. Instead, he got to his feet, turned Alex around, and lathered his hands again, then he slowly soaped Alex's back and the soft curve of his buttocks. Sliding his hands gently between Alex's legs, he parted them and carefully washed out his hole, examining it for any sign of tearing following their explosive sex earlier. It was fine, but Josiah took his time soaping and rinsing it out, teasing with his fingers as he worked, opening him up again. Alex moaned and leaned his arms against the shower wall, sticking out his bottom in clear invitation.

"Not yet," Josiah said. He moved on, locating the fading yellow and purple bruises on Alex's back from the beating he'd received at the show. He kissed those gently, too. He also found some older scars on Alex's back, faded and white. He traced them with his fingertips. "Also from the accident?" he asked.

"No," Alex said in a very quiet voice. "Tyler."

"He whipped you?" Josiah fought down a wave of rage.

"Yes. I don't think he intended to mark me, but he lost control."

GHOST EYE

Josiah's jaw tightened, and he made a silent vow that he would one day have revenge on Tyler for all that he'd done to this beautiful man.

Alex sensed his mood and turned. "It's okay. It was a long time ago," he said, stroking Josiah's tense jaw.

"I *will* make him pay," Josiah promised.

"Shh. I don't want Tyler to spoil tonight for us. He's ruined too much of my life as it is. Come on – my turn now." Lathering his hands with soap, Alex gently began his exploration of Josiah's body, stopping at the long scar that snaked up the outside of Josiah's arm.

"Rosengarten," Josiah said softly.

Alex kissed along the length of the scar from top to bottom and back again. He continued on to the round, squat scar on the side of Josiah's torso, and bent to kiss that, too.

"Bullet. Also Rosengarten," Josiah said.

Trailing suds slowly over Josiah's body, Alex carefully soaped his cock, making it hard again in the process, and then his balls, taking his time, playing with them gently.

Josiah sighed and leaned back happily.

Alex turned Josiah around and began washing his back. He found the burn on Josiah's hip. "Rosengarten too?"

"Yeah," Josiah grunted.

"And here?" Alex ran his fingers over the jagged scar on his shoulder blade.

"Nope – knife fight when I was a kid. Got stitched up by a druggie Quarterlands doctor, which is why it looks like that. He could barely see straight, let alone sew."

Alex kissed it, then moved on to the old bullet wound on his shoulder.

"Showdown with militia in Germany," Josiah explained. He hadn't realised just how many scars there were on his body until Alex had mapped them all, one by one, including the couple more he'd acquired during his years working at Inquisitus.

When Alex was done, Josiah leaned forward to place his hands on the wall, capturing Alex between his arms. He held him under the warm spray and kissed him again as the water pounded down on them both.

They were both squeaky clean by the time they finally left the shower. Josiah grabbed a towel from the heated rail and dried Alex carefully, before Alex reached for a second towel and insisted on doing the same for him. Then Josiah took his hand and led him to the bedroom. As soon as they reached the bed, Alex sank down on his knees in front of him and began kissing, licking, and teasing Josiah's hard cock.

"No." It took all Josiah's willpower to stop him.

Alex looked up questioningly.

Josiah put a finger over Alex's lips. "I want to do something for you. Is that okay?"

Alex smiled and nodded.

Josiah pulled back the duvet and guided Alex onto the bed on his front, with a pillow under his hips. "Just relax and let me do this," he said. "It'll be good – I promise."

Alex gave a happy sigh and rested his head on his hands.

Josiah slid between Alex's legs and pulled his buttocks apart. Then he dipped his head and licked between them. Alex gave a startled mewl of pleasure. Josiah grinned – he'd always loved rimming, and he knew he was good at it. He took his time, sliding his tongue deep into the dark cleft, enjoying the scent of Alex, the feel of him, and the way he whimpered with pleasure. He wondered if anyone had ever rimmed Alex in all his years as an IS. Had anyone ever paid attention to his pleasure, or had it always been about theirs? Josiah was determined to give Alex the best rimming of his life. Alex gasped, panted, and writhed ecstatically, so Josiah knew it was working. He licked inside Alex for a long time, until he was a boneless heap, then he drew back.

Alex glanced at him over his shoulder and opened up wider, clearly inviting Josiah to fuck him.

Josiah shook his head again. "Turn over," he instructed, helping Alex to lie on his back with a pillow beneath his head. Then he wrapped his mouth around Alex's cock. Alex gasped and bucked up into him. Josiah paused for a moment, giving him time to settle.

"I should be looking after you," Alex whimpered.

"No," Josiah said firmly. "You've been taking care of other people for a long time. It's time someone took care of you."

Alex's eyes were suddenly wet, but he didn't turn away to hide them; instead, he smiled up at Josiah through his tears, as open and honest as he'd promised.

Josiah kissed him gently, then moved back down and took his cock in his mouth again. It might have been ages since he'd done this, but he was very good at taking care of the men in his life. He loved giving pleasure, reducing his partner to a quivering wreck under his caresses, and lovingly bringing him to climax.

He felt the moment Alex abandoned himself to the sensation, surrendering to his skilful tongue. He felt Alex's balls tighten, but he continued sucking until Alex had pumped out his come. Alex tried to twist away, but Josiah held on to him and swallowed, savouring the taste — it'd been so long since he'd had a man's hard cock in his mouth and his come in his throat. He didn't want to miss any part of the experience.

Alex flopped back onto the bed, exhausted and sated. Josiah climbed in beside him and pulled the duvet over them both.

"I should..." Alex moved his hand down to Josiah's cock.

"No." Josiah caught his hand and held it, gently. "I wanted this to be all about you."

"Why?" Alex asked, gazing at him blankly.

"Because you deserve it."

"You don't know that."

"Yes, I do. You screwed up once, years ago, but you've more than paid for that," Josiah told him emphatically. "You deserve to be looked after, and cared for, and treated like you matter. After all those years of servitude, it was time — past time — that someone served you. It was my honour, my pleasure, and my privilege."

Alex buried his head in Josiah's neck with a muffled sob.

Josiah stroked his hair gently and let him cry it out. "I see you, Alex," he said softly as he held him. "I see *you*."

Chapter Nineteen

NOVEMBER 2088

Alex

Mick very deliberately locked the SUAV doors as it screeched away.

Alex looked up at him in stunned silence, shocked by the sudden turnaround in his fortunes. His hip hurt from where he'd been shoved into the vehicle; he tried to lever himself up to sit on the seat behind, but Mick pushed him down.

"Runaways don't get to travel in comfort. You can stay on the floor, where you belong."

"Please, Mick, don't take me back there," Alex begged. "Don't take me back to Tyler. I'd rather die."

"Well, dying's not an option for you, sadly," Mick said with a shrug. "You're a piece of scum, Alex – you always have been and always will be – so you can suck it up and learn to live with being an IS like the rest of us."

"He doesn't whore you out like he does me, Mick."

The guard shrugged. "We're all whores in our own way – anyone who has a chip under their skin. You want to believe you're special and different, but you're not. That kind of arrogance is what Tyler wants to squeeze out of you, and he will, eventually. It'd be easier if you just gave in – running away hasn't done you any favours."

"I tried to give him what he wants – you saw that – but it wasn't enough for him."

"No – you *pretended*, and he saw through you. Tyler wants the real deal – he'll know it when he sees it."

"And you're taking me back to him? Knowing that?"

Mick nodded, slowly. "I am, Alex. I am. You see, you had everything, and you threw it all away. The rest of us never had anything to begin with, so why should I feel sorry for you? I want you to be what I am, to feel it, the same way I feel it – not to pretend, but to know what it's really like."

"Mick..."

"Shut up. We're done here." Mick threw the hood over Alex's head again and fastened it around his neck.

Alex stared into the darkness, wondering if he could endure what was coming next.

They drove for a long time, and then he heard the sound of the SUAV crossing over a stretch of water. He assumed they'd reached Ghost Eye, and that he'd soon be back in Vertex Tower, leading that soul-destroying life again. His little taste of freedom, as terrifying as it had been at times, had simply served to remind him of what he'd lost.

If he'd jumped onboard Paul Andrews's boat he'd be in France by now, starting a new life. Yet... he couldn't regret holding his father's hand and telling him that he loved him. It had been worth it for that – if his father died, at least he wouldn't have it on his conscience that he'd failed him one last time.

The vehicle came to a halt, and his stomach lurched in terrified anticipation. He heard the door being opened, and he was dragged out and propelled into a building. He wasn't sure where he was, but it didn't sound or feel like Ghost Eye. He wasn't taken to a lift – he was escorted along a cool, tiled floor and into a room and then forced onto his knees.

There was a long silence, and then suddenly the hood was yanked off. He found himself kneeling in front of Tyler's white leather sofa in

the living room of The Lighthouse, in Lewes, where he'd first met him a year ago, in a different life.

Tyler was sitting on the sofa, gazing down at him. He didn't look smug or pleased with himself. He looked furious. He was wearing a black shirt and a pair of black jeans, and there were dark shadows under his eyes, as if he hadn't slept in days. His major-domo was standing behind him.

Sneaking a glance around, Alex noticed there were two guards he didn't know by the door, and Mick had taken up position by the huge French windows that looked out over the golf course. Next to him was Ted. His spirits rose a fraction to see at least one friendly face. Ted didn't – couldn't – smile, but their eyes met, and he took comfort from Ted's presence.

"So, the prodigal returns," Tyler snapped. "Aren't we lucky?"

Alex said nothing, because there was nothing to say.

"And he's uncharacteristically silent," Tyler mused. "No whining, Alexander? No self-justifications? No begging for forgiveness, or mercy, or special treatment? No '*but it was an accident*?'" he mocked in a sing-song voice.

Alex shook his head, looking down at the floor.

"Well, maybe your little escapade has taught you something, then," Tyler grunted. "It's certainly taught me something. I under-estimated you. You managed to evade my men for far longer than I expected. Do you have any idea the money I had to spend getting you back? The resources I had to throw into finding you? Or the time I wasted doing it?"

Alex still said nothing.

Tyler leaned forward and backhanded him across the jaw.

He went flying, his bound hands preventing him from breaking his fall, blood trickling down his chin.

"I asked a direct question, and I expect an answer," Tyler barked.

"Sorry, sir," he croaked.

Tyler loomed over him, grabbing hold of his hair and pulling him back, so that he was kneeling in front of him again. "This is where I want you, so please move back into position after I hit you," he said, in a bizarre parody of politeness. "I will be hitting you again, obviously."

GHOST EYE   347

Alex made no reply; he just stayed where he'd been placed, with his head down.

"I had to call in a lot of favours to keep it quiet. I'm legally obliged, of course, to report the escape of a convicted felon. You're not just any IS, Alexander – you were sentenced to serve seven years for your crime. So that makes you an escaped prisoner, and therefore not only my problem but the state's, too."

"I'm sure Martin Bagshaw took care of that for you," Alex said sarcastically. Tyler backhanded him again, and he fell sideways, onto his aching hip.

"You may speak only to answer direct questions," Tyler instructed, as he struggled back into a kneeling position. "And it's not that simple. I have to account for you and report on your welfare regularly. If you'd been found by anyone other than my men, or if you'd told the press your pathetic 'story' and the authorities had found out I hadn't informed them of your escape, there would have been serious consequences for me."

"I would have loved to tell the media my story, but I assumed you'd know someone who could hush it up for you," Alex said.

Tyler delivered another backhander. "Listening to clear instructions has always been a problem for you, hasn't it?" he said as Alex crawled back into position.

"Yes, sir," Alex said, his jaw throbbing painfully.

"I had to get in men, dogs, helicopters, and search specialists. That was very expensive and very annoying. So you can understand why I'm angry with you."

Alex wasn't sure if that was a question or not, so he just nodded again.

"I even went to see your father," Tyler said.

Alex looked up, his eyes blazing.

"Ah, you didn't know that." Tyler sat back, gazing at him thoughtfully. "I went to see him the night before he had his stroke. I told him you'd escaped, and I reminded him what I can legally do to an IS that runs away, especially one serving out a prison sentence in my custody. He was most distressed."

"*You* caused his illness," Alex hissed furiously. "You made him so upset he had a stroke."

"You can't make someone have a stroke by giving them unwelcome news." Tyler shrugged. "He was already in a bad way – due to months of stress, strain, and the shame of what his youngest son did to him. If anyone caused his illness, it's you."

"You bastard." Alex got to his feet and lunged. He couldn't do much except scream, and kick, and attempt to bite Tyler, but it felt good all the same. Mick and the major-domo pulled him off, threw him onto the floor a safe distance away, and held him there. Alex glared at Tyler, his chest heaving angrily. "He was your friend, once. You grew up together. Don't you have any feelings for him?" He saw a flicker of guilt in Tyler's eyes and knew he'd hit a nerve.

"You're right," Tyler said quietly. He stood up and adjusted his shirt where it had been snagged in Alex's attack. Then he crouched down in front of him and lightly touched his bruised jaw. "I never intended to harm your father, Alexander. This has never been about him – it's about you."

"When it's about me, it *is* about him. He's my father."

"Ah, it's touching that you believe he still loves you, after what you did to him and the rest of your family. You really do believe that, don't you?" Tyler rubbed his thumb gently over Alex's chin.

"Yes," Alex replied stubbornly.

"He disowned you," Tyler reminded him.

"I know." Alex felt the fight go out of him. He hung his head again.

"Poor, unloved Alexander," Tyler said, getting up and moving back to the sofa. He sat down and gestured to his men. They dragged Alex back into his former position, kneeling in front of Tyler. "I never wanted to hurt your father. I didn't plan his illness, but I have to admit it worked out well for me. I wondered if you'd have the balls to show up at the hospital; I'm both surprised and impressed that you did. It was stupid, but brave. I like that."

"I don't care what you like," Alex snapped defiantly.

Tyler nodded thoughtfully. "I know, and that's the problem. Mr Drummond did warn me that the approach I was taking with you wouldn't work, and he was right." He glanced at the major-domo. "He

GHOST EYE

carries that strap in his belt because running a huge household of indentured servants requires constant discipline. None of my indies are safe from the strap – and we make very sure they know it."

Alex thought back to Mick's words in the SUAV on the way here, about how he was the same as the rest of them. Now he understood why Mick didn't care about his plight.

"That's right, Alexander. All my ISs have been beaten for some infraction or other. When they first arrive, Mr Drummond comes down hard on them for the smallest thing – it helps them learn much faster. Once they understand that they're very small, very unimportant cogs in a very big wheel, they're happier here. It's like dogs understanding their role in the pack – a few bites, and they realise who's in charge. My ISs quickly learn not to question my authority; it's easier that way."

"You rule by fear, pain, and intimidation," Alex accused. "You go on and on about how much you hate what my family did to your father, but we treated him well – none of our indies are ever beaten."

"I know – *noblesse oblige* and all that." Tyler rolled his eyes. "Your family loved playing at being the lords of the manor, smiling down benignly on your sweet little indies, kindly helping them out and asking only for their total adoration in return. I cut through all that crap – this is the true system, precisely as men like your grandfather designed it. I know, because I grew up in it. I'm just stripping away the pretence."

"You're using it, that's all. You're using the system to accumulate more wealth and power for yourself, not to help anyone else."

"Of course. That's what the system is for. I should know – it created me." Tyler grinned. "You exploit, or you *are* exploited, Alexander – and I know which I'd rather be. Nobody will ever – *ever* – treat me as my father was treated. I've made sure of that." His eyes burned fiercely, and Alex realised that that was the crux of who George Tyler was. "I'm not just a product of the system – I'm its end game. Your grandfather built an empire on my father's back. That empire kept him and his family in luxury for years. I learned from that, Alexander, and I learned well."

"My grandfather would never have envisaged the IS system ending up like this," Alex said.

"Then it's a failure of imagination on his part, but I suspect that if the wily old bastard were still alive now, he'd be doing exactly what I'm doing." Tyler smiled bitterly. "My father worked his fingers to the bone for your grandfather's company – you didn't see him, coming back late, night after night – and for what?"

"So you got a shot at a better life than him," Alex retorted. "And you did. His hard work earned you an education that he couldn't have afforded otherwise."

"And I'm putting it to good use. Now, before we go any further, we have urgent business to take care of. We must make sure you're chipped again." Tyler held out his hand, and the major-domo gave him a syringe.

Mick held Alex down while Tyler pushed the needle into his wrist. Then he stepped back, and they both watched as the red light pulsed into life under his skin. Alex slumped back onto the floor.

"So, what do I do with you now?" Tyler mused. "I gave you special treatment, Alexander, because you *are* special. You're my pet project." He put his hand on Alex's hair and stroked it. Alex tried hard not to recoil in revulsion.

"I thought I could break you – mentally and emotionally – but Mr Drummond informs me that doesn't work without some physical element, too. I was too soft on you, Alexander, and you repaid me by running away and causing me all this trouble."

"You gave me to Jake Harper, and he beat me and raped me," Alex reminded him. "That was pretty damn physical."

"But he wasn't *me*," Tyler snapped. "It has to be me. Mr Drummond is right – I gave you too much special treatment. I didn't crush you hard enough, fast enough; that's why you ran away."

"It's really not."

Tyler waved his hand dismissively. "You forgot what you are, and I didn't make it clear enough. My mistake – and yours – so..." He turned to a little bag lying on the sofa beside him. "We need to remind you. This should help."

He took out a thick iron collar and held it up. Then he waved his

hand again. Mick held Alex in place while the major-domo took hold of his coat and pulled it off his shoulders, then ripped open his shirt and pulled that back, too, so that both his coat and shirt were tangled around his cuffed wrists.

Tyler leaned forward and stroked Alex's bare neck. "You took off my ID tag; that makes me sad. I liked seeing it on you, but I'll like seeing this on you better. You're a convict – you should look like one."

He clamped the thick metal around Alex's neck and locked it into place. The collar was heavy and instantly felt restrictive and claustrophobic.

"That's better. I like how that looks on you." Tyler nodded. "That should help to remind you, every day, that you belong to me. You're not free – you can't walk out of the door and go on some little escapade in the big wide world. I own you, and the state endorses that. You're an IS – and the sooner you embrace that fact, the easier it'll be on you. Understand?"

Alex gazed at him mulishly. "Yes, sir," he said in a dull tone. He had tried playing along with Tyler, and he'd tried escaping, but there was no getting away from the basic, obvious fact that Tyler owned him, and nothing was going to change that.

"The problem is, as always, that I don't want you just to pay lip service to it – I want it to be real for you," Tyler told him fiercely. "I want you to believe it to the point where I could leave the door open, remove your tracking device, and give you a duck, and you still wouldn't try to run away. That's what I want from you. I know I own you, and you know I own you, but I want you to really feel it and believe it. I want you to know that being an IS isn't just who you are – it's all that you are."

"I know that's what you want, but I don't know how to give it to you," Alex pleaded despairingly. "I tried – I honestly tried."

Tyler laughed. "I know you did, but you were born to *own* indies, not *be* one. We have to get into your head, flick a switch, and make you see that that's not who you are now – and we will do that, I promise."

Alex felt a shiver run down his spine. He gazed helplessly at Tyler, wondering how he was going to achieve that and dreading finding out.

"You're scared – that's good." Tyler nodded. "Now, obviously, you

have to be punished – and I think we need an audience for that, don't you?"

He stood up and clicked his fingers, and Solange was escorted into the room by one of the guards. She was wearing a black woollen dress that reached to her knees, and a pair of red boots, and she looked as immaculate as ever. Alex scanned her for signs of abuse or harm, but she looked well, so he thought it unlikely that Tyler knew the role she'd played in his escape.

"Solange, here, was devastated when you ran away." Tyler smirked. "Look, Solange, my dear – our darling Alexander has returned to us. Isn't that wonderful?"

"Yes, sir," she murmured, managing a wan smile.

"Well, go and say hello. You must be so pleased to have him back – you've been so lonely without him to keep you company in Vertex Tower, haven't you, sweetheart?"

"Yes, sir." Solange walked obediently over and crouched down on the floor in front of him. He wondered how he must look, kneeling here with this thick metal collar around his neck and bruises over his jaw, his coat and shirt stripped from his back and hanging from the cuffs around his wrists. He gazed at the floor in shame, unable to meet her gaze, but she lifted up his chin and made him look at her.

Her eyes were dark pools of sorrow. "Hello, Alex," she said. "I'm so glad you're safe." Then she kissed his forehead, and he wished he could tell her what had happened and explain why he hadn't used the precious gifts she'd given him to win his freedom.

"Solange has been fretting about you. She's upset that you ran out on us," Tyler said.

"Yes. It's good to have you back, Alex," she told him, holding his face gently between her hands and gazing at him sadly.

"Of course, Alexander has to be punished, Solange," Tyler said.

She swallowed hard and then nodded. "Yes, of course. He shouldn't have run away like that and caused us all this worry," she replied mechanically.

"That's right. Go and stand over there, by the fireplace, where you can get a good view," Tyler ordered, pointing.

GHOST EYE

She gave Alex one last pitying look, then stood up and walked over to the fireplace opposite the sofa, as instructed.

Tyler held out his hand, and Drummond stepped forward and handed him a long leather whip. This wasn't the strap that he always carried on his belt – this was an altogether more sinister item.

Alex sat back on his heels, trying to brace himself for what was to come.

Tyler undid his shirt cuffs and slowly folded them back to the elbows.

Alex watched, his mouth dry.

Tyler pointed at the sofa with the whip. Removing Alex's belt, Drummond unfastened his jeans and yanked them down to his knees along with his boxer shorts. Then, he and Mick picked Alex up and placed him on the sofa, with his knees on the centre seat and his chest facing the back. Drummond unlocked his handcuffs and stripped his coat and shirt away, then Mick took hold of his right wrist, and Drummond the left. They stood at opposite ends of the sofa and stretched him out, holding him down so that his chest rested on one of the upright cushions. Now, his shoulders, back, buttocks, and upper thighs were exposed.

He shook as the cool air caressed his bare skin, aware of how many people were witnessing his punishment.

Tyler paced around behind him. "Why am I going to punish you, Alexander?"

"Honestly? Because you hate me," Alex replied quietly.

Tyler gave a wry chuckle. "True enough," he said. There was a brief pause, and then the whip whistled through the air and tore into Alex's back.

He screamed – Harper's belt was nothing in comparison to the pain of this whip, designed precisely for the purpose of inflicting pain. He was still in shock from how much the first stroke had hurt when the second fell. He screamed again. He tried pulling his arms away, to at least give pause to the raw, agonising pain as each new burning stroke was painted on his flesh, but Mick and Drummond held him tight, keeping him in place against the back of the sofa. He was desperate for respite, if only for a second, but Tyler's whip was unrelenting. The

room was silent save for his screams and the sound of the whip beating on his skin as Tyler struck him over and over again.

Sweat dripped into his eyes. He threw his head back to clear it. He no longer cried out at each stroke – he was screaming out one long, continuous howl of pain instead, his chest aching.

"I will break you, Alexander," Tyler promised behind him. "Nobody escapes from me. Nobody."

Alex could hear the note of angry pride in his voice, making it clear just how personal this was.

Tyler redoubled his efforts, hitting even harder.

Alex stopped screaming. He could barely breathe. He could hear a wild, ragged, rasping sound in his throat as he struggled to take in air. The thick iron collar was strangling him, and he began to choke.

"Sir..." he heard Drummond murmur. "That's enough, sir."

"It's never enough," Tyler snapped, hitting out again.

Alex was dimly aware that Tyler had lost control. The whipping had stoked his rage into a frenzy, and he was lost to reason. He suddenly understood that Tyler would whip him to death, and none of these people would try to stop him, because they were all too scared.

The whip rose and fell on his shoulders, his buttocks, and the backs of his legs. He couldn't take the pain anymore. The world began to spin, going dark as he fought to breathe, and then from some great distance he heard a woman's voice, screaming.

"STOP! You're killing him! Please... stop!"

There was silence. Mick and Drummond released his arms, and Alex fell sideways, taking deep, gasping gulps of air. There was blood splattered on the sofa, staining the white leather with bright red droplets; he stared at it stupidly before realising it was his own. He also realised, through a haze, that the whipping had only stopped because Solange had thrown herself onto Tyler's arm. She was still hanging from it, trying to stop him from raising the whip again. Tyler gave an irritated growl and threw her backwards, and she landed on the floor with a thud. Throwing the whip to one side, he walked angrily towards her.

"Do you think I don't know?" he snarled, taking hold of her beautiful hair and pulling her to her feet. "Do you think I don't know that

you helped him? What kind of an idiot do you think I am?" Still holding her in place by the hair, he hit her across the face – once, twice, three times, making her squeal. Then he grabbed her arm and raised it up.

"You cut the tracker out of his wrist and put it in yours. Did you seriously think we didn't figure that out? Did you imagine, for just one second, that we didn't go over every inch of that security footage, so we could establish precisely what happened? You helped him, Solange, and you betrayed me, and by God you're going to pay for that."

Out of the corner of his eye Alex saw Ted running forward to protect her, but he was too late. Tyler drew back his hand and delivered a swinging blow to Solange's jaw. She went flying across the room, headfirst into the ornate stone fireplace. There was a sickening crack, her head jerked backwards... and she fell to the floor, with blood trickling down her face. She lay in a crumpled heap, unmoving.

Tyler nudged her with his foot. "Get up," he ordered. "I'm not done with you yet."

"She's not faking it – she's hurt," Ted cried, crouching down beside her. "Christ... she's..." He put his ear to her chest and his fingers to the side of her neck. "She's not breathing." He looked up, the blood draining from his face. "You stupid fucking bastard, you went too far! You've killed her."

"Don't be ridiculous. She's fine," Tyler snapped. "Drummond?"

Drummond moved to examine Solange while Tyler stood there, his chest heaving as he struggled to recover from his all-consuming rage.

Alex was trembling violently from head to toe from the shock of the beating, and his vision was blurred by sweat, but he saw Drummond look up at Tyler and shake his head.

"Her neck is broken, sir," he said. "She's dead."

Chapter Twenty

OCTOBER 2095

Josiah

Josiah awoke in the small hours and felt the warmth of Alex's body pressed against his own. He smiled, pulled him close, and kissed him. Alex was lazy and happy in his arms, and they were both wrapped up in a little bubble of bliss. Josiah knew it couldn't last, but he didn't want to think about the reasons why, for now. He just wanted to enjoy it while he could. Alex sighed and rested his chin on his shoulder, his hand slung carelessly over his hip.

Josiah fell asleep again, but when he awoke the next morning, he was alone. Then he knew the bubble had burst; their night was over, and it was time to face reality.

He pulled on his bathrobe and slippers and made his way down the stairs. He was about to go into the kitchen when Alex called out a cheery "I'm in here" from the direction of the dining room.

He found Alex sitting at the table, wearing only Josiah's shirt from the night before and a pair of boxer shorts. The shirt was three sizes too big for him, his hair was tousled from sleep, and although he was a thirty-year-old man, he looked like a kid playing dress-up. In front of him, on the table, he'd spread out some cardboard, and on top of that was an array of strange items: pots of gunk, sheets of sandpaper, and a variety of different-sized paintbrushes. In the centre of the cardboard

were the remains of the shattered vase, and he was bent over them, busily working.

Josiah paused in the doorway.

"Any reason why you're wearing my shirt?" He raised an eyebrow.

Alex looked embarrassed. "I like being able to smell you on it," he admitted.

Josiah gave a little smile and dropped a kiss on his messy hair.

Alex looked up at him happily and gestured to a tray on the sideboard containing a teapot, a little jug of milk, a couple of mugs, and a spoon. "I think it's still hot. I'm sure I did a refill about ten minutes ago," he said.

"A refill? What time did you get up?" Josiah picked up the tray and, sitting down at the table opposite Alex, poured the tea. It wasn't remotely hot. He had a suspicion Alex had no idea when he'd refilled it.

"Early. I don't know. I remembered it was a bit of a mess down here after last night..." He shot Josiah a knowing grin. "So, I decided I'd clean up, and that's when I found the broken vase. I was sad, because I know how much it means to you, so..." He waved his hand at the shattered pieces of the vase in front of him.

"You can't mend it, Alex," Josiah said incredulously. "It's shattered into smithereens."

"Yes, but it doesn't have to stay that way," Alex replied determinedly. "It can be mended." He pointed at the golden glue he was brushing onto one of the shards.

"Well, I suppose so, but it'll look pretty ugly all patched up, and I don't think it'll be much use. A vase has to hold water," Josiah pointed out.

"Trust me," Alex said with a wink. "I did a workshop on this years ago. I've had to improvise a bit, but did you know just how much shit Peter had in the garage? I'm assuming it's not your shit, because it's mostly car related, and we all know how you feel about moving vehicles of any description." He grinned happily. "Anyway, I took a good look through it, and I think this will work, together with some of the stuff I bought yesterday." He nodded at the box on the floor next to him. "I'm having to make it up as I go along, but I

like that. It's when I'm at my best." He bent his head to his work again.

Josiah sipped his cold tea and watched, lazily. Alex had deft fingers, and he seemed to know precisely what he was doing. It was fascinating to see the expression of concentration on his face as he worked, and how delicately he could hold a brush. This was the real Alex. The man in his bed last night and the man working on the broken vase this morning were the real deal, regardless of what deception or misdirection had transpired before. He was humming, and he looked so happy and absorbed that Josiah wished he could freeze this moment in time and keep him this way forever, but he couldn't. He cleared his throat.

"We need to talk," he said.

Alex glanced up. "Ah, those four little words that always ruin everything."

Josiah shot him a rueful smile. "Alex, last night was wonderful, amazing... but I don't want you to have any false hope. I can't wave a magic wand and make everything okay. If I could, I would, but it isn't in my power."

"I know that." Alex focused his gaze on the vase again.

"I wasn't sure how you thought this would end."

"I'm hoping it doesn't have to end anytime soon." Alex glanced up at him. "I assume we still have a little longer until you find Elliot's killer and have to hand me over for the dreaded probate to take its course."

"Yes, but... you'll still be an IS."

Alex shrugged. "I came to terms with being an IS a long time ago."

"I haven't," Josiah said honestly. "I don't know how I'll be able to give you up, when the time comes."

"You'll have no choice." Alex put down his brush with a sigh. "I'm used to that, but for a man like you I can see it's more difficult. We know we don't have forever, so let's just make the most of now." He reached across the table and put his hand over Josiah's.

"I've never been very good at accepting the things I can't change," Josiah admitted.

Alex squeezed his hand. "What's the alternative?"

"I could... we could..." Josiah hesitated. "I have the Kathleen Line – the escape network, Alex. I could get you to France."

Alex shook his head. "We both know you can't do that, Joe. I'm the most expensive and well-known IS in the country. If I go missing, there'll be hell to pay, and if you came with me... well, the press would go nuts, and the government would dig up everything on you. Then what would happen to Elsie, and your friend Liz who made this vase?" He nodded at the broken pieces in front of him. "And what about all the people you save, Joe? If you leave with me, the Kathleen Line falls apart, and all those people lose a lifeline. Think of it... all those 'Bens' out there, desperate for help, with nowhere to turn..." He shook his head again. "I know the press thinks I'm a selfish shit who doesn't care about anyone but myself, and maybe I was once, a long time ago, but that's not who I am now. Besides, how long would we last with every bounty hunter in Europe looking for us? We'd be on the run, looking over our shoulders the whole time, and they'd catch up with us eventually."

Josiah leaned back in his chair and finished his tea, considering Alex thoughtfully. "There's more to find out about you, isn't there?" he mused. "I haven't fully unwrapped the mystery that is Alex Lytton yet, have I?"

"No." Alex picked up his brush.

"Damn it – I hate mysteries."

"No – you love mysteries," Alex corrected. "You love unravelling them, piece by piece, and solving them. That's why you're such a good investigator."

"Talking of which – a couple of days ago, you said that you couldn't reveal what this was all about without first telling me something that would make me upset and angry," Josiah reminded him. "Well, I was pretty upset and angry last night, so I'm assuming that now you're ready to tell me what's really going on and what you've been playing at all this time?"

Alex met his gaze slowly, and then nodded. "Yes," he said softly. "It's time. Why don't you go and take a shower, get dressed, and make us some breakfast while I finish this – and then I'll tell you."

"Hmm, we sleep together once, and now you're the one giving all the orders," Josiah teased, getting up.

Alex gave an absent smile, but Josiah wasn't sure he'd even heard him – he was engrossed in his work again.

Josiah did as his IS commanded. He ran up the stairs and tidied up the bathroom, clearing away their discarded clothes from the previous night. Then he took a hot shower, singing to himself happily the whole time, before wrapping a towel around his waist and standing, bare-chested, in front of the mirror to shave. His gaze went to the chain around his neck with the wedding ring hanging from it. Frowning, he clasped the ring and held it for a long time, in an agony of indecision.

"It's time," Peter's voice said softly.

"Yes," he said. "I know."

"You have someone new to save now."

"I wish it were that easy."

"You can do it," Peter murmured encouragingly.

Josiah reached up slowly, unfastened the chain, and removed the ring from around his neck for the first time in seven years. It should have been difficult, but it wasn't. It just felt... right.

"Goodbye, Peter," he said, opening the vanity unit drawer and placing the ring inside.

"Goodbye, my love," Peter said.

Josiah was sure he felt the soft whisper of a kiss on the back of his neck, where the chain had been, and then... Peter was gone.

He was surprised to find that now the time had come, he wasn't sad. He was done with sadness. He still had a life to live... and Peter was right – he had a new man to save. He closed the vanity unit drawer decisively.

When he'd finished shaving, he dressed himself in silver-grey suit trousers and a white shirt, slinging the jacket on the bed. He decided not to bother with a tie, for the first time in years. Then he jogged back downstairs and made breakfast.

Alex was still sitting in the dining room, working on the vase, when Josiah returned with a tray full of food. He hadn't showered or dressed, but he must have gone upstairs at some point, because propped up at

the far end of the table was the *Halo of Fire* picture that he usually kept in his bedroom.

"So – what do you think?" he asked, pointing at the vase.

Josiah put the tray down on the table and examined it, without touching. It was now mended, the broken pieces held together by gold lacquer. It didn't look the same as before, but it was striking and lovely in a different way. "It's beautiful," he said, surprised. "How the hell did you do that?"

"It's an old Japanese art form called *kintsugi*," Alex told him proudly. "That basically means 'to repair with gold' – the idea is that the piece is more beautiful for having been broken. You don't try to disguise the breaks – you highlight them." He gestured at the snaking gold seams around the vase. "Apparently, some collectors loved the way it looked so much that they deliberately broke things so they could be mended like this." He laughed.

Josiah whistled as he examined the vase. "It really is exquisite."

"There's a whole philosophy attached to *kintsugi* – it's about embracing the flawed." Alex put his arm around Josiah's back and hugged him. "I'll admit it's an idea that hits close to home for me."

Josiah bent his head and dropped a kiss on his lips. "So – is there a reason why that picture is here?" he asked, pointing at the *Halo of Fire*.

"Yes, there is," Alex said. "But let's eat first."

He chatted about art, vases, breakfast... anything and everything, keeping up a continuous stream of talk as they ate. Josiah said nothing, sensing once again that he was building up to something important.

When they'd finished their breakfast, Alex pushed back his plate and took a deep breath. He wasn't nervy, like he'd been last night – instead, he was intensely still, and that was just as unsettling.

"Come on, Alex, you can tell me – whatever it is," Josiah encouraged softly.

"I know." Alex nodded rapidly, as if trying to convince himself. "It's just... it's been the most important thing in my life for so long. I've carried it with me for years, and I've been so worried about getting it wrong, or choosing the wrong time, or the wrong person. I know I'll likely only get one shot at it."

"Just tell me," Josiah said firmly. "I'm ready to hear whatever it is you have to say."

"Before I start, I want you to know that what happened between us last night was real. I don't want you to doubt me about that."

"Okay," Josiah accepted slowly. "I know that."

"Good, because I don't want you to think I'm using you."

"Alex, is this about my job?" Josiah demanded, automatically switching into investigator mode.

"Yes." Alex leaned forward and touched his hand. "Joe, you once told me that you didn't care if a killer was the prime minister or an IS – that your job is to catch them, whoever they are."

"It is," Josiah said tightly. He sat back in his chair and stared at Alex's pale face. "You know something that might lead me to Elliot's killer, don't you?" he demanded.

"Yes." Alex nodded. "I know two specific pieces of information, but I'm not going to tell you them right now."

"For God's sake, Alex! How can you still not trust me?" Josiah demanded, banging his hands on the table. "I thought you wanted to bring Elliot's killer to justice. That's what you said the other day."

"I said I wanted to bring *a* killer to justice," Alex corrected him. "I didn't say it was Elliot's killer."

Josiah stared at him. "Then who...?"

"This isn't about Elliot, Joe. It's never been about Elliot. Not for me. I will help you find Elliot's killer if I can, but it'll have to wait. I'm sorry if that sounds like blackmail, but it's the only leverage I have."

"Leverage? What do you want?" Josiah asked sharply. "Are you trying to win your freedom – is that what this is about? Because that's not in my power, Alex. You know that."

"No." Alex shook his head firmly. "It has nothing to do with that."

"Then why do you need leverage?" Josiah asked, puzzled.

"Jeffrey Mead was right – I did ask him those questions about how murder investigations work. He was an investigator, you see, if not a very good one." Alex made a face. "Still, he was the best I could do at the time."

Josiah sat back. "You weren't trying to find out how to cover up a murder – you wanted to find out how to get a murder investigation

opened," he said, slowly piecing together all the different parts of the puzzle.

"Yes." Alex nodded. "I didn't care about myself after she was killed. I just knew I had to live long enough to find an incorruptible investigator to take on the case – if such a person existed. I wasn't sure it would be you, but I'm glad it is, because you're probably the only one who can do it."

"She?" Josiah leaned forward. "Who was she, Alex?"

Alex looked down, his shoulders suddenly shaking.

Josiah realised Alex had been holding on to this for so long that he was almost scared to let it go. If anyone could understand that, it was him. "Alex?" He squeezed his hand gently.

Finally, Alex collected himself and looked up again. "I didn't want you to go after Tyler for what he did to me – for the prostitution, and the blackmail, and the beatings," he said softly. "But I needed to tell you about them so I could find out if you'd stand up to him, and if you'd stand up to your boss and the whole bloody system to bring him down, because I think that's what it'll take. You didn't let me down, Joe – and I'm sorry, I really am, because I'm asking you to put your career on the line for this, and probably your life, too, but I need you to do your job. I need you to bring a killer to justice, because she deserves that, and because she's waited a very long time."

"What happened, Alex?" Josiah asked quietly. "You need to tell me everything if you want my help."

Alex nodded and began speaking rapidly. "You know I escaped, but you don't know how. You asked me the other night if I had any friends who'd kill for me, and I told you I don't – but I did have a friend who was willing to die for me. She helped me get away, at great risk to herself. She gave me the nanopad with Elsie's number in it, and she gave me some cash cards. I almost made it, but then my father had a stroke, and I couldn't leave without seeing him one last time." He gazed downwards, blinking repeatedly, then looked up again. "Tyler's men captured me at the hospital and took me back to his house in Lewes – the one we went to the other day. Then Tyler whipped me so hard he left those scars on my back that you saw last night."

"The fucking bastard." Josiah half rose out of his chair, but Alex pulled on his arm to make him sit back down.

"That's not important... but she was there. She was his IS too. She tried to stop him beating me to death, and he lashed out and hit her. She went flying head first into the fireplace and broke her neck."

Josiah remembered Alex standing by the fireplace at Tyler's house, staring fixedly at a spot on the carpet. A shiver crept up his spine as he realised that was where it had happened.

"And she died?"

"Yes. He killed her. Tyler killed her, and then he disposed of her body and silenced everyone who was there that night. He got away with it, Joe. He got away with it, because she was just one more expendable IS that nobody gives a fuck about. Elliot Dacre dies and the whole country is up in arms, but she was killed, too, and nobody cared."

"I care," Josiah told him firmly. Now Tyler's determined effort to seduce him the other day made sense. Tyler had been trying to find out what he knew about this poor woman's death.

"It's not that I don't care about Elliot's murder," Alex said wearily. "He was a stupid, harmless old fool who never really hurt anyone and didn't deserve to die, but he has plenty of people pursuing justice on his behalf. She only has me. So any help I give you in finding Elliot's killer will have to wait until I get justice for her first. Those are my terms."

"I see." Josiah steepled his fingers together and nodded, slowly.

"And that's what I've carried with me all these years, Joe. That's what kept me going, all this time." Alex sat back in his chair, looking utterly exhausted. "I'm sitting here asking you to bring George Tyler to justice for what he did to her. Then I'll have done my duty by her, and she can rest in peace, and nothing else matters to me but that. Will you do it?" he begged anxiously. "I hate to ask you this after last night, but I have to. Will you get justice for her, Joe? Will you?"

"Of course I bloody well will." Josiah leaned across the table and spoke in a low, hard voice. "Catching killers is what I do, and nothing – *nothing* – would give me greater pleasure than bringing that bastard to justice."

Alex swallowed hard, and then managed a faint smile. "Thank you," he said. "You don't know what this means to me."

"Yeah – I think I do," Josiah replied softly. "I'll take on the case, Alex, and I will nail George Tyler. I promise you that. Now tell me... who was she?"

Alex picked up the *Halo of Fire* picture and opened up its back with trembling fingers.

"I'm an IS, and I'm not allowed to own anything, as you know. I've kept it hidden, so nobody would see it, but I also had to make sure it was nearby. I had to remind myself that the reason I'm still alive, the reason I didn't kill myself years ago, the reason I've kept going for all this time... is to get justice for her."

Underneath the hard cardboard spine of the photo frame was a folded-up square of paper. Alex smoothed it out with his fingers and handed it to Josiah. On it was a photo of a beautiful woman in her early twenties. She had soft brown skin, pretty brown eyes, and striking curly hair that hung like a cloud around her lovely face. She was wearing an oversized white tee-shirt, and there was a wistful, faraway expression in her eyes.

"Her name was Solange Alajika," Alex said, his voice breaking. "And she was my friend."

Chapter Twenty-One

NOVEMBER 2088

Alex

There was a long silence, and then all hell broke loose. Ted launched himself at Tyler, shouting, screaming, and lashing out with his fists. He landed a punch to Tyler's face before Drummond and Mick jumped on him and wrestled him to the floor. Tyler wiped away a fleck of blood from his cut lip, while Mick wrapped his arms around Ted to keep him still. All the fight went out of Ted, and he deflated into a huddle beside Solange. Mick released his hold on him a fraction, and Ted reached out a shaking hand to stroke Solange's hair.

"Sorry, baby," he said. "Sorry I didn't get to you in time. Sorry we didn't get our happily ever after. So sorry, my love. So sorry."

Alex was too badly hurt to move. He lay on the sofa in shock, wondering if this was actually happening, or if he was dreaming. Solange was a little heap on the floor; all he could see of her was the black dress, a cloud of hair, and a little puddle of blood. He tried to clear the fog from his brain and grasp what was happening. Solange couldn't be dead; she'd been standing over there by the fireplace just a few minutes ago, alive and well. He struggled to remember why she was now lying on the rug with blood congealing on her head.

He'd been bent over the sofa, screaming. He must have passed out briefly – he'd been struggling to breathe with this thick collar around

his neck, and the pain, the terrible pain, and she'd... Solange had tried to stop Tyler from killing him, and Tyler had hit her. She'd cracked her head against the fireplace and broken her neck, and now she was dead. Solange was dead. The knowledge finally reached him, like the blade of a knife being pushed slowly into his heart. He choked out a sob.

"We need to make some decisions," Tyler told Drummond in an undertone, taking hold of the major-domo's shoulder and leading him away from Ted. That brought them closer to Alex, and he heard every quiet word they said.

"We could call an ambulance – say she fell," Drummond said. "We'll have to clear up this mess first." He jerked his head at Alex, lying on the blood-streaked sofa.

"There will be questions," Tyler said. "A post-mortem. Apart from the fatal injury, her face is bruised."

"You've got Bagshaw," Drummond reminded him.

"He's an IS Agency compliance officer. This is a little outside his remit."

"We have a couple of IAs onside," Drummond suggested.

"Still risky – we couldn't depend on one of them being assigned to this case," Tyler said in quiet, rapid tones. "Solange was off-grid for the first few years – because of him." He glared at Alex. "I made her sign a contract, but I didn't register her with the IS scheme, or give her a microchip and ID tag, because I didn't want Alexander knowing what she was when I sent her to Oxford. That's illegal. I chipped her later, but if someone started poking around, asking the wrong kind of questions, there's a lot that could come to light. This is a string that could unravel a very long way, and we have too much to lose."

"Then what do you suggest?" Drummond asked.

"We cover it up. We go back to her roots and dispose of her in a way in which her people would approve." Tyler gave a tight smile. "Have you ever heard of something called the Quarterlands Splash?"

"Isn't that what the Quarries do with their dead?"

"Yes, and it's what we'll do with her. Go and get something to weigh the body down, and then we'll take a trip to the deepest section of water we can find and let her sink to the bottom without a trace."

"There are witnesses, sir," Drummond pointed out, glancing around the room at Mick, Ted, the two security guards, and then at Alex.

"We'll take care of them the usual way. There are only two we really need to worry about, I think."

Drummond's gaze flickered to Ted and then back to Alex. "Agreed."

"I'll take care of them both," Tyler said grimly. "You take care of the others – you can have all the money you need and make whatever threats you like to balance the equation."

Tyler went back over to Ted, who was still lying on the floor, sobbing, being half restrained and half comforted by a shocked Mick. Tyler waved Mick back and then crouched down in front of Ted. He put a hand on his shoulder. "You have a decision to make, Ted," he said gently. "I know how much you cared about Solange, and..."

"Cared about her? I loved her! We were going to get married one day, when our contracts were over."

"I understand." Tyler nodded sympathetically. "And I know your heart is broken right now, but she's gone, and you have to decide what's best for you and your family."

"What?" Ted looked up at him sharply.

"Nothing can bring Solange back, but she wouldn't want you to throw your life away, would she?"

"I don't..." Ted shook his head, confused.

"You've got a choice." Tyler took a handkerchief out of his pocket and handed it to him. "You've got family back in the Quarterlands, haven't you? Your mum and a little sister?"

"Yes... but..." Ted appeared too shocked to take any of this in, but Alex could see where Tyler was going with it.

"Well, we could get them out of there, buy them a little flat somewhere – nothing fancy, but a million times better than they have now."

"Are you trying to buy my silence?" Ted demanded contemptuously.

"Yes, of course." Tyler shrugged. "It's a straightforward business transaction. We get your family out of the Quarterlands, and we promote you, get you away from here, give you a fresh start somewhere else in the Tyler empire. I have a beautiful estate in Scotland, and I

GHOST EYE

could use a good security guard up there to help take care of it. I could make you deputy head of security, and we could find your family a place nearby, so you could visit them regularly. I'd give them an income to live on."

"Or?" Ted asked. "There's a great big 'or' to this deal, isn't there?"

"Obviously." Tyler gave a tight smile. "Or you can join her."

"Join her?"

"You're a loose cannon, and I can't have that," Tyler said apologetically.

Ted sat back on his heels, realisation flooding in. "So it's the carrot or the stick?"

"That approach has always worked for me." Tyler shrugged again. "What's it to be? A promotion, a good life for your family, and a fresh start for you, far away from here – or do you want to follow Solange?"

Ted stared at him.

"You'd also have to ask yourself whether you'd be believed if you said anything. You know how things operate around here. You know how many people I own – both officially and unofficially. You know this could crush you and your family. Why not accept the deal?"

"Because it's blood money," Ted hissed.

"A court case wouldn't be good for my reputation," Tyler told him firmly. "So, I really can't allow that. Solange would say you were a fool for throwing away the chance of a better life for your family out of misguided principle or misplaced pride – you know she would."

"Fine. Whatever. You always win," Ted said. "I don't stand a fucking chance." He lowered his head.

"Good man." Tyler put a hand on his shoulder. "You've made the right choice – your family will thank you for it. Now... I'm sorry, but I have one more thing to ask of you."

Ted looked up again, a weary expression on his face. "What?"

"You're going to come with us, Ted. We're going to give her a proper Quarterlands send-off, and I'd like you to do the honours."

"What?" Ted repeated blankly.

"We're going to give her the Quarterlands Splash – that's what it's called, isn't it? You, me, Mick, and Drummond are going to take

Solange out in a duck and do that for her. I think that's what she'd have wanted, don't you?"

"No," Ted said tightly. "All she wanted was for you to stop tormenting that poor bastard over there and leave him alone." He nodded at Alex. "And for us to serve out the rest of our time in this hellhole and then leave, with our heads held high and a bit of money in our pockets, so we could stand a chance of a decent life."

"Then you have to adjust your expectations," Tyler said briskly. "These things happen. I've had it happen to me. You have to find a way to use it to your advantage. So get up and help, or join her in the water. Your choice."

The two men stared at each other for a long time, and then, finally, Ted clambered shakily to his feet.

"You've made the right decision," Tyler said. "I'll see things go very well for you and your family from now on." Ted looked defeated, his shoulders hunched. "Good man." Tyler said softly. Then he beckoned one of his security guards over to lead Ted away from the body.

Tyler looked down at Solange, an unreadable expression in his eyes. Kneeling, he touched her face gently. "Damn it, girl. Why did you help him?" he asked, in such a low whisper Alex almost wondered if he'd imagined it. Tyler grimaced, his fingers gently caressing Solange's cheek. "Sorry, sweetheart," he murmured. Then he straightened up and was all business again.

Drummond returned with what they needed to dispose of Solange's body. Alex watched as he and Mick wrapped her in the rug she was lying on, added bricks to weigh it down, and tied it tightly around her body.

Tyler appeared beside him and gently stroked his hair. "I'm not done with you, yet, but I have to take care of this right now," he murmured in Alex's ear. He took a key from his pocket and unlocked the heavy collar around Alex's neck. "A shame – I wanted you to wear this for much longer," he said regretfully.

Alex took several deep, gasping breaths as Tyler removed the collar and handed it to Drummond.

Tyler jerked his head at the two nameless security guards standing by the door. "You two – take Alexander to the blue bedroom, lock him

inside, and stand guard over him," he ordered. "I'll deal with him later."

Alex screamed as the guards peeled his bleeding body off the sofa. He couldn't walk, so they slung his arms over their shoulders and dragged him out of the room. The last thing he saw as they passed Solange's body was a long curl of her hair that had escaped the rug and was resting pathetically on the floor.

The next few weeks passed in a painful blur. Alex was locked in a bedroom with an en-suite bathroom and attended daily by Dr Parker. He was bandaged, given antibiotics and sedatives, and put on a drip, but he refused to eat. What was the point? Solange was dead, so Tyler didn't have that leverage over him anymore. He couldn't bear the thought of spending the rest of his life as that murderous bastard's whipping boy. His life wasn't worth living, so why live it? If he could have thrown himself out of the window he would have, but it was locked down tight, and he didn't have the strength to even go to the bathroom unaided. Besides, he was watched day and night – one guard stayed in his room with him at all times, and another was posted outside his door. In his befuddled state, it took him several days to wonder why there was a guard in his room, but then he realised – there was no smartwall in here. Clearly, the Lewes bedrooms weren't set up to entertain "guests" in the same way as the Vertex Tower ones were.

He started to heal, but slowly. Most of the time he drifted listlessly in and out of consciousness, the days and nights blurring into one. He woke up one time to find he had a visitor – Tyler was sitting on the side of his bed, holding his hand.

"Hey, Alexander." Tyler smiled down at him. "I came to see how you're doing."

"Why should you care?" Alex croaked.

"I do, though." Tyler sighed. "I know we've had our differences, you and I, but I care. I must apologise – I didn't mean to hurt you so badly when I punished you. You did deserve to be punished, but I went too far. I was upset about your escape attempt."

"Go away." Alex mustered up all his strength and pulled his hand away. "What you gonna do? Whip me again? Go ahead. I don't care."

"You're upset, I can see that – but you need to eat."

"I don't. If I can't escape from you one way, I'll do it another."

Tyler nodded thoughtfully. "You know I can't let that happen."

"Why not? I'd have thought you'd be glad of it. One less witness to worry about." Alex exhaled wearily.

"You're the most famous IS in the land. You can't starve to death on my watch, Alexander. Even I couldn't cover that up."

"So this is all about you, as usual. And there was me thinking you actually cared about my welfare."

"You must eat," Tyler repeated emphatically.

"Or what? You'll hurt Solange? No... wait." Alex gave a twisted smile and turned his head away.

"There are other people you care about," Tyler said. "Your father... your brother."

Alex turned his head back slowly. "Leave them alone."

"I will. Of course I will, just as long as you start eating." Tyler put his hand on Alex's hair and tenderly brushed it away from his face.

Alex closed his eyes, wishing it were his father's hand.

"Think about it, son." Tyler stood up, leaned over, and pressed a kiss to the side of his head. "Think about it."

Alex did think about it. He didn't want any harm to come to Noah or Charles, but what could Tyler do to them? The man was a ruthless operator who seemed able to think up any number of gruesome traps for people, but if Alex was lucky, he'd die of starvation before Tyler had a chance to harm them.

He was tired of living. He'd seen too much death: his mother, Peter, and now Solange... He wanted to leave all this pain and suffering behind and join them. There was nothing left for him here.

His wounds healed, but he had no energy. He ached all over and was always cold. Dr Parker insisted on putting him in an armchair in front of the window with a blanket tucked around his knees, so he

spent his time staring out at the beautiful island below, surrounded by silver-grey water, wondering where they'd dumped Solange's body.

A few days later there was a knock on the door, and, much to his surprise, Ted entered the room.

"Leave us alone for a few minutes, will you, mate?" Ted asked the guard. The man nodded and stepped outside.

Ted took a seat in the armchair opposite Alex.

"Tyler sent you," Alex said listlessly. "There's no way they'd have let you in alone with me otherwise."

"Yeah," Ted admitted. "He wants you to start eating again, and he's right."

"Did he really manage to buy you so easily?" Alex asked, looking away from Ted and back out of the window again. It was raining outside, and droplets of water were sliding down the windowpane.

"Don't be like that, Alex. You know I didn't have a choice," Ted said. "Not really. Solange would have known that, too. Tyler was right about that. She'd have done the exact same thing if it'd been me that died. She was a realist – always was."

"She was my friend," Alex said softly. "The first friend I ever really had."

"And she was the first girl I ever really loved," Ted returned sadly. "But she's gone, and she isn't coming back."

"Where is she, Ted? Where did you throw her?" Alex demanded, jerking his head at the grey world outside the window. Ted made no reply, so Alex turned to look at him properly for the first time. He was pale and gaunt, his thin features even thinner than usual, giving him a sharp, ferret-like appearance. "You do know why Tyler had you go with them to dump her body, don't you? You do understand why he did that?"

"Yeah, I reckon it's so I can't change my mind later and tell the cops what he did."

"You helped dispose of her body, so you're complicit in the coverup of her murder."

"Technically speaking, I think Tyler would argue it was manslaughter," Ted said. "I don't think he intended to kill her."

"He certainly intended to hurt her, though," Alex retorted. "You

can't beat up people like that and not expect there to be consequences. If she hadn't stopped him when she did, I think he would have killed me. She saved my life."

"I dunno. You're worth a hundred and sixty million quid to him. I don't think he'd have killed you." Ted gave a wry smile.

"I'm not sure he was thinking straight. He was too angry."

"Maybe." Ted shrugged. "Look, Alex, I'm here to say goodbye. Tyler's sending me up to Scotland tomorrow, and... and I'm gonna see my family again." He gave a strained smile. "Please don't be angry with me. Solange would have wanted some good to come of her death; you know she would."

"Yes. She would." Alex looked out of the window again, the grey November day matching his mood.

"I don't like to think of you here, Alex, slowly dying like this," Ted said.

Alex shrugged. "I want to die, Ted. I can't stand this for another second. I can't be Tyler's whore and whipping boy anymore. The sooner I die, the better."

"Solange wouldn't have wanted that."

"Solange wanted me to escape, and this is the only possible way out for me now." Alex stared dreamily out of the window. He thought he could see her out there, drawn in the patterns made by the scudding rain clouds as they hurried across the sky. She was wearing a black dress and smiling at him, beckoning him to join her.

"Alex."

He came to. Ted was crouching in front of him, patting his face. "Look, Alex, I'm not smart like you, and I'm not strong like you, either."

"Strong?" Alex repeated blankly. "When was I ever strong?"

"All the time," Ted said gently. "I've never seen anyone as strong as you. I was there, remember? I saw every single thing Tyler did to you. I don't know anyone else who could have endured that without cracking up, or giving up, or both."

"Well, I'm giving up now," Alex told him distantly.

"I hope you don't. Here." Ted pushed a piece of paper into his hand.

Alex blinked away tears as he saw that it was a still photograph of Solange – the one Ted had taken on the suite nanopad many months ago without her knowing. "It's my favourite shot of her," Ted said. "I don't know if Tyler will allow you to keep it, but I wanted to give it to you anyway. Don't forget her, Alex."

Alex folded up the picture and put it in his dressing gown pocket. "I won't," he promised. "I couldn't. But it doesn't matter. I'll be going where she went soon."

Ted leaned forward, and Alex was surprised when he pressed his lips against the side of his head and spoke into his ear in a low, fierce whisper. "You have to keep going for her, Alex. You have to get justice for Solange. You'll figure out a way, one day. I'm not smart enough or strong enough to do it, but you are." Then he drew back and spoke in his normal voice. "Goodbye, Alex. I'm not sure if I'll ever see you again."

"Goodbye, Ted," Alex said softly.

After Ted had left, the guard returned and resumed his position at the door. Alex sat there for a long time, gazing out at the thunderous grey skies outside. He couldn't see Solange out there anymore; the clouds were just clouds.

He took the photo out of his pocket and smoothed it out. It was a beautiful image of her – he could see why Ted liked it so much. She looked so sweet and vulnerable, unaware of the camera, lost in thought. He remembered the day he'd first seen it, and her words from that conversation came back to him, as clear as if she were in the room.

"You have to find something to keep you going, or you'll fall apart."

Maybe it was a delusion, but he could swear she was here, standing somewhere just behind his right shoulder, speaking directly to him.

Tyler had killed her, and then he'd covered up her murder and dumped her body as if she were nothing. She'd had a sad life and an even sadder death, and nobody was ever going to bring George Tyler to justice for it, because of who he was. Who was there, in the whole world, who could take on Tyler and win? Was it even possible? Ted seemed to have faith that Alex could somehow do it, but Alex didn't see how. He was an IS, helpless and without friends.

For now.

He gazed at the picture again, reflectively. Tyler held all the cards right now, but that might not always be the case. He would have to be patient, play a long game, and endure God knew what suffering in the meantime, but one day, his chance might come. When it did, he'd have to seize the opportunity with both hands. Could he do that? Could he somehow keep going in the hope of achieving justice for Solange? Was he strong enough? It would be easier to let go and slip away into the peaceful escape of death. And yet... he'd made so many mistakes in his life. Maybe this was his chance at redemption?

Find something, Alex – find something, hold on to it tightly, and never let it go.

He folded the photo once more and returned it to his pocket. Then he turned to the guard standing by the door.

"I'd like to have something to eat now, please," he said.

Several days later, he was strong enough to get dressed. He took a shower and washed himself slowly. He still felt weak, and when he looked in the bathroom mirror he barely recognised himself in the gaunt-faced man who gazed back.

He stood naked in front of the mirror and mapped his emaciated body with his hands. His ribs and collarbone jutted out starkly, his pale skin stretched, thin and fragile, over them. He turned around and looked over his shoulder. The wounds from the whipping were fading, but some of the cuts were so deep he knew he'd be scarred for life. He looked at his reflection again, searching his face, and finally found himself in the clear, cold set of his eyes. This was who he was now. This was the new Alex. He would bide his time, for as long as it took, until he could seek justice for Solange.

He slowly pulled on a pair of soft grey sweatpants and a white tee-shirt. He was so thin that his hip bones protruded through the material, and he had to tie the pants tightly around his shrunken waist to keep them up.

When he returned to the bedroom, he found he had a visitor. Tyler was standing by the window with his back to him, gazing out. He was

wearing one of his usual off-duty outfits – plain black chinos and a black turtleneck.

"I'm glad you have your appetite back," Tyler said, not turning around.

"Yes," Alex said tonelessly.

"It's for the best."

"If you say so."

"Of course." Tyler turned to face him. "You're important to me, and not just because of how much you cost. I don't want you dead."

"No – where's the fun in that?" Alex raised an eyebrow. "Far more fun to have me alive where you can toy with me, like a cat with a rat."

"A rat?" Tyler grinned. "That's how you see yourself?"

"Why not?" Alex sat down in the armchair, exhausted by the exertion of getting dressed.

"We can have a fresh start," Tyler said. "Begin again."

"No." Alex waved a weary hand dismissively in the air. "We really can't."

There was a long pause, and then Tyler sighed. "Look, I know you're upset, but she's gone, and I can't bring her back. You have to let her go."

"Is this where the carrot and stick come in? I heard you that night, speaking to Drummond. You said you'd handle Ted and me. Well, you've solved the Ted problem, so now I assume you're here to handle me. What are your carrot and stick for me, George?"

"Ah." Tyler sat down in the armchair opposite with a wry smile. "I'm afraid that you require more complex handling, Alex."

"Alex. You called me Alex."

Tyler shrugged. "Why not? It's what you like to be called, isn't it?"

"Yes, which is why you never have."

"Well, like I said – a fresh start."

"How does it go, this fresh start of ours?" Alex demanded. "You enjoy tormenting me too much to give that up, but I know something that could potentially ruin you, so that makes me very awkward to have around."

"I doubt it'd ruin me," Tyler said sharply. "It'd be inconvenient to deal with if it ever got out, yes, but it wouldn't ruin me."

"Maybe. Maybe not."

Tyler's expression hardened. "Don't think you can play me, Alex, because you can't. I will always win."

Alex felt his own resolve harden in response. "You killed someone I cared about. She's dead because of you. I can't ever forget that, so please don't think I ever will."

Tyler's eyes flashed. "For God's sake! I didn't mean to kill her – it was an accident."

Alex threw back his head and laughed manically.

Tyler watched him, a bewildered look on his face.

Alex shut off his laughter abruptly. "*It was an accident*," he said mockingly. "Sound familiar, Tyler? *It was an accident.*"

"Shut up," Tyler snapped.

"Why – you wouldn't accept that excuse from me, so why should I accept it from you?" Alex demanded.

Tyler's expression darkened. "You see, this – here – is why you need special handling. I tried to bring you to heel, to train you – to break you down and build you up again. All I ever wanted was to make you right, because you've been wrong your entire life, haven't you? You've always been twisted inside, and you hate that about yourself as much as I do. I wanted to help you, Alex, but you wouldn't accept my help."

"Given the nature of it, you can hardly blame me," Alex responded wryly.

"Well, it's time for me to finally concede defeat." Tyler threw his hands in the air. "You must see that I can't have you walking around, knowing what you know, holding it over my head and threatening me with it." He grimaced. "I need the help of professionals. I've made some enquiries, and I believe I've found the right place." He stood up. "It's a shame I didn't manage to break you myself, but I'm a busy man, and I really don't have the time to devote to it. So I'm going to pass you over to a facility that can do it for me. I'm sending you away, and when you come back, you'll be different. This nasty, selfish, sarcastic young man will be gone." He leaned over Alex, a grimly satisfied look in his eyes.

It took all Alex's strength not to shrink back into the chair, away from him.

GHOST EYE

"In his place will be a nice, polite, obedient IS, eager to do his houder's bidding. You'll be happier then, Alex – much happier. It'll hurt, I'm sure, in the short term, but in the long term you'll feel so much better about yourself." He pressed a kiss to Alex's head, tousled his hair affectionately, and then straightened up again. "Goodbye, Alex. Next time I see you, you'll be broken, and then you'll do all those things I asked of you before. You remember what they were?"

Alex remembered all too well.

"You'll do them willingly and happily – without any trace of hesitation, reluctance, or resentment – and then we can truly start again." Tyler gave one last, terrifying smile, and left the room.

Alex was woken at 6 a.m. the following morning and ordered to get dressed in a pair of jeans, a sweater, and a thick woollen coat. Then he was bundled outside into the dark, misty morning, where a helicopter was parked on the back lawn. Mick was waiting for him. He helped Alex in, then climbed in opposite him and closed the door.

As the helicopter took to the skies, Alex looked down at the damp island below, with its beautiful glass house set in the middle of the green golf course. He was sure he could see a light on in one of the windows, and a figure there, watching him leave. He raised a hand to deliver a derisive wave of farewell to George Tyler, then turned back to Mick. "Where are we going?" he asked.

Mick looked away, mumbling something.

Alex wondered why he wasn't taking the opportunity to gloat, and then he realised: Mick had worked with Solange for months – possibly years. He'd made her cups of tea, chatted to her, and had never exchanged a cross word with her. Alex realised that Mick was ashamed of his part in what had taken place down there, in Tyler's house, a few weeks ago. "You could have stopped it," he said quietly. "You all could have stopped it, Mick. All these years, you let him get away with it. You never once stood up to him and said *enough is enough*. What happened to Solange was inevitable, in a way."

"You don't understand," Mick said defensively. "You never have."

"Yes, I do. I really do, Mick," Alex sighed.

"I liked her, Alex. She was a good person. She always had time for me." Mick hugged his arms around his big body, looking suddenly small and lost, like a child.

"You could go to the police. You could tell them the truth about that night."

"Yeah, right." Mick shook his head. "I might as well throw myself out of this helicopter right now as do that." He jerked his head at the long drop below. "You know as well as I do that he's never gonna answer for killing her, Alex. Best we can do is make sure we stay alive long enough to get out and put all the crazy behind us."

"That's your plan?"

"It's all I've got." Mick gave him an apologetic smile. "I'm sorry for you, Alex, I really am. This place you're going... I can't imagine it's very nice." He gave a little shudder.

Alex wondered where on earth Tyler was sending him. But wherever it was, and whatever they did to him there, he'd survive, because Solange was depending on him. Without him, there would be no justice for her. He felt in his pocket for the folded picture. She was his strength, and he'd hold on to her until either the day he died or the day George Tyler was held to account for killing her, whichever came first.

The helicopter travelled south-west for well over an hour, until Alex estimated that they must be over Somerset or Devon. Then they landed on a huge, rolling lawn, in what appeared to be the middle of nowhere. Mick helped him out and escorted him across the lawn to a gravel path leading up to a large manor house.

"I gotta leave you here, Alex," he said, pulling on the big doorbell next to a massive oak door. "Good luck." He scurried back towards the helicopter.

Alex looked up and saw the letters carved into the stone lintel above the door, forming a single word:

Belvedere.

End of Book Two

Find out what happens next in
Book Three: The Lost Zone

Want to hear the full version of Ashton's haunting melody? 🎵

Join my newsletter, **Walter's World,** to receive this *Dark Water* extra. Your **FREE membership** unlocks exclusive content you can't get anywhere else:
- *Dark Water* bonus novella
- MM pirate novella
- Curated playlists
- Interactive world-building extras
- Regular subscriber-only surprises
- Giveaways and competitions

Your privacy matters: I'll never spam your inbox or share your data.

Sign Me Up to Walter's World! https://geni.us/ww-bm

Join thousands of readers already exploring the hidden corners of my fictional worlds.

Please leave a review!

If you enjoyed this book, you can help others discover it by leaving a review on Amazon and posting a recommendation on social media. I'm an independent author and not very well-known, so every review and recommendation makes a real difference.

Leave a review on Amazon: https://geni.us/GE-GEBM

Your support means the world and helps me keep writing.

Dark Water Book Three - The Lost Zone
It's Time to Choose: Justice or Love?

Alex Lytton has waited seven long years for justice—now, just as he stands on the precipice of achieving it, fate offers him an impossible choice: complete the mission that has consumed his life or flee with the man who has captured his heart.

With time running out, Alex must decide what matters most: justice or love?

Grab your copy of *The Lost Zone* here: https://geni.us/DW3-DW2

———

Read on for more information about *The Lost Zone* and a special letter from Xanthe Walter about the writing of *Ghost Eye*.

HELLO FROM XANTHE WALTER

Dear Reader,

Thank you for submerging yourself in *Ghost Eye*.

Want to know a secret? I like to nurdle plot points in my head while out walking, and you can just imagine how excited I was to slot together the past and present, seven years apart, leading to those big, bloody climaxes. Poor Peter! Poor Solange! And poor Alex and Josiah (yes, I'm mean to the characters I love!).

Did you guess who Ben was before it was revealed? Keep reading – there are more shocking revelations in Book Three. And as for Book Four... ;-)

Please don't spoil the plot points in this series for other people. It's much more fun to look superior, smile smugly, tap the side of your nose knowingly, and stay schtum.

Can I ask a favour? If you're loving this series, please help spread the word. Reviews, social media posts, and/or recommendations to friends—it all helps *Dark Water* find new readers.

Want to debate whether Alex and Josiah have a future together, who the murderer might be, or just to chat with fellow readers? Come join my friendly Facebook group, Xanthology. You'll find all my links on my Linktree: https://linktr.ee/xanthewalter

For exclusive content, giveaways, and a FREE spicy pirate novella, join Walter's World, my newsletter family: https://geni.us/ww-bm

Happy reading,

Xanthe

www.xanthe-walter.com

P.S. If you enjoyed *Ghost Eye*, just wait until you see what *Dark Water* has in store next. You can find Book Three here: https://geni.us/DW3-DW2

THE LOST ZONE

It's time to choose - justice or love?

Alex Lytton has waited seven long years for justice—now, just as he stands on the precipice of achieving it, fate offers him an impossible choice: complete the mission that has consumed his life or flee with the man who has captured his heart.

With time running out, Alex must decide what matters most: justice or love.

"Just when you think you have everything figured out, Xanthe Walter comes in and turns everything upside down and sideways."
Dani ☆☆☆☆☆

———

Dark Water. Deadly Secrets. Dangerous Love.

As Alex Lytton unravels the mysteries of Belvedere, he learns the skills he needs to survive. But his greatest test awaits on his return to Ghost Eye City, where he must convince his most dangerous enemy that he's no threat – by surrendering willingly to his demands.

Meanwhile, Josiah Raine vows to protect Alex at any cost. But as

he works tirelessly to bring two killers to justice, a shadow from Alex's past emerges with a terrifying new agenda.

With time running out, the truth leads them to the cold grey waters of a lost zone, where a long-submerged secret holds the key to the future.

Plunge into *The Lost Zone,* the thrilling continuation of the *Dark Water* saga.

Claim your copy of The Lost Zone here: https://geni.us/DW3-DW2

Warning: *The Lost Zone* contains **mature themes and explicit sexual content, including graphic scenes of sexual violence.** It is intended for readers 18+ only. For detailed content information, please visit the content advisory web page for *The Lost Zone* before reading. https://www.xanthe-walter.com/content-advisory/dark-water-book-3/

WELCOME TO WALTER'S WORLD!

Become a Xanthe Walter VIP and join an exclusive community of readers who get the inside scoop.

Your FREE membership of my **newsletter mailing list** unlocks a complete multimedia story experience:

🍃 **Exclusive Story Content**
• **Dark Water** bonus novella *Safe Harbour* (only read this after finishing the complete series!)
• **Bonus scenes** from across my story universes
• **Exclusive snippets** from upcoming books
• **FREE gay BDSM pirate novella** *A Willing Lad*

🎵 **Multimedia Extras**
• **Curated Spotify playlists** for each book in the series
• **Ashton's complete song** from *Ghost Eye*
• **Alex's photo stash** from *The Lost Zone*
• **Rising Radio** - listen to episodes of *News-Spec*

📰 **World-Building Deep Dives**
• **Flood map** showing London's lost zones
• *The Daily Lowdown*- a fully designed news site with headlines from Elliot Dacre's murder
• **Character profiles** and extracts

🎁 **VIP Subscriber Benefits**
• **First access** to cover reveals
• **Behind-the-scenes insights**
• **Special offers and giveaways** for subscribers only
• **Regular surprises** and exclusive goodies

Your privacy matters: I'll never spam your inbox or share your data with anyone.

Sign up to Walter's World and join thousands of readers already exploring the hidden corners of my fictional world. Sign up here - https://geni.us/ww-bm

ABOUT XANTHE WALTER

Xanthe Walter has been crafting MM romances for over thirty years, creating hundreds of tales about love, adventure, and angsty men falling for each other.

Xanthe specialises in genre-bending stories – vampire cops, paranormal pirates, BDSM romcoms... if she can mix up a few genres, she will! Her dystopian murder-mystery series, 'Dark Water', perfectly shows her love for blending genres and exploring emotional complexity.

When she's not gleefully plotting her next cliffhanger, you'll find her singing along to musical theatre hits, obsessing over Tudor history, and eating far too many scones.

She lives between London and Somerset with two cats who are excellent writing assistants, provided your definition of "assistance" includes strategic keyboard-sitting and delivering unwanted wildlife gifts at crucial plot moments.

Xanthe writes epic emotional rollercoasters, but she promises the landing is always worth the journey.

Come and join her on her friendly Facebook group Xanthology.

You can find all her links on Linktree: https://linktr.ee/xanthewalter

ACKNOWLEDGMENTS

First and foremost, to Emma—thank you for living this book alongside me for so many years and patiently waiting to discover the murderer's identity!

To Angela, who devoured every chapter I sent within a day and provided immediate feedback—thank you for the countless hours spent discussing every aspect of this story with such enthusiasm.

An enormous debt of gratitude goes to my trusted team of audiencers and betas who have been with me since my fandom days. Chris, Leslie, and dot—this book wouldn't exist without your unwavering support and guidance. To Lauren - a recent addition to my team but hugely valuable. Thank you for your laser sharp attention to detail.

To my incredible Team Xanthe—your practical help and support have been invaluable.

My heartfelt thanks to my wonderful friends in Walter's World, Xanthology, and on my personal Facebook page, whose constant encouragement has meant the world to me.

Special thanks to Jacci, my website designer, for creating such a beautiful site and patiently handling my creative manias and OCD suggestions with grace.

To Tessa, my editor—thank you for elevating this book beyond what I thought possible. And to Toby, my proof-reader—you are truly awesome in every way.

Finally, to my beloved Penny—demon crocheter, Photoshop wizard, and devoted mother to black labradors. Though you didn't live to see books three and four, I've woven a special tribute into their pages just for you.

Copyright © 2025 by Xanthe Walter

All rights reserved.

No part of this book may be reproduced in any form or by any electronic or mechanical means, including information storage and retrieval systems, without written permission from the author, except for the use of brief quotations in a book review.

This is a work of fiction. Any resemblance to actual persons, living or dead, or actual events is purely coincidental.

Made in the USA
Coppell, TX
08 December 2025

65027969R00231